T. W. Marshall

Christian Missions Their Agents, Their Methods, and Their Results

by T. W. Marshall

T. W. Marshall

Christian Missions Their Agents, Their Methods, and Their Results by T. W. Marshall

ISBN/EAN: 9783742808745

Manufactured in Europe, USA, Canada, Australia, Japa

Cover: Foto ©Andreas Hilbeck / pixelio.de

Manufactured and distributed by brebook publishing software (www.brebook.com)

T. W. Marshall

Christian Missions Their Agents, Their Methods, and Their Results

by T. W. Marshall

CHAPTER IV.

MISSIONS IN CEYLON.

It will be expedient to confine within comparatively narrow limits the history of Christian Missions in this Island. The brief period subsequent to the establishment of British authority, though that rule dates only from the commencement of the present century, will more than suffice to afford us abundant illustrations of the contrast which we have already traced in other regions.

A Protestant Missionary Society, assembled on a solemn occasion, and moved by an unwonted impulse of candour, appreciated in the following terms the work of the three great Powers which have held sway, either together or in succession, in the land of spices and pearls. « The exertions of the Roman

Catholics in the conversion of the natives having been greater than those of the Dutch, and those of the Dutch having greatly exceeded the British, it is in the same proportion that the three classes possess a permanent influence over the native mind. » (1) The admission is not without value, especially from such a source, but it might have been more complete. The influence of the British, as far as religion is concerned, has yet to be acquired; that of the Dutch, so long supreme in the island, has vanished without leaving a trace; while that of the Catholics, which preceded them both, has survived the dissolution of the one, and gained its peaceful triumphs in spite of the jealous hostility of the other. These three positions we shall now establish, by the evidence of Protestant witnesses of many creeds and various social position, but all familiar, from personal observation and scrutiny, with the facts which they record.

The first period of the history of Christianity in Ceylon we will dismiss, for the sake of brevity, with a few words. The Catholic Missionaries in this island, during the whole epoch of the Portuguese dominion, were such as we have already seen them in China and India; and there is perhaps no need to describe again a type of character, or to recount the details of an apostolic warfare, with which by this time we are sufficiently familiar. St. Francis was one of their number, and where he was we may be sure the Angels were not far distant. In his gracious

(1) *Report of the Society for Missions to Africa and the East*; 10th Anniversary, p. 79.

form the Cingalese recognised a prophet of the true God, and by his companions and their successors thousands were converted to the faith. « Illustrious examples of pious devotion to the Saviour's cause, » says a candid Wesleyan missionary in Ceylon, « were furnished by the missionaries of the Roman Catholic faith. » (1) Jesuits, Franciscans, and Oratorians rivalled each other in wisdom and charity; and so solid was their work, here as elsewhere, that neither afflictions nor temptations, neither the cruel persecutions of the Dutch, nor the more dangerous enticements of the English and Americans, have had any other effect upon the Catholic natives than to prove, as Protestants will presently assure us, their invincible constancy.

Ceylon, like every other land in which the faith has been planted, was fertilised by the blood of martyrs. As early as 1546, men who had come from distant lands with the message of peace found here a glorious death. In 1548, one of the kings of the island was converted, and the Franciscans already numbered twelve thousand native Christians in Columbo. » (2) In 1602, the sons of St. Francis welcomed a new band of auxiliaries, de Guzman, de Mendoza, and other fathers of the Society of Jesus, who came to share the burden of their toils. In 1616, Fathers John Metella and Louis Pelingotti of that Society, having penetrated into the interior, yielded up their lives in testimony of the truths which they preached. Four new victims hastened to offer them-

(1) *A Narrative of the Mission to Ceylon*, by the Revd William Harvard, *Introd.* p. 63.

(2) Henrion, tome 1, 2de partie, p. 465.

selves in their place. Sociro was the first captured,
and the first martyred. In the following year, 1628,
Matthew Fernandez and Antony Pecci embraced the
same lot. And the heathen, as a modern historian
observes, were not the most implacable enemies of
these generous apostles. De Lyma and Moureyra
were attacked at sea by the Dutch, and their vessel
burned. Moureyra, having cast himself into the
waves, was pursued by the Calvinists, and killed
with harpoons. Antony de Vasconcellos, who had
resigned the highest dignities to embrace the apostolic
life, died by poison in 1633; and in the following
year, Andrada perished in the same manner. (1) And
these generous martyrs were succeeded by others
who, in their turn, fought the good fight, and were
able to inspire even the effeminate Cingalese, as
Baldæus confesses, in words which shall be quoted
hereafter, with courage enough to welcome the same
fate. Let us hasten at once to later times, and to
events of which we may accept the history from
Protestant witnesses.

Mr Pridham, a recent writer on Ceylon, — whose
sentiments may be inferred from his own avowal,
that he greatly prefers « the tenets of Buddhism, »
with all its madness of idolatry and superstition, « to
the insensate and infinitely *more* debasing tenets of
Rome, » that is, to the religion of Fénélon and
St. Francis Xavier, — will first give us his valuable
testimony. It is curious to see this gentleman forced,
by a power which even prejudice so intense could
not resist, to utter blessings when his mouth was

(1) Cretineau Joly, tome III, ch. IV, p, 250.

filled with curses. M' Pridham, then, thus describes
one of the later Catholic Missionaries in Ceylon, the
Oratorian Father Vaz. « He went about from place
to place, through swamps and jungles, making many
converts among the heathen by the austerity of his
manners. His voluntary poverty was such that he
would not accept money; his modesty such, that in
confessing women he would avert his eyes; and his
temperance such, that besides frequently abstaining
from food, he lived on the coarsest diet. Catholicism
appeared to revive throughout Jaffna, and the Dutch
attributed it to the revival of some Jesuit in disguise. »

But the Dutch, whose only argument was violence,
caught the Oratorian, and shut him up in prison.
Here, says M' Pridham, « he applied himself to the
study of Singhalese, in which he made himself a
proficient. » Prisons, it seems, are but a clumsy
mode of fighting against God, as the Jews found
when they had taken Peter captive. Like him, Father
Vaz became free again; and as a deadly pestilence
was now raging, M' Pridham, who thinks the religion of Vaz « more debasing » than even Buddhism,
tells us what he did next. « He followed the sick
into the jungles, and building huts as well as time
and place would permit, there sheltered them from
the elements and the attacks of wild beasts : in a
word, he contrived to supply every want, temporal
and spiritual, performed the most menial services,
opened hospitals in the deserted houses, and dared
every thing for their relief. The result was that
numbers who were cured joined the Church, and
had their children baptized. The admirable conduct
of Vaz gained him the confidence of the King, who

was only prevented from rewarding him by being
assured that he was too disinterested to accept any
thing. » But M' Pridham was not permitted to stop
even here, and so he continues his instructive nar-
ration as follows. « To relate all the undertakings
of Padre Vaz, and to unfold the full tale of his
energy, boldness, austerity, and devotion, would be
incompatible with our design : suffice to say, that
the Dutch were never able to eradicate the faith thus
planted by his courage, and Catholicism continued
to increase in Ceylon till it arrived at its present
position. » (1)

Such were the evangelists who laboured in Ceylon.
If their Master had not blessed them and their work,
Christianity would be only an idle fable. But He suffered them and their spiritual children to be assault-
ed by the enemy, like their brethren in other lands,
because He knew they could bear the trial. It was
the Dutch Calvinists whom the Evil One employed
as his instruments to vex and torment them; let us
see how the Protestants of Holland fulfilled their
mission, and with what results.

The Dutch have not acquired a high reputation,
even among their co-religionists, as judicious or successful missionaries. « I never saw such cold calcu-
lating people, » says D' Joseph Wolff, as the members
of the Dutch Missionary Society. » (2) And as he saw
more of them, the impression was only confirmed;
for at a later period he once more declares, « There
is scarcely any where such a lukewarm set of people

(1) *Ceylon and its Dependencies*, by Charles Pridham Esq.,
vol. II, app. pp. 808-11.
(2) *Journal*, p. 39.

as the members of the Dutch Bible and Missionary
Societies; they are as watery as their country. »
Even their own countrymen seem to have avowed
the same opinion, for the Captain of a Dutch ship
of war told him, in confidence; « Our missionaries
in the Dutch Colonies made many converts, but
Government would not permit them to convert any
more, for when they were converted, they got drunk,
and refused to work on Sunday. » (1)

But Dr Wolff is not alone in his unfavorable estimate of Dutch missionaries. In India, in the great
Indian Archipelago, in Ceylon, in South America,
every where and always, they have been the same,
and have provoked the same comments. Even in Japan, where they so long possessed a kind of commercial sovereignty, their real character appears to
have been accurately discriminated. « The Dutch
assured the Japanese, » we are told by Golownin,
« that they were no Christians, and obtained permission to trade with them. » (2) « I took the liberty, »
says Count Benyowski, who visited that country
towards the close of the eighteenth century, « to ask
the king whether he thought the Hollanders were
Christians; and he replied, that merchants had no
religion, their only faith consisting in getting money,
while they gave themselves very little trouble about
the belief of a God. » (3) Their direct missionary
efforts have produced just the results which the spirit
imputed to them by this sagacious monarch would

(1) *Journal*, p. 14.
(2) *Recollections of Japan*, by Captain Golownin, ch. III,
(1819).
(3) *Travels of Comte de Benyowski*, vol. 1, p. 399. (1790).

be likely to secure. Thus M' Kolff, though a native of Holland, tells us, that in their island of Damma, « by far the greater portion of the inhabitants are either heathens, or individuals once Christians, who have *returned* to their former habits; » while of the Arru islands the same witness unwillingly reports, « Our religion has retrograded, while Islamism has advanced considerably. » (1)

The same facts are repeated, with exactly the same comments, by many English writers, in spite of their religious sympathies. Of Batavia, where the Dutch converts have long enjoyed « a translation of the whole Bible, » D' Morison writes as follows. « It is painful to remark that the native Christians of this city, if such they can be called, are sunk in deplorable ignorance and vice, and in no way remarkably distinguished from their heathen brethren, except by the formal abandonment of idolatry, and the equally formal adoption of the Christian name. » The same Protestant historian confesses, that although « in Amboyna and the surrounding islands there were upwards of fifty churches, » — the inhabitants having been « compelled by law » to profess Christianity, — « they were, after all, but baptized pagans; » and he adds, « it seems an absolute burlesque upon the New Testament to speak of the mass of the Dutch converts in Amboyna as Christians. » (2)

In 1853, M'Gerstaecker reports once more, that the

(1) *Voyages of the Dourga,* by D. H. Kolff; ch. vi, p. 93; ch. xii, p. 195.

(2) *The Fathers of the London Missionary Society,* by John Morison, D. D., vol. 1, pp. 71, 75.

Mahommedans are in every respect superior to the so-called Christians. He even affirms that the results of « conversion » have been, « in almost every instance, » so deplorable, especially in the augmentation of immorality, that « Government does not like to see Missionaries go amongst the people, and if it does not prevent their teaching, most certainly does not support it. » (1) Lastly, Sir John Bowring and Mr Oliphant confirm, with ample details, these gloomy statements. « The interests of trade, » says the former, contrasting the wordly spirit of the Dutch with the religious zeal of the Spaniards, « have ever been the predominant consideration among Dutch colonizers. » (2) « In carrying out their ruthless policy against the Christians, » observes Mr Oliphant, « the Japanese always found in the Dutch ready and willing assistants. » It was the latter who « bombarded, at the behest of the Japanese government, 37,000 Christians, who were cooped up within the walls of Samabarra. » And these eager Protestants, who not only denied that they were Christians themselves, but gladly assisted pagans in slaughtering those who were, have failed in securing the very prize for which they committed crimes almost unparalleled in human annals. At home, they have seen the fairest provinces of their kingdom severed from them; while in Japan, « they have not even had the profits of a lucrative trade to console them for the ignominy with which they have been treated ; on the contrary, it has steadily dimin-

(1) *Voyage*, etc., vol. III, p. 257.
(2) *Visit to the Philippine Islands*, ch. V, p. 94.
II.

ished in proportion as the indignities to which they have been exposed have increased. » (1) M' Southey will tell us hereafter that their conduct, and its results, were exactly the same in South America.

M' Temminck, who has written an enthusiastic apology of Dutch government in the East, declares, as if he desired to redeem their sullied reputation, that « religious toleration » makes their Indian possessions quite a « terrestrial paradise. » (2) We shall see immediately that Ceylon, under their government, formed no part of this apocryphal paradise; but before we return to our immediate subject, let us add, in conclusion, the following impressive statement, by an energetic American Protestant, of what the Dutch have really done in the Indian Archipelago. « For two hundred years and more, three millions of Christian Dutchmen have been the masters over seven generations of about fifteen millions of Mahometan and Pagan Malays, Javanese, and other races of the Archipelago, — not less than one hundred millions in all; and for what purpose? to fill the coffers of stolid men of Amsterdam and Rotterdam! » The whole fruit of their conquests in the East, he says, is this, « that after two hundred years the natives display the same ignorance of the religion which their masters profess to believe. » (3) Even literature and science owe them but little, for as the learned orientalist Mohl complained, in 1844, to

(1) *Lord Elgin's Mission*, vol. II, ch. II, p. 49.
(2) *Possessions Néerlandaises dans l'Inde Archipélagique*, par C. J. Temminck, tome I, ch. II, p. 214. (1846).
(3) *The Prison of Weltevreden*, etc., by Walter M. Gibson, pp. 133, 446.

the Asiatic Society of France, « We are still using the Japanese grammars and dictionaries published two centuries ago by the Jesuits, and the Dutch do nothing. » (1) And now let us see what they did in Ceylon.

In this island, as in Western India, the Dutch succeeded the Portuguese, from whom they wrested the possessions which they were themselves destined to forfeit in turn to the English. These children of Calvin found their new territories peopled by Catholics. « The Island of Ceylon, » says Mʳ Irving, with some exaggeration, « is said to have been so completely Roman Catholic when it came into the possession of the Dutch, that, unable to convert the natives to Calvinism, they took measures to promote idolatry... they are said to have sent to the mainland for priests to re-establish Buddhism! » (2) But this singular policy, with which these ardent Protestants inaugurated their reign in Ceylon, need not surprise us. We have seen even Anglicans, both lay and clerical, confessing that they prefer the Hindoo or Chinese idolater to the disciples of St. Francis, St. Augustine, and St. Paul. Let us continue, by the help of Protestant writers, the history of Dutch Calvinism in Ceylon.

« It cannot be predicated in favour of the Dutch, » says Mʳ Pridham, whose information will be very useful to us, « that they entered upon the task of propagating the Reformed religion either with equal ardour or from similar motives to the Portuguese. »

(1) *Rapport*, 10 Juillet, 1844, p. 70.
(2) *The Theory and Practice of Caste*, ch. v, p. 130.

M[r] Hugh Murray told us exactly the same thing of
the English in India, and we shall hear it again in
future chapters of this history. But the Dutch, finding Buddhism an impotent ally against Catholics,
proceeded to try the plan which has cost Protestant
Missionaries such enormous sums in every heathen
land. They could not convert the Cingalese by argument, but they might perhaps do so by bribes. « The
Dutch went about the business coolly, » says Lord
Valentia, « and held forth the temptation of requiring the profession of the Protestant faith as a *quali-
fication* for all public offices. » (1) « They sought, »
we are told by M[r] Christmas, who is of the school of
M[r] Pridham, — for we are compelled to employ witnesses of this class, — « to bribe the Cingalese to
adopt Dutch Presbyterianism by the offer of places
and situations. » (2) The offer was accepted, but with
such results as might have been anticipated. Thousands of Cingalese became Protestants, without ceas-
ing to be Buddhists; and as the universal hypocrisy
and corruption which such conversions generated
only added new crimes to those which were indigen-
ous in Ceylon, Lord Valentia remarks truly, that
« many of the vices of the Cingalese seem to be the
creation of their late masters. » But we must hear
other witnesses.

A Dutch protestant, who visited the island shortly
before his countrymen were dispossessed by the Eng-
glish, gives this frank description of them. « So far
from making any account of the Dutch, the inhabit-

(1) *Travels*, vol. 1, ch. vi, p. 261.
(2) *The Hand of God in India*, p. 111.

ants of Ceylon treat them with a kind of contempt; but the Dutch have the prudence to overlook such trifles, minding the main chance, the amity of the King of Candy, that he may not take it into his head to break with them, which would be a very sensible wound to their commerce in this charming island. » (1)

A Baptist missionary, who notices the significant fact, that « the Portuguese left most people, the Dutch most buildings, » thus estimates, in 1852, the results of their missions. « The Dutch filled their territories with christians who knew nothing of Christianity except the name. It is not uncommon even now for a native to say, in the same breath, that he is a good Christian and a good Buddhist. » (2)

Dr John Morison, the historian of the London Missionary Society, thus describes the Dutch Missions. « Of these missions it is difficult to speak in terms of high commendation, on account of the loose and unscriptural principles on which they were conducted. Though they increased to a large extent the nominal territory of Christianity, it is much to be feared that they did but comparatively little towards the real conversion of the heathen world. » And then he describes their method. « All that was required by the Dutch divines of a Cingalese convert, prior to baptism and admission into the Christian Church, was, that he should be able to repeat the Lord's Prayer and the

(1) *A Voyage to the Island of Ceylon in 1747, by a Dutch Gentleman*, p. 18. English edition.

(2) *Missionary Tour in Ceylon and India*, by Joshua Russell, ch. II, p. 11. (1852).

Ten Commandments; « announcing at the same time,
« that no native should rise to rank in the army, or
be admitted to any employment under the Government, unless he professed himself a member of the
Protestant Church. » The Cingalese, D' Morison
adds, « pressed into the communion of so profitable
a faith. » (1) The Dutch no longer needed to stimulate the progress of Buddhism, in order to spite the
Catholics; it was enough to induce a Cingalese to
profess himself a Protestant, and his adhesion to
Buddhism was effectually secured. Calvinism accepted this compromise, and by the close of the seventeenth century, « the Dutch ministers in Ceylon had
baptized three hundred thousand of the inhabitants. »

It is true, as we shall see immediately, that they
were precisely such « converts » as Protestantism
has made in China and India, that they still practised
all the rites of heathenism, and were a scandal even
to their own countrymen by the new vices which
they now displayed. But still these nominal conversions continued during the whole period of the Dutch
occupation. At one time by constraint and violence,
at another by an organised system of bribery of
which the details were prescribed by legislative
enactment, they multiplied the disciples of the « reformed religion. » And the masters of Ceylon were
content with a process which produced such satisfactory numerical results, though it made Christianity a bye-word among the heathen, an object of
hatred to those who affected to embrace, and of scorn
to those who openly rejected it. « The vices, the

(1) Vol. I, p. 66.

cupidity, and the flagrant immorality of the Dutch
administration, as well as of their private conduct, «
says M. de Jancigny, « tended necessarily to cast
discredit upon their official profession of faith. » (1)
At length the inevitable hour of their downfall arrived, and then was revealed, to their confusion and
dishonour, the result of their presence in Ceylon.
But that result is too curious and instructive, as well
as too characteristic of the real influence of Protestant missions in pagan lands, to be dismissed with a
passing allusion.

The Dutch had two main objects during their occupation of Ceylon, both of which they pursued with
a keen avidity and an unscrupulous injustice second
only to that which distinguished their commercial
traffic; the first was to force the natives to become
Protestants, the second to crush or extirpate the Catholics. The first aim was partially accomplished,
after a fashion which shall be more fully described
presently; the second utterly failed. But we must take
the history of that failure from Protestant witnesses.

Sir Emerson Tennent, the highest authority on all
which concerns the island of Ceylon, and whose well
known work is justly commended by a Protestant
minister as « very impartially drawn up, » writes
as follows. « In 1748, it was forbidden to educate a
Roman Catholic for the ministry, but within three
years it was found necessary to repeat the same
prohibition, as well as to renew the proclamation
for putting down the celebration of the Mass. Not-

(1) *Ceylan*, par M. de Jancigny ; *l'Univers Pittoresque*,
tome VIII, p. 653.

withstanding every persecution, however, the Roman
Catholic religion retained its influence, and held good
its position in Ceylon. It was openly professed by
the immediate descendants of the Portuguese, who
had remained in the island after its conquest by the
Dutch; and in private it was equally adhered to by
large bodies of the natives, both Singhalese and
Tamils, *whom neither corruption nor coercion could
induce to abjure it.* » (1) Yet both were freely used,
though with no other result than to show, that the
pastors of this persecuted flock were worthy of their
vocation, and that their courageous disciples were
not unworthy of them. « The Roman Catholic priests
made their way into the low country, visiting in
secret their scattered flocks, and administering the
sacraments in defiance of the *plakaats* and prohibi-
tions of the Government. » And so the battle went
on. But the issue of such a conflict could never be
doubtful. Sir Emerson Tennent tells us what it was.
Father Joseph Vaz, to give only a simple example,
« in an incredibly short space of time added to the
Church upwards of *thirty thousand converts* from
the heathen. » In vain they bound the apostle in fet-
ters, martyred his disciples, or condemned them to
the galleys for life. In vain they devised those ingenious cruelties which forced even a Protestant minister to exclaim, in spite of his hatred of their
Catholic victims, — « Their blind, pharisaical vin-
dictiveness can only be cordially abhorred. » (2) But

(1) *Christianity in Ceylon*, ch. II, p 42.
(2) *Romanism in Ceylon*, by the Revd Edward J. Robinson,
p. 17. (1855).

this was their method of conversion, and they knew
no other. The persecution never slacked; « but the
proclamations of the Government, » we are told,
« were either too late to be effectual, or too tyrannical to be carried into force; and in 1717, only two
years after a renewed proclamation, the Roman Catholics were in possession of upwards of *four hundred
churches* in all parts of Ceylon. » Still the Dutch
pursued their policy of savage repression. They had
already prohibited all education to Catholics, and
now they forbade them, under terrible penalties,
« either to marry or bury; » and finally, as it was
possible to improve still further this too lenient code,
« freedom was conferred upon the children of all
slaves born of Protestant parents, whilst those of
Roman Catholics were condemned to perpetual servitude. » (1)

Such are the counsels which the enemy of man
suggests to the agents whom he employs to do his
work. But they come to naught, in Ceylon as elsewhere; and the Protestant historian of Christianity
in this island frankly confesses, that they only confirmed « the rising ascendancy of the Roman Catholics, whose numbers *had actually increased under
persecution*. They had churches in every district,
from Jaffna to Columbo; and in 1734 they extended
their operations to the Southern Province, and with
such success, that the Presbyterian clergy of Galle,
distracted by the impracticability or apostasy of the
natives, gave way before this accumulation of hostile
influences : from 1745 the district was left for some

(1) Sir E. Tennent, ch. II, p. 53.

years altogether without the services of a Protestant minister. » (1)

It is very satisfactory to have a Protestant narrator of so remarkable a history; but he has more to tell us. All the penal laws, futile as they were in their effects upon men whose faith made them invincible, were still in force. The Government still compelled Catholic parents, wherever they were within reach of the iron hand of the jailor, or the scourge of the policeman, to send their children to Protestant schools. By 1730, however, the native Christians had become strong enough to protest openly against this barbarous tyranny, and they publicly presented a petition to the authorities, in which they complained that they were compelled by violence « to send their families to be instructed in doctrines which they rejected. » They confessed that if, in the towns, they had hitherto submitted, it was only from fear of the merciless penalties; but that whenever, by a violence which they could not resist, their children had been « baptized by the ministers of the Reformed Church, they were in the habit of having the same children baptized a second time by a clergyman of the Church of Rome. » The « Consistory of Columbo, » composed of Protestant ministers, urged the Government peremptorily to reject this humble prayer of Christian fathers and mothers, who presumed to have a care for the souls of their little ones. They went still further, and besought the Government to deny, by virtue of its supreme pontifical authority, « the validity of baptism administered by a Catholic priest; »

(1) P. 58.

and to declare, that « none but Protestant headmen should be invested with authority in the different districts. » The civil authorities desired nothing better than to comply with this demand, but there was a difficulty through which they could not see their way, and which they proposed in despair to the Protestant ministers; they would gladly appoint only « Protestant headmen, » they said, but where could they find them? « It was practically impossible, » the government sorrowfully replied, « as the number of Protestant converts had become too scanty to afford a sufficient field for selection. » (1) The « Consis- of Columbo » had asked for too much.

However, « the prayer of the Roman Catholics was rejected, » and it was not until the Christian natives rose in insurrection, — for though it is sometimes a duty to suffer persecution for the faith, it is sometimes also a duty to resist it, -- that the frightened Government gave way. The enemy was already knocking at their doors, and their long reign of cruelty and fraud was drawing to a close. As early as 1756, the English had made themselves masters of the whole coast of Ceylon, and in 1796 the colony was annexed to the British crown. But before we speak of the new form of Protestantism which was now to be introduced, and of its fortunes in Ceylon, let us see what the English conquest revealed as to the final results of Dutch missionary operations in that island. They boasted that they had induced multitudes to embrace their religion, — let us enquire how far the assertion was true.

(1) P. 61.

Baldæus, the most celebrated, and apparently the
most upright of the Dutch missionaries, « candidly
states, » as Sir Emerson Tennent remarks, that his
converts were only « Christians in name » — *sine
Christo Christianiti.*

« They could refute the popish errors concerning
purgatory, the mass, etc., » says this Calvinist Missionary, but unfortunately their religion was confined to such negative formulæ; for, as Baldæus
reluctantly admits a few pages later, « though they
bear the name of Christians, they still retain many
of their pagan superstitions. » (1) And his testimony
is the more valuable, because he was describing the
fruits of his own labour. He could teach them, he
admits, to argue against some of the most sacred
doctrines of Christianity, but he could never persuade
them to accept even those meagre and distorted fragments of it which constituted his own religion. Like
the Protestant missionaries in India, he could plunge
them into the pit of atheism, but all his efforts could
never draw them out again.

Yet even such confessions hardly prepare us for
the prodigious facts which are unfolded in the following statement of the Rev. Mr Palm. « Of 182,226
natives enrolled as Christians at Jaffna, but sixty-
four were members of the Church, » — he means the
Protestant Church; « of 9,820 at Manaar, only five
were communicants; and in the same year (1760) at
Galle and Matura there were only thirty-six members
out of 89,000 who had been baptized! » (2) It appears,

(1) In Churchill's *Collection of Voyages*, vol. III, p. 737.
(2) Tennent, ch. II, p. 65.

therefore, from this remarkable statement, that out of more than *two hundred and eighty thousand* nominal Christians, *who had all received baptism,* not more than one hundred and five were regarded, even by teachers who had so many motives for exaggerating their number, as Christians in any sense whatever.

But even this is not all. We have seen that thousands of the natives of Ceylon, moved partly by the attraction of bribes and partly by the fear of persecution, enrolled themselves as Protestants, while in secret they continued to practice their own idolatries; but there is still a fact to be noticed of which the force and gravity would only be impaired by any reflections which we could offer. While in health, the Buddhist affected to be a disciple of the « reformed religion, » and even assumed the character with tolerable success; but when sickness or peril overtook him, his conscience, upon which Protestantism had failed to exert even the faintest influence, began to reproach him, and he hastened to appease the gods whom he had offended by the semblance of adhesion to a worship which in secret he despised. « A large proportion of these nominal Christians, » says Sir Emerson Tennent, « have been betrayed into apostasy *in times of sickness and alarm.* »

We shall see, before we conclude this chapter, what manner of men the Catholic natives have proved, and how *they* have manifested the effects of true conversion; but now we are speaking of those whom the Dutch admitted into the ranks of Protestantism. « It is a remarkable fact, » says a writer who has been already quoted, « that notwithstanding

the hundreds of thousands of Singhalese who were
enrolled by them as converts, the religion and discipline of the Dutch Presbyterians is now almost
extinct among the natives of Ceylon! Even in Jaffna,
where the reception of those doctrines was all but
unanimous by the Tamils, *not a single congregation
is now in existence* of the many planted by Daldæus,
and tended by the labours of Valentyn and Schwartz.»
The religion, he adds, and here we may conclude
this sketch of Dutch Missions in Ceylon, « has long
since disappeared almost from the memory of the natives of Ceylon. » (1)

And now we come to the English epoch, and to
the missionaries of the Established Church, and of
the various sects which she has begotten.

The English had scarcely begun the administration
of their new conquest when they perceived, with
that infallible good sense which rarely deceives them
when their interests are at stake, and which enables
them to restrain their docile bigotry even in its fier-
cest mood, that Ceylon would not be worth holding
on Dutch principles, and could not be governed by
Dutch maxims. They gave religious freedom to Canada, as Burke remarks, because they feared to lose
it; (2) they refused it to Ireland, because she was
within arm's reach. In Ceylon they wished to pursue
their commercial operations in peace, and the Catholic natives had shown that they could neither be
bribed nor terrified. Still there was a momentary
conflict between prudence and prejudice, and it was

(1) Tennent, ch. II, p. 71.
(2) « Government itself lately thought fit to establish the Roman Catholic religion in Canada. » *Works*, vol. IX, p. 221.

not till 1806, under the government of Sir Thomas Maitland, and at the urgent solicitations of the Chief Justice, Sir Alexander Johnston, that the old persecuting laws were finally repealed, and religious toleration proclaimed. After ten years hesitation, they thought it best for their commercial interests to leave the Catholics alone.

The first fact which occurs in the history of the English period is perhaps the most curious in the whole chapter. Expecting, from their experience of the past, to be still persecuted by the Government, the Dutch « converts » now lost no time in announcing themselves, by way of precaution, as *English* Protestants, to the number of 342,000! « M' Lambrick, the first Church of England missionary at Cotta, recounts that he one day asked a native of Cotta of what religion he was; and the answer was, *Buddha's*. So then you are not a Christian? Oh, yes, to be sure I am; I am a Christian, and of the Reformed Dutch religion too. » (1) But as soon as they comprehended that the Dutch reign was over, they transferred their allegiance to that new religion which they now heard of for the first time. It was always safe to be of the religion of their masters. When, however, they ascertained, by the new enactments, that they were « no longer to be *paid* for apostasy, » and that « a monopoly of offices and public employment » was not to be reserved for the submissive professors of the state religion, they showed at last their real character; and then was enacted one of the most notable scenes in the annals of Protestant Missions.

(1) Tennent, ch. vi, p. 313.

The hour of freedom had come for these poor Cingalese, and while the Catholic natives stedfastly adhered in this new era of tranquillity to the faith which
they had professed through long years of torment
and suffering, the so-called Protestants flung away
with joy the hated disguise, and the Church of England lost her 342,000 members before she had even
time to count them. « Almost with greater rapidity
than their numbers had originally increased, they
now commenced to decline. In 1802, the nominal
Protestant Christians amongst the Tamils of Jaffna
were 130,000; in 1806, Buchanan, who then visited
Ceylon, described the Protestant religion as *extinct.* » (1) We have seen that at the same moment
D'Claudius Buchanan described the *Catholic* churches
of Ceylon as thronged with worshippers. « The whole
district, » he says, speaking of Jaffna, « is now in
the hands of the Romish priests from the college at
Goa. » (2) It was no doubt, an unwelcome fact, but
he was obliged to confess, « they have assumed quiet
and undisturbed possession of the land. » What then
had become of the 342,000 Protestants? Sir Emerson
Tennent supplies the answer. « Vast numbers had
openly joined the Roman Catholic communion, to
which they had long been secretly attached, and the
whole district was handed over to the priests from
the college of Goa. » In the other districts the defection « was equally deplorable, and numbers of Protestants were every years apostatising to Buddha. »
Finally, « within a very few years, *the only Christ-*

(1) Tennent, ch. III, 86.
(2) *Christian Researches in Asia*, p. 44.

ians who were to be found in the Peninsula were the members of the Church of Rome. » (1)

The English Protestants, then, — for we have heard enough of their predecessors, - to whom the Dutch had bequeathed a doubtful heritage, which had already vanished when they put forth their hands to grasp it, did not gain much by the legacy. They had no alternative but to begin the work anew, and this time with other weapons, and by a different process. It was too late for persecution, even if they had wished to try that feeble and exploded method; and moreover, the new race of preachers were more humane than the terrible « Consistory of Colombo. » They resigned themselves, therefore, to the employment of milder means. At first the Church of England, by an unusual privilege, had the field all to herself; but wherever she is, the unwelcome forms which dog her steps in every land, the *diræ facies* of her kinsfolk and rivals, are sure to appear sooner or later in their accustomed procession. And so, before many years had elapsed, all the sects which we have seen striving, with feigned words of amity, to trip up each other in China and India for the instruction and amusement of the heathen, were gathered together in Ceylon. Each had its own partisans, whose eager sympathies followed it across the sea, and who never ceased to transmit to it from their remote dwellings

(1) P. 86. Captain Knox, who was four years a prisoner in Ceylon, noticed of the Catholic natives, that their religion « bred in them a kind of love and affection towards strangers, and men shall hear them oftentimes upbraiding the highlanders for their insolent and rude behaviour. » *Captivity in Ceylon*, ch. II, p. 150. (1818).

the gold without which it would have refused even to attempt a task in which gold was to be the chief agent. The Americans alone, as Lord Torrington has told us, had received long ago 100,000 l., and they have received a good deal more since. What the others have absorbed we need not stay to calculate. It is probable that in this one island Protestantism has expended, how vainly we shall hear presently, as much as would suffice to maintain all the Catholic Missions throughout the earth for a quarter of a century. But Protestant Missions, we know, are expensive, and their agents would smile with pity at the indecent poverty of St. Paul, who lived on alms and had apparently only one cloak, or of his Catholic successors, who have often none at all.

But it would be unreasonable to expect that respectable fathers of families, having complicated social duties to discharge, should condescend to the meagre outfit with which apostles have braved the longest voyage. When St. Francis was preparing to start for India, St. Ignatius made him accept a waistcoat on discovering that he did not possess one : it is true that he took off his own to supply the want. Yet St. Ignatius, unlike the agents of English or American religions, who seek to mend their fortunes by assuming the title of « missionaries, » « was of a race so noble that its head was always invited to do homage by a special writ, » (1) even in the proud court of Spain. The scantiness of apparel which such men accept would be altogether incongruous and unseemly if proposed to missionaries of the modern school. It

(1) Ranke, book II, ch. 1, vol. 1, p. 121.

is their own friends who protest most warmly against the unjust demand; and not content with repudiating on their behalf all claim to the apostolic character, declare, with almost perplexing frankness, that they too easily yield to the seductions of covetousness and luxury. « In India I supported the Missionaries, » said M' Leith in 1833, and the House of Commons printed his words; « but I say that they have not followed the Gospel. Christ said, ' *Leave all* and follow Me; ' they say, ' *Take all*, and follow Me. ' » The statement is harsh, but apparently true, and not less true in Ceylon than in Hindostan. An historian of Protestant Missionary Societies, who chronicles with impassioned eulogy all their works, thus depicts their mode of life in Ceylon. « A poet's imagination could scarcely conceive a spot more suited for the residence of a Christian Missionary. » Perhaps you conclude that he is noting the facilities which its position offers for the conversion of the neighbouring pagans? He has no such thought; he is only contemplating with wistful admiration the « spacious lawns » (1) with which the missionary mansion is adorned, and all those picturesque and attractive appendages which sometimes provoke the surprise of the heathen, but rarely their respect. Let us not enquire, however, too curiously into the domestic life which is deemed an appropriate mode of existence for a Protestant missionary, in Ceylon as elsewhere; or at least let us be content to take the account from their own associates, who know more about it than we do, and are more impartial witnesses.

(1) Smith's *History of the Missionary Societies*, vol. II, p. 641.

The Rev. Howard Malcolm, who visited Ceylon among other places, and was deputed by the American Board of Foreign Missions to report on the operations of his missionary brethren, fulfilled this part of his inquisitorial functions in these words. « Rulers and princes, at some stations, *are unable to live as the Missionaries do.* It is altogether undesirable to see carved mahogany sofas covered with crimson silk, engravings, cut glass, silver forks, etc. in the house of a Missionary; the house itself resembling our handsome country seats!.... Several Missionaries have confessed to me that, on their first arrival in the East, they were shocked at the style in which they found their brethren living. Yet they had been carried away by the current. And so, generally, will be their successors. » (1) We comprehend, therefore, that even the ample largesses of the generous subscribers at home, profuse and abundant as they are, are not superfluously liberal. Protestant Missions, we have already observed, are expensive.

But other witnesses, less reserved than M' Malcolm, and writing for the public rather than for a Missionary Board, are willing to introduce us into the interior of the pleasant « country houses » in which he was a familiar guest, though he prudently leaves his readers at the door. These unofficial visitors afford us an opportunity of contemplating their opulent hosts in the tranquil repose of their daily life. The scenes which they reveal are worth noting. « In Persia, China, India, *every where,* » says one who dwelt

(1) *Travels in S. Eastern Asia,* vol. II, p. 319.

amongst them in many lands, « I found them living quite differently from what I had imagined. They live quite in the manner of opulent gentlemen, and have handsome houses fitted up with every convenience and luxury. The Missionaries repose upon swelling divans, — their wives preside at the tea-table, — their children feast on sweetmeats and confectionary; in short, their position is one incomparably pleasanter and freer from care than that of most other people; they get their salaries punctually paid, and take their places very easily. »

The picture is too instructive not to merit closer examination. « In places where several Missionaries are settled, they have what are called ' meetings, ' three or four times a week, supposed to be devoted to business, but which are little else than parties at which their wives and children appear in tasteful dresses. At one of the Missionaries houses the meeting will be a breakfast, at another a dinner, at a third a tea party; and you will see several equipages and servants standing in the court-yard. There is, indeed, on these occasions, some little talk of business, and the gentlemen remain together perhaps half an hour discussing it; but the rest of the time is passed in mere social amusement. » (1) It is satisfactory to know that, by the alms of worthy persons who suppose they are assisting to convert the heathen, the revenues of the Missionary Societies steadily increase. They have evidently need of all their wealth. Let their subscribers, however, only continue faithful, and there is no danger lest the peaceful enjoyments

(1) Ida Pfeiffer, *Voyage round the World*, pp. 221-2.

of their agents should be curtailed, or their pleasant career compromised.

But it is time to enquire what they have actually accomplished towards the conversion of Ceylon. They will tell us themselves. They do not always conceal the truth, seldom, except under compulsion, or when writing to their official employers, who would promptly resent all superfluous and unprofitable candour as a perfectly useless indiscretion, and perhaps reply to their imprudent servant, as his offended lord did to Cassio, — « I love thee, but never more be officer of mine. » Indeed they confess that it is the proper function of their foreign agents to do abroad what « the highly salaried travellers » do at home, and to furnish, as a well known Anglican minister observes, « the anecdotes which form the great staple of a good deputation's talk, » and « the lovely traits of piety » which stimulate fresh subscriptions; and they do it with so much vigour, and relate such moving tales of the results accomplished in various lands by English or American gold, that, as their Anglican censor pleasantly remarks, « it puzzles one's philosophy to account for the fact that the same means do so little at home. » (1) It is true that they sometimes venture to resent, but rarely without inconvenient results, the hard service exacted from them. Thus, in 1830, two Protestant missionaries presumed to remonstrate against, « those monstrous errors and misrepresentations with which the Annual Report abounds; » and they were both immediately dismissed for the indiscretion. « Excite-

(1) S. G. O., *The Times*, April, 19, 1860.

ment, « they dared to say, « not principle, is the
leading feature of missionary zeal in England; and,
as a natural consequence, pleasing statements from
Missionaries, rather than facts, are sought after to
fan the flame. » (1) And then, as if they felt that they
could not compromise themselves more fatally, these
honest missionaries resolve to unburden their souls,
whatever it may cost. « The want of strict truth in
the Annual Reports, and the encouragement that is
given to the Missionaries to send home too favourable reports of their labours to the Society, these
things cause our hearts to ache. The Directors seem to
judge of people by what they *say*, not by what they
do. Hence the enquiry is not, What are the *labours*
which a missionary is carrying on at his station? but,
What sort of *letters* does he write to the Directors? »
It was natural that the indignant « Directors » should
chastise such improvident candour by prompt dis-
missal.

Another missionary agent, who served for some
years an Anglican association called « the Patagonian Missionary Society, » dared on a certain occasion to rebuke « the selfishness and arrogance of
missionary labour, » and frankly confessed, « the
whole missionary work seems to me to be a strange
compound of piety and irreligion. » This gentleman
also was dismissed, with circumstances of great
cruelty, when he declined to countenance what he
considered the immoral projects of his « society, » —
which included the « purchase of natives from their
chiefs, » who were to be discreetly located, « where

(1) Quoted by Forbes, *Unrefuted Charges*, etc., p. 35.

they could not run away; « the « making Keppel Island
a cattle colony; » « entering into mercantile speculations by trading between Monte Video and Stanley; » (1) and other equally ingenious modes of
acquiring nominal disciples, and preparing what the
judicious « secretary » called « a graphic account »
of imaginary conquests, by which fresh funds might
be obtained to pay his own salary, and save the
Patagonian Missionary Society from premature extinction.

But to return to Ceylon. Here also are found
some few sufficiently independent by character or
position to brave the indignation of « the Directors; »
and so, in their moments of frankness, they thus
describe the character of their converts, and the
manner in which they are recruited. « I have reason
to believe, » says the Rev. M' Percival, in 1854,
« that converts have in some cases been again and
again baptized by the same minister, being presented
by a mercenary catechist on special days, to swell
the number of candidates, and induce the belief that
the work of conversion was steadily advancing. »
And then he explains the secret motive of these ingenious catechists. « One so zealous and successful could
not but be well reported, and eventually as certainly
benefited by promotion. » (2)

The annalist of Protestant attempts to convert the
heathen, though anxious to exaggerate their success,
writes as follows of their result in Ceylon : « This
mission has now been carried on for between thirty

(1) *Tierra del Fuego*, by Captain W. Parker Snow; vol. II,
p. 313. *The Patagonian Missionary Society*, p. 8.
(2) *The Land of the Veda*, ch. xvii, p. 406.

and forty years with much fewer trials and hind-
rances than most of the Society's missions, yet its
progress has been small, as regards its great and
primary object, the conversion of souls to Christ.
Perhaps an utter indifference to all spiritual religion,
rather than hypocrisy, describes the state of heart
of most of the nominal converts. • (1) And this account is confirmed, with graphic brevity, by another
Protestant historian of Missions in Ceylon. • Heathens, Mahometans, and Roman Catholics, • says
Dr Smith, who always ranks these three classes together, as identical in their spiritual state, • were all
bigoted to their respective systems; the greater part
of the Protestants were *perfectly indifferent* about
the religion which they professed. • (2) And presently he declares of the Protestant *converts*, — • They
are Buddhists in belief, but politically Christians. •

Heber, who visited Ceylon officially, had long before remarked in his mild phrase, • there is among
the Cingalese and Tamul population a very large
amount of nominal Christians; • (3) but it was
reserved for later travellers to reveal their true character. The English, we shall see, were destined to
be, if possible, even less successful than the Dutch,
though they imitated their policy so far as to hold out
temporal rewards as an incentive to conversion. The
Rev. George Bisset, the secretary of the • Columbo
Auxiliary Bible Society, • reported with satisfaction to
the parent society, — • far from any disgrace attach-
ing to those who are converted to Christianity, • —

(1) *Hist. of Prop. of Christianity*, vol. II, p. 365.
(2) *Hist. of the Missionary Societies*, vol. II, p. 479.
(3) *Indian Journal*, vol. II, p. 216.

us in India, — « their private reputation is increased,
and their political capacity enlarged ; new situations
of rank and emolument are brought within their
reach, and the native Christian may aspire to a promotion from which the heathen, under this Government, has been long excluded. » (1) The Cingalese,
however, declined to embrace Anglican Protestantism
even on these favourable terms. The proffered liber-
alities of the English were still less persuasive than
the brutal menaces of the Dutch, except in the
case of famished and degraded outcasts, who now
compose the Protestant congregations of Ceylon, and
who are thus described even by their masters and
teachers.

    « The greater part of the Cingalese whom I desig-
nate nominal Christians of the Reformed Religion, »
says M͏r Harvard, a Wesleyan Missionary, « are little
more than Christians by baptism. They have no objection to the Christian religion, » and so they baptized them, « but for their amusement are apt to
attend the Buddhist festivals. Numbers of them make
no difficulty in asserting that they are *both Buddhists
and Christians.* » (2)

    But they are not always so candid. Sometimes
they think it more prudent to be Protestants in public,
and Buddhists only in private. « Amongst those who
profess Christianity, » says Colonel Forbes, « considerable pains are taken to conceal the unhallowed
rites which they secretly practise. » (3) « I consider

    (1) Owen's *History of the B. and F. Bible Society*, vol. II,
p. 272.
    (2) *Narrative*, etc., Introd. p. 61.
    (3) *Recent Disturbances in Ceylon*, p. 39. (1850).

the return officially made to the Government altogether ridiculous, » says Colonel Campbell, speaking
of the Church of England Missionaries, « but the
Cingalese have shown great readiness to assist these
reverend gentlemen in building their houses. » And
then he gives a particular instance. « The village
where these gentlemen reside contained 1,644 nominal Christians, but the greater part of them were
Christians in name only ... most of them continue
to worship devoutly, or rather to fear, the host of
devils they firmly believe in. » (1) « A converted Buddhist, » says another British officer, « will address
his prayers to our God, if he thinks he can obtain
any temporal benefit by so doing; but if not, he
would be just as likely to pray to Buddha, or to the
devil. » (2) « Nominal Christians often join in idol-
atrous devotional exercises, » says another Protestant official, « with apparently as much zeal as the
professed Buddhist. » (3) Mr Sullivan, a capable and
impartial witness, notices the still more singular fact,
that they will pass in the same hour from the Protestant service to the abominations of their own idolatry,
so little impression has the former produced upon
them. « The Cingalese, » he says, from his own
observation, « will attend chapel, listen with attention,
and apparently assent with understanding, but he
will go from chapel to his idol, from the preaching
of Christianity to the abominations of his degrading
profession, without the slightest trace of change ef-

(1) *Excursions in Ceylon*, vol. I, ch. VI, p. 121.
(2) Baker's *Rifle in Ceylon*, p. 85.
(3) *Ceylon : an historical Sketch*, by Henry Marshall, F. R. S.
E., etc. p. 236.

fected. » (1) « It is a subject of general regret to the
missions, » says Mʳ Bennett, an enthusiastic advocate
of the missionaries, « that, although in the immediate neighbourhood of a nominally christian population, scarcely one native family out of a hundred,
unless immediately connected with them, abstains,
on religious principle, from the ceremonies and
practice of devil worship. » (2) And all these witnesses, who thus disclose the incurable impotence of
Protestantism, are themselves enthusiastic Protestants. Let us turn from these official writers to the
missionaries themselves, who thus confirm their unwelcome evidence.

The Rev. James Selkirk, a Church of England missionary, reports of his colleague Mʳ Browning, that
« the multiplicity of his labours, and the little success he met with, were such as greatly to depress
Mʳ B'ˢ mind. » But Mʳ B. and his friends had other
vexations. « We are constantly pained, » adds Mʳ Selkirk, « to behold *vast numbers* infatuated by the
mummeries of popery. » (3) It was, no doubt, try-
ing, but the contrast might have suggested other
emotions than empty regret or restless mortification.

« The Church of Rome, here as elsewhere, » observes Sir Georges Barrow, « sweeps into its fold
all it can get. » (4) Apparently the Church of Eng-

(1) *A Visit to Ceylon*, by Edward Sullivan, ch. vii, p. 75.

(2) *Ceylon and its capabilities*, by J. W. Bennett Esq., F. L. S.,
late Ceylon Civil Establishment, ch. vii, p. 61.

(3) *Recollections of Ceylon*, by the Revᵈ James Selkirk,
ch. vii, p. 201.

(4) *Ceylon, Past and Present*, by Sir George Barrow, ch. vii,
p. 168. (1857).

laud tried to do the same, and no one blames the attempt; but why should it be laudable when it failed, and criminal only when it succeeded? « The Roman Catholic priests, » says Captain Percival, « with their usual industry, have taken advantage of the current superstitions to forward the propagation of their own tenets. » (1) He does not explain his meaning, nor need we attempt the unprofitable task; but he also is very angry at the « vast numbers » of their converts, whose real character and manner of life other Protestant witnesses, quite as prejudiced as Sir George Barrow and Captain Percival, but somewhat more candid, will describe to us presently. Meanwhile, let us hear Mr Selkirk again.

« Very few of the heathen, » he says, « i. e. native Kandyans, could be induced to come to hear the word preached, or, if they came for a short time, to be regular in their attendance. » This was in 1826, let us see if things improved as time went on. In 1827, « there were several things to discourage. Some of those who were communicants were seldom at church, except on that particular Sunday on which the Lord's supper was administered, » — which was probably very rarely. But they did not always come even then. « On one occasion there was not one of the communicants present, though notice had been regularly given the Sunday previous. » And these were the flower of their converts.

Years pass by, and still no improvement is recorded. « The Buddhists, » Mr Selkirk sadly relates, « remain prejudiced and bigoted to their own system of

(1) *Account of the Island of Ceylon*, ch. IX, p. 226.

error. The Roman Catholics continue stedfast in
their perversions of the Scriptures, and adherence
to vain superstitions : and the majority of Protestant
Christians, both European and natives, are lament-
ably indifferent to vital godliness. » (1) Is it possible
to avow more candidly, that Protestantism is the least
influential form of religion known amongst men?

In 1830, « the state of things had not much altered
for the better. » In 1835, for we need not give the
whole dismal history, year by year, « out of 580
souls, in 123 families, » — this was a Church of England mission, — « 80 children were unbaptized,
and in between thirty and forty families the parents
were living together unmarried. By far the greater
part of the whole visited are utterly careless, and live
as if they had no souls, and act as if they believed
with their heathen neighbours that there was no
God. » (2) Yet these were the « converts, » who
furnished the materials for « annual reports, » and
whose instruction and maintenance costs England
every year a kings's ransom.

Again; of the « nominally Protestant Christian
population of the southern and middle parts of Ceylon, » he says, « the worship of the devil is still
practised among them. »

Once more; if any one doubts the accuracy of Colonel Campbell's frank statement that « the return
officially made to the Government is altogether ridiculous, » let him weigh the following really horrible
account of the same Protestant missionary. « The

(1) *Recollections*, etc., ch. VII, p. 204
(2) P. 217.

Government native preachers, called Proponents, have sometimes baptized two or three hundred infants and elder children at a time. « They are paid, it seems, in proportion to the number, and therefore lay hold of all they can catch, employing as « sponsors » any one, pagan or not, who may be passing by; while these official baptists, who save the missionaries much labour, are themselves, says Mr Selkirk, « persons as ignorant of Christianity, as if there were no such religion in the world, and who perhaps have never been baptized themselves. » And then, as if this deplorable caricature of Christian missions were not sufficiently complete, he adds this frightful fact : — « Indeed, *almost all the Buddhist priests* in the *maritime provinces are persons who have been baptized in their infancy.* » (1)

It appears, moreover, that not only have multitudes of Buddhist priests received Protestant baptism, and therefore been celebrated as converts at English missionary meetings, but that others, who have not enjoyed the same advantage, are fully recompensed by more appreciable benefits. « The Government, » says Mr Dennett, in 1843, « allows a monthly stipend to forty two Buddhist priests. » (2) And twelve years after, Mr Baker is still able to notice the same amazing facts. « In Ceylon, » he tells us, « we see a protection granted to the Buddhist religion, while flocks of missionaries are sent out to convert the heathen ! We even stretch the point so far as to place a British sentinel on guard at the Buddhist temple in

(1) P. 515.
(2) *Ceylon and its capabilities*, ch. LI, p. 415.

Kandy, as though in mockery of our Protestant
church a hundred paces distant. » (1)

And these have been the only results, beyond the
luxurious maintenance of a vast number of missionaries and their families, of all the Church of England
and other Protestant missions in Ceylon, up to the
present hour. In 1849, Mʳ Pridham, who, it will be
remembered, prefers Buddhism to the Catholic Faith,
gives this report. « The results of the Church of England Mission have been almost entirely of a *negative*
character. *Christianity itself has made but lee-
way.* » (2) And this eternal sterility, which marks
all the operations of the Church of England, not only
in Ceylon but in every other land, is still more significant when we consider, that her missionaries, some
of whom are of course educated and zealous men,
have in several cases convinced the Buddhists of the
irrational folly of their religious tenets. « Its ministers, » as Mʳ Pridham observes, « have succeeded in
sweeping away a vast mass of the prejudices which
formerly confronted them. » Yet they can only succeed in making them infidels, never in making them
Christians. They persuade them sometimes to reject
the religion of Buddha, but cannot induce them to
accept their own in its place. They can destroy,
here as elsewhere, but have not yet learned how to
build up.

It is so great an advantage to be assisted to a
knowledge of these instructive facts by such a witness as Mʳ Pridham, — just as in our enquiry

(1) *Eight Years Wanderings in Ceylon*, ch. xi, p. 352.
(1855).

(2) *Ceylon*, etc., p. 441.

about India we received so much valuable aid from
M' Kaye, — that we will refer to him once more.
We have heard Protestant Missionaries denouncing
with considerable energy their own converts in Ceylon, but it appears that the day arrived when they
were inclined to retract their former censures, not
as unjust, but as weak and insufficient. « A minute
and careful examination of the native converts generally, » says M' Pridham, « has led even the Missionaries to form a *less* favourable opinion as to their
sincerity than they formerly entertained. » (1) And
the Rev. M' Tupper confirms this gloomy conclusion
in1856, when he says, that « all accounts agree in
reporting unfavourably of the state of Christianity
among them. Every one whom I asked said, it was
generally a hollow profession. » (2) They did not say
so in writing home to their employers, who would
have refused to receive such imprudent confessions,
but they relieved their minds by saying it to every
body else. M' Tupper considers, however, that in
spite of the unvarying experience of the last sixty
years, and the possession of every temporal and political advantage, they are not without motives, « to
encourage Missionary work; » a conclusion which
we shall presently see additional reasons for declining to adopt.

In the same year, 1856, the Rev. D' Hawks, who
examined all the facts on the spot with a candour not
unusual in Americans, says; « There are missionaries of various sects engaged in efforts to evangelise

(1) P. 442.
(2) *Out and Home*, by the Rev⁴ W. G. Tupper, M. A., p. 128.
II. 1.

the native heathen, *but with what success did not appear.* » (1)

And this is the language of every Protestant writer, except a few of that class who, in the words of an impartial witness, « become missionaries from interested motives, and whose relations of conversions and victories in the spiritual warfare are, to any one who has visited the scene of their exertions, as unfounded as they are mischievous. » (2) M' Baker also, than whom no traveller has enjoyed better opportunities of judging, honestly admits, in 1855, after more than half a century of missionary exertion, « the stationary, if not *retrograde*, position of the Protestant Church among the heathen; » and eloquently laments that England should have ruled so completely in vain over « the conquered nations (of the East), who have been subject to her for half a century, but know neither her language nor her religion! » (3)

In 1857, for lapse of time brings no change, M' Binning, a vehement Protestant, repeats once more that « Christianity has, as yet, gained but little footing among the natives of this island, » and that « the work of evangelisation seems to be scarce begun » (4) after the toils of half a century! Lastly, M' Sullivan declares from his own experience and observation, « supported by the testimony and opin-

(1) *American Expedition under Commodore Perry*, by Francis L. Hawks, D. D. ; ch. III, p. 120.
(2) Sullivan, ch. VII, p. 75.
(3) *Eight Years*, etc., ch. XI, p. 351.
(4) *Two Years Travel in Persia, Ceylon*, etc., by Robert B. M. Binning Esq., vol. I, ch. VII, p. 101.

ion of unprejudiced persons, whose long residence amongst them has made them acquainted with all their habits, that scarcely *one* real convert, whose belief is sincere and lasting, annually rewards the labours of the hundreds who are engaged in the spiritual warfare. » And this fact he proclaims because, he says, « it is the duty of travellers to offer the fruits of their experience, and to expose the almost utter uselessness of a system that... squanders sums which, if expended at home, would bring to perfection fruit that has been implanted in a good soil. » (1)

Perhaps all further evidence of the character and results of Protestant Missions in Ceylon may be deemed superfluous, but we must not conclude without quoting the testimony of so capable and impartial an authority as Sir Emerson Tennent. All his sympathies were with the men whose failure he thus describes. « The Clergy of the Church of England are indefatigable in their labours amongst the heathen; but although the section of the peninsula which is occupied by their mission contains a dense population of upwards of thirty thousands Tamils, the number who ordinarily attend their ministrations *seldom exceeds an average of twenty individuals.* » (2) And this is confirmed by a writer, formerly an Anglican missionary in Ceylon, who repeats, in 1848, the statement of another Anglican clergyman, « a man of great uprightness and untiring zeal in his work, » who declared in his presence, — « I do not believe that there are six real converts in the whole island. » (3)

(1) *A Visit,* etc., ch VII, p. 76.
(2) *Christianity in Ceylon,* ch. IV, p. 168.
(3) *Dublin Review,* vol. XXV. p. 104. (1848).

The Americans also, by far the most energetic in their methods of operation, confess, that after all their enormous expenditure, and « after thirty years of toil and devotion, they have enumerated not more than 680 *nominal* converts, who have been, at one time or other, received into communion with their churches; and the number now in connection with them is but 357! » This is certainly a feeble result compared with the 300,000 whom the Dutch reckoned, especially as even the fidelity of these is extremely doubtful and precarious. « Of the whole number, » adds Sir Emerson Tennent, « one seventh has been eventually excommunicated for their relapse into heathenism, and even of the remainder the Missionaries modestly remark that the proportion who are ‘ real Christians ’ can only be known to God. » (1) « The Church of England Missionaries, » he repeats, « speak with equal humbleness of their own labours during the past. »

A curious example of the real character of the so-called converts is furnished in the official reports of the American Board for Foreign Missions, in the year 1837. « During the year, » they inform their subscribers, « forty-nine were received in to the churches, and twenty-four were excommunicated. » (2)

If, lastly, we enquire what the Wesleyans, whose published reports are far from manifesting the same spirit of humbleness, have effected, there are not wanting Protestant witnesses to tell us. « It is certain, » says an English officer, who appears to have

(1) P. 170.
(2) P. 282.

been much struck by the « superabundance » of missionaries of this active sect, « that their exertions
and privations are greatly exaggerated. Their religious zeal seems directed to the inculcation of their
own peculiar tenets, rather than to the general diffusion of the light of Christian knowledge. Instead of
constantly visiting and residing at the various out-
stations, where the bulk of the uninformed population
dwell, they confine their wanderings within the limits
of the most desirable places of residence in the
island. » (1) This infirmity we shall find imputed to
them in other regions also, and especially in New
Zealand and America.

But it is fair to the Wesleyans to admit, that this
avoidance of hardship is no distinctive peculiarity of
their sect. A Protestant writer, who spent eight years
in Ceylon, and who deplores very candidly « the
enormous sums hitherto expended, with little or no
results, upon missionary labour, » gives us the following information. « For many years I have traversed the wildernesses of Ceylon, at all hours and at all
seasons. I have met many strange things during my
journies, *but I never recollect having met a missionary.* » He means a Protestant missionary, for he
continues thus. « Nevertheless, although Protestant
missionaries are so rare in the jungles of the interior,
and, if ever there, *no vestige ever remains of such a
visit,* still, in spots where it might be least expected,
may be seen the humble mud hut, surmounted by the
cross, the certain trace of some persevering priest of
the Roman faith. These men display an untiring zeal,

(1) *Rambles in Ceylon,* by Lieut. De Butts, ch. xiv, p. 279.

and no point is too remote for their good offices. Probably they are not so comfortable in their quarters in the towns as the Protestant missionaries, and thus they have less hesitation in leaving home. » (1) The explanation is somewhat inadequate, but let us return to the Wesleyans.

The Rev. D' Brown has described their operations, especially those directed by a certain D' Coke, who seems to have been a sort of ruler among them. « The schools which were so numerous, » he says, « and so numerously attended, were after some years found to be in a very inefficient state, and to have done little good. In some places the congregations continued good, but in Columbo, and others of the principal stations, they fell off greatly ; they were small, fluctuating, and very discouraging. Even the children educated in the schools, *when they grew up frequented the idol temples*, and scarcely a youth was to be seen at chapel, unless he was still a scholar... Disappointment, in short, was felt in every department of the mission. » (2)

This plan of schools was tried, as in India, by all the sects, and with precisely the same results. They could make atheists, but they could not make a Christian. « In Jaffna, » we are told by Sir Emerson Tennent, « while the educational labours of the American mission have produced almost a social revolution throughout the province, » — it appears that their schools were organised with skill, and maintained at enormous cost, — « the number of their *nominal* converts has barely exceeded 600, out of 90,000

(1) Baker, p. 360.
(2) *Hist. of Prop. of Christianity*, vol. 1, p. 515. (1854).

pupils ! • And again, speaking of the general results obtained, by all the sects, throught the agency of literary or educational efforts, he thus appreciates the costly failure. « As an instrument of conversion to Christianity, the press has hitherto been productive of but limited success in Ceylon... The moral results have been limited and unsatisfactory, though industriously applied to the multiplication of the Scriptures and Scriptural tracts, and to the preparation of school-books for the educational establishments. » (1) The Americans appear to have surpassed all others in prodigal expenditure. « The boarding school system, » we learn from an official report, « has been carried to a greater extent than in any other field to which the Board has sent missionaries. » The contributions forwarded from the United States, in the single year 1858, ranged from 20 to 350 dollars for *each* pupil in the Batticotta school; yet, in spite of a liberality which it is difficult to estimate but impossible not to admire, not one per cent. of these favoured pupils, though instructed with energy and skill during a long series of years, has made even a nominal profession of Christianity! Wealth, talent, and perseverance, combined with unquestionable humanity and benevolence, have utterly failed to obtain results which divine grace alone, without these human aids, has power to accomplish. In Ceylon, as in every other land, Protestant missionaries have employed a leverage powerful enough to move a world, and after the convulsive efforts of half a century have not succeeded in lifting a straw.

(1) Ch. vi, p. 263.

They tried also, as a last resource, — and in this
the various sects appear, as usual, to have com-
peted with each other, — hospitals, orphanages, and
other eleemosynary institutions, which are thus alluded to by Captain Laplace, who commanded the
Artemise on her voyage of scientific discovery. « The
numerous philanthropic institutions, destined to propagate Christianity and civilization among the natives,
the charitable establishments, in which a few sufferers
find relief in their misfortunes, only serve to hide
from the eyes of the vulgar the wretched condition
in which the population of Ceylon languish, although
their destiny has been confided for many years to
that which claims to be the most philanthropic nation
in the civilised world. » (1)

And now that, by the aid exclusively of Protestant
witnesses, we have traced the history and results of
Protestant Missions in Ceylon, — Dutch, American,
and English; it only remains to enquire in conclusion, what the Catholic Missionaries have done, and
what sort of converts *they* have rescued from the
cruel bondage of Buddhist superstition and idolatry?
The same witnesses will tell us.

We have heard already, from Protestants of various classes, not only that « vast numbers, » of the
natives of Ceylon have been converted to the faith,
and, as M' Selkirk lamented, are being « daily converted; » but that, in the words of Sir Emerson Tennent, « neither corruption nor coercion could induce
them to abjure it. » « Their numbers actually increased under persecution, » says the same writer;

(1) *Voyage de l'Artémise*, tome III, p. 78.

« they continue stedfast in their adherence » to the faith, says M' Selkirk, though up to 1848 there were only thirty Catholic Missionaries to serve 400 churches, and nearly 200,000 Christians; they are « bigoted » to their creed, adds D' Smith, by which he means constant and inflexible.

Baldæus had confessed long before, that « the most cruel persecutions of the kings of Jaffnapatam » could not shake the faith of the Catholic converts, though, as he observes, « they baptized many of the new converted natives with blood, after they had received the baptism by water. » (1) And the history continues the same to the end, for Sir Emerson Tennent declares, that, « their ranks are said to be daily increased by an accession of fresh converts from the heathen. » (2)

Nor has any Protestant writer ventured to give any other account of them. The Catholic Missionaries, they complain with one voice, succeed in winning the allegiance of their hearts and souls, while their unsuccessful rivals only reckon converts who deride their religion even while they nominally profess it, go out from a Protestant sermon to « worship devils, » and boast that they are Buddhists and Christians at the same time. « The ascendancy exercised by the Romish priests over the minds of their flocks, » says M' Pridham, « is very complete in the places where that religion chiefly obtains, far exceeding that of their Buddhist predecessors. » The Rev. James Cordiner, Protestant Chaplain to the Garrison of Columbo, sorrowfully records, that « a great body of the inhabitants

(1) In Churchill's *Collection*, vol III, p. 716
(2) Ch. III, p. 115.

now continue, voluntarily, firm in their adherence
to the Church of Rome. « Of the Catholic clergy
he candidly confesses, « they are indefatigable in
their labours, and are daily making proselytes. »
Their chapels, built and endowed by the contributions of the *natives*, « — not of the Government,
nor of the Missionary Societies, — « are neat and
well furnished. » (1) « And they are continually
building new ones. Fifteen Catholic churches were
in progress of erection in 1857, in the single province
of Jaffna. « It is unquestionable, » says an official
writer already quoted, who had noted all these
facts, « that the natives became speedily attached to
their ceremonies and modes of worship, » — that is,
to their faith and practice, to call things by their
proper names, — « and have adhered to them with
remarkable tenacity for upwards of three hundred
years. » (2)

Such is the first feature in the contrast between
Catholic and Protestant converts in Ceylon, but there
are others, still more worthy of our notice. « One
remarkable circumstance is observable in their converts, » says Sir Emerson Tennent; « that the number
of *nominal* Christians is infinitely smaller amongst
the Roman Catholics than amongst the professors of
any other church in Ceylon. » (3) But this is too
momentous a distinction to be left to the testimony
of a single witness, however competent and impartial.
We could hardly have ventured to anticipate that

(1) *A Description of Ceylon*, by the Rev⁴ James Cordiner, A. M.,
vol. I, ch. v, p. 154.
(2) Sir E. Tennent, II, 68.
(3) *Id.*, III, 90.

Protestants would exalt the superiority of Catholic
converts, yet Providence has arranged this also, and
in using them to proclaim their numbers to the
world, has forced them to confess their virtues at
the same time. It is a Wesleyan Missionary, — full
of the most extravagant prejudice, so that he is not
ashamed to call an image of our Lady and the Infant
Jesus, « a female idol with a child in its arms! » —
who thus describes, in obedience to a power of which
he was unconscious, the Catholics of Ceylon. « It is
but justice to this class of native Christians to state,
that in general they are more detached from the
customs of the pagan inhabitants; more regular in
their attendance on the religious services of their
communion; *and their general conduct more consistent with the moral precepts of Christianity,* than
any other religious body of any magnitude on the
island. » (1) But this gentleman was so impressed
by their marvellous constancy, under all trials and
temptations, that he could not restrain his reluctant
admiration. The following example might well excite
the astonishment of one who was familiar only with
Protestant converts. « More than two centuries, » he
says, after the Portuguese had been driven out, « two
small colonies of Roman Catholic Christians, the fruit
of the Portuguese Mission, were discovered embosom-
ed in the Kandyan jungles. Though unsupplied
with priests, they had continued a separate people,
and preserved their attachment to the Christian name
and ordinances. A copy of the New Testament,
translated into the vernacular tongue by an European

(1) Harvard's *Narrative*, Introd. p. 67.

Catholic priest, was found in their possession; and notwithstanding the errors of their system, the author cannot but avow his conviction, that such a translation, in connection with the singular preservation of the congregations referred to, furnishes a strong presumption of the purity and sincerity of those who laid the foundation of the work. » (1) Certainly so wonderful a fact might well suggest this conclusion, and we have reason to be surprised that this was all the effect it produced.

The superior morality of the Catholic natives was also generously attested by Sir Alexander Johnston, Chief Justice of Ceylon, who honorably confessed to the Archbishop of Goa, « that in a circuit he had lately made though the island, there was not a single Catholic brought for trial. »

All the Protestant witnesses appear to notice with surprise, some with peevish displeasure, another striking contrast between their own adherents and the disciples of the Catholic faith. Sir Emerson Tennent, after deploring « the trifling aggregate contributions » of the Protestant converts, says; « The Roman Catholic converts are by far the most willing to contribute from their own means to the support of their clergy and churches, and *their* donations for these purposes are on a scale of extreme liberality. » And this liberality is displayed by all ranks alike; although, as Mʳ Bertolacci observes, « poverty prevails in Ceylon more than in many other countries, because there are so very few manufactures carried on in it. » (2) « All the fishermen, » says a Presby-

(1) Harvard's *Narrative*, Introd. p. 64.
(2) *View of Ceylon*, by A. Bertolacci Esq., p. 205.

terian writer, « are said to be Roman Catholics, and
the tithe they pay to be worth 10,000 l. a year. » (1)
« Many of the Romanist churches in Columbo, » says
Mʳ Pridham, « have been built from the funds wrung
from the earnings of the devoted fishermen. » He says
« wrung, » though he knows the gift is one of voluntary charity, and does not stop to consider
what makes them « devoted. » Mʳ Selkirk, though
not less influenced by angry prejudice, says; « The
Roman Catholics of the Fisher-Caste are building a
new church at Negombo entirely at their own expense. They *refuse to take money* which people of
other castes, though Roman Catholics, are willing to
subscribe. They give up the produce of their fishing
one day in the week for this purpose. » (2) Mʳ Selkirk, though a missionary, calls this « a specimen of
the zeal of the Roman Catholics which might put
Protestants to the blush. » Mʳ Robinson also, though
he loses all self-possession when he speaks of Catholics, was so struck by the same class of facts, that
he uses exactly the same expression : « The zeal of
some of the poor Roman Catholics in Ceylon might
put many English Protestants to the blush. » (3) We
shall presently hear even a pagan Cingalese making
the same remark.

It is worthy of notice, and a sufficient refutation
of Mʳ Pridham's unwise calumnies, that the natives,
from whom their Catholic pastors have no need to
« wring » the contributions which their zeal sponta-

(1) *Six Years in India*, by Mʳˢ C. Mackenzie, vol. III, ch. IV,
p. 110.

(2) *Recollections*, etc., p. 394.

(3) *Romanism in Ceylon*, p. 163.

neously offers, will sometimes build churches even
in places where there is no Catholic missionary, in
the hope that their unsolicited munificence may induce one to compassionate their need; and the writer
who records this striking and unexampled fact, and
who once lived amongst them, says; « We know of
a single priest who, under not extraordinary circumstances, baptized more than 112 adults in the
course of one year. » (1)

But besides building churches out of their poverty,
and at the instigation solely of their own pious zeal,
we learn from Protestants to Whose honour they
dedicate them. It appears that Mr Selkirk, in spite of
his dislike of the « mummeries of popery, » sometimes ventured to enter the Catholic churches. « Of
course I could not understand the service, » he says,
but « the name of ' Maria ' came often over, and
some of them repeated at intervals the name of
' Jesus, ' in a very feeling manner, and smote their
breasts, crying out, ' My sin, my great sin. ' » We
who do « understand the service » have no difficulty
in comprehending, even from this defective account,
what these good people were doing, and Whose
praises they were celebrating.

And now we have sufficient Protestant evidence of
these facts, — that the Catholic natives of Ceylon
exist every where in great numbers, that new conversions occur « daily, » that nothing can seduce
their constancy, and that they are moral, diligent in
prayer, subject in all sincerity to their pastors, and
profuse in sacrifices and alms-deeds. It is not from

(1) See *Dublin Review*, vol. XXV, p. 106.

Catholic witnesses, to whom we have no need to apply, that we learn this, but from men who record it with grief and dismay. We cannot be surprised, then, to learn, and this may be our final observation, that even the heathen Cingalese, both educated and ignorant, easily discriminate between them and the nominal Christians of the Protestant sects.

The Journal of « Bishop Chapman of Colombo, » of the year 1850, — for all the facts we have noticed remain unchanged up to the present hour, — records the following instance of the estimate which the heathen themselves have formed of the results of Protestant conversion. A Kandyan chief, invited by an Anglican Missionary to allow his son to be baptized, gave him this answer. « What! would you have me make him a drunkard? » (1) Another Protestant writer, in 1854, gives a recent example still more curious and instructive, and one which will render all further testimony superfluous.

Mr Knighton, who was familiar with the interior as well as with the maritime provinces of Ceylon, relates in his interesting work four conversations which he had with an educated Buddhist, Marandhan, a Kandyan Colonel, who was « a fine specimen of his class, » and whom he endeavoured to convert to Christianity. Marandhan remarked to him that he had observed « the rancorous hatred between Protestants and Roman Catholics, » and continued thus : — « Well, with respect to these two great bodies of Christians, I have observed this — and I am sure you will not be offended at my mentioning it. »

(1) *Colonial Church Chronicle*, vol. V, p. 269.

Knighton. « Certainly not, any observations of yours on the subject I should be glad to hear. »

M. « Well, this : — Protestants *talk* most of their religion, Roman Catholics *believe* most. The former *seem* more enlightened on the subject, the latter *put their trust* in Christianity more firmly and more unhesitatingly. *Many* of the former seem to be sceptics, and *none* of the latter. Of this, too, I feel certain, that, generally speaking, the latter will make more sacrifices for their religion than the former. »

The Kandyan, — who was apparently a keen observer, and whose remarks upon the contrast which he had detected go some way towards explaining the failure of Protestant missions in all lands, — then instanced a recent case, an abortive attempt to collect subscriptions for a Protestant missionary from among the planters, and went on thus; —

« Considering the number of planters in this province, how small a proportion was willing to aid the original purposes of the scheme in carrying it out! I saw the list in the newspaper, not one twentieth part of the entire planting population, and yet all had been applied to! Now, had they been Roman Catholics, instead of Protestants, do you think that result would have followed? »

K. « Probably not. The unhappy disunion amongst us was the cause, however, of the failure of the scheme. »

M. « Another result of private judgment! »

K. « Perhaps so. We are wandering, however, from Buddhism. » (1) The conversation was appa-

(1) *Forest Life in Ceylon,* by W. Knighton, M. A., vol. II, app. pp. 411, 12.

rently taking an unpleasant turn, and Mr Knighton hastened to divert it into a safer channel. He found it easier to attack Buddhism than to shield his own religion from the assaults of so intelligent an adversary.

We have been told that the heathen in other lands are quite as observant of « the unhappy disunion » which is the characteristic of Protestantism as the natives of Ceylon. The Chinese replies to the missionaries of the various sects which present their conflicting religions for his acceptance, « You must have as many Christs in Europe as we have gods in China; » and the Hindoo says, as M^r Le Bas told us, « I should like your Christianity better if there were not quite so many kinds of it. » Let us hear what Protestant writers relate of the same mode of reasoning in Ceylon.

« I cannot but regret, » says Major Forbes, « the numerous and perplexing divisions of the Christian community. » (1) He had seen what were their bitter fruits, which a more philosophical writer thus describes at large for the admonition and instruction of his co-religionists.

« A serious obstacle to the acceptance of reformed Christianity by the Singhalese Buddhists has arisen from the distinctions and differences between the various churches by whose ministers it has been successively offered to them. In the persecutions of the Roman Catholics by the Dutch, the subsequent supersession of the Church of Holland by that of

(1) *Eleven Years in Ceylon*, by Major Forbes, vol. I, ch. v, p. 112.

England, the rivalries more or less apparent between
the Episcopalians and Presbyterians, and the peculiarities which separate the Baptists from the Wesleyan Methodists — all of whom have their missions
and representatives in Ceylon — the Singhalese can
discover little more than that *they are offered something still doubtful and unsettled,* in exchange for
which they are pressed to surrender their own ancient superstition. Conscious of their inability to
decide on what it has baffled the wisest of their
European teachers to reconcile, they hesitate to exchange for an apparent uncertainty what has been
unhesitatingly believed by generations of their ancestors, and comes recommended to them by all the
authority of antiquity; and even when truth has
been so far successful as to shake their confidence in
their national faith, the choice of sects which has
been offered to them *leads to utter bewilderment* as
to the peculiar form of Christianity with which they
may most confidingly replace it. » (1) If the experience
and observation of Sir Emerson Tennent had issued
only in this pregnant statement, it would have been
impossible to over-estimate its value.

We have already seen, in reviewing the history
of Protestant missions in other lands, and we shall
meet with fresh examples in every chapter of this
work, that the most evident effect of the presence
of Protestant missionaries in pagan countries is to
render their conversion impossible. The instincts of
human nature suffice to condemn a form of religion
which cannot unite even its own disciples in a

(1) Sir E. Tennent, ch. v, p. 196.

uniform profession; and the heathen only smiles at
the pretentions of a doctrine in which he detects the
inconstancy, contradictions, and incoherence which
betray even to his dull eye its earthly origin. He
knows that whatever be truth, *this* it cannot be. And
Protestant travellers, affrighted by the unwelcome
portent which confronts them at every step in their
wanderings, have contended with one another in
uttering cries of warning, rebuke, or entreaty, which
attest indeed the mortal influence of the evil they
deplore, but do not even suggest a remedy. « In
Ceylon and in India, » says one who had visited
many lands, and brought away the same sorrowing
conviction from each, « the Protestant Church has
no chance in competition with the Roman Catholic.
The importance of the precept, *In veste varietas sit,
non sit scissura*, is fully recognised by the latter
Church, which admits of no schism to affect its form
of worship, thereby offering a marked contrast to
the varied forms and conflicting doctrines of the
Protestant faith, that not only weaken and nullify
her at home, but utterly confuse and astound the
ignorant heathen abroad. » (1) And another writer,
— for all who have no private interest to serve use
the same language, — after noticing that the only
converts made in Ceylon are Catholics, thus explains
the sterility of the Protestant missions. « Among the
confusion arising from our multitudinous sects and
schisms, the native is naturally bewildered. What
with High Church, Low Church, Baptists, Wesleyans,
Presbyterians, etc., etc., etc., the ignorant native is

(1) *A Visit to Ceylon*, by Edward Sullivan, ch. VII, p. 78.

perfectly aghast at the variety of choice. » (1)

And now we may ask, since it is the only enquiry which remains to be satisfied, what explanation do Protestants offer of this new example, attested by themselves, of the contrast between Catholic and Protestant missions to the heathen? Most of them, it appears, maintain in this case an absolute silence, and are content to acknowledge a fact which the researches of their own friends have disclosed. They proclaim the complete and unchanging success of the Catholic, the perpetual failure of the Protestant missionaries, — and then they are silent. But Sir Emerson Tennent, though too upright and intelligent to countenance any disingenuous pleadings, and though he sharply rebukes both English calumny and Dutch cruelty, is of too ardent a temper not to attempt at least some solution of the problem. He puts aside, first of all, as might be expected in such a man, the immoral fictions of writers like Hough and Cordiner, who try to obscure an unwelcome fact by boldly asserting, that the Catholics « compelled the natives of Ceylon to adopt their religion. » « I have discovered nothing, » says Sir Emerson, « in the proceedings of the Portuguese in Ceylon to justify the imputation of violence and constraint; but unfortunately as regards the Dutch Presbyterians, their own records are conclusive as to the severity of their measures, and the ill success by which they were followed. » But if the earlier Catholic missionaries disdained such criminal and profitless measures, even when the civil authorities were, in some instances,

(1) Baker, *Eight Years*, etc., ch. xi, p. 361.

men of their own faith; much less could they dream
of adopting them during the last two centuries,
when they were themselves the objects of ceaseless
and unsparing persecution. Yet it is precisely during
the latter epoch, under the Dutch and English go-
vernments, that their successes have been most
conspicuous.

We are not surprised, then, that a writer like
Sir Emerson Tennent, should refuse to adopt an
explanation at once so inadequate and so arbitrary.
He suggests, however, in grave and temperate language, two considerations, which appear to have
impressed his own mind, and which deserve our
respectful notice. The inflexible stability, as well as
the superior morality of the Catholic natives, may,
he thinks, be partly attributed to « the over-ruling
influence of the Confessional, and the unintermitted
control which it exerts over the feelings and the actions
of its votaries. » And then he adds, — « in fact, if
any evidence were wanting to substantiate the real
ascendancy thus acquired and maintained by the
Church of Rome, it would be found in the munificence with which the natives contribute habitually
for its support. »

With this statement we find no fault. No doubt
the Sacrament of Penance produces the same healing
effect in Ceylon as in other lands. No doubt they are
happy who taste its salutary power, whether in
Ceylon or elsewhere. But the use of this Sacrament
is the *effect*, not the *cause* of conversion. Men seek
the tribunal of penance when their consciences are
enlightened, they abhor it while enslaved by self-
love. They come to it of their own free will, moved

by divine grace, and the deep searchings of the
heart. But so far is the « over-ruling influence of
the confessional » from explaining the conversion of
pagans, — though it may partly account for their
subsequent constancy and virtue, — that it would be
more reasonable to regard it as an additional impediment to their adoption of a religion which imposes,
upon all its disciples alike, so wholesome but mortifying a discipline. The confessional, Sir Emerson
Tennent may be assured, makes men excellent Christians when once admitted into the Church, but it
deters no small number from entering. The Sacrament of Penance has, fortified the Cingalese in the
practice of religion, but it was not the Sacrament of
Penance which first led them to embrace it.

The second suggestion of this excellent writer has
less claims to our respect. It is the « goudy ceremonial » of the Catholic Church, he says, which has
retained the Cingalese in her communion. But let
us quote his own words. « There is palpable evidence
to establish the fact, that once enrolled as Roman
Catholics, the imagination of the Cingalese became
excited, and their tastes permanently captivated by
striking ceremonial and pompous pageantry. » This
is a common Protestant explanation of the triumphs
of Catholic Missionaries. It has been applied to their
work in all parts of the world. It was this, says
Count Hogendorp, (1) which fascinated the Japanese.
He says it boldly, as if no one could deny it, though
he very well knew that tens of thousands of Japanese
were converted by men who had no other earthly

(1) *Coup d'œil sur Java*, par le Comte de Hogendorp, ch. XI,
p. 389.

possessions than a cassock, a crucifix, and a breviary. And what is true of Japan is equally true of every other pagan land. Does Sir Emerson Tennent suppose that Father Joseph Vaz, for example, when a fugitive in the swamps and jungles of Ceylon, converted thirty thousand idolaters by « pompous pageantry? » Did St. Francis Xavier, whose ecclesiastical apparatus was limited to a hand-bell and a catechist, convert seven hundred thousand souls by « gaudy ceremonial? » Did the Venerable John de Britto gain his tens of thousands in the forests of Marava by the splendours of an imposing ritual? Was it by the aid of such accessories that the martyred apostles of China and Corea, whose churches were huts and their vestments rags, won their triumphs? Was it « pageantry » which rescued 1,500,000 South American Indians from the worship of demons? Was it « ritual » which caused the Holy Name to be adored on the banks of Lake Huron, by the borders of the Ohio and the Mississippi, and again, at a later date, in the plains of Oregon and the valleys of the Rocky Mountains? Is it by a « gaudy ceremonial » that the Franciscans are at this moment renewing their ancient victories in the far interior of Brazil, or the Lazarists in Syria, or the Jesuits in Columbia, or the Marists in the islands of the Pacific? What, then, shall we think of a cause which strives to cloak its eternal humiliation, and to excuse its perpetual misadventures, by a plea which it knows to be false, and by attributing the conquests which it vainly envies to means which it was absolutely impossible to use, and which would have been utterly inadequate and ineffectual even if they had been employed?

The solitary explanation which Protestants venture to suggest of the triumphs of Catholic missionaries, attested in every land by their own witnesses, but every where denied to themselves, deserves further consideration. Let us examine it once for all, that we may not have to notice it again. It is their *only* argument; and yet it is at variance, not only with historical facts, but even with the universal practice of man, both heathen and christian, and with the instincts of his nature. And first, it is at variance with facts.

There is not so much as one example, literally not one, in the whole history of missions, of the heathen being attracted towards the Catholic religion simply by its ritual accompaniments. Only wilful ignorance, or incurable petulance, could attribute the conversions in India or China to such a cause; while in every other land in which missionary operations are now in progress, the poverty of the Catholic evangelists has become a proverb. In the islands of the Pacific, of which we shall have to speak hereafter, we hear of Catholic missionaries wanting even the common necessaries of life, and of their Bishop using « the back bone of a whale for his episcopal throne. » In America, even at the present day, they have not always food to eat; though in some provinces, as in Texas, Oregon, and California, it is habitually of the coarsest kind. In South America, they willingly share the life of the poor Indian, who honours them in spite, perhaps because, of their apostolic poverty; and obeys them, as his fathers obeyed theirs, with loving reverence. An American Protestant, who not long ago visited the Valley of

the Amazon, — in whose distant solitudes he encountered Catholic missionaries whom he describes,
with generous enthusiasm, as the very ideal of apostolic teachers, — makes this observation; « I was
amazed at the *poverty* of the church, and determined, if I ever went back, to appeal to the Roman
Catholics of the United States for donations. » (1)
And this is confirmed by an English officer, who
traversed the same remote regions, where he found
Catholic missionaries honoured with « the greatest
respect and deference,» even by natives who «showed
no deference to any one but the Padre, » but where
he describes almost every church which he saw, from
the Andes to Para, as little better than « *a huge
barn.* » (2) Yet we are asked to believe that the
Church wins souls to God only by the fascinations
of a « gaudy ceremonial. »

But this popular explanation contradicts, not only
the facts which are admitted and proclaimed by
every competent witness, but also the most notorious
phenomena of heathen life. The pagan, though he
has reared many a gorgeous temple, and decorated
it with such skill as his knowledge of art allows,
has never even conceived the idea of devising a specious ceremonial as a substitute for a more active
and intellectual worship. Every where he retains, in
spite of his fall, the primitive traditions of *sacrifice,
prayer,* and *mortification.* The very Hindoo would
despise the imposture of a hollow ecclesiastical pageantry. He does not even worship idols, if we may

(1) Lieut. Herndon's *Valley of the Amazon,* ch. xi, p. 225.
(2) *Narrative of a Journey from Lima to Para,* by Lieut.
W. Smyth, ch. viii, p. 148; ch. xi, p. 213.

believe Protestant writers, but « symbols of the Almighty's power; » (1) and Sir William Hooker affirms generally of the Buddhist devotee, that he « attaches no real importance to the idol itself. » (2) His worship is demonology, but still it is worship. He comprehends, unlike the Protestant, those great principles which the latter alone of all mankind seem to repudiate in their practice, — the sovereign rights of the Creator over His creature, the obligation and efficacy of penance in a fallen race, and the principle of *sacrifice* as the essence of worship. Hence it is easier to convert him than the children of Luther and Calvin, who have lost even these primary no-tions. The disciples of Buddha and Confucius, of Brahma and Mahomet, nauseate, in spite of their spiritual penury, the sapless food of pageantry and ceremonial, as incapable of appeasing the famine of their souls. And they have shown, in many a land, that they know how to discriminate between the solemn ritual which veils and symbolises the august mysteries of the Christian Altar, and those chill forms of Protestantism which symbolise nothing; — dreary accompaniments of a religion which rightly eschews ceremonial, because it has nothing to hide and nothing to reveal, because it begins and ends with man, and contains no deeper mystery than the varying accents of the human voice. And thus it comes to pass, as we have read in this chapter, that the heathen will hurry immediately from a Protestant service to the adoration of his own divinities, because

(1) *The Wonders of Elora*, ch. XIV, p. 347.
(2) *Himalayan Journals*, vol. I, ch. XIV, p. 324,

he has detected that in the former there was not
even the semblance of *worship*. He has hardly been
conscious that so frigid a ceremony, in which he
has seen only a man reading out of a book to other
men, often without much sign of interest on either
side, had even the pretence to be a religious service.
He has perceived in it nothing but a tedious and
unmeaning formality, which he has deemed, like the
Hindoo, only a new eccentricity of his incompre-
hensible rulers. Yet he has confessed, at the first
glance, on entering the humblest Catholic oratory,
that *there* men were offering *worship*. In both cases
his instinct has guided him aright.

There is no form of religion in the world, as De
Maistre has shown, save only Protestantism and
Islamism, of which *sacrifice* is not the chief act.
« Ubi *corpus* fuerit, » said our Blessed Lord, « ibi et
aquilæ congregabuntur; » (1) in which divine words
we have, so to speak, the whole distinction between
the Catholic and Protestant religions. And a learned
English writer tells us, that even « to the Hindoo the
ideas of a *Sacrifice*, an Incarnation, and a Trinity
are already familiar : » (2) so that when the true
notion of these divine mysteries has been unfolded
to his consciousness by men whose manner of life
corresponded with his own conception of what befits
a teacher of religion, he fell on his knees and adored,
confessing the supreme majesty of that tremendous
Altar and Sacrifice by which, as the last of the prophets had foretold, the Name of God should become

(1) St Luke, xvii, 37.
(2) *Life of Baler, Emperor of Hindostan*, by R. M. Caldecott
Esq., p. 336.

« *great among the Gentiles.* » (1) *This* is the secret
of conversion, and not the ritual which does but
feebly minister to it.

Ou the other hand, the religions of the so-called
Reformation, upon which the heathen looks, in every
land, either with unmoved apathy or with angry
contempt, are thus described even by their most
eminent advocates. « The characteristic badge of the
Protestant world, » says Menzel, « is religious indifference. Every thing depends in the Protestant form
of worship upon the preacher for the time being. For
the Catholic, all his churches are alike, and he con-
ducts his devotion without the priest, as it makes but
little difference what priest officiates. Hence there
prevails, if I may so say, an undisturbed equanimity
of devotion every where among the Catholics. Among
the Protestants, however, every thing depends upon
the personal character of the preacher; for his sake
alone, and only when he is present, do people go to
church ; people regard him alone, are concerned with
him alone, because nothing else in the Protestant
church attracts attention. » (2) He only stops short
of the confession, which could not be expected from
him, that this is the very apostasy predicted of old,
which should set up *man* in the place of God, and
having « *taken away the Daily Sacrifice,* » should
bring in « the abomination of desolation. » (3)

And we have seen that such an impression exists
even in the heathen mind with respect to it. Every
where they doubt whether Protestantism be really a

(1) Malachias, i, 11.
(2) *German Literature,* by Menzel, vol. 1, p. 147; (ed. Felton.)
(3) Daniel, xi, 31.

religion at all. « They marvel, » says M′ Forbes,
« whether the English have any religion. » The Persians, M′ Walpole and others tell us, make the same
remark. The Turks, as M′ Warburton noticed, call
them « the prayerless. » The Chinese, as D′ Morrison
complained, « are irreverent, and laugh. » The Kurds
claim the English as co-religionists, because « they
keep no fasts and say no prayers; » and even the
Druses, the atheists of Syria, have learned to consider
the Protestant religion, as we shall be told hereafter,
« a species of freemasonry which very much resembles their own. » Why, then, does Sir Emerson Tennent attempt to explain the success of Catholic and
the failure of Protestant missionaries by a suggestion
which deals only with the surface of things, and
leaves their substance untouched? The true explanation lies deeper. It is not a question of ritual, but of
doctrine. The Catholic succeeds, not only because his
vocation, his gifts, and his faith, are all from God,
but because he can erect an Altar *on which He is
really present;* the Protestant fails, because even the
heathen detect that he is only a man like themselves,
and though he affects to be the minister of a divine
religion, can entertain them with nothing more divine
than the sound of his own voice.

One more observation we may offer, before finally
quitting a subject to which it will not be necessary
hereafter to recur. It there be in the world a class of
men who, in a certain sense, are absolutely indifferent
to « ceremonial, » although obliged to use it, and
who in celebrating the mysteries of their holy religion
are almost unconscious of its presence, the Catholic
belongs to that class. Whether he assists at the Holy

Sacrifice, which constitutes the chief act of his religion, or at any other of the divine offices which
attract him with irresistible power to the house of
prayer, his eye and heart are fixed, not on sensible
objects, but on that Awful Presence, — *stupendum
supra omnia miraculum*, — which at one time is
veiled in the Tabernacle, at another manifested to the
gaze of the faithful. Vestments, music, and incense
—whatever meets the eye or ear — he hardly notes,
for there is something there which speaks to the soul,
and taxes all its powers. Let the accompanying ceremonial be meagre or imposing, it is with the mind of
a Christian, not of an artist, that he marks its presence; all he asks is, that it shall not distract him —
the rest, in the presence of those stupendous mysteries, is of little import. Like Mary and Salome, he is
thinking of the Body which he has come to adore,
not of the « sweet spices » which he has brought to
anoint it. He provides indeed, out of reverent love,
the « fine linen, » the « myrrh and aloes, » (1) and
whatsoever else his devotion may inspire or the
Church appoint, for in this august action she leaves
nothing to human caprice or invention; but all these
accessories of his worship, from the least to the
greatest, — the cloud of incense, the blazing lights,
the swelling choir, and the jewelled robes, — have
no worth and no significance but as offerings to Him
who gives them all their value by deigning to accept
them. « All these are signs and symbols; for the
devotion to the Blessed Sacrament is the adoration of
the Uncreated Majesty..... Verily there is no pomp

(1) S. John, xix, 39.

but that of a believing and loving Heart, which pays
welcome or respectful court to this Sacramental
King. When we gaze therefore upon the white robes
of the Immaculate King, the lights and flowers of the
sanctuary seem to fade away, and there open before
the eyes of faith interminable regions of various
splendour and consummate beauty, over which as
Man He is at this moment wielding His far-reaching
sceptre of dominion. » (1)

It is true that this is not the idea which Protestants
entertain of Catholic worship, but Protestants are
hardly competent judges in such a matter. For them,
— who consistently despise « ceremonial, » because
they abolished long since the Daily Sacrifice, and cast
the Altar to the ground, — only that which meets
the eye and ear has any meaning, and even this they
pervert or misconceive. When Mr Selkirk enters a
Catholic church in Ceylon, and tells us, « of course
I could not understand the service, » he accurately
represents the qualifications which Protestants bring
to the critical examination of Catholic worship. When
Dr Clark notes the breathless devotion of a congregation in Seville Cathedral, and then adds with contempt, that it was some « picture » which his roving
glance had detected that they were really worship-
ping; (2) he knew not that he was probably the only
person in that silent throng who was even conscious
of its presence. When another Episcopalian clergyman goes to a High Mass at St. Peter's, celebrated by
the Sovereign Pontiff, and then hurries home to write

(1) Father Faber, *The Blessed Sacrament*, book IV, § 2, p. 432.
(2) *Glimpses of the Old World*, by the Revd I. A. Clark, D.D.

in his journal, « Alas! no religious feeling could for
a moment be connected with it! » (1) — he only
proves that he was looking for *man*, and listening
for man's voice, where the company of the faithful
saw God alone. It is ever thus with spectators of this
kind. Like the Jews who thronged the streets, going
up to the Passover, they see a Child seated on an ass,
and a Maiden by His side; but they hurry on, and
know not that it is the Lord of Heaven and His Immaculate Mother whom they have just passed by. The
« Sacramental King » is as effectually hidden from
the sectary, as the Incarnate God was from the Jew.
They wander into the temple, they hear the music, and
see the lights, — for they can exercise sensual functions, — but of what is really going on in that place,
what mean those bended knees and downcast eyes,
why that ministrant is covered with cloth of gold and
demeans himself like one standing in the court of
Heaven, — all this is as completely hidden from them
as if the Cross had never been lifted up on Mount
Calvary, nor the *Pure Oblation* known amongst men.
And so they smile on one another, and then go home,
like Mr Selkirk, to talk of « the mummeries of popery. » So utterly unconscious are they of that which
is the joy and life of all other Christians, as it is the
supreme blessedness of the Angels in heaven, — so
effectually have they banished God even from their
temples, in order to enthrone man in His place, —
that they can only scoff while men who have known
Him from their childhood upwards are holding their
breath in His Presence, so deeply absorbed and

(1) *Memorial of the Holy Land*, by the Revᵈ George Fisk, p. 25.

entranced by that coming amongst them of the Holy
One, though His majesty be clouded by the sacramental veils, that they forget, not only music and
incense and vestments, but even the intrusion of these
jesting critics, who with unbent knee and head erect,
in all the wisdom of complacent ignorance, are passing sentence upon them.

If it were possible for aliens to know, for one
brief hour, what is the Presence of God in the Church,
and how it is manifested, they would comprehend
at last, that the « ceremonial » which they deem so
important an element in Catholic worship has no
charm either to beguile Christians or to convert the
heathen. They would learn also to rebuke and detest
the light judgments of foolish men, whom the Prince
of the Apostles calls, in terrible words which only
an Apostle might use, « irrational beasts, *blaspheming those things which they know not.* » (1)

And now we may conclude. We have heard
enough of the history of religion in Ceylon, and of
Protestant comments upon it. The evidence which
might have been obtained from Catholic sources has
been excluded, in spite of its interest and import-

(1) 2ᵈ Sᵗ Peter, II, 12. Since « the Blessed Sacrament is the
greatest work of God, the most perfect picture of Him and the
most complete representation of Jesus, it must needs follow that
it is the very life of the church, being not only the gift of Jesus,
but the very living Jesus Himself... It is the central devotion of
the church. All others gather round it, and group themselves there
as satellites; for others celebrate His mysteries, this is Himself.
It is the universal devotion. No one can be without it, in order to
be a christian. How can a man be a christian who does not worship the living presence of Christ? » Father Faber, *The Blessed
Sacrament*, book IV, § 7, p. 541.

ance, because it is proposed in these volumes, for
obvious reasons, to leave historical proofs to Protestants alone. It is from *them* we have learned how the
native Catholics of Ceylon have resisted, during three
centuries, both the savage assaults of persecution
and the politic benevolence of heresy. From them
also we have learned what is the character of their
own converts, and how exactly they resemble those
whom they have gained in other lands. We may
be satisfied with their unwilling testimony; and
if we add, in conclusion, a few words from one
whose name is honoured in many a Christian household throughout Ceylon, it is only as an example of
the revelations which we might have obtained abundantly from similar sources.

In December, 1832, Bishop Bettachini, the Vicar
Apostolic of Jaffna, gave the following account of
occurrences within his own Vicariate, which includes
only the northern portion of the island. « The number of conversions, of Gentiles and Protestants, during the past year, amounts to 501. » Of Trincoma-
lee, he says; « It is the residence of a Lombard
Priest, Dom Vincent Cassinelli, who is much esteemed by all parties. A considerable number of
conversions from Protestantism is made here every
year, so many indeed, that the Methodists, who had
a station here, have been obliged to give up the contest for want of proselytes. » Of Chilau, this is his
report. « A large church, with three naves, is in
course of erection here, sufficiently spacious to ac-
commodate five thousand persons. » There are no
contributions from missionary societies, nor gifts
from official patrons, but religious zeal supplies

their want. « Men and women, » says the Bishop,
« boys and girls, have set to work with incredible
zeal. The judge of the district, who is a convert
from Protestantism, has given upwards of 40 l. as
his subscription. The chief merit of the work is due
to Dom Froilano Oruna, a Spanish Benedictine, who
has acquired marked influence over the population. »
Of the mission of Valigamma, close to Jaffna, the
Bishop notices, that though the Protestants have immense institutions, « an extensive printing establishment, a large college for the education of boys, a
large seminary for girls, in both of which pupils are
received gratuitously, ninety schools, two doctors,
eight or nine ministers, and several catechists, » —
who are all maintained by subscriptions from England and America, — the results, by their own
admission, have been so nugatory, that « it is probable they will soon disappear altogether. » Lastly,
he thus mentions their attempts to corrupt the Catholic natives, by offers of books and money. « When
the Protestant ministers visit them, to distribute
their books among them, these good Christians not
only reject with contempt the poison offered to them,
but often confound the distributors by various embar-
rassing questions, which render the apostles of error,
who are at a loss to answer them, objects of
scorn. » (1)

The facts referred to by the Bishop in these extracts are once more confirmed, in 1860, by an authority who shall be our last witness. « From the latest
published Reports of the Protestant missionary So-

(1) *Annals*, vol. XIV, p. 164.

cieties, it appears, that the Protestant Native Converts, of all sects, in the whole Island, amount only to 4,259. » And even this scanty number is constantly diminishing, in spite of the various attractions held out to them. Thus in the single Vicariate of Columbo, in the course of the year 1857, 411 adult Protestants were received into the Church; in 1858, 422; and in 1859, 289; making a total of 1,122 adult Protestant converts in three successive years, in one only of the ecclesiastical provinces into which Ceylon is divided. (1)

Once more we have applied the divine rule, *By their fruits ye shall know them.* Let the reader, who will have observed that all our evidence has been derived from Protestants, condemned to awaken the conscience of others by publishing facts which produced no effect upon themselves, draw his own conclusions. It is no new thing that Almighty God should employ the enemies of the Church to proclaim their own humiliation and her glory; but it seems to be His will, not only that the hopeless sterility of Protestantism, in spite of the talents and even the virtues of some of its professors, should be everywhere manifest, but that everywhere there should be a Protestant historian to detect and record it. They will accompany us in all the lands which we have still to visit, and in each they will tell us the same tale — of wealth idly wasted, and labour leading to nothing. Every where they find God absent from their councils, every where they proclaim the dreary void which that absence creates. Missionaries, tourists, and offi-

(1) *Madras Catholic Directory for* 1860, pp. 178-180.

cials go forth from England or America, in the gaiety
of their hearts, to chronicle the baneful influence of
the Ancient Faith, and to sing the triumphs of the
new; and when at last their books are published,
the world is amazed to find, that they have unconsciously obeyed the inspiration of God rather than of
their own hearts, and that the glories of the Catholic
Church are divulged by her most unscrupulous enemies, and the impotence of Protestantism elaborately
proved by the most enthusiastic of its own disciples.

CHAPTER V.

MISSIONS IN THE ANTIPODES.

We have now, for the first time, to speak of regions in which, by a singular exception, the Protestant preceded the Catholic Missionary. In Australia and New Zealand, during a long course of years, the agents of English missionary societies conducted their operations in the presence of friendly witnesses alone. No competitors were there to impede their free action, no rivals to dispute their influence. Three nations of pagan and uncivilised men, whose lands seemed to have long invited a new possessor, had opened their gates to England and her emissaries. With unlimited resources, and backed by the whole power of one of the greatest empires on earth, they had only to reign in peace, and command these deserts to revive and

flourish, like a field on which the dew of heaven has
descended. Here, at length, was an opportunity of
showing what the « reformed religion » could effect,
in a sphere where its dominion was supreme and
uncontested, towards the conversion of the gentiles.
It had often boasted its power, the moment had arrived to test it. Australia, New Zealand, and Tasmania were added to the long catalogue of Britain's
colonial conquests; let us see whether she has
played in them a nobler part than in India or Ceylon.

We should only echo the complaint of her own
sons, if we were to say, that of two out of the three
England has made a moral cesspool. But this familiar reproach, which, on the one hand, is harsh and
unjust for want of due limitation, on the other, takes
no account of far more real crimes than those which
it too hastily condemns. It was surely no unpardonable offence, unless we deny the fundamental maxim
of Roman jurisprudence, to banish from the society
which they had outraged the felon and the homicide.
But it was cruel and impious to treat these unhappy
outcasts like brutes condemned to the slaughter, and
to provide for them, in the land of their exile, only
shambles and an axe. More than any of the sons of
men they needed—for it was all which now remained
to them—the hope of reconciliation, and the promise
of the future. Their bodies they had forfeited, and
could henceforth move hand or foot only at the bidding of the taskmaster; but their souls were free,
and in that freedom they could still seek after union
with God, still propitiate a Judge who wipes away
the tears which He has caused to flow, and in the

very act of chastising has already begun to pardon. Yet
the first ship which bore away its freight of despair,
—of bruised hearts, and woful memories, and fearful
expectations, — would have left the shores of England without even a solitary minister of religion, but
for the timely remonstrance of a private individual!
The civil authorities deemed their work complete
when they had given the signal to raise the anchor
and unloose the sails — the rest was no concern of
theirs.

Half a century later, the same disgraceful fact re-
curred. « An oversight equally remarkable took
place, » says Judge Burton in 1840, « upon the recent expedition to Port Essington. » On this occasion
also, « H. M. S. Alligator sailed from England with
upwards of five hundred souls, unprovided with any
minister of religion. » (1)

But this is not all. In Australia, as in India, they
neither provided ministers themselves, nor would
suffer others to supply the defect. Among the emigrants to the new continent were some of those
children of Ireland, whom Providence seems to have
dispersed through all the homes of the Saxon race,
that they might one day rekindle amongst them the
light of faith which their own long misfortunes have
never been able to quench. To these exiles it was necessary to convey the succours of religion. The first
Catholic priest who arrived in Australia on his mission of charity, and whom the policy of self-interest
should have persuaded the authorities to greet with
eager welcome, was treated with derision, and « was

(1) *State of Religion and Education in N. S. Wales*, p. 72.

directed, « as one of his most energetic successors relates, « to produce his ' permission, ' or hold himself
in readiness for departure by the next ship. » (1)
He was alone, and therefore a safe victim; while
his presence was irksome to men who seem to have
felt instinctively that his proffered ministry was the
keenest rebuke of their own cruelty and profaneness.

Dut we need not pursue the details of a history
which is absolutely uniform from its opening to its
final chapter, and which contains only two facts, —
the one, that not even a solitary native of Tasmania
or New Holland has ever been converted to the faith;
the other, that the aboriginal tribes of the first have
utterly ceased to exist under British rule, while those
of the second are rapidly dying out. Such, as we
shall see more fully hereafter, has been the invariable
destiny of the savage, in Australia, in North America,
in South Africa, in Polynesia, — wherever he has
found Protestant masters; while in the Philippines,
in Oceanica, and in Western and Southern America,
he has dwelt in peace and prosperity, nay, has
increased and multiplied under Catholic rulers. Let
us briefly trace this history in Australia, and the influence of Protestant missions, conducted with every
advantage which power and wealth could impart,
upon her aboriginal tribes.

The subject is meagre, and need not detain us
long. A few characteristic facts will suffice. They are
Protestant witnesses who will tell us, once more, the
familiar tale of worldly and covetous missionaries, of
the immorality of the English colonists, of money

_____

(1) *A Reply to Judge Burton*, by W. Ullathorne, D. D., p. 10.

squandered in vain, and of final and admitted failure.
D' Lang, the Protestant historian of New South
Wales,—who reports, in 1852, « there is as yet no
well authenticated case of the conversion of a black
native to Christianity, » — will assure us that this
result is not due to insufficiency of temporal resources. « In the year 1828, » he says, « when the whole
population did not exceed 36,598, (of whom about
one half belonged to other communions,) the cost of
the Episcopalian establishment of the colony exceeded
22,000 l. » And apparently even this failed to satisfy
the class amongst whom it was distributed. « Accounts
of the most discreditable character were trumped up
by individual chaplains, who had ample salaries and
allowances of every description besides. In this way
the two Episcopalian chaplains in Sydney presented,
one an account for 700 l., and the other an account
for 500 l., which were both paid them, in addition
to all their regular and accustomed demands. » (1)
Archdeacon Scott, he says, after failing in business
in England, then acting as a clerk or secretary, finally
merged into an ecclesiastical dignitary, and was sent
out with a salary of 2,000 l. And though these revelations may be fairly attributed to sectarian animosity,
this Presbyterian witness is at all events perfectly
candid, and does not conceal « the cold-blooded and
unnatural indifference which, I am sorry to acknowledge, the Church of Scotland evinced at that period,
and for many years thereafter to the moral and religious welfare of her people in the colonies. »

(1) *History of New South Wales*, by John DunmoreLang, D. D.,
vol. II, ch. XI, p. 465. (1852.)

Perhaps the excessive opulence of the Episcopalian clergy may partly account for certain characteristic facts which we may notice at once, for the
sake of getting rid of them. When D' Broughton,
who was their bishop, was examined by a Committee
of the House of Commons as to his success in converting the aborigines, the following opinion was eli-
cited from him. « Have you found it absolutely impossible to instil into their minds any adequate idea of the
Deity and of Christianity? Of Christianity, certainly,
I should say. » (1) It is only fair to the Wesleyan
witnesses, before the same Committee, to say, that
they emphatically repudiated this opinon, and apparently with reason. A scientific writer, who had examined the question as a physiologist, gives his verdict
in favour of the Wesleyans. « Examination and
comparison have shown, » he says, alluding to the
physical characteristics of the Australian race, « that,
instead of peculiarities, strong analogies are found
to the skulls of white men. » (2) And another capable witness confirms this *dictum* of science by the
conclusive fact, that there was not wanting evidence
of distinct « religious traditions » among them. (3)

Indeed a large number of writers on Australia appear anxious to refute the discreditable plea of
D' Broughton. « They are as apt and intelligent, »
says Sir George Grey, who had carefully studied
their habits and character, « as any other race of

(1) *Parliamentary Papers*, vol. VII, p. 14, Cf. p. 201.
(2) *Physical Description of N. S. Wales*, by P. E. de Strzelecki, § 7, p. 335.
(3) *Savage Life and Scenes in Australia and New Zealand*, by
George French Angas, vol. II, ch. VII, p. 231.

men I am acquainted with. » (1) « Their belief in
spirits is universal, » we are told by M' Angas.
« Certain it is, » says M' Marjoribanks, « that they
believe in the immortality of the soul, and the existence of evil spirits. » (2) « There is no doubt whatever, observes M. de Rienzi, after careful investigation, « that the Australians are capable of being
civilised. » (3) « There is some reason to think, »
adds M' Dennett, « that the aborigines believe in the
metempsychosis; » (4) an opinion confirmed both
by M' Parker, who held the office of Protector of
Aborigines, and by Mgr. Salvado, who has dwelt
among the tribes of the interior, and gives conclusive
proofs of their remarkable aptness. (5) « The work
of evangelising them may be unpromising, » says
M' Young, a Wesleyan missionary, « but it presents
no greater difficulties than those which, in other
parts of the heathen world, have been overcome. » (6)
Finally, M' Gerstaecker, an experienced German traveller, in proving the « abilities and talents » of the
Australian native, gives this decisive example. He
visited a school, in which native children not only
« read the New Testament with a great deal more
expression and emphasis than children commonly

(1) *Journals of Two Expeditions in Australia*, vol. II, ch. XVIII,
p. 374.
(2) *Travels in New South Wales*, by Alexander Marjoribanks,
ch. IV, p. 92.
(3) *Oceanie*, par M. G. L. Domeny de Rienzi, tome III, p. 517.
(4) *Wanderings in N. S. Wales*, by George Bennett Esq.,
F. L. S., F. R. C. S., vol. I, ch. 5, p. 131.
(5) *Mémoires historiques sur l'Australie*, par Mgr. Rudesindo
Salvado, 3me partie, p. 258. (ed. Falcimagne, 1854.)
(6) *The Southern World*, ch. V, p. 111. (1854).

exhibit in English village schools, » but afterwards
gave an explanation « which proved the excellent
memory of the children. » (1) Here was surely
some material to work upon. Dr Broughton, however, had decided that he and his wealthy colleagues
could do nothing with such people. We may, therefore, put aside the Episcopalian clergy, but not without noticing two facts which identify them with their
class in every other land.

Dr Broughton, who thought the Australian incapable of receiving truths which are addressed equally
to every creature of God, was more solicitous about
the progress of the Catholic religion in New South
Wales than about the conversion of savages; and
distinguished himself chiefly by sending home fretful
protests against the « schismatical » archbishop of
Sydney for using a title which Dr Polding had received
from the successor of St. Peter, and Dr Broughton
from the successor of Henry VIII. The Catholic prelate took no notice of his invectives, which hardly
provoked any other comment than the remark of a
French writer in the *Correspondant*, that « an Anglican charging a Catholic with schism is like Ishmael
calling Isaac a bastard. »

The second fact referring to Dr Broughton and his
colleagues is the following. It appears that there was,
not long ago, a sort of conference of Protestant
bishops at Sydney, at which a majority expressed a
quasi-official opinion in favour of the doctrine of
Baptism, the adoption of which they cautiously
recommended to their ecclesiastical inferiors. The

(1) *Voyage*, etc., vol. III, ch. II, p. 88.

« clergy of Australia, » however, immediately resolved, that « the construction put by the Bishops,
if imposed, would be tantamount to a new article of
faith. » The laity also protested against the innova-
tion, while the clergy of Van Dieman's Land solemnly
addressed their bishop to record « their regret, that
after the decision of the Privy Council, and two
Archbishops, » he should entertain such unsound
views. (1) In the presence of such facts we have
surely no reason to marvel, when Count Strzelecki
informs, us, that « the attempts to civilise and christianise the aborigines *have utterly failed.* » (2)

When we have mentioned one or two examples of
the efforts made, and of their result, the tale will be
complete. « Efforts prodigal indeed in zeal and money, » says Colonel Mundy, speaking of the Australian native, « have been made to civilise and christianise him, but they have hitherto met with signal
failure. » The Colonel then quotes a Missionary Report, referring to « the greatest of all the mission
stations on this continent, » at which large sums
had been expended, during nine successive years,
in feeding, instructing, and preaching to the natives. « Amongst all those young men, » says the
Report of the year 1842, « who for years past
have been more or less attached to the Mission,
there is only one who affords some satisfaction and
encouragement. » (3) And the results of all this

(1) *New Zealand and its Inhabitants*, by the Revd Richard
Taylor, M. A., ch. xx, p. 304.
(2) *Physical Description*, etc., § 7, p. 350.
(3) Colonel Mundy's *Australasian Colonies*, vol. I, ch. vii,
p. 241.

care, and of an education prolonged through many
years, are still more darkly depicted by Mr Hood,
in the following year, 1843. « It is said that cases
have occurred of persons who when young had been
educated at the Mission, murdering their children in
after years. » (1) M. de Rieuzi mentions the case of
one who was brought up from childhood by a beue-
volent Englishman, sent to England, and exhibited
at many public meetings as a specimen of the success
of Protestant education; but who, on his return to
the colony, fled to his native forests, where he lived
in a state of nudity, and was finally executed for
rape. (2) Yet the missionaries had, no doubt, done
their best, though with little effect upon scholars
many of whom, as Colonel Mundy observes, « learned
merely by rote, but all enjoyed the good feeding: the
words Missionary and Commissary were synonymous
terms with them. » Like their brethren in other
lands, the missionaries could feed, clothe, and instruct, but they could not convert.

Another expensive trial was made in the Mission
of Lake Macquarie. « The great cost of this mission, »
says Dr Lang, « and the peculiarly unpromising
character of the field, very speedily induced the
Society to abandon it. » (3)

Another case at Lake Colac, in which the Wesleyans were agents, is thus described by Mr Byrne,
in 1848. « An extensive tract of land, and annual
assistance in the shape of a money grant, was afforded by the Government, the total amount of the

(1) *Australia and the East*, by John Hood, ch. vii, p. 207.

(2) *Océanie*, tome III, p. 507.

(3) *History of N. S. Wales*, vol. II, ch. xi, p. 507.

latter since 1836 approaching 5,000 l. But here
again the Executive recognised the inutility of all
attempts for the civilisation of the aborigines; and
the grant to the Colac Mission is now only 100 l.
per annum, a sum that merely enables it, under the
superintendence of the Rev. M' Tuckfield, to linger
out its existence without a hope of any advantage
being obtained by it. » (1) Indeed M' Young, a Wesleyan minister, confesses, six years later, that « the
work had to a great extent been abandoned as a
hopeless undertaking. »

As early as the year 1842, « the expences of every
Mission to the Aborigines within the Colony, » says
one of its historians, « amounted to 51,807 l. We
must honestly say that little or no value has been
rendered for it. » He quotes also a missionary who
made the following singular report. « In whatever
direction I go, even at a distance of forty or sixty
miles, the parents conceal their children, as soon as
they hear that a missionary approaches their camp ;
and when I have come upon them by surprise, I have
the grievance to observe these little ones running into
the bushes, or into the bed of the river, with the
utmost rapidity. » (2)

But these discouraging facts were not always so
candidly admitted. If the natives avoided the missionaries, the latter did not on that account abandon
their lucrative functions. A few years ago the colonial
journals related, with appropriate comments, the
case of a Protestant clergyman, who regularly re-

(1) *Twelve Years Wanderings*, etc., vol. I, p. 367.
(2) *History of N. S. Wales*, by J. H. Braim Esq., Principal
of Sydney College, vol. II, ch. vi, p. 237.

ceived during some years a grant towards the support
of a mission which he was supposed to be conducting in the interior, and of the progress of which he
forwarded annual reports; but who was accidentally
discovered at last to be engaged in the peaceful pursuits of agriculture, which his stipend as a missionary had sensibly aided, and to be the pastor of a
« mission » which had no existence whatever, except
in his own ingenious reports.

We have heard enough, however, to prepare us
for the final account which is given in 1853 by
M' Gerstaecker, who says, « The missionaries have
given up the work of conversion in despair; » and
in 1858 by M' Minturn, the latest traveller in these
regions, who once more declares, — « All missionary efforts among them have failed; they are, in fact,
rapidly dying away, and disappearing before the
white race. » (1)

And this is the only result, as far as the natives
are concerned, of the English dominion in Australia.
They had a nation to convert; they have only created a desert. « Another ten years, » says M' Byrne,
« and an aboriginal native will be as great a curiosity in Sydney, or within the boundaries of the colony, as he is at present in Europe. » (2) Of the
same fact in Van Dieman's Land, we are told, « the
extermination of nearly a whole race has been the
work of twenty years. » (3) Of the new colony of
Victoria, M' Westgarth says, that whereas in 1834

(1) *From New York to Delhi*, ch. III, p. 21.
(2) Vol. 1, ch. v, p. 279.
(3) *The Catholic Mission in Australia*, by W. Ullathorne,
D. D., p. 47.

there were from 20,000 to 25,000 natives « within
the limits of the present Victoria, » they have dwindled away so rapidly under English rule that « they
now stand at 2,500 for the *whole* of Victoria, » —
nine tenths having perished in twenty years, — and
that even this feeble remnant has been relegated to a
barren tract « useless to the colonist. » (1) Lastly,
of New Zealand, M' Paul says, « the New Zealanders
are annually on the decrease, and will no doubt in
the course of time, perhaps 40 or 50 years, become nearly if not entirely extinct; » (2) a fate
which Lord Goderich reported to Governor Bourke
was inevitable, though, he added, it was impossible to speak of it « without shame and indignation. » (3)

« It seems, indeed, » says the Rev. D' Lang, with
great composure, in reviewing these results of Protestant colonisation, « to be a general appointment
of Divine Providence, that the Indian wigwam of
North America, and the miserable break-wind of the
aborigines of New Holland, should be utterly swept
away by the flood-tide of European colonisation,...
and the miserable remnant of a *once hopeful* race

(1) *Victoria and the Australian Gold Mines*, p. 51.

(2) *Australia, Tasmania, and New Zealand*, by R. B. Paul,
p. 252. (1857).

(3) *New Zealand, its advantages and prospects*, by Charles
Terry, F. R. S., F. S. A., p. 112. « Within the first two or
three years after the establishment of the Society's settlement at
the Bay of Islands, not less than one hundred at least of the natives had been *murdered* by Europeans in their immediate neighbourhood. » *The British Colonization of New Zealand*, published
for the New Zealand Association, p. 167. (1837).

will at length gradually disappear from the land of
their forefathers. » (1)

Yet there are lands, as we shall see hereafter, in
which the wigwam of the Indian still stands, except
where it has been replaced by a more solid edifice;
and in the Catholic islands of Oceanica, as well as
by the banks of all the rivers which flow from the
Andes to the Ocean, — by the Amazon and the
Orenoco, by the Rio Negro and the Parana, and the
thousand tributaries which mingle with their mighty
streams, — his race dwells in peace, and calls upon
the true God. Even in the northern continent, where
the Indian in contact with Protestantism » has not
ceased to degenerate, » as M. de Tocqueville observed,
and where the savages diminished by *seventy-four
thousand* between 1850 and 1856; the populations
under Catholic influence, as we shall learn in a later
chapter, » still thrive or increase, » and an American
officer could report to his Government » the prodigious work effected by the missionaries » in the far
West, and even declare of one of the most powerful
tribes, » *They are hardly Indians now.* » But in
these cases the teachers of the savage were men who
carried with them from Europe no treasures but the
Cross of Christ and the Gospel of salvation, and
therefore were able, as we shall see when we trace
their history, to gain millions of barbarians to such
a degree of civilisation and prosperity as excited the
admiration even of a Southey and a Voltaire.

We have now exhausted the religious history of
Australia, as far as the natives are concerned, and

(1) *History of N. S. Wales*, vol. I, ch. II, p. 26.

have no motive to enquire curiously about its other inhabitants; yet a few words may be added upon them also, before we pass to the missionary annals of New Zealand. Dr Lang has described, with his accustomed frankness, both the clergy and the people; though we may well believe there are some exceptions to the character which he depicts. Of the missionaries he gives this report. « There were instances — repeated instances — of men, who, although it was *known* that their characters were blasted at home, were nevertheless recommended as fit and proper persons for the colonial field. » (1) And the people appear, if we may believe his account, to be worthy of such pastors. Mr Lancelott, (2) and other writers on the Antipodes, deplore in energetic terms the profound immorality of « the most influential citizens, » while Dr Lang thus speaks of « the higher classes of colonial society. » « Even their profession of Christianity is unquestionably far more hurtful than beneficial to the cause of pure and undefiled religion. In short, the influence of no inconsiderable portion of the higher classes in N. S. Wales has all along been decidedly unfavorable to the morals and religion of the country. »

« The extent to which the labouring classes of emigrants become contaminated, » observes Mr Henderson, in 1851, « is immense.... Education, in most cases, is in a most lamentable state; in fact, in the greater part of the country there is none, except what

(1) Vol. II, ch. XI, p. 492.
(2) *Australia as it is*, by F. Lancelott Esq., vol. II, ch. v, p. 72.

parents themselves can bestow. » (1) This applies to
N. S. Wales; while of Van Dieman's Land M' Puseley reports, in 1838, that « the number of offences
committed in the city of Hobart, with a population
of only 23,000, exceeds by fifty per cent. that of
Liverpool, with its 296,000 inhabitants. » (2)

On the whole, Protestantism does not seem to
have redeemed in Australia its misadventures in other
lands. It has failed, in spite of every temporal advantage, to convert even a solitary pagan; while its
own professors, in large numbers, have practically
abandoned Christianity. And Protestants have not
omitted to contrast these results with those which
mark the influence of an older and purer faith. Thus
D' Lang is angry with Sir Thomas Brisbane, who
must have been the most candid of Australian governors, because he bluntly replied to a « Presbyterian
memorial » for public aid, on the ground that it was
given to Catholics, that « it would be time for the
Presbyterians to ask assistance from the government
when they showed they could conduct themselves as
well as the Roman Catholics of the colony. » (3)
M' Hood also, a perfectly impartial observer, ventures
to suggest to his co-religionists, that « the Protestant population will do well to imitate their Roman
Catholic brethren in their exertions on behalf of the
rising generation; » and whereas M' Henderson has
told us that education amongst the Protestants is at
the lowest ebb, M' Hood candidly observes, « the

(1) *Excursions in N. S. Wales*, by John Henderson Esq.;
vol. II, ch. xi, p. 288.
(2) *Australia and Tasmania*, by D. Puseley, p. 196.
(3) *Hist. N. S. Wales*, vol. II, ch. xi, p. 461.

Roman Catholic Church, with its usual exemplary
zeal, has pushed schools and seminaries into every
corner of the colony. » (1) « *They* lose none of their
members, » says M' Draim, with evident regret,
« nor abate any of their zeal. »

Finally, Colonel Mundy makes the following observation upon those incessant religious divisions
which are not less conspicuous in the Antipodes than
in China, India, Ceylon, and every other land in
which the new religion has displayed its multitudinous forms. « The Roman Catholics here, as generally in these colonies, appear to have increased in
number and consequence at a much greater ratio
than other denominations. The reason is obvious.
Union is strength. The Protestants are split into
sects — every man must set up a creed for himself. » (2)

If there is a fact still more remarkable than these
ample and almost perplexing confessions of Protestant writers in every land, of which we have already
heard so many, it is surely the singular composure
with which they offer their evidence, and then turn
away as calmly as if they had been recording only
the averages of a price-current, or the variations of
the thermometer. They are loading with infamy their
own religion, and do not even seem to be conscious
of it. They address to more thoughtful and anxious
hearts the most formidable admonitions which man's
experience can offer or receive, and recite them with
cool monotonous indifference as if they had no mean-

(1) *Australia and the East*, ch. x, p. 325.
(2) *Australasian Colonies*, vol. III, ch. II, p. 42.

ing or significance. They suggest to others deep counsels and prompt action, remaining themselves indifferent and unmoved ; ready to repeat to morrow
without emotion the avowals which they made yesterday without regret.

The only Protestant admission of success on the
part of Catholic missionaries in civilising the natives,
after the long and fruitless efforts of their unsuccessful rivals, is recorded by a candid American writer
in these words. « The Roman Catholic clergy have a
native missionary establishment at Victoria Plains,
where they make the natives useful by taking every
means of civilising them. A very good feeling exists
between the natives and the Roman Catholics. » (1)

Yet the Catholic missionary, here as elsewhere,
had to contend with that almost insuperable obstacle,
found only in pagan lands tenanted by Protestants,
the contempt or aversion of the heathen for a religion
which he had already learned to despise, before the
professors of a holier creed presented themselves to
him. If the Apostles had appeared every where, each
accompanied by a lady, and most of them by a group
of children; eagerly solicitous, like other men, about
money, luxury, and ease; contradicting one another
in every discourse, and distinguished from their
pagan hearers only by the profession of truths of
which their own daily life was the most effective
refutation ; — in other words, if they had been protestant missionaries; — Christianity would hardly
have extended outside the walls of Jerusalem, and
would not have attracted much attention within them.

(1) *Voyages to India, China*, etc., by W. S. Bradshaw ; cb. VI.

In spite of the formidable difficulty which apostles must now expect to encounter in all lands, and especially in those which are under the dominion of England, the Benedictines have commenced in Western Australia one of those generous undertakings, so often initiated by the first followers of St. Benedict, in converting the ancient barbarians of Europe. On the 2nd of June, 1859, more than forty Benedictines, — the first Vicar General of Australia, now an English Bishop, had been a member of the same illustrious Order, — attended, under the guidance of Bishops Serra and Salvado, at the solemn benediction of a new monastery in the district of Perth. From that hour hope dawned upon the native of Australia. Bishop Serra has lately communicated to his friends in Europe this account of the present condition of his community.

« The example of their habits of industry has already been followed by many natives, who, abandoning their erratic life, have turned their attention to the cultivation of the soil, *and are now living upon its produce.* Moreover, as every Benedictine foundation is traditionally known as a nursery of learning as well as an asylum of penance and prayer, a college has been established under the direction of the Fathers, and, amongst the pagan youths who have been gratuitously received as pupils, three young Australians have already been sent to Rome to complete their education. » (1) Perhaps this remote colony of England, hitherto abandoned to utter darkness, may be destined to receive from the child-

(1) *Annals,* May 1860, p. 120.

ren of St. Benedict the same inappreciable blessings
for which the mother country is indebted to the family of the same glorious Saint.

Even the Protestant inhabitants of the colony appear to anticipate, without deriving any satisfaction
from the prospect, that the Benedictines will not
labour in vain. Thus a colonial journal quotes with
disapprobation a recent letter of the superior, « as
showing the untiring and unsparing energy of the
Church of Rome in proselytizing within the territories of Great Britain. » Considering that Great Britain has done nothing for the inhabitants but deprive
them both of their lands and their life, the complaint
seems a little unreasonable. « Our plan of proceeding, » says the Bishop, as quoted by the protestant
journalist, « is as follows. We shall join the first
savage tribe which we meet; we shall go with them,
and share their nomad life, until we are able to fix
them in some favourable situation, when we propose
to teach them, by our example, how to obtain their
subsistence by agriculture. When we have thus attached them to the soil, we shall begin to speak to
them of religion, and initiate them in ecclesiastical
knowledge, in order that we may find in the sons of
Australia future missionaries who may assist us in
instructing their still savage brethren. When we have
the good fortune to see new fellow-labourers arrive
from Europe, we shall locate them in the monastic
huts already established, leaving them to bestow
their labour on the tribes already attached to the
soil. This will leave us at liberty to advance further
into the interior, and to win other tribes to the faith
of Jesus Christ. If we can in this manner establish a

chain of monasteries, the conversion and civilisation of Australia will be complete. »

A still later account by Mgr. Salvado informs us that these hopes had begun to receive their accomplishment. The natives only laughed, he says, when they first saw the monks ploughing and sowing; but when they gathered in the first crop, these agricultural toils appeared to them worthy of imitation. And whereas protestant missionaries relate, that the native children run away, or hide themselves, at their approach; the Benedictines commend both the zeal with which their parents send them for instruction, and the remarkable aptness of the scholars. They record also that five Australians had already left for Europe to complete their studies, and add the astonishing fact, that two others had actually been admitted as novices in the Convent of the Most Holy Trinity *della cava*, in the kingdom of Naples. (1)

On the whole, we may conclude that Bishops Serra and Salvado would not agree with Count Strzelecki, who was acquainted only with Protestant missions, that « all attempts to civilise and christianise the aborigines have utterly failed; » nor with the Rev. M᙮ Young, that « it is a hopeless undertaking; » nor with M᙮ Gerstaecker, that « they have given up conversion in despair; » nor, least of all, with D᙮ Broughton, who assured the House of Commons, that « it was impossible to instil any idea of Christianity into them. »

And now let us come to New Zealand. In reading

(1) *Mémoires historiques sur l'Australie*, 2ᵐᵒ partie, pp. 145, 198.

the accounts which Protestant writers of various
sects have given of the history of their own religion
in this colony, our first impression is one of astonishment. So eager do they seem to proclaim to the world
the turpitude of the very men whom they profess to
esteem as the preachers of a « scriptural » faith, that
we are compelled to remind ourselves, from time to
time, as we listen to their scornful invective, that
they are partial and reluctant, not hostile or prejudiced witnesses. It seems incredible that writers of
so many creeds and classes, but all more or less
warmly interested in the success of Protestant missions, many of them ardent advocates of the missionaries, and not a few their personal friends and associates, should have consented to make revelations
which are certainly without parallel, except perhaps
in the records of the same class of agents in South
Africa and Polynesia.

The story of Protestant missions in New Zealand
opens after this manner. « I have a manuscript account, » says one who belonged to the class which
he describes, « which I drew up myself, from unquestionable authority, so early as the year 1824, of
every missionary that had set foot in New Zealand
up till that period, as well as of every important
transaction which had occurred till then in connection
with the New Zealand Mission. » (1) It is not often
that history is written by a witness at once so competent and so impartial, and it is impossible not to
anticipate with some curiosity the results of such
careful observation. He goes on thus, addressing

(1) *New Zealand in* 1839, by J. D. Lang, D. D., p. 30.

himself to Lord Durham, who at that time held high
office under the crown of England. « I am confident,
my Lord, it would be impossible to find a parallel,
in the history of any Protestant Mission since the
Reformation, to the amount of inefficiency and moral
worthlessness which that record presents. Indeed,
Divine Providence appears to have frowned upon the
New Zealand mission all along, and blighting and
blasting from Heaven seem to have rested upon it
even until now. » And then he adds these examples
from his manuscript record, in order to justify such
a denunciation. « *The first head of the New Zealand
mission was dismissed for adultery; the second for
drunkenness; and the third, so lately as the year
1836, for a crime still more enormous than either.* » (1)

This account was published in 1839, and other
witnesses will presently carry it on to our own day;
meanwhile, let it be noticed that Dr Lang finishes in
1839 as he began in 1824. « There is still, » he says,
« a most flagrant abuse tolerated and practised by
the *great majority* of its members, of sufficient
magnitude to neutralise the efforts even of a whole
college of Apostles. »

Such is the dark opening of a history which
resembles rather the shameful records of a criminal
calendar than the annals of Christian missionaries.
In New Zealand, Protestantism was *alone*, free to
develope according to its nature and instincts. Let us
see what it became, and what it has done for the
noblest race of barbarians in the southern hemisphere,

(1) *New Zealand in* 1839, by J. D. Lang, D. D., p. 30.

during the half century of its uninterrupted intercourse with them.

A protestant naturalist and physician, Dr Ernest
Dieffenbach, declares, that « of all the natives of the
Polynesian race the New Zealanders show the rea-
diest disposition for assuming a high degree of civilisation. » (1) It was permitted by Providence, for
reasons which we cannot penetrate, that the christian
religion should first be announced in this promising
field by the agents of Protestantism. The mission of
New Zealand was founded by Mr Marsden in 1814,
after unsuccessful attempts by others in 1800, and
1807. (2) « He was originally, » we are told,
« brought up as a blacksmith; » (3) but became
ultimately an episcopalian minister in N. S. Wales,
where for many years he combined the two functions
of preacher and agriculturist. Having amassed a considerable fortune as a sheep farmer, without prejudice to his spiritual character, and having acquired a
very accurate knowledge of the value of land, of
cattle, of crops, and of a good many other things, he
seems to have paid a visit to New Zealand on behalf
of the Church Missionary Society. The directors of
that institution showed considerable discrimination
in the choice of an agent who knew, by long experience, how to blend together in a prolific union the
arts of the clergyman and the farmer. His first step
proved that they were not deceived in him, and
Mr Marsden inaugurated the nascent mission by pur-

(1) *Travels in New Zealand*, by Ernest Dieffenbach, M. D.,
vol. II, ch. IX, p. 139.
(2) *New Zealand*, by Edward Brown Fitton, ch. I, p. 17.
(3) *The Gospel in New Zealand*, by Miss Tucker, ch. IV, p.36.

chasing 200 acres of land, chosen by himself, for 12 axes. (1) The transaction was perhaps not apostolic, but the directors of the Church Missionary Society would have smiled at so unreasonable an objection : it was not even honest, for the poor savages, as they afterwards complained, did not know the value of their land; but it was an excellent bargain, and a very good beginning of the New Zealand mission.

Unfortunately, however, Mr Marsden's felicitous contract suggested to others, quite as capable as himself of appreciating the keen negotiation, a spirit of eager commercial enterprise which soon led to very notable results. The Episcopalian and Wesleyan clergy, who now congregated with startling promptitude in this land of promise, rivalled each other in « purchases » the fame of which traversed half the globe, and began to fill the ears of busy and thoughtful men in the marts and cities of England. It penetrated even the courts of law, and found an echo within the walls of parliament. This was the term of its progress; for then arose such an outcry of many voices, such a chorus of mingled laughter and indignation, that the Government had no alternative but to adopt instant measures to thwart the exorbitant cupidity of the missionary societies and their agents. A little later, and a large part of the soil of New Zealand would have passed into the hands of the Church of England and Wesleyan missionaries. Let us examine, solely by the aid of Protestant witnesses,

(1) *New Zealand*, by J. L. Nicholas Esq., vol. II, ch. vii, p. 193.

the process by which this appropriation was being
gradually effected, until the hour in which it was
fatally checked by the inexorable edicts of the Colonial
Secretary.

We have seen that the acquisitiveness of which
we are about to trace the results was first manifested by M' Marsden, the founder of the New Zealand mission. His example was fruitful; and only five
years later, in 1819, as we learn from D' Morison,
the historian of the London Missionary Society, « five
missionaries and artisans » — they not unfrequently
cumulated these professions — « purchased thirteen
thousand acres for forty-eight axes. » (1) For thirty
years this lucrative commerce continued; the parties
to the contracts being, on the one side, men who
called themselves missionaries, and on the other,
ignorant and inexperienced savages, to whom they
had introduced themselves as messengers from God.
« In many cases, » says M' Terry, « the natives were
quite unconscious of what they had really conveyed
by these ready-made deeds;... tracts of land larger
than counties in England were sold or conveyed for
comparatively a trifle, on half a sheet of paper. Already thirty-two millions of acres are claimed. » (2)
Between 1830 and 1835, at Hokianga and the Bay
of Islands alone, « twenty-seven square miles were
purchased *by missionaries*. » (3)

« At first, M' Byrne informs us, « these purchases

(1) *The Fathers of the London Missionary Society*, vol. II, app.
p. 598.
(2) *New Zealand*, etc., p. 73.
(3) *The Story of New Zealand*, by Arthur S. Thomson, M.D.;
vol. I, p. 268.

were made for little more than a nominal consideration;
a few beads, a musket, some blankets, and a little powder and ball, were sufficient to purchase tracts which
were measured, in the language of the Missionaries,
by miles. » (1) Let us give a few examples of a covetousness which is described by Protestant writers as
so eager and unscrupulous, that even when detected
it knew not how to blush, and which, when finally
baffled and rebuked, and compelled in many cases
to disgorge its prey, resented the loss of its spoils
rather than the public exposure of its fraudulent
greed.

Among the many missionary claimants up to 1841
were the Rev. J. Matthews, for 2,503 acres; the
Rev. R. Matthews, for 3,000 acres; the Rev. T. Ait-
ken, 7,670 acres; Rev. W. Williams, 890; M' Clarke,
19,000; M' Davis, 6,000; M' Fairburn, 20,000;
M' Kemp, 18,000; M' King, 10,300; M' Shepherd,
11,860; and finally, for we cannot reckon them all,
the Rev. H. Williams, at first for 11,000, (2) and
afterwards, as Dr Thomson reports, for 22,000 acres.

The last named gentleman should not be confounded with the crowd of obscure competitors in
this active commerce. He was conspicuous among
the missionaries whom, as M' Earp playfully told
the House of Commons, « the natives regarded as
having *done* them. » « The Rev. Henry Williams,
the chairman of the Church Mission in New Zealand, » we are told by M' Wakefield, « under the
pretence of securing a piece of land for a native teach-

(1) *Twelve Years*, etc., vol. I, p. 48.
(2) Terry, p. 122.

II.   6

er, had obtained an assignment *to himself* of forty
acres of the best part of the proposed site. » (1) And
he appears to have displayed similar talents during
a long series of years. In 1852, Dʳ Shaw relates that
he passed « miles of barren district » in the neighbourhood of Auckland, the unproductiveness of which
he found, on further enquiry, was due to the speculative schemes of its reverend owner. « It was
explained, » he adds, « from the fact of an Archdeacon Williams, one of the missionaries, who had
got possession of it, and would not sell it; thereby
putting an end to cultivation and rural industry in
that part of the country. » (2) Dʳ Lang speaks of a
Reⱽ. Mʳ Williams, whom he calls « the ordained
head of the New Zealand mission, » who became
ultimately an Anglican bishop in that colony. If it
was the same individual, his career may be regarded
as a pleasing example of continuous and progressive
prosperity.

But Mʳ Williams, if never surpassed, was sometimes equalled by his missionary colleagues. « Mʳ Shepherd, » we learn from a Protestant historian, « bought
a large tract of eligible land, having a frontage of from
four to five *miles* on one of the navigable rivers in
the Bay of Islands, for two check shirts and an iron
pot. » (3) Mʳ Marsden, if his life had been prolonged,
would have been tempted to envy his successors. But
Mʳ Shepherd was not satisfied with one such bargain,

(1) *Adventure in New Zealand*, by Edward Jerningham Wakefield Esq., vol. 1, ch. vii, p. 190.

(2) *Notes of a Ramble in Australia and New Zealand*, in 1852,
by John Shaw, M. D., F. G. S.; p. 289.

(3) Lang, *New Zealand in* 1839, p 34.

and knew how to accomplish still more brilliant operations, when spiritual engagements left him leisure, by the aid of check shirts and iron pots. He has, we are not surprised to hear, « *another* estate towards the North Cape, where he is at present stationed as a Missionary. » Indeed the success of these gentlemen has been so complete, that we are told of Mr Fairbairn, Mr Williams, and others, that the very timber on their ample estates was « worth half a million sterling. »

These examples of the skill of Christian missionaries in the discharge of their profitable stewardship are instructive, and it is only too easy to add to their number. The Rev. Richard Taylor, who has written a book about New Zealand, full of unction and running over with texts of Scripture, is thus described by Mr Wakefield in 1845. « The Rev. Richard Taylor, who only went to New Zealand in the year 1838, was a claimant before the Land Commissioners of 50,000 acres of land! » (1) In Mr Taylor's book we only read of his zeal for the Gospel, and his tender interest in the salvation of the natives. It is true that he soon abandoned the care of their salvation to other people; but perhaps this was only because so extensive a landowner might reasonably aspire to greater dignities at home. It is true also that, ultimately, the decision of the authorities deprived the ex-missionary of more than forty-eight thousand acres of his claim; and Dr Thomson notices that a well known periodical « suggested he should have his picture hung up in

(1) *Adventure*, etc., vol. II, ch. XIV, p. 344.

the Church Missionary Society's hall, with the words
' fifty thousand acres ' under it. » (1) Yet if you read
his book, you will be almost tempted to think that he
went to New Zealand to preach the Gospel to the
heathen.

The Rev. William Yate, also a « Church Missionary, » deserves our particular notice. He too has
written a book on New Zealand. Three missionaries,
he says, were sent to that colony with an annual
allowance of 300 l., an income which he considers
despicable, and is surprised they should be expected
to do any good with such « necessarily inadequate
means. » Yet such a sum, which would suffice to
maintain twenty-five Catholic missionaries for a year
in China or India, was surely recompense enough
for men who had so many other means of adding to
their income, and of whom their colleague thus
speaks. « So far did some of them dishonour the
self-denying doctrines of the Cross, which they had
been sent here to teach, that no less painful a plan
could be adopted than an ignominious erasure of their
names from the list of the Society's labourers. » (2)

Mr Yate's own admiration of the same self-denying doctines was no doubt perfectly sincere; and it
was probably before he had learned to value them
that he permitted himself some occasional relaxation
of their strictness, after a manner which was thus
revealed to a Committee of the House of Commons.
Mr Yate used to prohibit the natives, the House was
informed, from selling their pork to the whalers, not

(1) Vol. II, p. 156.
(2) *An Account of New Zealand*, by the Rev⁰ William Yate,
ch. IV, p. 168, 2ᵈ edition.

from any unkind feeling towards those adventurous
mariners, but because he preferred to buy it himself
at one penny per pound, and then to sell it at five (1)
The sentiments which M' Yates expresses in his book
justify us in assuming that he afterwards regretted
his transactions in pork, which he probably felt had
been more advantageous to himself than to the whalers whom he mulcted, or to the natives whom he
instructed so persuasively in « the self-denying doctrines of the Cross. »

Such, according to their own testimony, were the
Protestant missionaries in New Zealand, for more
than thirty consecutive years, and such the examples which they afforded to its aboriginal inhabitants. These were the Riccis, the Verbiests, the de
Brittos, and the Xaviers of Protestantism. In 1842,
M' Heaphy still deplores in energetic terms « the rapa-
ciousness of the Missionaries. » (2) In the same year
M' Terry reproaches them with the fact, that « many
of the Missionaries are now possessors of very large
property. » (3) As late as 1845, we find a member
of the Legislative Council once more lamenting that
« many of the Church Missionaries undoubtedly are
traders and land-jobbers. » (4) « Scarcely one of the
servants of the Church Missionary Society, » — they

(1) *Parliamentary Papers.* M' Earp's evidence, vol. VII,
p. 156. M' Earp told the Committee, « That has been the case a
great deal in the past history of the Missionaries. »
(2) *Narrative of a Residence in various parts of New Zealand,*
by Charles Heaphy, ch. I, p. 5.
(3) *New Zealand,* etc., p. 180.
(4) *New Zealand and its Aborigines,* by William Brown, ch. II,
p. 89.

were all Anglican ministers,— says Mr Wakefield in
the same year, has been free from this blemish of
self interest. »(1) And this is the language of all the
witnesses, of every sect. « The missionaries of the
Church Missionary Society in New Zealand, » says
Dr Lang, « have actually been the *principals* in the
grand conspiracy of the European inhabitants of the
island to rob and plunder the natives of their land.»(2)
Yet we shall presently find these « traders and land-
jobbers, » not only speaking complacently of themselves as devoted and self-denying missionaries of the
Cross, but reviling their Catholic rivals in terms
which only such men could use, and opposing them
by arts which only such men could employ.

   Some, no doubt, were better than others ; but all
the authorities represent the Church of England missionaries as the least scrupulous of any. When
Mr Earp was examined by the House of Commons,
and asked by Lord Jocelyn if there was any difference
of character « between the Wesleyan and Church
missionaries, » he replied ; « There is nothing to
choose between them. I think the Church missionaries have the predominance; they have made much
larger speculations in land than the Wesleyans. »

   Yet some of the latter had proved formidable rivals
to Archdeacon Williams, Mr Shepherd, Mr Taylor,
and the other Episcopalian clergy. Dr Lang tells us
that Mr White, a Wesleyan missionary at Hokianga,
was obliged to retire In consequence of detected « immorality, » and adds; « this reputable individual is

(1) *Adventure in New Zealand*, vol. II, ch. XVII, p. 449.
(2) *New Zealand*, p. 33.

now a merchant of the highest class. « Nor does any
amount of exposure correct the frailties of these singular missionaries. As late as 1850, — for time,
which changes all human things, does not change
them, — we have the following curious account of
the Rev. Walter Lawry, « General Superintendant
of the Wesleyan Mission at Auckland. » It is one of
his own colleagues who thus describes him.

« He lends money, and now has money out at the
modest interest of 20 per cent. » It is his delight, he
adds, « to watch the market, and to buy, sell, lease,
and mortgage to the best advantage; so that he is
now owner of land and houses, and one of the weal-
thiest men in Auckland. » What follows is still more
impressive. « He is doing as much business as ever;
almost every week we hear of some fresh purchase
or sale.... He now talks of going to England. He is a
graphic narrator, and has a fund of interesting material, *and may produce a good impression on behalf
of those missions.* But I pray God we may see his
face no more, unless he get re-converted. » (1) In
the next chapter we shall find Mr Lawry, as we
might have anticipated, invoking maledictions upon
Catholic missionaries, and quoting Holy Scripture
against them.

Even in 1857, nearly fifty years after Marsden
made the first missionary contract in New Zealand,
Mr Hursthouse thus describes his Anglican successors. If he uses the language of jest and irony, who
can blame him? « It appears that the Church Mis-

(1) *A Voice from New Zealand*, by Rev⁴ Joseph Fletcher,
Wesleyan Missionary at Auckland, pp. 2, 3.

sionary gentlemen had come to like New Zealand.
The natives were still addicted to cannibalism and to
preserving each other's heads; but the natives were
' missionary christians, ' attentive in chapel, and not
bad workmen in the glebe. Their lines had fallen in
pleasant places. Liberal of the Society's converting
blankets and tobacco, they had already acquired for
their thirteen confederated chiefs some 300,000 acres
of land. » (1)

« Several missionaries, « M' Didwill had previously
observed, in 1841, « claim tracts of from one to six
hundred thousand acres in different parts of the country. » (2) In 1845, M' Hawes told the House of
Commons, that, besides being land-jobbers, « they
had, at least some of them, become more or less *traders* also. » (3) And so notorious had their character now become, that M' Charles Duller, writing
officially to Lord Stanley, did not hesitate to speak
of them as men who would not dare even to offer
any defence of their own conduct. « The Missionaries are not in a state to encounter public discussion of their past proceedings, and would entertain any terms offered to them in a very mitigated
spirit. » (4) They, had become at last a jest and a
proverb!

Finally, even D' Dieffenbach, their familiar friend

(1) *New Zealand, the Britain of the South*, by Charles Hursthouse, vol. I, ch. 1, p. 37.
(2) *Rambles in New Zealand*, by John Carne Bidwill, p. 86.
(3) *Report of the Debates of the House of Commons on the
state of New Zealand*, p. 115.
(4) *Eighteenth Report of the Directors of the New Zealand
Company*, p. 42.

and constant advocate, was contrained, by his own
experience and observation, to speak as follows of
men whom he desired only to praise. « The Church
Missionaries in the Bay of Islands possess large pro-
perties in these districts, which is perhaps the reason
that they have not long ago gone into the interior,
where they would have been far more usefully employed than in the Bay of Islands, which is principally a shipping place. Some of the stations occupied
by them are nearly deserted by the natives, and they
have therefore no congregations, unless they choose,
like St. Antonio, to preach to the fishes. » But in
default of congregations they had their estates, which
they probably considered a satisfactory compromise.
« Their efficiency would undoubtedly have been
greater, » D' Dieffenbach mildly observes, « if they
had shared the adventurous spirit of the settlers, and
had lived amongst the interior tribes. » But such a
life had no attractions for them, and « the consequence has been that many of the older missionaries
have become landed proprietors; and many, by other
pursuits, such as banking, or trading with the produce of their gardens or stock, have become wealthy
men... Some of these persons *are now retiring on
their property.* » (1) Their sons also, hereditary
merchants, learned to imitate the virtues of their
fathers, and « the relatives of the Church Missionaries, » Colonel Mundy relates, « contracted for the
supply of provisions » to the army and fleet, « and
their sons did undoubtedly reap a rich harvest. » (2)

(1) *Travels in New Zealand*, vol. II, ch. v, p. 75.
(2) *Australasian Colonies*, vol. II, p. 222.

Such is one of the most characteristic chapters in
the history of Protestant missions. We shall find
many like it in the lands which we have still to visit,
as we have already found others in China, India, and
Ceylon; but we will only so far anticipate the
evidence which has still to be adduced as to observe
here, that the same witnesses whom we have just
heard will tell us presently, in spite of vehement
prejudices, that the Catholic missionaries in this land
have been conspicuous for the evangelical purity,
zeal, and disinterestedness which they vainly search-
ed for in their Protestant rivals. To these true
apostles of Jesus we owe an apology for even comparing them, though by way of contrast, with such
emissaries as England has sent to New Zealand during fifty years, to represent her religious opinions. Yet
these men professed to be « missionaries of the Gospel, » and teachers of the « self-denying doctrines of
the Cross. » Most of them have written books exalting
their own apostolic triumphs, and challenging the
admiration of their partisans at home. How far they
deserved it, we have seen, from their own confessions, or the narratives of their friends. Perhaps even
their warmest advocates, — though they have eagerly
read the romantic biographies in which such men as
Marsden, and Taylor, and Yate, and Leigh, and
many others, are depicted as « angels of light, » —
may at last comprehend their true character, and
the hollowness of their religious profession, if they
will only refer to the *Acts of the Apostles*, and
contemplate for a moment the model there exhibited
of the Christian Missionary. Let them at least interrogate their own hearts, and say whether the men by

whose labour God has in various ages converted the heathen to the knowledge of His Son were ever such as these? Let them tell us, whether they can imagine St. Paul claiming thousands of acres in Thrace, or an estate in the suburbs of Corinth; St. Barnabas bartering domestic utensils for a vineyard in Cyprus; St. Augustine robbing the Saxons of their pork to sell it to the Welsh; St. Boniface lending money at twenty per cent. on the banks of the Danube; or St. Francis Xavier a thriving cattle-dealer on the shores of the Persian Gulf?

In this lamentable history there is, however, one consolation. The day of retribution came at last; and England nobly disavowed, by the voice of her rulers, the turpitude of her missionaries in New Zealand. Some of them indeed had anticipated the coming storm, and « retired on their property; » but their cupidity, as Mr Brodie notices, led to « the enactment of a law declaring all titles to lands purchased from natives invalid. » (1) Many who were striving to emulate their prosperous predecessors were rudely interrupted in their dreams of wealth, and even compelled to abandon the prey which they thought they had secured. « Many of the purchases, » says Mr Chamerovzow, though *he* includes the colonists as well as the missionaries in his reproaches, « have since been declared invalid by the local government, being repudiated by the native owners, on the plea of inadequate compensation,.... wilful double-dealing, or actual fraud. » (2) « The Church of England mis-

(1) *Remarks on the Past and Present state of New Zealand,* by Walter Brodie, p. 52. (1845).

(2) *The New Zealand Question,* by Louis Chamerovzow, ch. I, p. 4.

sionaries, « says a writer in 1860, — for it is a notable feature, as we saw in India and China, of Protestant missions, that their *latest* annalists are as full
of rebuke as all who preceded them, — « claimed
216,000 acres of land ; » and the arts by which the
reverend claimants had appropriated them are sufficiently revealed by the fact, that the final judicial
award compelled them to resign 150,000 ! « Archdeacon Henry Williams and some others, » adds the
same authority, were at length admonished, but not
till it was found that the English public would no
longer tolerate their proceedings, « that they must
either give up their excessive grants of land, or leave
the service of the mission. The Archdeacon chose the
latter course... When he had suffered suspension for
five years, he was restored » — to become once more
a guide to the heathen, and an ornament of the Anglican Church in New Zealand.

The missionaries had now no alternative but to be
content with their salaries, and to trade or speculate
only through the agency of others. But the Societies
at home had prepared at least a partial compensation,
by arranging that the wealth of their agents should
vary as the number of their children. The tariff of
missionary rewards, we learn from D⁥ Dieffenbach,
was on the following scale. « When the question of
providing for the children of the Missionaries was
brought before the Committee of the Church Missionary Society in London, two hundred acres for *each
child* was thought to be a liberal allowance. » He
adds that « *ten* acres of arable land must be regarded
as sufficient for all reasonable wants of an individual. » But we have seen that the revenues of the

missionary societies are large, and the benevolence
of their subscribers inexhaustible. (1)

One circumstance only remains to be noticed. The
too prosperous career of the Missionaries in New
Zealand attracted attention, as we have observed,
even in the assembly of Parliament. In a debate
which took place in the House of Commons in 1845,
« the conduct of the Catholic missionaries, » of
which we shall hear more presently, was contrasted
by more than one speaker with that of the Protestants. The late Sir Robert Inglis, the official apologist
of the Church of England, on all occasions and
against all adversaries, offered to the House of Commons this explanation. « It must always be recollected, » he said, « that, after no length of time, could
the Roman Catholic missionaries have to provide for
families. » The same thing, happily for the progress
of Christianity, was true of the first Apostles; but it
was not to be expected that Sir Robert Inglis should
introduce this consideration to the notice of the
House.

A more candid and better informed critic, who
had seen both classes of missionaries at their work,
while he laments that the Protestant teachers « were
very censurable, » adds the very reflection which
Sir Robert Inglis prudently suppressed. « The Roman
Catholic missionaries, » Dʳ Thomson remarks,
« would not take advantage of the trade; for the
missionaries of this church in other countries have
generally obeyed the spirit of the holy injunction to

(1) In like manner. « the Chaplains of New South Wales were
gratuitously presented with 1600 acres *per child.* » *Excursion in
New Zealand,* p. 50.

the first Christian missionaries in the world : ' Take
nothing for your journey, neither staves, nor scrip,
neither bread, neither money, neither have two coats
apiece; ' » — a contrast which we have seen emphatically traced by another witness, when he told the
House of Commons, « Christ said, *Leave* all; they
say, *Take* all. »

And now that we are sufficiently acquainted with
the missionaries themselves, it is time to enquire
what has been the result of their labours. In the first
place, it is undeniable that a large number of the
natives have gradually been induced, like the Cingalese during the Dutch occupation, to profess a nominal christianity. Irresistible motives have conspired
to provoke their external acquiescence in the religion
of their masters. From them they have learned many
European arts, tending to augment their ease and
enjoyment; and « their fine intellect enables them at
once to perceive the great value of these crafts. » (1)
From them they learned the value of land, and of its
products , for which they quickly understood the
strangers would be their surest customers. « The
success of the Missionaries in New Zealand, » observes Mr Drown, « is chiefly referable, not by any
means to a wish on the part of the natives for religious instruction, but to their hope of selling their
land, building houses, or general trading. » (2)

The same observation has been made by many
other writers. « Utilitarian motives, » says Colonel
Mundy, « have undoubtedly been very powerful

(1) Brown's *New Zealand*, ch. II, p. 60.
(2) P. 90.

auxiliaries to their reception of the Christian faith. » (1) « The greater part of the so-called Christian natives, » M' Caroc Bidwill informs us, « have only been attracted to become converts by the easy mode of life which they enjoy at the missionary establishments. » (2) « They seem to understand little, and to care less, about the principles of the Christian creed, » says another independent witness, but they appreciate the « many useful arts » which the missionaries can teach them, and easily understand that it is « their policy to support and encourage the missionaries. » (3) « Many have been the supposed converts to missionary instruction, » says M' Polack in 1840, « from the crafty feeling of bettering their present condition. » (4) « We are growing old, » is an expression which M' Wakefield sometimes heard amongst them, « and want our children to have protection in people from Europe. » (5) « The natives, » says M' Hay, « are anxious to be placed under the protection of British law, and would be willing to receive any person vested with power to enforce it. » (6) « All, » says D' Thomson, « looked upon the missionary and his effects as their own property. » (7) And so well was this understood by the

(1) *Australasian Colonies*, vol. II, ch. IV, p. 133.

(2) *Rambles in New Zealand*, p. 36.

(3) *Rovings in the Pacific*, by a Merchant long resident at Tahiti, vol. I, ch. IX, p. 227.

(4) *Manners and Customs of the New Zealanders*, by I. S. Polack Esq., vol. II, ch. XXII, p. 235.

(5) *Adventure in New Zealand*, vol. I, ch. IV, p. 73.

(6) *Journal of the Royal Geographical Society*, vol. II, p. 134.

(7) Vol. I, p. 316.

authorities in New Zealand, that when a new tribe
announced their adhesion to the missionary party,
Mr Forsaith, who held the office of « Protector of
Aborigines, » contented himself with reporting to
the local government that it had « nominally embraced Christianity. » (1) What the profession was
worth we shall see presently.

It is evident, then, that far from encountering even
the preliminary difficulties which commonly impede
the progress of Missions in heathen lands, every thing
tended in New Zealand to promote and accelerate it;
so that Mr Brown reproaches the missionaries, with
apparent reason, that « they have themselves to
blame that success has not been much greater. »
Every human aid which could promote that success
was freely placed at their disposal. If a new mission
is to be opened, the Governor does not disdain to accompany the missionary in person, and goes to in-
duct him, surrounded by such pomp and circumstance as his *quasi*-regal office permits; (2) and thus
forcibly admonishes the « fine intellect » of the natives that the power which they may never more
hope to resist, and from whose patronage alone they
can henceforth expect grace and favour, is permanently enlisted on the side of their Protestant teachers. To them they must now look for prosperity,
for instruction in domestic arts, and even for daily
employment. The very agents selected from amongst
the natives as « catechists » or « assistant preachers »
are thus described by Mr Wakefield. « The principal

(1) *Parliamentary Papers*, vol. XXX, p. 173. (1846).
(2) See Sir George Grey's *Overland Expedition from Auckland
to Taranaki*, 1850.

teachers under the Missionaries are generally their
house-servants at the same time, black their shoes,
clean their windows, make their beds, groom their
horses, and cook their dinner. » And we cannot be
surprised that barbarians whose acuteness has become a proverb, and who enjoy daily opportunities
of exercising it, should reflect seriously upon the
ample resources which they perceive to be at the
disposal of their masters. They may be ignorant of
the exact annual revenue of the various missionary
societies, but they have detected that it is large
enough to justify the shrewd calculation, that even
the generous living of the missionaries will not wholly
exhaust it, and that a considerable surplus will be
applicable to their own wants.

It was remarked by M' Terry, in 1842, that « at
the enormous annual expense of above fourteen
thousand pounds, in the twenty-fifth year of its
establishment in New Zealand, the Church Missionary Society only provide for the religious and
scholastic instruction of the Aborigines *eight* Missionaries, and sixteen Catechists. » (1) Many years
later, we are told by D' Selwyn, of whom we shall
have to speak more fully hereafter, that the result
of one appeal for pecuniary contributions to the New
Zealand mission was this, — that « the post for some
days seemed to rain bank notes. » (2) The Wesleyans also, as the Rev. M' Turton relates, had spent
80,000 l. before 1844. (3) Lastly, the Canterbury

(1) *New Zealand*, etc., p. 189.
(2) *The Melanesian Mission*, by G. A. Selwyn, D. D., Lord
Bishop of New Zealand, Letter 1, p. 51. (1853).
(3) Brown's *New Zealand*, app. p. 273.

settlement, the latest missionary enterprise in this colony, was conducted from its very origin with such
careful financial forethought, that « one third of the
entire proceeds of the ' Land Sales ' is appropriated, » we learn from M' Hursthouse, « to religious
and educational purposes; » (1) and in 1850 the
projectors cheerfully estimate their eventual share
from this source at one million sterling. (2)

The natives, then, had manifold and urgent motives for close alliance with the Protestant missionaries. So clearly did they perceive that they had
every thing to gain and nothing to lose by the nominal profession of Protestantism, that considerations of interest overcame, in the case of large numbers, the repugnance with which the avarice of the
missionaries had inspired them. It was indeed
strongly suspected, as M' Tyrone Power observes,
that « a struggle for temporal advantages » chiefly
influenced the latter; (3) or as D' Dieffenbach relates, « that the missionaries sought to convert them
only with a view to their own aggrandizement; » (4)
but if the natives could share in the benefits by
which a more active commerce was sure to be accompanied, they were willing to overlook this defect
in their religious teachers, and even to do their best
to imitate it. In this, as all the witnesses affirm, they
were entirely successful. The natives still said, indeed, and sometimes even in the presence of the

(1) *New Zealand*, etc., p. 155.
(2) *Canterbury Papers*, p. 7. (1850).
(3) *Sketches in New Zealand*, by W. Tyrone Power, D. A.
C. G., ch. xvii, p. 147. (1849).
(4) *Travels*, etc., vol. I, ch. viii, p. 169.

missionaries, that « their only reason for coming
to New Zealand was that it was a better country
than their own. » (1) But this conviction did
not deter them from profiting by their instructive
example. With what fatal results that example has
been attended is sufficiently revealed in the following
passages. « They have become covetous, suspicious,
and unfortunate, » says D[r] Dieffenbach, the friend
and associate of the Protestant missionaries. « They
have lost a great part of their hospitality and politeness, and their refusing aid when the stranger is
most in want of it, or exacting exorbitant recompense for it, makes travelling now very annoying. »
M[r] David Rough, another Protestant traveller, who
was on a certain occasion the guest of « Archidea-
con Brown, » relates that « the demands made were
so exorbitant, » even for the smallest services, that
his host lent him « his own men rather than suffer
us to submit to imposition. » And so little ashamed
were these « Christian » natives of their new vice,
that, as M[r] Rough adds, they openly boasted of
« their success in exacting high pay. » (2) « Instead
of enjoying themselves with song and the merry
dance, as formerly, » says M[r] Brown, « they are
absorbed in thinking of their next bargain with the
Europeans. » « How is it likely, » asks another Protestant writer, « that their avarice should be subdued,
when they saw those people *who came to preach the
Gospel* grasping to obtain large landed property, and

(1) D[r] Lang's *New Zealand*, p. 42.
(2) *Narrative of a Journey through part of the North of New
Zealand*, by David Rough, p. 18.

those who were guilty of downright vice ? » (1)

It appears, too, that they had already learned to quote the Protestant Bible in defence of their greed and impurity. M' Fox gives examples, in 1851, such as the following. « One of them, whom the governor was upbraiding with having sold his land three or four times over to different parties, justified himself by quoting the passage, ' After thou hadst sold it, was it not thine own? ' And a very intelligent native, to whom I was pointing out the impropriety of having three wives, replied ; ' Ob, never mind, all the same as Solomon ! ' A much more serious misapplication of the Scripture, occurred during the late war, when many of them tore up their Bibles to make wadding for their guns. » (2) Even the native « preachers, » whom the missionaries somewhat imprudently deputed to represent them in the interior, and who were of course the flower of their « converts, » « raised a very considerable income, » we are informed by M' Shortland, « in the shape of iron pots, boxes, blankets, and fire-arms, as fees for performing the ceremonies of marrying, burying, etc. » (3)

It would be easy to multiply these melancholy statements, which for the honour of our race and nation we would have gladly suppressed, if they had not been already recorded by a crowd of Protestant writers, — but we may content ourselves with adding the testimony of M' Wakefield, than whom no writer

(1) *Letters from Wanganui*, p. 30. (1845).
(2) *The Six Colonies of New Zealand*, by William Fox, p. 82. (1851).
(3) *The Southern Districts of New Zealand*, by Edward Shortland, M. A., p. 268. (1851).

on New Zealand has enjoyed better opportunities of
estimating the native character, and the effects of
Protestant missions upon it. « The most disagreeable
and saddening remark, » says this intelligent writer,
« which I made, was this, that the natives appeared
to have entirely abandoned their primitive and beautiful hospitality, the great redeeming point in the
character of the most ferocious and treacherous heathen native, whom no influence of any sort has yet
changed for the better, or perverted from the customs
of his fathers. Every village (of the ' christians ')
reminded me of the ' touters ' on the pier at Bou-
logne, seeking to pounce on an unfortunate traveller.
Instead of the former dignified reception, with a
house assigned you by the chief, the whole population rushes at you; but you soon find that, whichever you may choose, you have to pay for each small
kit of potatoes, for the carrying of water, or of fern
for your bed, and even for every stick of fire-wood
before you are allowed to burn it. » (1) And this
account is confirmed, in 1859, by the latest writer
on New Zealand, who, while noticing that even at
that date « their religion consisted more in words
than deeds, » still adds the same sign of declension,
—that« Christian natives were less given to hospitality than the heathens. » (2) What they have become
at last, we shall learn at the close of this chapter.

Such, as their own friends attest, is the first and
most obvious result of the action of Protestant Missionaries upon the natives of New Zealand. Let us,

(1) *Adventure in New Zealand*, vol. II, ch. xiv, p. 358.
(2) Dr Thomson, vol. II, p. 164.

enquire, in the next place, and still from the same
impartial witnesses, what is the nature of the religion
which they have been induced to profess, how far it
resembles Christianity, and what influence it exerts
over their habits and character. As the evidence is
copious, and, in spite of the diversity of the witnesses, absolutely uniform, it will perhaps be most
convenient to follow the order of dates. D⟨r⟩ Lang has
traced for us the results of Protestant Missions in
New Zealand up to 1839; other authorities, equally
competent and unexceptionable, will carry on the
history to the present hour.

Already, in 1832, a writer in the *Asiatic Journal*,
after a review of some of the facts which we have
been considering, pronounced this verdict upon the
missionaries in New Zealand and the islands of the
South Sea. « We have come to the painful conclusion,
that the presence of the Missionaries in New Zealand
and Otaheite has been productive of more mischief
than good. » (1) And in the same year, M⟨r⟩ Earle,
who indignantly reproaches their wordly and uncharitable lives, and exposes the real character of their
« converts, » emphatically declares, — « I never saw
one proselyte of their converting. » (2)

In the year 1835 we come to M⟨r⟩ Yate, a Church
of England missionary, whose operations as a dealer
in provisions have already been noticed. Here is a
conversation which he relates between himself and
one of his male converts.

---

(1) *Asiatic Journal*, vol. VIII, p. 106. New Series.
(2) *Nine Months Residence in New Zealand*, by Augustus
Earle, p. 201.

M' Yate. « What is the new heart like? » Answer;
« Like yours, it is very good. »

« Where is its goodness? »

« Answer; « It is altogether good : it tells me to
lie down and sleep all day on Sunday, and not to go
and fight. »

« When did you pray last? »

« This morning. »

« What did you pray for? »

« I said, O, Jesus Christ, give me a blanket, in
order that I may believe. » (1)

This view of the proper objects of prayer seems to
have been universal with Protestant New Zealanders.
Here is a letter which M' Yate received from one
of his neophytes, and his book contains similar specimens of their epistolary style. « M' Yate — how do
you do? Sick is my heart for a blanket. Yes, forgotten have you the young pigs I gave you last summer. My pipe is gone out, and there is not tobacco
with me to fill it : where should I have tobacco?
Remember the pigs which I gave you : you have not
given me any thing for them. I fed you with sucking
pigs; therefore I say, do not forget. » (2) M' Yate
was evidently doomed to be reminded of an animal
with which his missionary career had made him too
well acquainted.

Advancing to 1840, we come to M' Polack, and
to the careful and minute account which he has given
of New Zealand and its inhabitants. « The attempts
to instil a real belief in the Christian religion into the

(1) *Account of New Zealand*, ch. v, p. 222.
(2) P. 271.

minds of the benighted natives, « he says, « has
hitherto decidedly failed » — after an experiment
which already lasted twenty-six years, aided by
every human advantage which it was possible to possess. Not a few, he adds, have professed Protestantism, with the hope of « bettering their present condition ; but almost in every instance, where a contrary
conduct ensured present benefit, the adults have
renounced their lately received opinions, and held
aloof from their instructors. » (1)

In 1841, we have three witnesses, of very different
characters, but all conversant with the natives and
with their habits. M' Bidwill, though a friend and
advocate of the missionaries, says; « I have certainly
observed that the ' missionary ' natives are the most
impertinent and least willing to work. » (2) M' Bright,
a member of the medical profession, is more emphatic.
The converts, he says, « keep the Sabbath, » go to
church, and even « subscribe to the Church and Wesleyan missionaries; » and then he adds, « they are,
however, no more honest in their general transactions
than the rest; » and again, « the slight hold religion
has of them is frequently attested by their aberrations
under common temptations. » Once more; « I should
say that more than one fourth of the native population can read and write their own language, and
that they have a sense of moral obligations. Further
I would not give them credit, as it is doubtful whether
piety has entered the soul. » (3) Lastly, a Catholic

(1) *Manners and Customs*, etc., vol. II, ch. xxii, p. 235.
(2) *Rambles*, etc., p. 20.
(3) *A History of New Zealand*, etc., by John Bright, M. R.
C. S., ch. vi, p. 127.

missionary, the Abbé Petitjean, who visited the natives at Wangaroa this year, whom he found « almost
entirely Protestant, » and making habitually the most
ludicrous perversions of the Bible, says; « Will it be
believed that these poor people did not know that
there is one God in Three Persons; that the Word
became Man and died for us; yet their teachers
have been in New Zealand for more than twenty
years! » (1)

In the following year, 1842, D' Dieffenbach,
though he endeavours to make the best possible case
for the missionaries, gives this account of the effects of
Protestant conversion. « Instead of an active warlike
race, they have become eaters of potatoes, neglecting
their industrious pursuits... and they pass their lives
in eating, smoking, and sleeping. » In several places
he indicates that they retain as Protestants their
pagan customs, and that they exhibit the influence
of their new religion chiefly by a superstitious and
irrational observance of the ' sabbath, ' which « the
ill-judged directions of the missionaries » (2) have
taught them to regard as the capital tenet of Christianity.

At the same date, M' Heaphy, who had visited the
various provinces of New Zealand, thus recounts the
results of his observation. « I estimate the good which
the Missionaries have done as about the same which
would have resulted from the settlement, for the same
period, of a like number of respectable settlers of
various avocations; with the exception that the sett-

(1) *Annals*, vol. II, p. 154.
(2) *Travels*, vol. I, ch. VII, p. 110.

II.   r

lers would probably have taught the natives many
useful arts, and introduced industry amongst them,
which the Missionaries have not. » And presently he
adds, « much of what the missionaries have endeavoured to teach the New Zealanders has had any but
a good effect upon them. » (1)

In 1843, Mr King, an unusually candid missionary, says; « The number of natives under Christian
instruction is very large, but the number of those
who are decidedly Christian is very small. » (2) Yet
twenty-nine years had now elapsed since the Protestant missionaries entered New Zealand, and they had
to deal with perhaps the most apt and intelligent race
of barbarians in the world.

The year 1843 furnishes six witnesses. The American Commodore Wilkes, who commanded the United
States Exploring Expedition, relates that « *perhaps*
those who have become somewhat attached to the
Christian religion may be a *little* improved, » — but
he confesses that he only heard of a solitary instance
of such improvement. « The Missionaries of the
Episcopal Church, » he adds, « appear to keep aloof
from the natives, and an air of stiffness and pride
seems to prevail. They appear to be doing but little
in making converts. Most of the natives have morning
and evening prayers, but their practices and character
show any thing but a reform in their lives. » (3)
Mr Brodie notices in the same year, as a proof of the

(1) *Narrative*, etc., ch. v, p. 52.
(2) *Polynesia and New Zealand*, by the Right Revd M. Russell, ch. x, p. 361. (2d edition).
(3) *United States Exploring Expedition*, by Charles Wilkes,
U. S. N., vol. III, ch. xii, pp. 400, 401.

feeble influence of Protestantism, that Dᵣ Selwyn and
his colleague Dᵣ Williams tried in vain to prevent
their own followers from fighting. (1) Mᵣ Brown at
the same date observes, — and his position gave him
unusual opportunities of judging,—that « the Church
Missionaries in particular » — meaning the Episcopalians — « have not found their way to the hearts
of the natives, and are not so much respected as they
ought to have been. One powerful cause of this has
been their adoption of a peculiarly hard and illiberal
system of dealing with the natives in commercial
matters, which has produced a highly unfavorable
contrast in this respect with the conduct of the other
settlers. » (2) Thirty years, it seems, had effected no
change in their character.

Mᵣ Wakefield confirms, in his well known work,
the same facts. Of the so-called Christian natives he
says, « they appeared to be tamed without being
civilised; » and he gives examples of the imprudent
boasts and exaggerations by which the missionaries
too often attempted to deceive their supporters at
home. Hongi and Waikato, two New Zealand chiefs,
were sent over and exhibited by them to English
audiences as « perfect and very devout Christians; »
but as soon as the former, enriched by the presents
of his credulous admirers, returned to his own
country, « he appeared in his true character as an
ambitious and blood-thirsty warrior. » One of his
first acts was to destroy « the Wesleyan Mission at
Wangaroa. » But without multiplying these character-

(1) *Remarks*, etc., p. 39.
(2) Ch. 11, p. 84.

istic details, let it suffice to quote the following impressive statement, in which Mr Wakefield appreciates the historical results of Protestant missions in New Zealand. « It was a matter of constant observation, among all classes of settlers, that the results of the missionary system of instruction were not by any means satisfactory. At Wellington no less than at Wanganui, and at other places where there were no white settlers, this fact began to startle the impartial observer. The only good result that appeared to have been obtained, was the strict and rigid adherence to the mere forms of the Christian religion. But it was hardly a matter of doubt that the conversion penetrated no deeper than the mere forms. *As a body they were distinctly inferior in point of moral character to the natives who remained with their ancient customs unchanged...* At some places, such as Patea, where their religious enthusiasm was carried, in form, to the most extravagant pitch, they maintained the very worst character for honesty, and courtesy to a stranger. It must be remembered that no white man had dwelt there. The Missionary system had therefore enjoyed a fair trial, without the interference of civilization. » (1)

In the same year, another Protestant witness writes as follows from Wanganui. « I state my belief that the Missionaries have done very little, if any thing, towards the improvement of either the civil or moral condition of the Maoris. It will be urged, that the natives must be better than before, as they are nearly all Christians. Truly as far as the name they

(1) *Adventure*, etc., vol. II, ch. I, p. 11.

are — but what else? I appeal to any one who
knows any thing of them, whether they are one jot
more moral or more civilized than their neighbours
the ' *Devils* ', as the unchristian natives are styled
par excellence; whether, in fact, you would not
sooner, at any time, trust or believe a ' *Devil* ', rather
than a ' *Missionary?* ' • (1) Another witness from
the same place, and in the same volume, says of the
Protestant converts, — • generally speaking, they
are distinguished from the unconverted natives as
rogues, thieves, and liars. • (2) A third declares
that • Polygamy is still not uncommon, the principal
chief at Putiki having three wives, *all Missionaries.* • (3)

Lastly, still in the same year, Dʳ Selwyn tell us
of • a native *teacher* who relapsed into sin, • and of
a Chief who told him, that • his own backwardness
of belief was owing to *the bad conduct of the baptized
natives.* • (4) Thirty-one years had now elapsed.

In 1846, Mʳ Fitzroy, a friend and companion of
the Missionaries, reports still more unfavorably.
• Religion • he says, • has lost much of the limited
influence which was acquired previous to 1840. •
And then he explains his meaning. Hitherto, the
Protestants had at least none but friendly witnesses
of their failure, in this chosen field of their operations.
This advantage they were now losing for ever.
• Roman Catholics • Mʳ Fitzroy adds, • have entered
the field which was exclusively Protestant till

(1) *Letters from Wanganui,* p. 8.
(2) *Ibid.,* p. 35.
(3) *Ibid.,* p. 21.
(4) *Church in the Colonies,* Number vii, p. 44.

1838. » (1) It was apparently high time, and we shall see presently what welcome they received.

In 1847, M' Augas, a friend of D' Dieffenbach, still notes the force of the old superstitions, and records that « even those natives who have embraced Christianity, » are subject to their influence, and especially to « the dread of the supposed power of witchcraft. » (2)

In 1849, — such a history should be pursued to the end, — a British officer visits New Zealand on service. He is amazed to find himself fighting against « Protestant natives, » of whom he probably knew nothing but from the florid narratives of missionary records, and this is his reflection upon the curious fact. « It appears to me unaccountable, but it is nevertheless true, that nearly the whole of the natives who took part with John Heki against the Government in the Bay of Islands *were Protestants.* » (3) Heki himself was a notable specimen of the influence of Protestant « conversion, » and deserves a moment's notice. « This man was *educated* by the missionaries, » says D' Thomson, « and had acquired a deep knowledge of the Bible; he was baptized in the presence of the British Resident, and the tears he shed on the occasion showed how keenly he felt the solemnity of that Sacrament. » And what was the effect of Protestantism upon this noble savage, « whose mind was of the order found in the front

(1) *Remarks on New Zealand in 1846*, by Robert Fitzroy, ch. VII, p. 63.

(2) *Savage Life*, etc., vol. 1, ch. IX, p. 331.

(3) *Reminiscences of Twelve Months service in New Zealand*, by Lieut. H. F. Mc Killop, R. N., p. 86.

rank of intellectual progress? » Here is the answer.
« He fell back into heathenism, and took delight in
religious disputes; he argued against the truths of
Scripture, and confounded Christians with their
own weapons. » And that the miserable form of
Christianity presented to him, and especially its
incessant divisions and the malice displayed in them,
produced this effect, is proved by his own expressive
taunt; « One bee-hive is very good, several are trou-
blesome. » (1)

In 1850, Mr Brunner thus describes the Anglican
Mission at Taramakau. « The natives here are members of the Church of England, and attend service
regularly; but they appear to be very ignorant of its
nature or meaning. » (2)

The year 1851 supplies three valuable witnesses.
The first is Mr Shortland, a friend of Dr Selwyn, and
apparently himself a missionary. This gentleman
gives us a description of the higher class of « converts, » whose special merits had earned for them the
lucrative distinction of being employed as assistant
preachers of Protestant doctrine, and by the aid of
whose superior intelligence it was proposed to act
vigorously upon the native mind. Mr Shortland employs one of them, who had been « educated in the
house of an English Missionary, » to preach for him
on Sunday. It was a rash experiment. « I afterwards
saw cause, » Mr Shortland observes, « to regret that
I had not dissuaded him from undertaking an office
he was little qualified to discharge. » Of another

(1) Dr Thomson, vol. II, p. 96.
(2) *Journal of the Royal Geographical Society*, vol. XX, p.358.

« native preacher » of the same class, he says, « as
parts of his composition were often very absurd,
I thought it right to forbid him the use of extempo-
rary prayer, and to confine him to our old forms. »
But it was only by threatening to dismiss him altogether, which would have involved the loss of his
salary, that he restrained his dangerous improvisa-
tion. Speaking generally of the whole class, he writes
as follows. « The Missionaries anticipated good results from sending out the best instructed of their
young converts as preachers and missionaries among
the more distant tribes, whom they were unable
themselves to visit. The attempt seemed at first
crowned with extraordinary success — vast numbers
being daily added to the body of professing Christians
— and very favorable reports on the subject were
constantly forwarded to the Society in England. But
after a year or two it was discovered that great
abuses had been introduced into the practice of the
Christian religion by these native missionaries. » (1)
Mr Shortland has told us, what we might safely have
assumed, that only the « best instructed » were employed in these functions, and these were the best!
We have already seen that they « raised a very considerable income, » by levying contributions in kind
from the flocks entrusted to them by the English missionaries.

Mr Fox, in the same year, gives further examples
of the veracity of the missionary reports, and of the
real character of missionary converts. « An intelligent clergyman, » he says, describes Rauperaha, one

(1) *The Southern Districts of New Zealand*, p. 268.

of the most conspicuous of these converts, as « now to be seen every morning in his accustomed place, repeating those blessed truths which teach him to love the Lord with all his heart. » We can imagine the sensation which this pleasing picture would create at a missionary meeting in England, and the lavish donations which it could not fail to provoke. Unfortunately, however, the virtues of this eminent convert existed only in the imagination of the « intelligent clergyman. » Only « a few days before his death, » M⟨r⟩ Fox tells us, « two settlers called to see him. While there a neighbouring missionary came in, and offered him the consolations of religion. Rauperaha demeaned himself in a manner highly becoming such an occasion; but the moment the missionary was gone, he turned to his other visitors and said, ‘ What is the use of all that nonsense? that will do my belly no good. ’ He then turned the conversation on the Wanganui races, where one of his guests had been running a horse. » (1) Captain Cruise relates a parallel story of the chief Tooi, who had been long in England, where he was exhibited as a model convert; (2) and M⟨r⟩ Hursthouse informs us that his fellow-christian Rauperaha used to say of Captain Fitzroy, the Governor, who was as easily beguiled as the intelligent clergyman, — « he is soft, he is a pumpkin. »

M⟨r⟩ Fox sums up his own observations in these remarkable words; — « I am often asked what the effect of the influence of the Missionaries has been. My

(1) *The Six Colonies*, p. 73.
(2) Captain Cruise's *Journal*, p. 38.

answer is, up to a certain point beneficial — beyond
that, *injurious in a very high degree.* » Of their converts he gives a description worthy of careful study,
and which we only omit for the sake of brevity.

Our last witness for this year, the thirty-seventh
of Protestant efforts in New Zealand, is a gentleman
engaged in commercial pursuits, and who gives, from
actual observation, an account of the missionaries
themselves which we can hardly venture to quote in
full. « It is right that the world should know; » he
says, « that there have been as many wolves as
shepherds amongst the folds. » And then he continues
thus. « I esteem and venerate holy men who act according to their profession, and am aware that no
man is infallible; but when one yields to the ' old
man ' the corrupt portion of his nature, and finds
himself incapable of subduing his sensual passions, let
him resign the sacerdotal character, and not doubly
pollute his soul and body, bringing contempt on
the missionary cause, and standing forth to the heathen a mocking comment on the Word of God. »
We can hardly be surprised, when this gentleman
adds, — and the examples of Rauperaha, Hongki,
and other chiefs may assist us to believe him, —
that « instead of improving the native character, the
missionaries have superinduced upon their other bad
qualities hypocrisy of the deepest dye. I speak dis-
passionately when I say, that I conscientiously believe the moral character of the natives has not been
improved by missionary intercourse. » (1)

We have almost exhausted our witnesses. In 1834,

(1) *Rovings in the Pacific*, vol. I, ch. IX, p. 223.

another Protestant traveller thus describes a scene
in a church. « The service consisted in singing a
psalm, rapidly reading a chapter, and as rapidly
reading some of the Church prayers. I fancied I saw
a resemblance to the lifeless formality with which
some of our Cathedral daily services are attended. » (1) We almost expected this familiar image.

In the same year, we have one of those conclusive
testimonies which leave nothing to be added. The
Rev. Robert Young, who went to New Zealand as a
« deputation » from the Wesleyan Society, and had
no personal interest in the work which he was only
charged to examine and appreciate, thus describes its
real character, exactly forty years after it had been
commenced by Marsden's advantageous purchase.
« In many cases their Christianity is merely nominal. They feel not its saving power. » (2)

In 1855, an English lady, of a class which only
exists in England and America, produced a book
which she entitled « The Gospel in New Zealand. »
It need not detain us long. When the natives scoff at
her missionary friends, whom she depicts as at least
equal to the first Apostles, she calls them « barbarians, whose extermination seemed far more desirable
than their conversion » — a sentiment in which zeal
seems to triumph over charity. But she says other
things more worthy of notice. Speaking of an epoch
more than twenty years subsequent to their establishment, she relates how « the Missionaries mourn-
ed over the unfruitfulness of their labours as to the

(1) *A Summer's Excursion in N. Z.*, p. 178.
(2) *The Southern World*, ch. vii, p. 161.

conversion of souls, « and then comes the following
passage, in which we might suspect a lurking irony,
if she were capable of jesting on so grave a subject.
« It had been comparatively easy, » she remarks,
« to dig their fields and plant their gardens, — and
it was pleasant to gather the abundant produce, —
to drop a peach stone into the ground, and ere long
to enjoy the delicious fruit; but » — and then she
confesses, in a language peculiar to herself, that their
spiritual husbandry was much less fruitful.

Let us hear this lady once more. In spite of her
wish to represent her missionary friends as almost
more than mortal in their virtues, she draws but a
gloomy picture of their success, and terminates her
lamentations with this characteristic discourse.
« The dangers of Popery are added to those of
worldliness! The efforts made by this false religion
are unceasing; and though in those districts that
have long had the blessing of Scriptural teaching, they
have failed in producing much lasting effect, » — we
shall learn more on that subject presently, — « yet
in the newer districts they have been but too successful among the half-awakened, and the remaining heathen, and cause our Missionaries much
anxiety. » (1)

In 1857, Mr Paul fitly sums up the history of
Protestantism in New Zealand by the usual announcement, that « the New Zealanders are annually on
the decrease ; » and ventures to prophecy that the
final result of the English rule will be, that « they

(1) *The Gospel in New Zealand*, by Miss Tucker, ch. x, p. 117;
ch. xx, p. 253.

will become nearly, if not entirely, extinct. » (1)

Lastly, in 1859, the whole series is closed by various and pregnant testimonies, of which it will suffice to notice only a few. Dr Thomson, whose sympathies were all on the side of the Protestant missionaries, thus describes the final result of their labours after fifty years of costly effort. *Thirty six per cent*, he says, of the surviving population are still avowed pagans; while of the nominal Christians this is his candid account. « The Christianity of many of them is a rude mixture of paganism and the cross, an adoption strengthened by superstition more than a conversion. Missionaries will deny this : but Christian natives, suffering under sickness, *frequently appeal to their old gods for health*, » — the reader will call to mind the same extraordinary fact in Ceylon, — « and healthy Christians dread violating the tapu, lest the gods who watch over that code should punish them with sickness. » (2) And then he sums up the whole history of half a century in these impressive words, — « The work of Christianity in New Zealand is only begun. »

In the same year, 1859, an official document was published at Auckland, by order of the colonial government, and with the revelations contained in that document we may at length determine, without the risk of error, the real influence of Protestant missions in New Zealand, after an expenditure which we may imagine, but can hardly estimate. And first, this curious paper, which professes to investigate the

(1) *Australia*, etc., p. 252.
(2) Vol. I, part. II, ch. IV, p. 317.

true causes of the rapid decrease of the native population of the islands, attests the grave fact, that it
had already dwindled at that date to 56,409, — so
that nearly *seven eighths* had disappeared, if Cook's
estimate were true, since the white man set foot in
New Zealand.

Secondly, all the witnesses concerned in obtaining
materials for the solution of the problem proposed to
them are perfectly unanimous on these points, —
that nothing can now arrest the decay of the population, and that universal immorality and misery are
its chief determining causes. « An increasing taste
for spirit drinking, » says Mr Hulse, « is prevalent
among both sexes, but more particularly with the
young, who resort to all kinds of devices to obtain
it. » « In my opinion, » observes Mr Fenton, by
whom the evidence was collected and printed, « the
social condition of the Maories *is inferior to what
it was five years ago.* Their houses are worse, their
cultivation more neglected, and their mode of living
not improved. The mills in some places have not
run for some time, and the poverty of the people
generally is extreme. At the same time there has
appeared a remarkable activity of mind, directed to
the development of political ideas. » « There is reason
to fear, » he adds, that nothing can save « a population which has once reached such a state of decrepitude as that exhibited by the Maori inhabitants of
this country. » Lastly, one of the missionaries, and
they are all of one mind, declares, that « the greatest
cause of decrease is uncleanness, outwardly and in-
wardly, in diet, dress, and habitation, in body and
mind, *in all their thoughts words, and actions.* »

Such have been the effects of Protestantism upon
this noble race, and to this climax Dr Thomson
points when he says, « The work of Christianity in
New Zealand is only begun. » That work will probably be at length complete when there is no longer
a New Zealander in existence, and paganism will
have disappeared when the last pagan has perished
from the land.

The facts which have now been traced for us by
so many Protestant witnesses, each independent of
the other, and all recording the results of personal
observation, do not require any comment. This was
the fruit of half a century of missionary labour. This
was all that Protestantism could do, as its own
agents confess, with such human aids and appliances
as never missionaries possessed before, for perhaps
the noblest race of barbarians now extant. To uproot
their heathen virtues, which might at least have
earned a temporal reward, and to substitute for them
new and strange vices, — indolence, treachery, and
avarice; to teach them, by their own example, that
the Christian religion was so worthless, that even its
ministers might be types of selfishness, luxury, and
worldliness; to abuse their simplicity by mean craft,
and rob them both of their land and its produce,
with a Bible in one hand and a fraudulent contract
in the other; and finally to cheat souls which were
capable of supernatural virtue by a narrow and
superstitious formalism, or corrupt them into systematic hypocrisy; such, as their own associates
eagerly attest, has been the work of Protestant missionaries in New Zealand. Yet even this is not all.

There was still another evil, the same which has

made England a bye word throughout Christendom,
which it was possible to carry across the sea, and
transplant even in her most remote dependency. The
war of sects, the licence of crude and shifting opinion,
the strife of texts, and endless discord of opposing
creeds, — it was necessary that New Zealand should
possess them all. Fatal gift! against which even
pagans would have lifted up the cry of fear and
supplication, if they had known what it would bring
in its train. But this is the final chastisement which
ages of impenitence have brought upon the heathen
world in these last days, and which not even
Apostles — though they were as wise as St. Paul,
as mighty as St. Gregory Thaumaturgus, or as fervent as St. Francis Xavier — could now avert from
them. Protestantism is the last scourge of heathenism.

Let us see, before we conclude this history, what
the missionaries themselves relate of the effects of
religious divisions in New Zealand. « We need not
wonder; » says Dr Selwyn, « at the controversies
which are raging at home, when even in the most
distant parts of this most remote of all countries, in
places hitherto unvisited by English Missionaries, »
— he is speaking of *Ruapuke*, to which only *native*
teachers had been sent, - « the spirit of controversy
is every where found to prevail, in many cases to the
entire exclusion of all simplicity of faith. » (1) Such
is the phenomenon upon which, in conclusion, we
must offer a few remarks.

The fact admitted by Dr Selwyn is illustrated, in
still more energetic language, by a multitude of wit-

(1) *Church in the Colonies*, No VIII, p. 23.

nesses. Even in the most retired spots, observes
Mr Brunner, in 1850, « though in some places there
are only *six or seven* natives, yet they have separate
places of worship, — Church of England and Wesleyan, — and are always quarrelling about religion. » (1) « Contention, animosity, distrust, and
intolerance, » says the Rev. Elijah Hoole, « are but
the mere outlines of that state of feeling which at
present exists among our divided people. The spirit
of Christianity is lost in the form, and the very form
itself has become the subject of incessant and angry
dispute. These, together with other circumstances of
a painful character, have contributed to destroy much
of that missionary influence which it is of the utmost
importance to possess. » (2)

In earlier times they made war on each other in
tribes, and now that they are restrained by the strong
hand of Government, they display their ferocity in
sects. « Tribes hereditarily hostile, » says Dr Thomson, « adopted through jealousy different modes of
faith; and these converted New Zealanders were
ready to abuse each other for religious creeds they
did not understand, and the precepts of which they
daily disregarded. » « Schismatic differences have
already arisen among the natives, » says Mr Polack
in 1840, « who have ranged themselves on different
sides. In 1837, a serious fight, during which several
persons were shot dead or wounded, arose between
the Wesleyan neophytes and the sticklers to the old
belief. » « I found, » says Mr Shortland ten years

(1) *Journal of Royal Geographical Society*, vol. XX, p. 361.
(2) *Year Book of Missions*, pp. 213, 222.

later, « that the professing Christians were divided
between the Church of England and the Wesleyans,
the two parties being very hostile to each other. »
« The most revolting religious feud was going on at
Waimate, » Mr Wakefield relates in 1845, « between
near relations in two septs of this tribe — Wesleyan
and Episcopalian — when I passed through the district. » « The whole population of natives, » he adds,
« struck me as being *in the most repulsive and pitiable condition*. They were all ' missionaries, ' but
divided in their creeds. The most dreadful religious
schisms occured daily between the nearest relations.
And this virulence of dispute, on the most abstruse
as well as the most trifling points of religion, both in
form and doctrine, I found very much replacing the
strict puritan observances and adherence to absurd
exaggerated forms. »

In the province of Otago, Mr Paul says that even
the colonists fought with « a virulence that turns the
sanctity of their professed Christianity into ridicule,
and makes religion a subject of discussion for arous-
ing the worst passions of man. » « The minds of the
natives, » Mr Brown reports, « are perfectly distracted. The first effect is the rejection of the teaching *of
both parties*. It is lamentable, however, to think that
the influence of religion has no sooner subdued and
eradicated their savage feuds and enmities, than that
very religion is converted into an occasion of strife
and bloodshed.... The natives are now at open war
with each other; they have forsaken their own animosities for the no less deadly hatred and enmity
engendered by the teaching of different professors of
the same meek and merciful religion ; and unless

some effectual remedy be devised for the growing
evil, all the good that Missionaries have ever done
may soon be as nothing compared with the evil
which threatens to accompany it. »

« I had heard that religious differences prevailed
to a serious extent, » says another writer, « but I did
not believe it possible that these differences should
lead to such defined separation. » (1) The agents of
the Missionaries, we are told by one who held the
office of Protector of the Aborigines, « busied themselves with making proselytes with more of the native
than the christian spirit, and have caused a schism
between the inhabitants of almost every settlement,
one party styling themselves children of Wesley, the
other the church of Paihai. The distraction of their
minds thus caused has essentially interfered with
their happiness, by producing ill feeling and separation among members of the same family. This would
seem to suggest the expediency of not sending missionaries *of different breeds* among the same tribe at
least, as they must neutralise each other's labours,
and may possibly cause an uncertainty of belief in the
minds of the natives, ultimately destructive of the
cause they seek to promote. » (2)

Finally, the Rev. Mr Turton, a Wesleyan missionary, completes the narrative in these terms. « We
have the awful sight of father and son, mother and
daughter, hating each other with a mortal hatred. In
some cases they are dividing themselves into *separate
pas;* in other cases into separate divisions of the same

(1) *A Summer's Excursion,* p. 148.
(2) *Parliamentary Papers,* vol. XXX, p. 153. (1846).

pa : and in one village, within eight miles of this settlement, has the party spirit risen so high between near kinsmen, that one of these *pas* has erected a fence across the Kainga, and lined it thickly with fern, not as a break-wind or shelter, but, as he told us, *that the one party might not be able even to look upon the other.* » (1)

Such are the gifts of Protestant England to her colonies. To sow in all lands the tares which the enemy has planted in her own, — to present Christianity to the heathen as the symbol of confusion and disorder, the fruitful mother of jealousy and hate, — to strip the savage of the new virtues which he was ready to assume, and revive the old enmities which he was willing to forget ; such is the terrible mission which she has chosen for herself. It is her own children who fling this reproach at her ; it is her own agents and emissaries, regretting too late their fatal success, who cry to her from every region of the earth, from every island which the sea has cast up to its surface, and seem to pray that her ships may pass far from their shores, and carry elsewhere their cargo of pestilence and death. But the prayer comes too late ; the seal is opened, the plague let loose ; « the waters have become wormwood, » and souls shall die « because the fountains of waters have been made bitter. » (2)

Let us return for a moment to the story of New Zealand, that we may bring it to an end. « You Europeans are not even agreed amongst yourselves, »

<hr>

(1) Quoted in Mr Brown's *New Zealand*, app. p. 261.
(2) *Apoc.*, VIII, 11.

said a powerful chief, « as to what is the true religion. When you have agreed amongst yourselves
which is the right road, I may perhaps be induced
to take it. » (1) Who will cast the first stone at this
barbarian, or convict him of error? « Had there been
one uniform creed and priesthood, » says Colonel
Mundy, as if determined to justify the argument of
the savage, « one cannot doubt that the success of
the Christian Missions would have been incalcu-
lably greater — perhaps literally catholic, universal,
throughout the native population of these islands.
The observant Maori cannot be blind to such open
and wide schism, nor deaf to the virulence of sectarian animosity. » He is, in truth, neither blind nor
deaf. If this be your boasted religion, he says, and
these its fruits, we are better without it. Even pagans can judge such a mockery of Christianity. « They
say, and they are right in saying it, » exclaims a
Protestant missionary, as if some strong spirit forced
the avowal from him, « *that heathenism in love is
better than Christianity without it.* » (2)

We have still to speak of the efforts of an individual whom, for several reasons, it was inexpedient to
compare with his companions. It would be indecent
to confound the respected name of Dr Selwyn with
that of his predecessors and colleagues. Most Eng-
lishmen are familiar with his honorable career. Distinguished even in youth by the manly energy of
character which made him pre-eminent amongst all
rivals both at school and college; exhibiting all the

(1) *New Zealand*, by William Swainson, H. M. Attorney General, p. 36. (1856).
(2) Mr Turton, quoted in Brown's app. p. 268.

qualities which compose the highest type of excellence recognised by his countrymen and co-religionists ; Dr Selwyn had only to make his own choice
amongst the various dignities which popular sympathy awards to its favorites. In the army, he would
have risen to high command ; the bar would have
admitted him amongst its leaders ; having selected the
ecclesiastical profession, he naturally became a bishop. Anglicanism could not desire a better representative. Let us follow Dr Selwyn to New Zealand, and
see what his talents and virtues have enabled him to
effect, after many years of labour, as the acknowledged head, both by character and position, of Protestant missions in that colony.

We have seen already that, like Heber and Mid-
leton in India, he contents himself with recording as
an unwelcome fact those implacable religious divisions which Anglicanism every where generates, but
for which he does not even affect to suggest a remedy,
and which others declare are mainly due to his own
influence. « He has not rested satisfied, » says a
member of the New Zealand Legislative Council whom
we have already quoted, « with promulgating the
doctrines of Christianity, but has waged war on his
fellow-labourers, by denouncing their teachings as
unsound. » Dr Selwyn had perhaps good reason for
denouncing his various rivals in New Zealand, and
for warning the natives against their version of
Christianity; but as the Episcopalians and Wesleyans had co-operated together as one body for nearly
a quarter of a century before his arrival amongst them,
had always recognised each other as fellow-ministers
before the heathen, and had even been accustomed,

we are told, during all that period • to partake
of the sacrament • together indifferently, — his admonition naturally provoked two comments; the first,
that it came too late; and the second, that it was a
far more severe condemnation of his own church,
and of her capricious inconsistency, than of the Wesleyan teachers, who at least had the advantage of
being always of one mind. We shall presently hear
both these arguments urged with great force, and
apparently with triumphant effect.

That Dʳ Selwyn has not succeeded, in spite of his
eminent natural gifts, in changing the character of
the New Zealanders, any more than Martyn succeeded in India or Tomlin in China, is sufficiently proved
by what we have already heard, as well as by his
own admissions. • Bishop Selwyn complains, • we
are told by Mʳ Fox, who refers to his own words,
• that the Missionaries can obtain no hold on the
minds of the natives, owing to the loss of influence
of the chiefs. They are, he says, ' a rope of sand;
the young men escape from all control. ' • (1) Even
his own • converts • appear obstinately indifferent to
the peculiar tenets which he has endeavoured to recommend to them, and especially to the most elementary notions of what he would call • church
principles. • Thus Dʳ Selwyn, after relating that on
a certain occasion a native chief insisted upon reading the prayers, while he himself preached the sermon, goes on thus· • This, you will say, was an unusual combination : a New Zealand war chief reading
prayers, and an English Bishop preaching; but you

(1) *The Six Colonies*, p. 59.

must not at present judge us by the ordinary rules of Church discipline. (1) Most people will be so little disposed to judge this occurrence harshly, that they will see in the concession made to the headstrong chief only a proof of Dᵣ Selwyn's good sense; but we may fairly observe, that while Catholic missionaries have no difficulty in fixing deep in the hearts of their converts, however rude and uncivilised, all the stupendous mysteries of the apostolic doctrine, Anglicans cannot so much as induce their own countrymen, much less the heathen tribes, to observe even the formal decencies of ecclesiastical discipline. The « war chief » probably thought himself quite as capable a minister of *such* a religion, which consists only in the utterance of words, as his episcopal colleague, and Dᵣ Selwyn had no alternative but to comply with his humour. No such anecdote, however, will be found in the annals of Catholic missions; and the Catholic convert of to day, though yesterday but a pagan savage, has already been taught by God both that religion has its sanctuaries, and that *he* may not dare to intrude into them.

As we are now speaking of Dᵣ Selwyn, not in the character which his many friends justly admire, but in that of an apostolic missionary, — for this is his profession, — we are obliged to notice the following characteristic fact. He is on a journey, not more arduous than common men undertake every day for business or pleasure, but still a journey, and he has left his family behind. A feeling of lassitude comes over him, and he tells us from what source he derived

(1) *Church in the Colonies*, Nᵒ vɪɪ, p. 8.

comfort and strength. « I consoled myself with a letter from M⁻ Selwyn, giving an excellent account of
herself and William, upon which I took heart. » (1)
Let it be freely admitted that such a sentiment is
perfectly natural and becoming in the mouth of a
Protestant bishop, even though a « missionary ; » but
if we would comprehend all that such language im-
plies, let us try to fancy St. Andrew or St. Bartholomew, or even the most obscure Catholic missionary
of the nineteenth century, gravely writing, that being
on an embassy from the Most High God, he was re-
freshed and « took heart, » because he heard good
tidings of his wife and family. In such words is revealed the whole difference between a mere man, amiable and educated, but possessing only the natural
virtues; and an apostle, filled with divine gifts,
and deriving from his union with God a higher
consolation than the purest domestic joys can ever
yield.

« How shall we preach to the world detachment
and contempt of earthly things, » said the great
apostle of China, in a treatise of almost incomparable eloquence and force addressed to the Literates
of that land, « if we do not contend against covetousness by holy poverty, and against voluptuousness by
chastity ? We resign freely that which is our own, in
order to teach the world not to covet what belongs to
another; and we refrain even from lawful marriage,
to admonish it against forbidden pleasures. There
will never be wanting fathers of families, to set an
example of domestic virtue, and yet many of these

(1) *Church in the Colonies*, N° vⅢ, p. 34.

II.   *

are more occupied in destroying religion than in extending it. Let some at least be altogether given to
the latter. We do not respect man for what he has in
common with the brutes. To aim at perfection is his
true calling. Man can more safely dispense with bread
that with justice, and the world would be better
without inhabitants than without religion. The importance of religion is, then, a sufficient motive with
some men to neglect marriage; but is marriage so
important that we ought to neglect religion for it?
Death itself should not hinder us from following the
Divine will; why, then, should the necessity of re-
nouncing marriage do so? Our office is to preach the
Faith in all the earth. If we fail in the West, we hasten
to the East; if they refuse to hear us in the South,
we turn to the North. We are not tied to one place; but
marriage binds a man and attaches him to his family.
Married persons may quit each other no more.....
The members of my Order are ready, at a moment's
warning, to carry the Faith to any region, though it
were distant thousands of leagues. They have not to
provide for a family. They have God for their father, all
men for brothers, and the world for a home. A virtue
as high as the heavens, as wide as the oceans, is it
not far above mere conjugal fidelity?.... We do not
contemn marriage; they who marry sin not; but
we who are missionaries abstain from it, while we
readily admit that not all who observe celibacy are
saints. » (1)

It is curious that, almost at the same moment
that Dr Selwyn was « taking heart » in his

(1) *Lettres Édifiantes*, tome XXV.

fatigues, the Catholic Bishop of New Zealand, whose character Protestant witnesses will presently expound to us, was writing home to his aged mother in France, not to complain of his solitude, or of all that he had left in Europe, but to ask her prayers, — the prayers of his own mother, — that God would grant him the grace of martyrdom, and let him finish his apostolic career by shedding his blood for his Master.

It remains only to allude to D' Selwyn's attempts to introduce « high-church principles » in New Zealand, and the results to which they have led. He is the first Protestant missionary by whom the experiment has been tried; and his own mode of action, the comments which it provoked in others, and its final results, are too instructive not to merit special notice.

Before D' Selwyn's arrival in the colony, the clergy of the established church, occupied chiefly in making their fortunes, and caring as little about « church principles » as the majority of their brethren at home, were hardly to be distinguished, except by their superior wealth, from Wesleyans, Independents, or Presbyterians. The different sects dwelt together in harmony, and were too keenly absorbed by more pressing interests to quarrel about their ecclesiastical distinctions. D' Selwyn was of another class; he had not come to New Zealand to make money, and he had a strong opinion about the « priesthood » and the « sacraments, » or at least about two of them. He bade his clergy tell the natives, for the first time, that the Weleyans were unauthorised agents, without orders or mission. Then arose that furious strife of

sects which has made New Zealand a battle-field from
one end to the other, and of which the effects have been
described to us by Dr Selwyn himself. But the Wesleyans were not disposed to retire from a field which
they had occupied for a quarter of a century; they
accepted Dr Selwyn's challenge, and they replied to
his arguments after this manner.

For more than twenty years, said Mr Turton, who
represented the Wesleyan body, and who conducted
the official correspondence with their new and unexpected adversary, your clergy have invariably co-
operated with us. Either they were wrong then, or
you are wrong now, unless the Church of England
has the privilege of changing its principles every
twenty years. The argument was forcible, and hardly
admitted of reply; but Mr Turton then proceeded to
discuss the probable effects of the new • church
principles • upon the natives. • They are shrewd
men, • he observed to Dr Selwyn, and will be sure
to ask, • Why have we not heard of this schismatical church before? Is this *a new Church of England*
that has lately sprung up? And what has this new
bishop been doing for the last twenty years, that he
could not hasten hither before now to warn us of
our danger? • Mr Turton seems to have felt that he
had a strong case, and was determined to make the
most of it; so he went on thus. • Your lordship has
placed the Church Mission, and her past operations
amongst the New Zealanders, in a most awkward
position. She must either acknowledge herself to
have been egregiously wrong in holding the least
sympathy with ' schismatics, ' or she must defend
the course which she has taken for the last twenty

years in the exercise of ' brotherly love ' towards the
Wesleyans. » (1)

Dr Selwyn was far too intelligent not to feel the
« awkward position » quite as keenly as his Wesleyan correspondent, and appears to have sought
escape from it in this way. In public he continued
to condemn the Wesleyans, while in private he did
just what his clergy had done « for the last twenty
years. » Familiar as we are with the Church of
England, and with her constant betrayal even of the
truths which she professes to uphold, it is difficult to
realise that such words as the following were written
by Dr Selwyn. « The Wesleyan Missionaries received
me in a most friendly and hospitable manner, and all
our *differences of system* seemed to be forgotten in
the one absorbing interest of the work in which we
were all engaged for the conversion of the heathen...
It was of little consequence whether these babes in
Christ were nourished by their own true mother, »
— meaning, apparently, the establishment in England and Ireland, — « or by *other faithful nurses*,
provided that they were fed only with the sincere
milk of the word. » (2)

Elsewhere he says, « I went to the house of
Mr Watkins, Wesleyan missionary, by whom I was
hospitably entertained. In the evening I catechised
his natives. » (3) But this assertor of « church
principles » could discern and acknowledge « faithful
nurses » any where. « I may confess, » he says,
writing from another place, « *the pleasure which*

(1) In Brown's appendix, p. 259.
(2) *The Melanesian Mission*, Letter I, p. 17.
(3) *Church in the Colonies*, N° VIII, p. 17.

I felt in kneeling down to family prayers in the
house of the resident Missionary, a minister, 1 believe, of the *Independent persuasion.* » (1)

These are not the only passages of the same kind in
Dr Selwyn's letters, but we need not add to them. The
Wesleyans and Independents were probably satisfied
that such an adversary was not likely to do them much
injury, and that « church principles » were far more
harmless than they had supposed. What Dr Selwyn's
explanation of these contradictions may be, we do not
stay to enquire. He has only done what Heber and
others did before him, and many more will do after
him; but he has added one more proof to the thousands which already existed of the real character of
the Anglican Church, and has shown that she only
differs from the various sects which have sprung from
her in this, — that while they form each a separate
community in order to enjoy the exclusive profession
of a particular heresy, she, in the person of her
bishops, professes them all at once, and has therefore
a right to be astonished that they should have
thought it necessary to leave a communion, possessing ample revenues, in which they might have held
any opinions whatever, without the superfluous cost
of endowing a new race of ministers to teach them.
She has had « bishops, » like Cranmer and Hooper,
who denied the Episcopate; she has « priests, » like
nine tenths of her present clergy, who deny the
Priesthood; and she is so tolerant of the privileges
of error, that after preaching, like Dr Selwyn, against
the enormity of schism, she always finishes, like

(1) *The Melanesian Mission*, p. 25.

him, by « feeling great pleasure » in going to prayers with schismatics.

We can hardly be surprised to learn that D' Selwyn, in spite of his energy and ability, has failed, like Middleton, and Heber, and other equally conspicuous Anglican ministers, even to correct the infirmities of his own flock. « Dishop Selwyn, » says D' Thomson, « complained with deep emotion of his flock's lukewarmness, and *they* whispered, in extenuation of their conduct, that they objected to exclusive clerical rule in church management. The members of the Roman Catholic church in New Zealand, although strong advocates of political freedom, bowed to the authority of a priesthood they revered, and with whom they regarded it wrong to dispute. » D' Selwyn, like his brethren at home, was less successful in appealing to the docility of his followers. « The English Church did not flourish, and the reason was obvious. At home it is supported by endowments and dignities which enable the clergy to rule, and make them leaders rather than servants of the laity ; in New Zealand there are few dignities and endowments ; and, as the lay members have no faith in the infallibility of their priesthood, they wished to have some share in the management of a church they as yet chiefly supported. » (1)

D' Selwyn had recourse to the only measures available to a Protestant bishop. « The bishop, perceiving this feeling, purchased and procured grants of land in the colony for endowments » — we have seen that, in his own words, it sometimes « rained

(1) Vol. II, p. 264.

bank notes. » And then he tried another scheme.
« He visited England to obtain from her Majesty a
government for the Church in New Zealand. » If
money and the aid of the state could not remedy the
« lukewarmness » of his flock, the case was hopeless.
« But the Secretary of State informed him, that the
settlers had now the law in their own hands, and
that a church constitution, if necessary, must originate with the colonial parliament. » And then he
went back, and summoned, in 1857, « a convention
of the English Church at Auckland for the purpose
of settling what should be done. » Dr Thomson
adds, « no interest was taken in its proceedings by
the public; » and even in the « Canterbury settlement, » destined to be exclusively Anglican, the same
undiscerning « public, » as we shall hear immediately, only interfered to place the established church
on exactly the same level as all the other sects. Is it
wonderful that men who cannot even conquer the
lukewarmness or hostility of their own nominal
flock, should fail to convert the heathen?

But the proceedings of so distinguished a person
as Dr Selwyn, and the fortunes of « High Church »
principles in New Zealand, deserve further notice.
We have seen that Dr Selwyn himself actively co-
operated in public, in spite of his theoretical views,
with men whom he continued to rebuke in private
as « schismatics. » He did more, — he gave up the
whole contest, when he found that he could not prevail, and assigned his reasons for doing so. « The
keen sighted native convert, » he told the University
of Oxford, « soon detects a difference of system, and
thus religion brings disunion instead of harmony

and peace. » It was necessary, therefore, to affect a
unity which did not exist, in order to re-assure « the
keen sighted native ; « and so, instead of insisting
any longer upon principles which, if they were
apostolic verities, should have been maintained at
the risk of life itself, D' Selwyn began to consort
with Wesleyans and Independents. « Above all other
things, » he said, « it is our duty to guard against
inflicting upon them the curses of *our* disunion, lest
we make every little island in the ocean a counter-
part of our own divided and contentious church. »
The Wesleyans, therefore, were glad to claim
D' Selwyn, as they had claimed all his predecessors,
as a witness to their value as « faithful nurses; »
and one of their number was able to appeal to a still
more consoling fact in the following words. « The
venerable and truly Christian Bishop of Melbourne
has publicly stated, that in that form of Christianity
designated Wesleyan Methodism there is a peculiar
adaptation to the population of this very remarkable
island continent. » (1) D' Selwyn had only admitted
them to be as good as himself; another Anglican bishop « publicly stated » that they were much better.

The assertors of « church principles » in England,
in spite of the zeal and ability of many among them,
have not been successful; in the colonies, and before
the heathen, they have been, if possible, still more
unfortunate. In New Zealand they established the
Canterbury settlement, with the avowed purpose
of displaying to the world the power and efficacy of
those principles. M' Cholmondeley relates in 1854,

(1) Rev⁴ R. Young, *The Southern World*, ch. xviii, p. 402.
II.   ۰.

and M' Fuller in 1859, the actual result of their
operations. If D' Selwyn deplored the « lukewarmness » of *his* followers, the gentlemen at Canterbury
had still less reason to be satisfied with the docility
of theirs. Even their « land fund, » from which, as
we have heard, they anticipated so much wealth, has
been forcibly diverted, by their own co-religionists,
to the support of « schismatics. » « The colonists
altered the previous rule, » says M' Fuller, which
gave « the third part of their land fund for the separate service of the Church of England, » and peremptorily decided that « the funds voted for educational
purposes » should henceforth be distributed, not by
a favoured sect, but « through the ministers of different religious bodies » (1) — which was probably
much less agreeable to the promoters of the Canterbury settlement. And this mortifying result was accompanied by another, — of which indeed it was
the direct correlative, — the growth of a population
which repudiated more and more energetically the
religious tenets of their founders; « the mass of the
people at large, » as M' Fuller observes, « being
decidedly of what are termed Low Church views. »

« From the first, » says M' Hodgkinson, speaking
of the same province, « the majority of the members
of the Church of England have opposed all Tractarian
doctrines and ceremonies. » (2) M' Cholmondeley,
though apparently one of their advocates, goes much
further in describing their failure. « The Maories,

(1) *Five Years Residence in New Zealand*, by Francis Fuller
Esq., ch. I, pp. 17, 21. (1859).
(2) *A Description of the Province of Canterbury*, by S. Hodgkinson, M. R. C. S., p. 15. (1858).

as such, « he says, « are disappearing; and the
young people look mean, squalid, and sickly, and
the children miserable in the extreme. » Of the
colonists he speaks as follows. « The truth at present is, that there is no religious character in the
British colonies : and those are especially indifferent
who in the old country belonged to the Church of
England. » Of Canterbury he says, « Often when at
church in Lyttleton or Christ-church, I have been
struck with the *English character* of the attendance
at divine worship; I mean, the pretence and hypocrisy of the whole thing. » And then he adds, « let
our church remain in her present unformed condition, and the sons of her people will become either
Roman Catholics, or Atheists and Materialists. » (1)

We have only one more remark to make on D' Selwyn and his missionary career, of which, as his
own friends relate, these are the deplorable results.
He is willing, we have seen, to hold close communion with the very men whom he calls, in technical
and professional language, fautors of heresy and
schism, and even to acknowledge them as « faithful
nurses » of the heathen; but he has evidently no
such spirit of forbearance towards the servants of
the Catholic Church. For them he has only bold
words of anger. Hear what he says. In one of his
journeys he comes to a Catholic Mission, so he takes
his pen, and writes quickly, — « *one of those blots
upon the Mission system — a Romanist station.* » (2)
Whether these words represent his own sentiments,

(1) *Ultima Thule*, by Thomas Cholmondeley, ch. xvi, p. 196;
ch. xviii, pp. 271, 281. (1854).
(2) *The Melanesian Mission*, p. 19.

or were only a concession to the prejudices of friends
and supporters at home, we cannot tell. In either case
they are disappointing. It is sad to hear from D' Selwyn language which even many of the least distinguished members of his sect would blush to use, and
which are equally repugnant to truth, piety, and
good taste.

And now we have only to add a brief account, or
rather to quote that which has already been published by Protestant witnesses, of the character of the
Catholic Missionaries in New Zealand, and the results of their labours. We have no need of partial
evidence on either of these points, for they are
avowed enemies whom Providence has employed,
without their knowledge or consent, to furnish ample
testimony to both.

It is not easy to conceive a more hopeless or im-
practicable project, as far as human means were
concerned, than that which was attempted by the
first Catholic Missionaries in New Zealand. Every
thing was against them, except the Power in which
alone they trusted. For more than a quarter of a century, the only form of Christianity with which the
natives were acquainted, and which was recommended to them by the irresistible authority of their
masters and rulers, was one of which the very
existence is a protest against the Catholic Faith. And
lest this should not suffice to prejudice them against
the new comers, no effort had been neglected by
their powerful and wealthy patrons to kindle betimes
a feeling of bitter animosity towards them. With
unscrupulous frand they had been represented as the
agents of a foreign state, whose secret object was to

seize the islands and kill or enslave their inhabitants. The natives were told, as Mr Wakefield informs us, that if the Catholics were once admitted, they would cut their throats or drive them out of their land. In a memorial which they were persuaded, no doubt by the missionaries, to address to William IV, they said, — « We have heard that the tribe of Marian is at hand, coming to take away our land; » (1) and they pray his majesty to protect them against these formidable pirates ! And when at length they arrived, a few defenceless foreigners, scowled upon by the government, and by every authority whom the natives were accustomed to fear; bringing neither money nor goods, and introducing a doctrine which was hateful to the ruling class, and which began by forbidding covetousness, lying, and impurity to their subjects; is it wonderful that, as Mr Bright mildly observes, « they were not much inclined » to them? « In their eyes, » the same writer adds, « much trade gives respectability of character; » and the first announcement of the Catholic Missionaries was, that they would not trade at all, and had nothing to trade with. It was impossible to invite more persuasively the contempt of the natives, or to convince them more effectually that they had nothing to gain, and every thing to lose, by mortally offending their masters and employers in order to

(1) *The New Zealand Question*, by L. A. Chamerovzow, ch. III, p. 69. Cf. *Colonial Constitutions*, by Arthur Mills Esq., p. 331; who relates that « thirty-five chiefs subscribed a declaration, constituting themselves into an Independent State » — expressly to resist the anticipated attack of the French, whom they had been told to expect!

propitiate auxiliaries so helpless and destitute as
these. The conclusion was obvious, and the natives
could not fail to adopt it.

Yet the Catholic Missionaries, in spite of their
weakness and poverty, had one thing in their favour.
It is the nature of man, whether savage or civilised,
to reverence purity and disinterestedness. He may
be unwilling to imitate, but he cannot refuse to admire them. This is the secret of the triumphs of
Catholic Missionaries throughout the world. Like
the first Apostles, they win their way by wisdom,
holiness, and charity. Their virtues have first dis-
armed the hand which was uplifted to strike them,
and then extorted respect for a religion of which
they were the fruit and evidence. And so in New
Zealand, as early as 1842, we learn from Dr Dieffenbach the significant fact, that, in one of the most
populous provinces, « the number of converts to each
creed is about equal, although the Roman Catholic
mission was established so much later than that of
the Church of England. » (1) But we must not anticipate this surprising result until we have first
shown by what manner of men, and in spite of what
complicated difficulties, it was accomplished.

We have seen that the natives had been induced
by their Protestant teachers to regard the Catholic
Missionaries, even before their arrival, as men of
blood, conspirators, and malefactors. The same unpleasant view of their character was still more diligently enforced upon them after they had commenced
their apparently hopeless task. « The Protestant natives, » says Dr Dieffenbach, « regard their Roman

(1) *Travels*, vol. 1, ch. xxvii, p. 407.

Catholic brethren as belonging to the devils. « Their masters, who could teach them nothing else, could teach them this; and it was natural they should attempt to do so, when even a missionary describes them thus, in 1853, not to a native, but to an English audience. « Satan had taken care, » says the Rev. Mr Strachan, « to strengthen all his natural defences by a fresh importation of auxiliaries from France. » (1) The Catholic Missionaries, according to this gentleman, were the agents of Satan. Let us see what other Protestant witnesses say of the character and mode of life of men whom an unsuccessful rival could thus describe.

Dr Dieffenbach, after noticing with evident repugnance the worldly and covetous habits of the men towards whom his own sympathies attracted him, frankly confesses, that, on the other hand, « the humble and disinterested manner of living of the Catholic Priests, and the superior education which they have generally received, have procured them many friends both amongst Europeans and natives, and also many converts amongst the latter. » And again; « in accordance with the spirit of the Roman Catholic Missionary system, they are generally without fixed places of abode, and the Bishop, whose diocese extends over several Archipelagos in the great ocean, is continually travelling from place to place, accompanied by priests. » (2) This is certainly more like St. Paul, who was « in travels oft, » not in a commodious yacht, but in the first vessel which came

(1) *Life of the Rev S. Leigh*, by the Revd A. Strachan, ch.xv, p. 439. (1853).

(2) *Travels*, ch. ix, pp. 163, 169.

to hand; and Dr Dieffenbach, who has told us how
the Protestant missionaries preferred to reside in the
Bay of Islands, rather than « go into the interior, »
seems, in spite of himself, to recur again and again
to the unwelcome contrast. But he is not the only
Protestant writer who indulges in such reflections.
Mr Augustus Earle, who gives a still more unfavour-
able account of the Protestant missionaries, cannot
refrain from instituting a similar comparison. « I
have visited many of the Roman Catholic missionary
establishments, » he says, « and their priests adopt
quite a different line of conduct; they are cheerful
and kind to the savage pagan, polite and attentive to
their European brethren; they have gained the esteem of those they have been sent to convert, and
however we may differ in some tenets of religious
belief, we must acknowledge the success of their
missions. » (1)

It appears that Mr Earle, like other travellers,
had occasion to deplore the churlish and inhos-
pitable behaviour of his opulent co-religionists. Thus
he notices, with pardonable disgust, that even on
a Christmas Day the missionaries shut their doors
against him and his party, whilst travelling in the
interior, and that even the savages spoke with contempt of their morose and uncharitable conduct.
Mr Rochfort also, at a much later date, makes the
same complaint, and adds; « I must say the Catholic
Missionaries are generally the more hospitable of the
two » (2) — in spite of the exiguity of their re-

(1) *Nine Months Residence*, etc., 171.
(2) *Adventures in New Zealand*, by John Rochfort, ch. III,
p. 28.

sources. We shall find Protestant tourists making the same observation in other lands.

But the writers on New Zealand have more to tell us about the character of the men whom Mr Strachan represents, without any misgiving, as the agents of Satan. The leader of the Catholic mission was Bishop Pompallier, a man beloved by all who have had the good fortune to know him, but who, though worthy to be numbered with those apostolic missionaries of whom France has produced so many, « was attacked, » as Mr Wakefield relates, « by both sects of Protestant missionaries in the most intolerant manner. » One of his own clergy observes, in 1840, — « Scarcely had we quitted the tribe of Mototapu when the Protestant ministers came to sow discord amongst its members. One of them made an attempt to degrade our venerable bishop by giving his name to impure animals. All the natives were indignant at this conduct. » (1) It is interesting to learn how this French prelate, who might have appealed to his own great nation for succour, rebuked by « patient continuance in well doing the malice of evil men, » and finally won the esteem and sympathy of all who were capable of appreciating a courteous gentleman and a devout christian. « The gentlemen of the club, » says Mr Wakefield, « and others who had enjoyed his acquaintance, spoke highly of his urbane manners, and his philanthropic views with regard to the natives. » He was something better than a philanthropist, who is often only a refined heathen, but we must leave our witnesses to use their own terms. « Bishop Pompallier, »

(1) *Annals*, vol. III, p. 26.

says one whose own accomplishments enabled him
to admire higher qualities in others, « is a man peculiarly adapted for the purposes of the mission of
his Church. By education a scholar, in manners
engaging, in countenance prepossessing and expressive, added to sincere and earnest zeal in the cause
he has undertaken,.... it may easily be imagined that
he creates no ordinary sensation among the Aborigines. » (1) « I would not attempt, » says the Presbyterian D' Lang, « to conceal my own serious
apprehension of M. Pompallier's success; » (2) but
he is satisfied with expressing his alarm, and does
not talk about « Satan. » A Sydney journal, on the
authority of New Zealand letters, observes at the
same date; « the Rev. D' Pompallier is said to have
made great progress in the conversion of the natives of
Hokianga, where the Wesleyan mission is... some
of the leading chiefs have promised his Lordship to
attend to his new mode of worship. » (3) It was probably these facts of which the authoress of the Gospel in New Zealand spoke, when she said, « they
cause our missionaries much anxiety. »

Happily the motives of their anxiety became more
and more urgent, as time went on. In 1841, M' Dright
writes as follows. « With those Maoris to whom the
Vicar Apostolic is known he seems popular. He has
converted the oldest chief in the Bay of Islands, his
sons, and people, although previously attendants on
the Church Mission. » (4) Perhaps it was such events

(1) Terry, p. 190.
(2) *New Zealand*, p. 43.
(3) *Asiatic Journal*, vol. XXIX, p. 189. N. S.
(4) *History of New Zealand*, ch. VI, p. 126.

as this which made D' Selwyn describe a Catholic
station as « a blot upon the Mission system. » But
M' Bright continues. « The Vicar Apostolic says he
had not been sent to trade, and that he is not a buyer
of land. » And these were the results of his abstinence
from such questionable pursuits. « When I embarked
to inspect a county on the East coast, I was surprised
to meet Moko, » a chief from the Bay of Islands,
« with about thirty of his people, men, women, and
children; during the passage, three times a day,
their discordant voices were raised together, chanting
the Mass, or some service of the Catholic faith. » It
was not the Mass, but that is of no consequence.
At Opo-tee-kee also he meets the same phenomenon :
« the very children were humming over some portions of Masses in their play. Twice a day the chapel
was crowded, chorussing together, although perhaps
not twelve of all of them had ever seen the Vicar or his
curés. » (1) So in another district, the same writer
tells us, — « the Vicar Apostolic settled down amongst
them, and before he could have attained their language he made converts, of whom most had subscribed to the Church Missionaries. » Even in the
Canterbury Settlement, destined to be the exclusive domain of Anglicanism, M' Rochfort informs us that
« there are many Roman Catholics, and their cathedral is the finest building in Wellington. »

M' Angas too, who is unable to record such facts
with composure, is not afraid of exciting merriment
in his readers by calling New Zealanders « a community of Jesuit natives. » Many of the Taupo na-

(1) *History of New Zealand*, p. 121.

tives, » he says, « are Catholics; » and then, unwilling to let their conversion speak for itself, he
suggests that it was « with the aid of beads and
crosses, » and other equally valuable « presents, » that
the missionary « succeeded in making numerous proselytes to the faith of Rome. » Yet Mʳ Angas knew
that however the Catholic missionary might surpass
his rivals in some respects, the power to bribe was
not one of them. At Motupoi also, « the chief is a
Roman Catholic; several of his people have also
embraced Popery, and at sunset they performed
their vespers in front of the chief's house. » (1) This
time Mʳ Angas says nothing about presents.

Again, at Kororarika, the American Commodore
Wilkes notices that the Catholic mission « was making
many converts, » — which he also attributes to « presents, » though the value of the crosses, religious
pictures, and other donations bestowed on the natives,
after their conversion, rarely exceeded the modest sum
of one penny. They would hardly have deserted their
Protestant masters for such a reward as this. Yet
even so intelligent a writer as Dʳ Thomson could
seriously suggest this as the true explanation of a
phenomenon which he notices in these words; « It
has been observed that Roman Catholic missionaries
have converted natives abandoned by the Protestants
as hopeless » (2) the secret of their success, he suggests, being « gifts » which were more likely to excite
the contempt than the cupidity of those to whom
they were proffered.

(1) *Savage Life*, etc., vol. II, ch. III, pp. 118, 121.
(2) Vol. I, p. 316.

Sometimes the writers on New Zealand, inspired by a candour which it is impossible not to admire, venture even to contrast the Catholic and Protestant natives, and always to the advantage of the former. Such statements almost exceed what we might fairly expect even from the most upright of our enemies. In 1854, a gentleman who made a tour in New Zealand gives this testimony. He is at Otaki, amidst a Catholic tribe, and says; « The resident priest I heard very well spoken of, and certainly the state of the mill, and every thing connected with it, evidenced the influence of a master mind. » The next village he arrives at is a Protestant one, and he goes on thus; « There was a very observable difference in dress and personal cleanliness between the natives here assembled and those at Otaki, much in favour of the latter. » (1)

Such testimonies are scarcely less honorable to those who offer them than to the objects of their generous praise. Here is another and still more striking example of the noble candour which sometimes distinguishes our countrymen. Sir George Grey, then Governor of New Zealand, addressed to Earl Grey, in 1851, a despatch which contains the following words. « The Roman Catholic schools in this country are exceedingly well conducted, and not only reflect great credit upon the Roman Catholic bishop and his clergy, but give them a great claim to any proper consideration which can be shown to them. » (2) Perhaps it was in consequence of the encouragement which such language afforded, that some of the na-

(1) *A Summer's Excursion in N. Z.*, p. 157, 165.
(2) *Parliamentary Papers*, vol. XLV, p. 12. (1854).

tive females, taught by Sisters of Mercy, whom the charity of Christ had moved to cross the great ocean, ventured to adress a letter to the sovereign of Great Britain, imploring aid for their generous teachers. It was no doubt with regret that succour was refused, and the petition unnoticed.

It is evident, then, without adding superfluous evidence, that the Catholic missionaries had outlived the dislike, and overcome the opposition, of their numerous and powerful enemies. Once more they had accomplished one of those triumphs in which there are victors but no vanquished. With calm patience they had pursued their way, aided only by Him to whom they had dedicated their lives, and esteeming the poverty of Jesus more than the riches of the world. If they had failed to gain a single convert, their very lives would have sufficed to prove the truth of their religion; for they were pure amidst corruption, patient in adversity, charitable towards all men, and especially towards those who reviled them, and so irreproachable in their humble and disinterested career that even calumny was abashed in their presence, and dared not sharpen its tongue against them. And so when the evil day arrived, and tribes which had nominally embraced the religion of their rulers thirsted for their lives, and rose up in fierce insurrection against them, the abode of the Missionaries of the Cross was still a sacred spot; and Colonel Mundy relates that « the missionary station presided over by Bishop Pompallier was the *only* portion of the town spared by the invaders. » (1) It was on the eve of the

(1) *Australasian Colonies*, vol. II, ch. vi, p. 179.

conflict, in which Protestant natives fought against
their teachers and destroyed their lives and property,
that the Captain of an English frigate offered a refuge
to the Vicar Apostolic, and a shelter where he might
hide his alarm till the danger was past. The friendly
offer was refused, in a letter which announced his
intention to commit himself to the guardianship of the
savages, and which disowned the apprehension which
he was supposed to feel in the apostolic words, —
« I fear nothing but sin. »

Finally, if we ask for the numerical result of
labours begun at so fearful a disadvantage, and continued under every trial and difficulty which could
beset missionary efforts, — so that success might
well seem impossible in a battle where all human
means of attaining it were on one side, and none on
the other, — one of the latest writers on New Zealand has furnished this surprising statement. In 1843,
the Catholics were already estimated by M⁴ Clarkson
as one twentieth of the population, while the Wesleyans, who had been thirty years in the field, and
had spent vast sums of money, were one seventh; but
in 1854, the Wesleyans, opposed at all points by
the Episcopalians with their enormous wealth and
official patronage, had dwindled to one eleventh, and
the Catholics, against whom all had combined in a
common hostility, had steadily advanced till they had
become one seventh of the whole population. (1)

It appears, however, that even this statement
underrates the fact; for while the Catholic missionaries represent their followers, good and bad,

(1) *A Summer's Excursion*, p. 14.

as amounting to about twenty thousand, we have
seen, by a recent official statement, that the whole
number of natives now remaining is only 56,049,
of whom thirty-six per cent, are avowed pagans. The
proportions are probably destined to be further
affected by the war now raging (1861) in this
ill fated colony, and which will perhaps only terminate when all the pagan and protestant natives have
been exterminated. It is surely a suitable conclusion
of the history of Anglicanism in New Zealand, that,
fifty years after it began, the natives are found once
more in arms against teachers whose influence, in
spite of their wealth and the use which they make of
it, has only become more feeble year by year, till at
length it appears to be utterly extinguished. « Despite
the remonstrances of the Bishop of New Zealand, of
the most influential clergy, and of those chiefs who
still remain loyal, the flag of the self-styled King of
the Maoris has been publicly hoisted » both in the
settlements of Auckland and Wellington; and even
this significant fact does not fully reveal the final
catastrophe, nor exhaust the incidents in the closing
chapter of Protestant missions in New Zealand.
« Among the most formidable symptoms is the reported tendency to ' recur to old barbarous customs ',
and the ' *decreasing influence of the missionaries.* ' » (1)

Such, in its broad outlines, is the history of Missions in New Zealand. The very savage, as he reviews
in his own mind, or relates to his children, its successive phases, though he may care too little about

(1) *The Times*, September 14, 1860.

his soul to act upon his convictions, easily detects on
which side is truth, on which side God and His holy
Angels. Two classes of teachers have claimed his
attention. In the one he has seen, through a long
series of years, and with rare exceptions, corruption,
vanity, and worldliness; in the other, purity, chastity, and a blameless life. « Their continence, » says
Dr Thomson, « produced a strange impression on the
mind of the natives » — accustomed to a different
exhibition of the Christian character. With the first
comers, as he knows to his cost, have been introduced
the myriad evils of confusion and disorder, of shifting
and incoherent doctrine, and passionate religious
strife; with the last came peace, unity, and love.
Finally, while the one could attract only nominal
converts — whose vices are attested by themselves —
by appealing to the coarse instincts of worldly interest and the grossest appetites of our nature; the
others, obliged to begin by inviting the half-civilised
native to abandon even the temporal rewards which
he had already earned, and for which they had no
recompense to offer him, have yet succeeded in winning him, not only from the darkness of heathenism,
but even from his lucrative association with the
various sects in which he had been previously enrolled.

We are far, however, from asserting that all the
native converts to the Faith are as yet intelligent and
consistent Christians, or that all afford unmixed
consolation to their pastors. Such a statement would
be a culpable exaggeration, which the spontaneous
testimony of their spiritual guides would suffice to
rebuke. Not all the disciples even in the primitive

uge, not all who heard the Voice of the Master
Himself, deserved this praise; and the modern missionary knows how to accept trials from which the
first apostles were not exempt, and must be content,
like them, to gather into his net both good and bad
fish.

Some of the converts from the Protestant sects,
though they reverence the unwonted virtues of their
new teachers, have been too deeply corrupted by
previous habits of hypocrisy and fraud to be easily
or effectually reformed. Christianity has long since
appeared to them a purely nominal religion, of which
the professors contrasted unfavourably even with
pagans, and whose very teachers and ministers were
to them only models of incontinence, cupidity, and
injustice. Some also, though rescued from such influences, are but partially instructed; while their
pastors, unable to cultivate the whole field which
lies before them, can sometimes only cast their seed
by the wayside, and then pass on, hoping, yet hardly
expecting, that they may one day find leisure to
watch its after growth, to tear away the noxious
plants which may threaten to choke it, or to bind up
the weak stems which may have been trodden under
foot. Yet it is pleasant to read the following account
of the best class of native converts by one who
knows them so well.

« I am often moved to tears, » says the honoured
Prelate to whom New Zealand owes so much, and
whose virtues even his adversaries have so often
confessed, « when I see the chief of some tribe come
many leagues through the forests to consult me on
some point which embarasses the delicacy of his

conscience. » (1) Here again we have an example of
that powerful « influence of the Confessional » which
Sir Emerson Tennent remarked in Ceylon, and without whose aid the Catholic Missionary knows that
all hope of confirming men in habits of virtue is vain
and chimerical. « Scarcely have they received instruction in the law of God, » Bishop Pompallier
continues to say, « when their only study is to con-
form their conduct to it. With what simplicity do
they open their mind to the minister of salvation,
and with what sincere attachment to us do they return the services we render them... They might be
taken, from their dress and appearence, for a band
of robbers; yet they are inoffensive sheep, who follow the footsteps of him whom Jesus has given them
as their shepherd. » The Bishop even adds, that
many who are not Catholics have learned how to
distinguish between « the *trunk*, as they call the Catholic Church, and the *severed branch* churches. »

So little difficulty have the true apostles in winning
these rude minds to the comprehension of « church
principles, » as well as of the other great evangelical
truths with which they are inseparably connected;
while their rivals, busy with ceaseless strife and filling the air with mutual reproaches, fail to teach
them even the doctrines of the Holy Trinity and the
Incarnation, make religion only the occasion of new
crimes, the Bible itself an excuse for committing
them, and after half a century of unblessed effort
have only forced the reluctant savage to accept a lot
more full of calamity and malediction than even his

(1) *Annals*.

original state, — the dread responsibilities of Christianity without its gifts and graces. And lastly, the
annalists of New Zealand missions confess, with sorrow and shame, that the natives, familiar with the
incessant divisions and unappeasable conflicts of the
Protestant sects, have at length delivered that memorable verdict, so often recorded against Protestantism by the instinct of pagan nations, — that verdict
which is at once the measure of its influence, the
monument of its results, and the summary of its
triumphs, — « You have taught us that Heathenism with love is better than Christianity without
it. »

CHAPTER VI.

MISSIONS IN OCEANICA.

.

In that wide waste of waters which for ages have rolled their floods between the Old and New Continents, and where once the sea-bird found no rest for his foot, a hundred islands, cast up from their deep ocean-bed by some convulsive throe, are now securely anchored. Once naked and unsightly, they have long since been clothed with grass, and flowers, and trees. Upon their low hills cluster the dark myrtle and the slender palm; and through their valleys, rich with spreading ferns, bright rivulets wind their course. Here the sugar cane and bread fruit grow untended, and a thousand edible roots, unknown in other climes, lurk in the untilled soil. To these fair islands, sheltered by coral barriers from the ocean

wave, men found their way, — from what land,
when, and how, only the angels know. By what
strange migrations they were peopled, history will
never tell. This is God's secret.

Yet science, which is never more honorably occupied than in the investigation of such problems,
has applied its patient induction to this; and if it has
not absolutely determined how the islands of Eastern
and Western Oceanica were peopled, has at least
suggested how they might have been. William Von
Humboldt considers that he has established the identity of the Malays and Polynesians ; and Prichard,
who adopts his conclusion, calls the latter « Malayo-
Polynesians. » (1) M. de Rienzi, indeed, is certain
that they came originally from the island of Borneo.
Other writers are of opinion that the natives of some
of the Pacific Islands can hardly be distinguished
from the Caucasian family. But Sir George Simpson,
Governor of the Hudson's Bay territories, — who
reports, in 1847, that « the whole group of the
Sandwich Islands is known to be slowly but surely
continuing to rise, to be still, as it were, in the
throes of creation, » — speaks as follows of the
origin of the Polynesian race, whose religious history we are to narrate in the present chapter. « From
what country, then, of Asia, did the Polynesians
spring ? Almost to a moral certainty from some
point, or rather points, between the southern extremity of Malacca and the northern limits of Japan. » (2) Many considerations, which need not here

(1) *Natural History of Man*, § 32.
(2) *Narrative of a Journey round the World*, vol. II, ch. I,
p 7

he noticed, combine to recommend this conclusion;
yet the origin of the Malays themselves is still uncertain, and while some look for their birth-place on
the South-eastern shores of China, Bopp thinks their
language derived from the Sanscrit. (1)

From the Polynesians themselves no aid has been
received in the discussion of this problem of ethno-
logy; and the Abbé Caret, referring especially to
the Gambier Archipelago, in which he long resided
as a missionary, warns us « not to ask of the population of these islands any explicit information concerning their origin; all your questions would remain
unanswered; on this subject their traditions are silent. Perhaps these tribes had their origin in the
remotest antiquity : it takes a very long time for a
people to forget the history of its origin. I have
heard the best informed of the natives euumerate as
many as fifty kings, who are said to have presided,
one after the other, in the government of the Archipelago. «

One source of information, which existed at an
earlier period, and from which a careful enquirer
might perhaps have constructed at least the fragments of a history, has been, in many of the islands,
imprudently destroyed, by men whose proceedings
will be presently recounted to us by competent witnesses. « One fault, » says the learned Mosblech, in
his treatise on the dialects of Eastern Oceanica, « for
which we can never pardon the Methodist ministers »
— he means the Protestant missionaries — « is their

(1) Mohl, *Rapports faits à la Société Asiatique*, tome II, ch. I,
p. 8.

having destroyed, by an irrational zeal, all the poetic compositions of this people. No one can be blind to the injury which they have thus inflicted upon science and history. The Catholic missionaries, guided by their intelligent chief the Archbishop of Chalcedon, who admirably appreciates not only what belongs to religion but also the things which relate to science, have acted with more caution. » (1)

It appears that the mythological, as well as the pastoral and erotic compositions of the natives, some of which were no doubt of questionable purity, but which had at least a scientific value, were violently suppressed by their English teachers, and not only suppressed but destroyed. With them perished all the lays and rythmical legends which they had received from their forefathers. What their new masters gave them instead, we shall see hereafter, and how far they have profited by the change.

But we must now enter, without further preface, upon the wide field which lies before us, and in which we shall once more trace, by the aid of the same class of witnesses, the impressive contrast of which we have already seen so many examples. It will be necessary to begin by dividing into groups the island world which we are about to visit, and in this task we have no choice but to adopt the classification which both history and geography prescribe.

Of the various groups which we are about to notice, and whose religious annals we shall find to be

(1) *Notice sur la langue de l'Océanie Orientale* ; Journal Asiatique, tome III, p. 441, 1ᵐᵉ série ; 1844.

preguant with those startling contrasts which urgently invite our consideration, — not only because they
decisively reveal the respective influence and character of Catholic and Protestant Missions, but because they remove to the clear region of historical
facts that old controversy which is obscure and unprofitable while it turns only upon cunning words
and distorted texts, — some have been visited by
Catholics alone, some have belonged exclusively to
Protestants, and others have been occupied by both.
In the first, religion has gained its accustomed and
undisputed victory; in the second, enormous expenditure has been attended by universal corruption and
admitted failure; in the third, heresy has waged its
usual warfare of violence and calumny, has been
combated by patient charity and long-suffering, and
has finally confessed its discomfiture and defeat.
This is the history which we are about to trace.

Let us begin with the Philippine Islands, and
those contiguous groups which lie nearest to the
main-land, whose happy fortune it was to be discovered by men who laboured for God rather than
for themselves, and who carried with them wherever
they went the faith which was the light of their own
souls, and the charity which obliged them to communicate it to others.

Argensola, the careful and conscientious historian
of these regions, whose intelligent candour has earned the applause, not only of the Council of the Indies
by whom he was employed, but even of his English
editors, has recounted all the details of that generous
apostolate which won the Philippines to the Cross of
Christ. From him we learn how the false Prophet

II.   9.

came to be honoured even in these remote islands of the East; how Persian and Arab conquerors carried thither the plague which had enveloped half the world, and from which it is the glory of the Roman See to have saved Europe by that long series of efforts which alone preserved Christendom from the destroying legions who had overflowed the earth from the Pillars of Hercules to the wastes of Tartary, and who once threatened to hang up in every temple of Europe the impure banner which they had already planted on Mount Sion.

Against such adversaries the first apostles of the Philippines lifted up the Cross, and though they fell, like their brethren in other lands, cut down by the sword of Moslem or Pagan, consumed by fire, or torn into fragments on the scaffold, they conquered even in death. The conflict did not last long; the decree had gone forth that here the Cross should triumph, and « the false and corrupt memory of Mahomet, » as Mendoza simply relates, « was with the Gospel of Christ easily rooted out. » (1) A few words will suffice to describe the events which led to this result.

The Philippines were discovered by Magellan, as Gemelli notices in his history of the Ladrone Islands, in 1521, but it was not till a later period that they were subdued and colonised by Spain. The inhabitants of the Ladrone group, for we may speak of them together since they have a common history, « had no notion of a Deity, » we are told by Le Gobien, « nor any religious worship, nor had they any temple,

(1) *Historie of the Kingdome of China*, vol. II, ch. XIII, p. 261 ; published by the Hakluyt Society.

priest, or forms of worship. » Their only religion consisted in « some irregular notions of a hell and a heaven. (1) » Towards the close of the sixteenth century, as we learn from Argensola, more than six thousand Christians had already been martyred in the single province of Ternate, « that so, » he adds, « the foundation of our faith may be in all parts cemented with the blood of the faithful. They dismembered the bodies, and burned the legs and arms in the sight of the still living trunks. They impaled the women, and tore out their bowels; children were pulled piece-meal before their mothers eyes, and infants were rent from their wombs. » (2)

Yet all these tortures were bravely endured by neophytes who had seen their pastors tread the same *Via Dolorosa* with unfaltering step, and even children learned to imitate the fruitful example of such teachers. A Portuguese vessel, sailing by the coast of Amboyna, picked up a crowd of fugitives swimming near the shore, « and having viewed them at leisure, » says Argensola, « found that none of them were above twelve years of age. Yet at this same time, when cruelty advanced God's glory, idolaters and Mahometans were converted, and our religious men preached and catechised without any fear of punishment, which they rather coveted, and thought themselves unworthy of. » He allows, indeed, that many apostatised, overcome by anguish, and this need not surprise us. In 1697, ten of the missionaries had been

(1) *History of the Ladrone Islands*, in Callander's *Terra Australis Cognita*, vol. III, p. 53.
(2) *Discovery and Conquest of the Molucca and Philippine Islands*, by B. L. de Argensola, book III, p. 65. (1708).

martyred in the Ladrone Islands, and for a time the
rest were obliged to fly, but it was only to return
when the storm had passed. (1) In the island of Say-
pan, Father de Medina, a man of illustrious birth, was
the first martyr, in 1670. In 1672, Sanvitores, also
belonging to one of the noblest houses of Spain — for
these men began by flinging away the wealth and
honours which others consume a whole life in endeavouring to acquire — was martyred in the island
of Tinian. By his first discourse, — unaided by the
the « ceremonial » which is supposed to be so effective in such cases, — he won fifteen hundred converts; and before he died had established the faith
in 13 islands, founded 3 seminaries, and baptized
50,000 idolaters. In 1699, idolatry had almost become extinct in the Ladrone Islands. Surely martyrdom was a suitable termination of such a career as that
of Sanvitores; who, it may be added, predicted the
future conversion of the islands of Oceanica, though
he was only acquainted with two of them, the Pelew
and the Caroline groups. (2)

In the Philippines the success of the missionaries
was so complete, that even at the close of the sixteenth century Mendoza could say, — « According
unto the common opinion, at this day there is converted and baptized more than four hundred thousand
souls. » In 1598, as an ardent Protestant observes,
in his account of the Voyage of Oliver Noort, and
speaking of what he calls the « Lusson » islands.
« There are few Spaniards, and but one Priest, which

(1) Gemelli, in Churchill's *Collection of Voyages*, vol. IV, p. 462.
(2) Henrion, *Histoire des Missions Catholiques*, tome II,
2de partie, p. 530.

is of great esteeme; and had they Priests enough, all
the neighbour nations would be subject to the Spaniards, » — for, he adds, « the Jesuits are in reputation with their converts as demi-gods. » (1) And this
work continued, until, as later Protestant writers
will presently tell us, the four million inhabitants of
these islands had embraced that Catholic Faith from
which they have never since swerved. Such is the
first chapter in the history of Polynesian Missions.
How far it resembles the same apostolic work in the
lands which we have already visited, and especially
in characteristic solidity and permanence, we shall
now learn from Protestant witnesses, whom Providence seems to have employed to this end, that
their co-religionists might the more readily accept
their testimony.

The Rev. David Abeel, — a Protestant missionary,
who seems to have wandered over the lands beyond
the Ganges, searching for something to do and finding
nothing, and whose book is simply a record of the
triumphs of Catholics and of the choleric disgust with
which he witnessed them, — thus writes of the Philippines. « The Church of Rome has here proselyted
to itself *the entire population*. The natives have become bigoted Papists. The influence of the Priests is
unbounded. » It is only fair, however, to this gentleman to add, that he considers the conversion of the
Philippines, accomplished by such men as Medina
and Sanvitores, a remarkable example of « the power
of the Beast. » (2)

(1) Purchas' *Pilgrims*, vol. I, lib. 2, ch v, pp. 75, 76.
(2) *Journal of a Residence in China*, ch, xvi, p. 328.

In the year 1858, M' Crawfurd, whose writings are well known in this country, and who was formerly Governor of Singapore, made the following declaration at a public missionary meeting. « In the Philippine Islands the Spaniards have converted several millions of people to the Roman Catholic faith, and an immense improvement in their social condition has been the consequence. » (1)

« Much credit, » says Sir Henry Ellis, in spite of incurable prejudice, « is due to the Spaniards for the establishment of schools throughout the colony, and their unremitting exertion to preserve and propagate Christianity by this best of all possible means, the diffusion of knowledge. » (2) « It is said, » observes the wife of the American navigator Captain Morrell, that in Manilla there are more convents than in any other city in the world of its size, and the general voice of natives and foreigners declares that they are under excellent regulations. » And then she describes their inmates. « They all seemed full of occupation. There is no idleness in these convents as is generally supposed » — and as her own account of the various works accomplished in them sufficiently proves. Moreover, « their devotions begin at the dawn of the day, and are often repeated during the whole of it, or until late in the evening in some form or other. » Altogether the effect produced on the mind of this lady was remarkably different from that which M' Abeel records. « I was born a Protestant, » she says, « and trust that I shall die a Protestant, but

(1) *Times*, 2nd December, 1858.
(2) *Journal of an Embassy to China*, ch. VIII, p. 442.

hereafter I shall have more charity for all who profess
to love religion, whatever may be their creed. » (1)

In 1833, M. de La Girouière, who spent twenty
years in the Philippines, informs us that the present race of missionaries are not unworthy to be
compared with their martyred predecessors. Thus
he relates how Father Miguel de San-Francisco, a
friend of his own, used to collect the young men in
his house, four at a time, keep them with him a
fortnight under diligent instruction, and then send
them in different directions to communicate to others
the lessons which they had received from his patient
charity. In this way he would contrive gradually to
leaven a whole district. M. de La Girouière also notices the important fact, that while Manilla and its
suburbs contain about 150,000 souls, the Spanish
and Creole population hardly amount to one tenth of
that number. (2)

In 1845, an American statistical writer addressed
to Mr Ingersoll the following account of the Philippines. « The colony is in a very flourishing condition.
Most of the native *Tagalos* and *Horaforos* have been
converted to the Catholic faith. There are three
Suffragan Bishops in the Provinces; one of them,
the Bishop of New Segovia, Island of Luzon, wrote
me in 1837, that his diocese consisted of upwards
of 600,000 christian souls. » (3) Let these facts be

(1) *Narrative of a Voyage*, by Abby Jane Morrell, ch. II, p. 44;
ch. V, p. 90.

(2) *Vingt années aux Philippines*, par P. de la Girouière,
p. 89. (1853).

(3) *Letter to the Hon. Charles I. Ingersoll*, etc., by Aaron
H. Palmer, p. 14.

compared with the history of Dutch or English
Protestant missions in the same part of the world.

The remarkable influence of the clergy, in spite of
the small proportion of Spaniards to natives, is
attested by many writers. In the early part of the
present century, M. de Guignes remarked, from his
own observation, that « the European priests are
greatly respected by the Indians, who always consult them in their various undertakings, and even
about the payment of taxes; » (1) which agrees with
what Mr Abeel says impatiently of their « unbounded
influence. » Sir John Bowring, in 1859, confirms
the testimony of M. de Guignes, and once more
reports of the clergy; « They exercise an influence
which would seem magical were it not by their
devotees deemed divine. » (2)

Dr Ball, an American Protestant traveller, agrees
with M. de la Gironière and others as to the character of the Spanish clergy. Of one whom he met at
Manilla, he says, « He has a fund of knowledge on
almost every subject, speaks six or seven languages,
and has declined an offer of the president of the seminary here, preferring to remain always in the capacity
of missionary. » (3)

Lastly, that we may hear every kind of witness,
and yet not encumber ourselves with superfluous
testimony, let us cite one more Protestant writer,
who tells us, in 1861, the impression which he had
formed of religion in the Philippines, in spite of the

(1) *Voyages à Pékin, Manille*, etc., tome III, p. 391.
(2) *A Visit to the Philippine Islands*, by Sir John Bowring,
L. L. D., F. R. S.; ch. xii, p. 210.
(3) *Rambles in Eastern Asia*, ch. xxiv, p. 200.

prejudices both of creed and country which threatened
to warp his judgment. M' Mac Micking, who spent
some years in these islands, where he only partly
unlearned earlier prepossessions, declares of the
natives, that « the warriors who gained them over to
Spain were not their steel-clad chivalry, but the
soldiers of the Cross; — the priests, who astonished
and kindled them by their enthusiasm in the cause of
Christ. » He confesses also that the suppression of
the Jesuits, who were banished from the Philippines
in 1768, « was attended with the worst effects to the
trade and agriculture of the islands. » The people, he
allows, are so truly what M' Abeel calls « bigoted
Papists; » that « religious processions are as frequently passing through the streets as they are in the
Roman Catholic countries of Europe. » And presently
he adds, « the church has long proved to be, upon
the whole, by much the most cheap and efficacious
instrument of good government and order; » while
even the common people « very generally learn reading by its aid — so much, at least, as to enable them
to read their prayer-books or other religious manuals.
There are very few Indians who are unable to read,
and I have always observed that the Manilla men
serving on board ships, and composing their crews,
have been much oftener able to subscribe their
names to the ship's articles than the British seamen
on board the same vessels could do. » (1) Lastly, he
admits that the present rulers and pastors of these
islands have in no degree degenerated from their an-

(1) *Recollections of Manilla and the Philippines*, by Robert
Mac Micking Esq., p. 45.

cestors. « The enlightened and benevolent government of Don Pascual Enrile, who was Captain General of the Philippines from 1831 to 1835 and his
entire administration, has left behind it the happiest
results for the people he governed, » — a statement
confirmed in 1859 by Lord Elgin's secretary, who
also visited Manilla, and found that « the advanced
views of Don Pascual Enrile have in many instances
been improved upon, and carried out by the present
governor. » (1) Of the clergy Mr Mac Micking speaks
as follows. « Most of the priests I have been in contact with appeared to be thoroughly convinced of,
and faithful to, their religion in its purity » — a large
concession from a Scotchman. Of « the present Archbishop of Manilla » he speaks with the utmost respect,
and especially of his « piety, and good feeling towards
all men, » though he naturally resents the refusal of
Christian burial to Protestants; and he sums up his
frank admissions by the following generous account
of the modern Spanish missionaries. « These good
men have penetrated where soldiers dare not enter
with arms in their hands, and in their case truly the
sword has given place to the gown, with good effects
to all concerned in the reduction of these wild Indians to the Roman Catholic faith, and the arts of
civilized life; for many hundreds of them, nay, I
believe thousands, are now peaceful cultivators of
the soil, which these good fathers have taught
them how to till, instead of living, as they formerly
did, at warfare with mankind, and solely on the
produce of the chase. » And they continue the same,

(1) *Narrative of Lord Elgin's Mission*, vol. I, ch. v, p. 82.

he says, up to the last hour; for whereas there are still in the remote mountains of Ylocos and Pangasinau some tribes of pagan Indians, « the well-directed energies of several enthusiastic missionaries, who have as yet only found an entrance among them, are likely to civilize and ameliorate their condition. » (1)

Eight years later, Sir John Dowring, in spite of scant sympathy with Catholics or their religion, — though he always writes with temper and moderation, and confesses that he « found among the clergy men worthy of being loved and honoured, » — relates that in the diocese of Ylocos, in 1859, there were 15,775 baptisms, and that the number of Christians was 337,218. (2)

Such have been the peaceful triumphs of religion in that part of Eastern Oceanica which Providence has confided, as if to show her inexhaustible fecundity, to the healing power of the Church, and the fruitful ministrations of her servants. Whole nations of savage men, numbering several millions, have been converted, civilized, and instructed by successive generations of pastors, and have never ceased to repay their apostolic labours by loving confidence, devout and obedient service, and unshaken constancy in the faith. Blessed are the feet of the messengers of peace, and blessed the lands to which they bear them. « Beautiful upon the mountains are the feet of him that sheweth forth good, that preacheth salvation, that saith to Sion : Thy God shall reign. »

(1) *Recollections*, etc., ch. xxxiii, p. 290.
(2) Ch. xii, p. 213.

We are now to pass to other scenes. We do not
stay to speak of Protestantism in the Philippines,
because it has no existence. « To our shame be it
said, » observes a British officer in 1859, « there is
no Protestant place of worship on the island; and
even the burial ground is in an unseemly position
and condition, and, I believe, unconsecrated. » (1)
Let us proceed, then, with our narrative. Thus far
we have spoken of evangelists who abandoned all
which the natural man craves, — home, parents,
and kindred, — that they might with greater freedom proclaim « the unsearchable riches of Christ. »
We have now to tell of others, who also assumed the
title of « missionaries, » but only in order to improve
their worldly estate. Each class was successful in the
object of its ambition; the one found toil and martyrdom, the other wealth and repose.

Let us go forth into the wide ocean, leaving far behind us the coasts of Asia, and we shall come to the
islands of which we spoke in the beginning of this
chapter. They have been called « the latest conquest
of modern navigators; » and it was natural that,
lying mid-way between East and West, they should
first be visited by the ships of those sister nations,
whose vast commerce seeks to link the two hemi-
spheres in one, by multiplying the stations between
them. England and America, rivals in a traffic which
embraces the world, and which is equally honorable
to the skill and enterprise of both, have carried their
flag to every islet to which the ocean gave access.

(1) *Hong-Kong to Manilla*, by H. T. Ellis, R. N.; ch. xiii,
p. 244.

With their mariners, a hardy and adventurous race, went men of another order, whose ostensible purpose was the conversion of the heathen. It was from England and America that they went forth ; and a writer of the latter nation, who warmly espouses their cause, and, unlike most of his countrymen, speaks of the Catholic Church in language which is always trivial and generally indecent, tells us why they went. « The divine command, ' Go ye and teach all nations, ' » he crudely observes, « was obeyed by that people who had been the most alive to its commercial advantages. » (1) The missionaries whom he defends, or at least most of them, appear to have obeyed the difficult precept from the same politic motive. We shall see them presently at their work.

A French writer, who had examined all the facts, as far as they were then revealed, which we are about to notice, observed a few years ago, that the Protestant missionaries in Oceanica appear to have aimed at establishing, in all its islands, « a theocratic and commercial fief for their numerous posterity. » The latter half of this design has been partly accomplished in some of the groups, the former has been wholly unsuccessful. Let us visit, in order, the scenes of their labour, and begin with the *Society Islands*, where they first commenced the operations which we are now to relate.

Most people have heard of the « missionary voyage of the ship Duff. » It was in this vessel, more hon-

(1) *History of the Sandwich Islands*, by James J. Jarves, ch. XI, p. 357.

oured than the sacred galley of Athens, or the bark
which carried the fortunes of Cæsar, that England
despatched to the favoured isles of the Pacific her
first missionaries. We need not recount here the well
known « instructions » addressed to « M^r and Mrs Wilson, » — the solemn injunctions laid upon the missionaries committed to their joint oversight, — nor
the hymns of triumph which heralded the parting
ship, and accompanied her on her way. Who is not
familiar with the tale? Who is ignorant that if it
provoked a smile in some, it has excited, during a
long series of years, the vehement sympathy of
others? Even as late as 1839, one of the most eminent of English Reviewers still speaks of the « voyage
of the Duff, » with a burst of uncontrollable enthusiasm, as « one of the manifestations of the pious zeal
of the nineteenth century, fraught with a promise
very different from that of the crusades of the middle
ages. » (1) The crusades, which saved religion and
civilisation, were, according to this authority, only
a trivial incident in human annals, compared with
« the missionary voyage of the ship Duff. »

Let us enter this historic vessel, and form some
acquaintance with her passengers and crew. Even
the latter, we are assured by the Rev. Dr Campbell,
in 1840, « were many of them as truly godly men as
the missionaries themselves; » whose « character
and vocation, » this historian of missions adds, « were
purely spiritual; » so that he exults, after the lapse
of so many years, in the consoling recollection, that
« Christianity, in her first approach to Polyne-

(1) *Quarterly Review*, July 1839, p. 176.

sia, appeared arrayed in her native purity. « (1)

Conspicuous as a leader among these celebrated
missionaries, whose praise is still in all Protestant
churches, was the Rev. Mʳ Lewis. It was this gentleman who was chosen by his colleagues as their
« first moderator, » (2) and who presided both at
their periodical devotions, and in the daily selection
and exposition of Scripture texts. Such a distinction
appropriately attested the rare merits of the future
missionary, and in the discharge of these grave duties he wore out the voyage, amid the applause of his
companions. Arrived at length in Tahiti, he justified
after this manner their good opinion. « For some
time, » says the Rev. Dʳ Brown, « his behaviour
towards the Tahitian females had been extremely indecent; »(3) and this was only the beginning of evil,
for a little later, as Mʳ Ellis, a well known missionary, adds, « Mʳ Lewis intimated to his companions
his intention of uniting in marriage with a native of
the island. Considering her an idolatress, » his companions protested against the proposed nuptials; (4)
and when the « first moderator, » defying their remonstrance, had espoused a pagan savage, their Sunday
journal records his apparition at chapel in these reproachful words, — « Mʳ Lewis and woman attended
the service. » Finally, he perished, apparently by

(1) *Maritime Discovery and Christian Missions*, by John Campbell, D. D.; ch. VII, p. 260.

(2) *Missionary Voyage to the South Sea*, ch. V, p. 46.

(3) *History of the Propagation of Christianity*, etc., vol. II,
p. 125.

(4) *Polynesian Researches*, by the Revᵈ William Ellis, vol. I,
ch. IV, p. 95.

the hand of his heathen relatives, being found lying
on his face, with his skull cleft asunder.

The next of this famous company is the Rev.
M⁕ Broomhall. He too was « a shining light » among
his fellows, great in the interpretation of Scripture,
and had been for some time, M⁕ Ellis says, « highly
serviceable to the mission. » (1) When M⁕ Lewis
lapsed, he was foremost in addressing to him the
most solemn admonitions. Unfortunately, he also, in
spite of his eminent qualities, as D⁕ Smith relates,
« successively connected himself with two Otaheitan
females, and with one of them he continued to coha-
bit till he quitted the island. » (2) Before his departure, we learn from the same Protestant historian,
« he seemed entirely devoted to the principles of infidelity ; » and his companions observe in their journal,
forwarded to the missionary society at home, that
« the state of M⁕ Broomhall's mind is very awful ; he
professes himself no Christian, neither desires to be
one. » (3)

The third in dignity of this too celebrated troop,
whose evangelical triumphs have been so often the
theme of missionary orations in England and America, and are still eulogised with enthusiasm by English writers, was the Rev. M⁕ Veeson. He also,
though able to manipulate texts as skilfully as his
friends, « cohabited with one of the Tonga women, »
as D⁕ Brown relates ; then began « mingling with
the heathen, and showing a strong disposition to

(1) *Polynesian Researches*, vol. 1, p. 103.
(2) *History of the Missionary Societies*, vol. II, p. 56.
(3) *Otaheitan Journals*, quoted in *Missionary Transactions*,
vol. I, p. 184.

learn their ways, in which he at length made a woful
proficiency, and threw off the mask of Christianity
completely. » (1)

The Rev. M' Harris, another of these earliest
« heralds » of English Protestantism, who introduced
Christianity to Polynesia « in her native purity » is thus
described by D' Russell. « It was manifest that he had
become paralysed by fear, his ardour quenched, and
his firmness shaken. » And these were not his only
infirmities. « He expressed his deep disgust with
the food and other matters. » Finally, after « the
frightened missionary had been on the beach all
night, » the people of the ship went to his aid, and
« found him in a most lamentable condition, and
almost deprived of intellect. » (2)

The Rev. Francis Oakes, who appears to have
also travelled in the Duff, « left the island a twelve-
month after, » we learn from D' Lang, « in consequence of some hostile demonstration of feeling on
the part of the natives, and settled as chief constable
at Parramatta. » (3)

Finally, of *eleven* missionaries, who seem to have
reached New Zealand, from which they again fled
for fear of the natives, we are told by D' Smith, an
eager partisan, that « instead of achieving any thing
for the honour of the Gospel, some of them afforded
melancholy proof that Otaheite would not have been

(1) *Hist. Prop. Christianity*, vol. II, p. 200.
(2) *Polynesia and New Zealand*, by the R' Rev⁴ M. Russell;
ch. v, p. 186. Cf Fanning's *Voyages round the World*, ch. x,
p. 131.
(3) *History of N. S. Wales*, vol. I, ch. v, p. 103.

eventually benefited by their continuance in that island. » (1)

Such, by the testimony of Protestant annalists, were the passengers by the ship **Duff**, and such the expedition « fraught with a promise » which casts even the crusades into dim shadow. And it is of such men that English clergymen and English reviewers could deliberately speak, a quarter of a century after their crimes and their apostasy, as « godly men, » busy with « manifestations of pious zeal, » and generous benefactors of their race.

But this is only the first scene in the Protestant missions of Oceanica; we shall find others quite as worthy of our attention, for they have the faculty of reproducing themselves, in the later history of the Society Islands, and especially in Tahiti, the chief member of the group. That history we will now examine, as it has been unfolded by Protestant witnesses.

Captain Laplace, the commander of the French frigate *Artémise*, who visited almost all the islands of the Pacific, noticed, in 1833, that « the methodist ministers have never dared to attempt the conversion of the frightful and sanguinary tribes of New Caledonia, New Hebrides, New Guinea, » etc. These formidable disciples they preferred to abandon to missionaries of another faith, who, as the same distinguished officer testifies, « have courageously ventured into the midst of them, and pursue their work with success at this moment, chiefly in New Caledonia, where they already count a considerable

(1) Vol. II, p. 41.

number of neophytes, whose habits they have succeeded in changing to an astonishing degree. » (1)

The Protestants, however, chose more tranquil
fields of labour, and selected for their first operations
an island which is thus described by M' Herman Melville. « The ineffable repose and beauty of the landscape is such, that every object strikes an European
like something seen in a dream; and for a time he
almost refuses to believe that scenes like these should
have a common place existence. » (2) Long before this
writer visited Tahiti, De Bougainville, who noticed
with admiration « the mild behaviour of the natives, »
had been « delighted with the beauty of its hills and
valleys, the verdure of its swelling acclivities, the
cool shades afforded by its groves, and the pleasant
associations connected with its grassy plains and
murmuring rivulets. » And, once more, De La Ri-
charderie bore witness, more than sixty years ago,
to that « sweetness of manner and benevolence of
disposition » (3) which all the earlier navigators
attest with one accord, but of which every vestige
has long since disappeared. The vices which now
make Tahiti a proverb, — theft, drunkenness, cruelty,
lying, covetousness, and fraud, — all date, as their
own friends will presently tell us, from the arrival
of the Protestant missionaries, and were almost unknown at an earlier period.

It was to a gentle and winning race, inhabiting
one of the fairest regions of the earth, that the emis-

(1) *Campagne de Circumnavigation de la Frégate l'Artémise*,
tome V, ch. iv, p. 425.

(2) *Omoo*, ch. xviii, p. 66.

(3) *Bibliothèque Universelle des Voyages*, tome VI, p. 370.

saries of the English missionary societies first presented themselves, in the guise of apostles, charged
with a message from heaven. The first effect of their
presence, as we have seen, was to introduce shameless incontinence, and to teach the natives how easy
it was even for its preachers to apostatise from
Christianity; the second, as they themselves confess,
was to destroy for ever the peace which their presence disturbed, and to kindle the flames of merciless
wars in every grove and valley which they visited.

« It is a very remarkable fact, » says the missionary
Williams, unconsciously pronouncing sentence upon
himself and his companions, « that in no island of
importance has Christianity been introduced *without
a war.* » (1) His own « converts, » he admits,
« acted with great cruelty towards their enemies,
hewing them in pieces while they were begging for
mercy. » Already they had become cruel and sanguinary, and the most impartial witnesses affirm,
that it was the missionaries who made them so.
« The new religion, » says Von Kotzebue, « was
forcibly established, and whoever would not adopt
it *put to death.* With the zeal for making proselytes,
the rage of tigers took possession of a people once so
gentle. » And presently he adds, « the bloody persecution *instigated by the Missionaries* performed
the office of a desolating infection. » (2) And again;
« Ambition associated itself to fanaticism. »

And this is confirmed in 1843 by the American

(1) *Narrative of Missionary Enterprises in the S. Sea Islands,*
by the Revᵈ John Williams, ch. xii, p. 49.
(2) Kotzebue's *New Voyage round the World,* vol. I, pp. 159,
169. (1830).

Commodore Wilkes, a disinterested but anti-catholic witness, who says, that a war which he found raging at Tongataboo was « a religious contest, » promoted by the Missionaries. In vain he remonstrated against their proceedings. « I was much surprised and struck, » he says, « with the indifference with which Mr Rabone spoke of the war. He was evidently more inclined to have it continue than desirous that it should be put a stop to ; viewing it, in fact, as a means of propagating the gospel! I had little hopes of being instrumental in bringing about a peace, when such unchristian views existed where it was least to be expected. » (1)

Catholic missionaries, in all lands, have been accustomed to offer the sacrifice of their own lives, but have never assisted in taking away life from others. When we come to speak of America, we shall find instances of Protestant « Missionaries » actually slaying the heathen with their own hands and exulting in the fact; meanwhile, let it be noted that, in the Pacific, as Williams admits, Protestantism has nowhere been introduced « without a war. » This is the first mark by which it may be known.

And how, it is natural to enquire, were the natives of Tahiti induced to profess a religion introduced by such teachers, and which they were encouraged to propagate by such means? Mr Williams, who was a principal agent in these proceedings, will tell us. « Some thought that by embracing Christianity, vessels would be induced to visit them ; many hoped by adopting the new religion to prolong their lives. »

(1) *United States Exploring Expedition*, vol. III, ch. 1, p. 12.

And then he quotes the speech of one of their chiefs,
who thus recommended the English religion to his
people. « Look at the wisdom of these worshippers
of Jehovah, and see how superior they are to us in
every respect. Their ships are like floating houses,
so that they can traverse the tempest-driven ocean
for months with perfect safety ; whereas, if a breeze
blow upon our canoes, they are in an instant upset,
and we are sprawling in the sea. Their persons are
covered from head to foot in beautiful clothes, while
we wear nothing but a girdle of leaves... Their
knives too, what valuable things they are ! how
quickly they cut up our pigs, compared with our
bamboo knives! Now I conclude that God who has
given to his white worshippers these valuable things
must be wiser than our gods, for they have not given
the like to us. *We all want these articles;* and my
proposition is, that the God who gave them should
be our God. » (1) It was impossible to reason more
sagaciously ; and having come to this conclusion,
they eagerly agreed to assist the missionaries in for-
cing all the other tribes to adopt a religion which
imparted to its happy votaries such beautiful clothes,
and such excellent knives.

But this point deserves further illustration. « When
Pomare embraced Christianity, » says Lord Waldegrave, « the whole island, in obedience to his will,
adopted the Christian religion. It was, however, only
a state conversion not understood, and therefore not
sincere. » (2) « The truth is, » says Dr Russell, « the

(1) *Narrative,* etc., ch. XXXII, p. 149.
(2) *Journal of Geographical Society,* vol. III, p. 182.

chiefs had already perceived so many temporal advantages connected with Christianity, that they became desirous, on secular grounds alone, to extend its principles among their dependants; » and he quotes the ingenious letter of Pomare the Second to the London Missionary Society, in which, after asking for a supply of missionaries, that acute monarch added, — « Friends, send also property, and cloth for us, and we also will adopt English customs. » (1) Mr Stewart, an American missionary, tells us of another Polynesian sovereign, who urged the President of the United States to send emissaries to her dominions, because « our harbours are good, and our refreshments abundant. » (2) Lastly, Mr Cargill, also a missionary, relates, that having asked a chief if he believed what he said was true, — « True! every thing is true that comes from the white man's country: muskets, and guns, and powder, are true, and the religion *must* be true. » (3)

The Protestant missionaries were now definitively established in Tahiti. From that hour, during many successive years, such accounts of their uninterrupted success were forwarded to England as might well stimulate the hopes and sympathies of their supporters. Idolatry, they reported, had given way before them; and so great was the devotion of their disciples, as the missionary records annually testified, that Tahiti became a watchword among all the advocates of missionary enterprise. « Our congregations

(1) *Polynesia and New Zealand*, ch. IV, p. 151.

(2) *A Visit to the S. Seas in the U. S. Ship Vincennes*, by C. S. Stewart, A. M., vol. II. Letter VII, p. 50.

(3) Dr Brown, *Hist. Prop. Christianity*, vol. I, p. 512.

increase, » said the Rev. Mr Osmund, as late as
1842, « and many are pressing into our churches.
For goodness of temper, general moral conduct, correct scriptural knowledge, decided attachment to the
gospel, and, in the aggregate, pleasing consistency
as church members, I am bold to say that they are
fit to be placed on a footing with any equal number
of professing christians, in any church, in any part
of the world. » (1) Every word of this statement
should be carefully weighed, for it was the common
language of the missionaries, in all the letters which
they addressed to the Society at home. How far it
was justified by facts, including their own secret
confessions, we shall learn presently.

Dr Russell, in his account of the Polynesian missions, observed, nearly twenty years ago, as if antici-
pating the disclosures which would one day reach Europe, — « It is almost inseparable from the duties of
an uninspired missionary to exaggerate the amount of
his success. » Already, even in his time, the unwelcome truth was beginning to be revealed. « An impression has been very generally produced, » he reluctantly admits, « that the European teachers have
to answer for *more evil* than will ever be compensated by their most zealous services. » (2) Let us
now review the facts which created this gloomy
impression, and we must receive them exclusively
from Protestant witnesses, since no other testimony
would suffice to prove them. We will follow, as in
former instances, the order of dates, which range

(1) *Hist. Prop. Christianity*, vol. II, p. 185.
(2) Ch. III, p. 113.

through a period of thirty years, from 1829 to 1859.

Our first witness is the Rev. William Ellis, a clergyman of the Church of England, well known by his various writings on China, Polynesia, and Madagascar, and accounted by no mean authority « an enlightened and accomplished missionary. » (1) M' Ellis considers the Catholic religion « one of the most absurd and fatal delusions which the powers of darkness ever invented for the destruction of mankind. » This is his deliberate estimate of the religion which, — to say nothing of St. Dominic and St. Francis, St. Bernard and St. Philip, — was preached in later times by Bossuet and Fenelon; admitted to be divine by Pascal, Leibnitz, and Grotius; and which has captivated in our own age the intellect and the affections of such men as Stolberg and Schlegel, Galitzin and Schouvaloff, Hurter and Overbeck, Newman and Faber. But M' Ellis has decided that it is an absurd delusion.

M' Ellis visited Tahiti. Speaking of the beneficial influence of his own presence in that Island, he says; « With what augmented joy must that honoured and distinguished saint, the late Countess of Huntingdon, in strict obedience to whose last bequest and dying charge the South Sea Mission was attempted, have viewed the pleasing change! » (2) We are, of course, not acquainted with the feelings of that amiable lady; but if her contemplation embraced the proceedings of the missionaries who travelled in the ship Duff, and who inaugurated the Mission in which she felt

(1) *Quarterly Review*, July 1859.
(2) *Polynesian Researches*, ch. x, p. 261.

so much interest, we may perhaps doubt whether her
joy was sensibly augmented. But less us examine
more closely M' Ellis's own operations, and endeavour to learn from his published statements what
he considers the true method of evangelising the
heathen.

« We instructed them, » he tells us, « not to consider Baptism as possessing any *saving efficacy*, *or
conferring any spiritual benefit*, but being on our
parts a duty connected with our office, and on theirs
a public declaration of discipleship. » (1) So much
for the Sacrament of Baptism.

« We felt no hesitation, » he adds, speaking of
the « Lord's Supper, » in using the roasted or baked
bread-fruit, pieces of which were placed in the proper
vessel. » And again; « We have sometimes been ap-
prehensive that we might be under the necessity of
substituting the juice of the cocoa-nut for that of the
grape » — which he confesses some of his colleagues
actually did. (2) M' Ellis has no doubt often read
St. Paul's Epistle to the Corinthians, and can perhaps explain, how that Apostle would « discern the
Lord's Body » in roasted bread-fruit and the juice of
the cocoa-nut. This Anglican missionary may certainly boast that he has effectually sequestrated the
only two sacraments which his church had retained.
Whether it is lawful for men thus to suppress the
ordinances of God, and to substitute for His sacraments new inventions of their own, M' Ellis would
probably consider a trivial enquiry.

(1) Ch. IX, p. 250.
(2) Ch. XI, p. 309.

Having thus dealt with the sacraments of Baptism and the Holy Eucharist, this clergyman of the Church of England next proceeded to abolish all creeds. « We did not, » he says, « present any creed or articles of faith for their subscription. » Perhaps some may be tempted to ask, the sacraments and creeds being now blotted out, what portions of Christianity Mr Ellis had reserved from the common destruction? This question we are unable to answer. He tells us, indeed, that in « the strict observance of the Sabbath the Tahitian resembled the Jewish more perhaps than the Christian Sabbath, » which he may possibly have considered an adequate substitute for sacraments and articles of faith; but we search his book in vain for any definite account of what he actually taught the people of Tahiti.

We learn from it, however, much more distinctly what he thought of the position of a missionary in such a land. « The only earthly solace, » Mr Ellis observes, « which a Missionary enjoys among an uncivilized people, except what he derives from his work, is found in the *social endearments* of the domestic circle. » And again; « The greatest trials the Missionaries experience are those connected with the bringing up of a family.... he experiences a constant and painful struggle between the dictates of parental affection and the claims of pastoral care. » (1) « *He is divided*, » said St. Paul, alluding to this very perplexity; and that sublime Missionary thus warned all who would give their whole hearts to God against this very snare. « I would have you to

(1) Ch. xviii, pp. 512-4.

be without solicitude. He that is without a wife, is
solicitous for the things that belong to the Lord, how
he may please God. But he that is with a wife,
is solicitous for the things of the world, how
he may please his wife : and he is divided. » (1)
Mr Ellis seems to have felt the inconvenience of this
position, which indeed ultimately deprived the Tahitians of his presence; for « the severe and protracted
illness of Mrs Ellis, » sent them home, though he had
protested twenty times in the course of his book that
nothing should ever separate him from this field of
labour, — he lived to visit many others, and to write
a book on each of them, — and so he adds, with infinite composure, — « we took our final leave of the
Polynesian islands, and the interesting people by
whom they are inhabited. » To what extent the
people had profited by his abode amongst them,
we shall learn more satisfactorily from other witnesses.

The very year after Mr Ellis published his book,
Von Kotzebue, an intelligent and perfectly impartial
authority, thus described, from actual observation,
the religion of Tahiti. « The religion taught by the
Missionaries is not true Christianity, though it may
possibly comprehend some of its doctrines, but half
understood even by the teachers themselves. A religion which consists in the eternal repetition of prescribed prayers, which forbids every innocent pleasure, and cramps or annihilates every mental power,
is a libel on the Divine Founder of Christianity. »
And then this celebrated navigator gives a descrip-

(1) I, Cor. vii, 33.

tion of the dark and tyrannical system under which the natives of Tahiti were already groaning at the time of his visit, and by which they were crushed till the happy interference of France released them from their bondage. « By order of the Missionaries, » he says, « the flute, which once awakened innocent pleasure, is heard no more. One of our friends having begun to sing for joy over a present he had received, was immediately asked by his comrades, with great terror, what he thought would be the consequence, should the Missionaries hear of it? » « The oppressed people, » he adds, and many witnesses confirm the fact, « even suffer themselves to be driven to prayers by the cudgel. » His final impression he records in these grave words. « The religion of the Missionaries has neither tended to enlighten the Tahitians, nor to render them happy. » On the other hand, « each Missionary possesses a piece of land, cultivated by the natives, which produces him in superfluity all that he requires. » (1)

In 1830, we have the evidence of a gentleman well known for the energy of his religious opinions, Captain, afterwards Lord Waldegrave. « The missionaries, » he reports, after much personal observation, « are all engaged in trade, which I am afraid interferes in some degree with their usefulness. At present they have the monopoly of cattle, so that the shipping are almost wholly supplied with fresh beef by them. They also appeared to deal in cocoanut oil and arrowroot. « Of their converts this ardent Protestant cautiously confesses, « the tenets of the

(1) *Voyage Round the World*, vol. II, pp. 172-203.

Gospel have not in many taken deep root. » (1)

The next year, 1831, gives us another witness of the same class, having, like Lord Waldegrave, no motive whatever but to tell the truth. Captain Bee-chey disclaims any but a friendly feeling towards the English Missionaries, but says he « felt himself called upon to declare the truth, » and not « to increase the general misconception, » created by missionary reports. The natives, he reports, like those of New Zealand, had already learned the vice of covetousness, and were accustomed to sell false pearls, « ingeniously made out of an oyster shell, » and to exult in the success of their fraud. « Without amusement, and excessively indolent, they now seek enjoyment in idleness and sensuality. » The Tiokeans, he reports, « are still reputed to be cannibals, notwithstanding they have embraced the Christian religion. » He shows also that the violent suppression of all innocent amusements, which marked this strange form of Christianity, extended even to the king's household. He was present at an entertainment given in his honour by Pomare, of whom we shall hear more presently, but « it was necessary that the vivo, or reed pipe, should be played in an under tone, that it might not reach the ears of an aava, or policeman, who was parading the beach, in a soldier's jacket, with a rusty sword; for even the use of this melodious little instrument, the delight of the natives, from whose nature the dance and the pipe are inseparable, is now strictly prohibited! » (2) Of the other islands of

---

(1) *Journal of the Royal Geographical Society*, vol. III, p. 180.
(2) Beechey's *Voyage to the Pacific*, vol.1, ch. IX, pp. 286, 307.

the Pacific, Captain Beechey gives a similar account, as we shall see when we come to speak of them.

In the same year, the Protestant author of the Mutiny of the Bounty thus speaks of the natives of Tahiti. After describing with admiration their earlier character, before the Missionaries had visited them, he says; « what they now are it is lamentable to reflect! All their usual and innocent amusements have been denounced by the Missionaries, and, in lieu of them, these poor people have been driven to seek for resources in habits of indolence and apathy : that simplicity of character which atoned for many of their faults has been converted into cunning and hypocrisy; and drunkenness, poverty, and disease have thinned the island of its former population to a frightful degree. » And then he shows, « on the authority of a census taken by the Missionaries, » that in thirty years the population had dwindled to less than one third! And even this was probably too favorable an account, for whereas Bligh reports that « the inhabitants of Otaheite have been estimated at above 100,000, » (1) Lord Waldegrave reduced this estimate, in 1830, to 8,000.

What follows is still more impressive. « All the smiling cottages and little plantations of the natives are now *destroyed*, and the remnant of the population has crept down (from the fertile grounds) to the flats and swampy ground on the sea shore, *completely subservient to the seven establishments of Missionaries, who have taken from them what little trade they used to carry on, to possess themselves*

(1) Bligh's *Voyage to the South Sea*, ch. vi, p. 80.

of it; who have their warehouses, act as agents,
and monopolise all the cattle on the island. » A few
years later we shall find the very Society which
employed them admitting these facts. Well might
this author add, — « How much is such a change,
brought about by such conduct, to be deprecated!
How lamentable is it to reflect, that an island on
which Nature has lavished so many of her bounteous
gifts, should be doomed to such a fate! » (1)

It was now the turn of the Tahitians to enjoy the
advantages which every where attend the presence
of Protestant missionaries. In China, as Mc Sirr has
told us, they augment their incomes by diligently
« attending auctions » ; in India, as a crowd of witnesses relate, « their cry is only, ‘ money ’ » ; in
Ceylon, they rejoice in « spacious lawns, » handsome country houses, » and « social meetings » ; in
the Antipodes, they deal in land and provisions ; in
Tahiti, they cheat the poor natives of their humble
commerce, « to possess themselves of it » — and it is
from their companions and advocates that we learn
these facts. Let us continue their history.

Once more, in the same year, a celebrated writer,
reviewing Captain Beechey's work, thus appreciated
the influence of the missionaries in Tahiti. « Unhappily, in eradicating idolatry, the missionaries, from
whatever cause, have failed to substitute any better
principles in its stead; and the only effect of the
change produced has been, to degrade Christianity to
the level of the most brutish idolatry, without making
one *step* towards raising these miserable idolaters to

(1) *History of the Mutiny of the Bounty*, ch. i, pp. 37-39.

the rank of Christians. The people, consequently, are as much barbarians and savages as ever, — or rather, *they are worse;* for they have borrowed from civilization nothing but the vices by which it is dishonoured. » (1)

In the next year, 1832, a writer in the Asiatic Journal, comparing the public and official reports of the missionaries with their private confessions, thus discloses the want of harmony between the two. « As a proof of what the Missionaries themselves *really* think of the Otaheitans, I will give you an extract of a letter written by them to a friend of mine. ' The Pitcairn islanders are arrived, but I am afraid their morals will soon be corrupted *by the Otaheitans* ' » (2)— whom Mr Osmund, it will be remembered, described, in an official report designed to attract fresh subscriptions, as models of « general moral conduct, correct scriptural knowledge, and decided attachment to the gospel. » The same writer adds the characteristic fact, that up to that year, 1832, « more than 100,000 l. sterling has been expended on the missions to the Society Islands» — that is to say, on the missionaries and their families.

In 1834, the London Missionary Society, unable to conceal the fatal evidence which was now multiplying on all sides, confess at last in their annual report, — « the tidings which have been received by late arrivals have been more unfavorable than any. » (3) And in 1835, Mr Williams, whose career

(1) *Edinburg Review,* No 53, p. 217.
(2) *Asiatic Journal,* vol. VIII. p. 107.
(3) *Report of London Missionary Society,* 1834 ; in *Asiatic Journal,* vol. XIV, p. 196.

shall be noticed presently, and whose accounts of triumphant progress had exactly resembled that which has been quoted from Mr Osmund, thus writes to the Directors of the same Society. « Although it would be much more pleasant to myself to state that the former prosperity continued, this is not my happiness on the present occasion.» All that he ventures to add, by way of apology, is, — « that in all the lamentable defections from Christian doctrine and purity which have taken place among us, I have never heard of one individual who has even thought of returning to the worship of their former gods. » (1)

The official reports of the missionaries were now beginning to agree with their private confessions, and with the voluntary testimony of more independent witnesses. The fact that the backsliding natives did not renew the worship of their wooden gods was but a feeble consolation; for, as the historian of Protestant Missions observes, « the truth appears to be, that in the Islands of the Pacific Ocean, idolatry had a very slight hold on the minds of the natives; » (2) and another writer declares the same thing of the Sandwich Islands, where « idolatry had, as if by miracle, given way, even *before* the coming of the mission. » (3)

The well known work of the Rev. John Williams, of which the thirty-fifth edition was published in 1841, now claims our attention. Mr Williams lost his life in one of the islands of the Pacific, and has

(1) Quoted in *Asiatic Journal*, vol. XVIII, p. 115. New series.

(2) Dr Brown, vol. II, p. 218.

(3) *Voyage of H. M. S. Blonde to the Sandwich Islands*, by Captain Lord Byron, p. 147.

been regarded by his admirers as a martyr. His
evidence, on several accounts, deserves particular
consideration.

We have already learned from him, that the form
of Christianity which he taught was not introduced
into any of the islands « without a war. » He next
admits that polygamy was sanctioned by the missionaries, even while legislating for its suppression. They
had admonished their polygamist « converts » to
select one of their wives, to whom they should be
united formally by a religious ceremony. The Injunction was apparently obeyed; but when, at a
later period, the natives repented of their first
choice, urging, as Mr Williams reports, that « had
they known it to be permanent, they should have
made a different selection, » (1) they were consider-
ately allowed to choose again, — a licence ·which
would somewhat obscure their apprehension of the
sanctity of Christian marriage.

Of the real character of the nominal converts,
Mr Williams, towards the close of his career, furnishes an accurate estimate, though not very consistent with his own earlier reports. Thus he had
described Rarotonga, at least twenty times, as a
kind of Paradise, and its inhabitants as model
Christians ; yet he confesses, in his book, that « as
vast numbers of those who professed Christianity
were influenced by example merely, no sooner had
the powerful excitement produced by the transition
from one state of society to another subsided, than
they *returned* to the habits in which, from their in-

(1) *Narrative*, etc., ch. VIII, p. 35.

fancy, they had been trained. « Of the converts of
« the whole Hervey Island group, » he says, « I do
not assert, I would not intimate, that all the people
are real christians; » and of another group, « I by
no means affirm that many, or even that any, of the
Samoans had experienced a change of heart. » (1) It
is only to be regretted that these confessions were
delayed until they were extorted by the unexpected
revelations of others.

But there were some converts whom Mr Williams
was unwilling to include in the general catalogue,
and of these king Pomare was the most conspicuous.
Mr Williams was his friend in life, and attended him
on his death bed. « I confidently hope, » he says,
« that *he* was a subject of Divine grace; » indeed he
was quite sure of it, for he adds, — « I visited him
in his last illness, and found his views of the way of
salvation clear and distinct. »

Unfortunately, however, the reports of more impartial witnesses do not permit us to share the cheerful conviction expressed by Mr Williams. « Pomare
was the first convert to Christianity, » Mr Ellis says,
« in the island of which he was king... during the
latter part of his life, his conduct was in many respects exceptionable; » which means, as Mr Ellis
goes on to remark, that he had « habits of intemper-
ance, and was also reported to be addicted to other
vices. » (2) On the other hand, this writer assures
us, in the peculiar phraseology of his class, that
Pomare « was not averse to devotional engagements,

(1) Ch. xxxii.
(2) *Polynesian Researches*, vol. II, ch. xviii, pp. 532-4.

and gave a steady patronage to the Missionaries. »

But we must endeavour to arrive at a more exact knowledge of the real character of this « subject of divine grace. » « Their zealous king, » D' Russell tells us, « was not the only native of Otaheite whose conscience permitted him to combine the worship of Jehovah with a relaxed code of morals. » « He was as dexterous a thief, » says M' Turnbull, « as any amongst them; » and yet he declares that « the Otaheitans are thieves in every sense of the word. » (1) The examples which he gives of Pomares « relaxed code of morals » do not certainly encourage a high opinion of that royal personage. But let us pursue our investigation. « The chiefs, » says the Hon. Frederick Walpole, who had been their guest, « were too powerful a body to be touched by the Missionaries who framed the laws; so as they, the Missionaries, only owed their existence to them, they allowed *them* to retain many of their old savage privileges » — including, as it appears from his graphic account, lewdness, theft, and drunkenness. (2) Lord Waldegrave also, after describing the house of this « subject of divine grace » as one of those unclean stews for which language has no name, or only one which cannot be employed, adds; « Pomare, the king, sat in the room, a witness of, and indifferent to, the addresses paid to his wife, or the open debauchery of his mother in law. » (3) On the whole, we are reduced rather to hope than to believe that the real character of Pomare justified

(1) Turnbull's *Voyage round the World*, ch. XI, pp. 281-3.
(2) *Four Years in the Pacific*, vol. I, ch. XI, p. 215. (1849).
(3) *Journal*, etc., ubi supra.

the sanguine estimate of Mr Williams. His « views »
may have been excellent, but his morals were detestable.

But it is time to leave this gentleman — not, however, without adding a word upon the manner of his
death. It is true that Mr Williams was killed by the
natives, as Captain Cook had been ; and it is impossible not to compassionate his dismal end, when we
are informed, that he was not only struck down in
the prime of life, but that « his body was roasted
and eaten. » (1) Yet history, while it deplores his
melancholy fate, can never admit his claim to the
title of « martyr. » If this unfortunate gentleman,
by his own or his childrens act, provoked the just
reprisals of men whom they had cruelly injured and
robbed, the frightful penalty may inspire sorrow
and regret, but nothing more. Mr Williams had been
conspicuous amongst those who, in the words of
Mr Leigtch Ritchie, « are said to have usurped many
of the functions of government, and to have taken
advantage of their position to obtain an undue share
of trade ; » (2) or, as another writer expresses it,
he was one of the missionaries « who are determined to get the whole commerce into their own
hands. » (3) He had even been publicly and officially
censured by the very Society which employed him
for his own share in such transactions, and especially
for his traffic in South Sea tobacco. He was « largely
engaged, » says Archdeacon Grant, « in private spe-

(1) *Incidents and Adventures in the Pacific Ocean*, by Thomas
Jefferson Jacobs, ch. xxvi, p. 235. New York, 1844.
(2) *The British World in the East*, vol. II, p. 416.
(3) *Asiatic Journal*, vol. VIII, p. 106.

culations; « (1) and M' Ebenezer Prout, his enthusiastic biographer, who seems almost disposed to
defend even this incident in his life, says; « M' Williams received a letter from the Directors, in which
his speculation was condemned, and his conduct
censured. But his spirit, though bowed down, was
not broken. » (2)

In 1841, the same Directors were obliged to
acknowledge that « some of the Missionaries have
from time to time been extensively engaged in
mercantile transactions, and the practice, besides
lowering the general tone and character of the mission, has, we fear, frequently brought them into
invidious and degrading competition with their
own people, whose interests happened to be embarked in the same line of traffic. » (3) And in all
these proceedings poor Williams appears to have
been fatally compromised. To augment his own fortune and that of his children had long been his chief
concern. Commodore Wilkes reports that he visited
« the tiny ship-yard of his son, M' John Williams,
who was taken by his father to England, and there
taught all the mechanical trades... by the aid of a
few natives he has already built himself a vessel
about twenty-five tons burden, which he proposes to
employ in trading among these islands. » (4) And
M' Walpole throws more light on this sad story,
when he tells us, that « *the son of a Missionary at
Tahiti* fitted out a brig, armed her, and, assisted by

(1) *Bampton Lectures*, Lect. VII, p. 239.
(2) *Life of the Rev⁴ John Williams*, ch. IV, p. 194.
(3) Quoted by D' Brown, vol. II, p. 184.
(4) *U. S. Exploring Expedition*, vol. II, ch. IV, p. 93.

a number of natives of Borabora, made a descent on
one of the Figie Islands, drove the people into the
mountains, *cut down all their sandal wood*, burnt
their villages, and made off. » (1) Whether this
man, who, it is added, « now enjoys a capital position at Tahiti, » was the son of Williams, is not
distinctly stated; but we have heard quite enough to
explain the tragic fate of the solitary « martyr » of
Protestant Missions. St. Austin once noticed the
claims of a martyr of the same class, but contented
himself with saying to his admirers ; « *Et cum
vivatis ut latrones*, *mori vos jactatis ut mar-
tyres.* » (2)

Resuming now the course of our narrative, we
come to the evidence of the Rev. Dr Brown, the Protestant annalist of missions to the heathen. In September, 1843, the Rev. William Day, he tells us,
admitted « the unchanged hearts, after the lapse of
ten years, and unaltered lives, of many who have
attached themselves to our ministry. » This tardy
confession relates to Upolu. Of his colleagues generally, Dr Brown says, as if he felt that it was useless
to deny it any longer, — « We apprehend that the
religion of their converts is often very superficial,
and is not even founded in any proper knowledge of
the principles of the Gospel. » Even the Directors,
he adds, « express in successive reports unfavoura-
ble views in regard to the moral and religious condition of the people ; and it is very unlikely they would
do so on insufficient grounds. » (3)

(1) *Four Years*, etc., vol. I, ch. XIII, p. 289.
(2) *Contra Litteras Petilian*, lib. 2. Opp. tome IX, p. 431.
(3) *Hist. Prop. Christianity*, vol. II, p. 183.

Nothing, in truth, could be more unlikely, seeing that they had continued to publish, as long as it was possible to conceal the truth, such reports as those of M' Osmund. The Rev. William Orme, foreign secretary to the London Missionary Society, had himself circulated an account of these missions, in order to obtain additional funds, which, but for its irreverence and puerility of language, might have been a description of the primitive saints and martyrs. D' Brown might well call it a « painful » exaggeration; and M' Timkin, a missionary in the Sandwich Islands, had the courage to confess, that it was « a picture of the South Sea Mission for which there is no original in the Pacific, and in our judgment will not be for a century to come. » (1)

D' Brown also speaks of the entrance of Catholic missionaries into these islands, to which we shall refer immediately, and avows his own decided opinion, that Louis Philippe was dethroned by the divine anger because he sent them to Tahiti — an account of that prince's downfall which we may venture to reject, since the whole influence of his policy was directed against, and not in favour of religion.

In 1840, we have the testimony of M' Bennett, an English naturalist, and an apologist, as far as truth would permit, of the missionaries. The latter, he says, « speak of the native character in terms of severe reprobation. » We have seen, however, that in their public reports they spoke of it with admiration. And then he describes the actual state of Tahiti, where he saw « scenes of riot and debauchery that

(1) *Hist. Prop. Christianity*, vol. II, p. 191.

would have disgraced the most profligate purlieus of
London. It was vain to attempt to recognise, in the
slovenly, haggard, and diseased inhabitants of the
port, the prepossessing figure of the Tahitian, as pic-
tured by Cook! »

M' Bennett appears to have been as much struck
with the prosperity of the missionaries as with the
squalid misery of their disciples. Their « tastefully
furnished dwellings » attracted his notice, as also the
fact that « the principal sugar plantations at Tahiti
are those belonging to Mess" Bicknell, Henry, and
Pritchard » — all missionaries.

Of Raiatea, where Williams resided « for many
years, » he gives this account. Chastity was unknown,
« either in the single or the married state; » not
« even the most devout members of the church » having any respect for that particular virtue. « The
worst effects of debauchery, » he adds, were apparent
on every side. We shall hereafter find the same witness celebrating the « modesty » and other graces of
Catholic converts of exactly the same class. (1)

In 1841, M' Francis Olmsted reports, that « Tahiti
is far behind any of the Hawaiian islands in industry,
knowledge of government, and religion. » (2) Yet the
latter, as we shall learn in due time, are in a sufficiently deplorable condition.

In 1842, the very year in which M' Osmund depicted the extraordinary virtues which raised the Ta-

(1) *Narrative of a Whaling Voyage*, by F. Debell Bennett Esq ;
F. R. G. S.; vol. I, ch. III, pp. 81, 87 ; ch. IV, p. 109 ; ch. VII,
p. 220 ; ch. XI, p. 350.

(2) *Incidents of a Whaling Voyage*, by Francis Olmsted,
ch. XXVI, p. 312.

hitians to a level with « professing Christians in any
part of the world, » — we have an account of these
regions by M' Daniel Wheeler, an American philanthropist, and a member of the Society of Friends. He
was also an occasional preacher, and we could not
desire a more valuable or unexceptionable witness.
His evidence is perfectly conclusive. « There is
nothing, perhaps, in Tahitian habits more striking or
pitiable than their aimless, nerveless mode of spending
life. » « Certainly, » he says elsewhere, « appearances,
as to the religious state of the community, are unpromising; and however unwilling to adopt such a
conclusion, there is reason to apprehend that Christian principle is a great rarity. » (1)

M' Wheeler was not the salaried officer of a missionary society, and, having no fear of resentful « directors, » could afford to speak truthfully. Of Rarotonga, which M' Williams once described in such
glowing colours, he reports; « Out of the whole population of the island, I understand not more than *one
hundredth part* are regularly initiated into church
membership. » (2) Of Eimeo, he says; « The same
compulsory system which obtains in Tahiti ensures
for the present in Eimeo an external attention to the
services of the chapel, but the very existence of this
detestable regulation indicates unsoundness. The fact
that the poor native is subjected to a penalty if he
absents himself from the chapel, and the sight of a
man with a stick ransacking the villages for worshippers, before the hour of service, — a spectacle

(1) *Memoirs of Daniel Wheeler*, app. p. 757.
(2) P. 778.

we have often witnessed, — are so utterly abhorrent
to our notions that I cannot revert to the subject
without feelings of regret and disgust. » (1)

In 1845, Mr Wilkes, also an American Protestant,
affirms, that « in spite of the devotion manifested
within the church, the conduct of the women after
the service was concluded left room for believing that
their former licentiousness was not entirely overcome
by the influence of their new religion. » He notices
too the exorbitant cupidity of the native traders, and
that the Missionaries, in spite of their official enco-
miums upon their flocks, « bring up their own children
to look down upon them. » « I no longer wondered,»
Mr Wilkes forcibly remarks, « at the character, which
I was compelled by a regard for truth to give, of the
children of missionary parents in Tahiti. » Speaking
of the Paumotu Group, he says, that the catechists
employed by the missionaries « are ignorant of most
of the duties enjoined upon a Christian »(2)—and yet
thinks they may be usefully employed! What this
gentleman says of the Catholic missionaries, we
shall hear at the end of this chapter.

In 1847, another American writer, Mr Herman
Melville, reports, that « the hypocrisy in matters of
religion, so apparent in all Polynesian converts, is
most injudiciously nourished in Tahiti. » He also
remarked, like Mr Wilkes, that the missionaries kept
their children aloof from the natives, from fear of
contamination; « and yet, strange as it may seem,
the depravity among the Polynesians, which renders

(1) P. 763.
(2) *U. S. Exploring Expedition*, vol. I, ch. xv, p. 328.

precautions like these necessary, was in a measure *unknown* before their intercourse with the whites.» (1) The examples of M⁣ʳ Lewis, M⁣ʳ Broomhall, and the other English missionaries of the ship Duff, were surely not unlikely to produce such results. If the natives had now become incurably immoral, they might at least plead the example of their Christian teachers.

In the same year, Dʳ Coulter, an English physician, after a second visit to this unfortunate island, says; « I found Tahiti much as I left it. There was only one difference, and that was, the natives were evidently fast breaking through their missionary and temperance laws. » (2)

In 1849, we have two witnesses, M⁣ʳ Pridham, who prefers Buddhism to the Catholic religion, and M⁣ʳ Walpole. The former gentleman assures us that « too many » of the missionaries in the Pacific, as well as in the West Indies and South Africa, « have deemed a sordid greed and agrarian acquisitiveness, audacious exaggeration and the vilest hypocrisy, impudent meddling and vulgar insolence, to be necessary components of the missionary character »; and that they « added by their own presence a plague to the evils they had come to cure. » (5) The latter, more temperate in form, though equally emphatic in substance, writes as follows. « On the Missionaries it is dangerous to touch; but with all humility I would beg they might be first examined at home, to see if the

(1) *Omoo*, ch. XLVI, p. 177; ch. XLVIII, p. 187.
(2) *Adventures on the Western Coast of South America*, vol. II, ch. XVIII, p. 289.
(3) *Ceylon*, etc., vol. I, ch. VII, p. 444.

preacher is fitted for his task... And let them not
relate to the world such very exaggerated stories of
hardships and dangers; the untruth of these makes
many doubt the truth of any part of the account. »
Of the results of their work he gives this account.
« It is sad, as the eye rests on the scanty congregation which now fills the churches, to think how all the
good they did is passing away;... that faults and errors mainly brought this about may hardly with justice
be denied. » Presently he adds, — « nothing remains
but many, alas! of the vices of civilisation, and most
of the follies of the savage... day by day, the Missionary loses his hold, he has no longer temporal
power to back his precepts. » (1)

Yet there was a time — a period of many years —
when these men exercised supreme influence over the
natives, and declared to them all which they themselves
knew of the Christian religion. Dr Smith tells us that
they had a chapel in Tahiti of such dimensions that
they used to preach from three pulpits simultaneously.
« Brother Henry occupied the east pulpit, and preached
from » — no matter what; « Brother Wilson, in the
middle pulpit, preached from; — Brother Bicknell,
in the west pulpit, preached from. — » (2) And this
was the end of all the preachings of Ellis, and Williams, and Wilson, and fifty more. The Catholics
came, freedom was given to the native, and straight-
way the chapel, into which the Tahitians had so
often been driven by the scourge, became a desert.

Let us hear Mr Walpole once more. « The mission-

(1) *Four Years in the Pacific*, vol. I, ch. VII, p. 162; ch. V,
p. 84.

(2) *Hist. Miss. Societies*, II, 77.

aries were beginning to feel much straitened; already
the effects of the opposition were sadly operating;
their mission at Papawa was *deserted;* and the house
was empty, save Pomare the First's chair, which was
stored up, as a relic, I suppose. » Lastly, that we
may not omit all allusion to the special characteristic
of Protestant Missions, M' Walpole tells us of the
Samoan Group, « as every variety of dissenters exists
among the teachers, some confusion must occur in
the but half-awakened mind of the savage, as one
sect succeeds another at the different missionary stations. » (1)

And as time progressed, the witnesses still continue unanimous in their reports. In 1851, — for we
are approaching the end of the history, — D' Lang,
himself a missionary, thus describes his brethren in
Polynesia. « Missionaries who had been sent forth
with the prayers of the British public, and the benediction of the London Missionary Society, to convert
the heathen in the numerous isles of the Pacific, were
at length found converted themselves into stars of the
fourth or fifth magnitude, in the constellations Aries
and Taurus; or, in other words, in the sheep and
cattle market of New South Wales. » (2)

In the same year, the Rev. Henry Cheever, also a
missionary, though he lauds, in other places, both
himself and his order, in a moment of forgetfulness
breaks out as follows. « Becoming missionaries has
not made them saints, nor procured them exemption
from the ordinary infirmities and peccability of men;

(1) Ch. xvi, p. 368.
(2) *Hist. N. S. Wales*, vol. II, ch. xi, p. 459.

nor do we find the odour of sanctity, nor that
imaginary halo of holiness with which certain memoirs have surrounded the Missionary's person and
office. » (1)

In 1853, Captain Erskine, though a warm advocate of the missionaries, notices with indignation
their intolerable arrogance, and « dictatorial spirit
towards the chiefs and people. » « One of the missionaries, » he says, « in my presence sharply rebuked
Vuke, a man of high rank in his own country, for
presuming to speak to him in a standing posture! » (2)
And lastly, in 1855, Mr D'Ewes still repeats what
so many equally impartial witnesses had avouched
before him, — « the native Christian population,
except in name and outward observances, know little
of the real spirit of Christianity. » (3)

In the presence of facts attested, during so many
years, by Protestant writers, we are prepared for the
following account of Captain Laplace. After expressing his astonishment at finding that the missionaries
still possessed « the finest houses, the best estates,
extensive coffee and sugar plantations, as well as
the monopoly of all the trade with Europe, » that
officer thus describes his impression of the actual
condition of the natives. « These people, formerly so
gay, so happy, and so clean, and at the same time
so generous towards strangers, have become gloomy,

(1) *The Island World of the Pacific,* by the Rev⁴ Henry
T. Cheever, ch. vi, p. 135.

(2) *The Islands of the Western Pacific,* by John Elphinstone
Erskine, Capt. R. N., ch. iv, p. 131.

(3) *China, Australia, and the Pacific Islands,* by J. D'Ewes,
Esq., ch. v, p. 144 (1857).

dirty, brutalised, cheats, and liars. Such is the condition to which, with whatever good intentions, the
Protestant Missionaries have reduced Tahiti and its
interesting population. » (1) And with this testimony
we may close the series, offering no other commentary than the unwilling confession which has
been already quoted from one of their own professional advocates ; — « the European teachers have to
answer for *more evil* than will ever be compensated
by their most zealous services. »

We must not, however, terminate the history of
religion in the Society Islands, and the adjoining
groups, without a brief allusion to the incidents
which compose its final chapter, — the entrance of
the Catholic missionaries, and the fortune which
attended them. In Tahiti, as in New Zealand, they
disembarked on a hostile shore, and it was not from
the heathen, but from their christian rulers, that
they received the first blow. However cold the reception which had greeted them in the Antipodes,
however arduous the trials prepared for them, they
had at least nothing to apprehend from actual violence. In New Zealand there was a responsible government, guided by the inflexible maxims of European
polity, and which, though irritated and unfriendly,
would neither delegate its office to others, nor tolerate in subordinates an unprofitable tyranny of which
the ignominy would have recoiled upon itself. In
Tahiti, on the other hand, the Missionaries were
both the founders and the administrators of the civil
government. The power which had crushed the na-

(1) *Campagne de l'Artemise*, tome V, p. 389.

tives, and stamped out their national life, — which
had robbed them of their possessions, decimated them
by war, and instructed them in new forms of lubricity
and fraud, — was not likely to spare defenceless
strangers, whose very presence was at once a reproach for the past and a menace for the future.
How the missionary merchants of Tahiti confronted
the new enemy, and what was the final issue of the
combat, we shall now learn from the same impartial
witnesses who have already been quoted.

The first Catholic missionaries, who, fortunately
for the progress of religion in Tahiti, were subjects
of a nation which does not suffer its citizens to be
outraged with impunity, belonged to France. They
had scarcely landed when they were seized, as Captain Laplace relates with an indignation which was
both christian and patriotic, flung on board a small
vessel, and driven out to sea without even the clothes
and provisions necessary for the voyage which they
were forced to undertake. But we must not leave
such facts to the testimony of a Catholic witness,
however honorable and trustworthy. American Protestants, who speak from personal knowledge of all
the details, will describe to us this singular warfare.
« Invariably treated with contumely, » says M' Iler-
man Melville, in 1847, « they sometimes met with
open violence; and, in every case, were ultimately
forced to depart.... and finally carried aboard a
small trading schooner, which eventually put them
a shore at Wallis Island, a savage place, some two
thousand miles to the Westward! Now, that the
resident English Missionaries authorised the banishment of these priests, is a fact undenied by them-

selves. I was also repeatedly informed, that by their
inflammatory harangues they *instigated* the riots
which preceded the sailing of the schooner. Melancholy as such an example of intolerance on the
part of the Protestant Missionaries must appear, it
is not the only one, and by no means the most flagrant, which might be presented. » (1)

We shall see, indeed, worse cases presently, confessed by the missionaries themselves. The Rev. Walter Lawry, one of their number, whose proceedings
as a usurer and general dealer in New Zealand have
been described to us by his own companions, but
who was gravely styled in missionary reports « the
patriarch of the Pacific, » reveals the feeling which
inspired them all. « This people, » he says, speaking
of Tonga, « might be moulded to any thing at present, » — we have seen what the unhappy people of
Tahiti had been « moulded to » by the same hands, —
« but if a Romish priest should land there, what will
become of our fair blossoms?» And presently he cries
out, — « May it please the Lord to preserve this field
from the Roman ' boar out of the wood. ' » (2) The
prayer of the usurer was not destined to be heard;
and Commodore Wilkes, who mentions examples of
the barbarity of Mr Lawry's colleagues, records with
regret the inevitable effect, that « their intolerance
caused much remark among the natives themselves, »
and no doubt hastened the rapid desertion of which
the first symptoms coincided with the arrival of the
Catholic missionaries, and the introduction of a new
era of freedom and peace.

(1) *Omoo*, ch. xxxii, p. 124.
(2) *Friendly and Feejee Islands*, pp. 19, 95.

But the honest disgust of the natives was not the only result of these proceedings. « These islands, » says a German Protestant, « like the Sandwich group, have to thank intolerant missionaries for the difficulties they got into with the French nation — difficulties that overthrew their whole policy, cost them the independence of their country, and brought death and misery to hundreds of families. » (1) It is now a matter of history, that the imprudent violence of the missionaries, blinded by a mistaken calculation of their own commercial interests, had so nearly provoked a war between England and France, that only the moderation of M. Guizot, whose national ardour was perhaps tempered in this case by religious sympathies, prevented the collision. Mr Pritchard, — the hero of a contest in which blood was shed, but, as usual, the blood of the innocent, by whose death the guilty were saved, — seems to have regretted his own share in these transactions. He received indeed an indemnity, and the rank of Consul; but we cannot speak harshly of one who so far repudiated earlier faults as to offer his own house, at a later period, as a residence for the Catholic missionaries. He had perhaps learned, from the events of which he was a witness, to appreciate them at their real value.

We have seen that the first Catholic missionaries were transported by their merciful rivals to Wallis Island. Entering it as fugitives, they immediately commenced amongst its fierce tribes the apostolate

(1) Gerstaecker, *Voyage round the World*, vol. II, ch. VII, p. 255.

which had been so rudely interrupted, though only
for a brief season, in the milder region of Tahiti.
« The Catholic missionaries have commenced their
good work, » says M' Wilkes, « and are reported to
have performed it effectually. » He might well say
so, for already, in his own words, « they have succeeded in gaining over half the population. » (1) A
little later, as we shall learn hereafter, they had converted every soul in the island. And this was not the
only fruit of their forced dispersion. « While in the
Feejee group, » says the same gentleman, « I learned
that a Catholic Mission had already been established,
that it was prospering, and that it had already been
the means of saving an English vessel from capture,
by a timely notice to the crew. » It was thus that
they revenged themselves on their English persecu-
tors.

Meanwhile, their rivals, though the day of their
downfall was now at hand, continued inexorable to
the last, — that is, till the artillery of France was
ringing in their ears, and Admiral Dupetit Thouars
had obtained « perfect equality for Catholic and Protestant missionaries. » Thus at Apia, in the Samoan
Group, they would not even suffer the Catholic missionaries to land, but drove them away at once, refusing, with their accustomed charity, even a small
supply of provisions; and the men whom they thus
expelled, but who shortly after found an entrance,
are thus described by an English gentleman, whose
dislike of their religion could not restrain a reluctant
confession of their virtues. « The priests at Faleata,

(1) *Exploring Expedition*, vol. III, ch. v, p. 149.

the district where they lived, were most polished, gentlemanly men, spoke several European languages, and displayed so high a tone of feeling in their conversation, that one felt, alas! how, under such influence, their baneful doctrines would spread. They have already many converts, and gain more daily : there was certainly more tolerance and good feeling among them than in the other mission, *nor between the men themselves could a comparison be dared.* »(1)

What was the final issue of the combat which had already passed through its first phase, we shall see at the end of this chapter, not only as respects the Society Islands, but all the other groups of Eastern and Western Oceanica. Meanwhile, it is pleasant to hear from Mr Walpole, that as soon as the French missionaries had triumphed in Tahiti, by obtaining permission to announce to its afflicted people « the liberty wherewith Christ has made us free, » not only did they attract « every reverence and respect, » but all the dismal superstitions which had hitherto usurped the place of true religion gave way to innocent joy and peace. The whole island seemed to celebrate its resurrection from the grave, and, in the touching words of Mr Walpole, — « The native girls, no longer restrained by the wholesome dread of the missionary, used to assemble and dance in all the joyousness of recovered liberty. » It is a Protestant who describes this national festival in honour of the downfall of Protestantism. How complete that downfall was, we learn from the Rev. Henry Cheever, a Protestant missionary, who announces, in character-

(1) *Four Years*, etc., ch. xvi, p. 369.

istic language, in the year 1850, that « the roaring lion and raging bear of Frenchism and Romanism *have nearly devoured the Society Islands* » — a climax which Mr Cheever considers especially odious, on account of the comparatively limited commerce of the French nation. « There has never been, » he complains, « but one cargo of goods imported from France! » (1) It was intolerable to be defeated by people who did not even possess any « goods. »

Let us now quit for a time the Society Islands, cross the equator, and going northwards we shall reach a group lying in the 20th parallel of north latitude, of which the religious history is still more remarkable than that which has just been related. In the Sandwich Islands, which we are now to visit, the same facts occur again, but on a larger scale, and with still more impressive results.

It was in 1820 that the American Missions were first established in these islands. « They are actually inhabited, » we are told by Mr Caswall in 1854, « by large numbers of Americans, and the aborigines are rapidly wasting away. The government is, in fact, in the hands of Americans. » (2) For forty years they have now ruled in the Hawaiian group, with what success we shall soon learn. Meanwhile, let it be observed, that if they have failed, like the English in Tahiti, it has not been for want of means. In 1844, they had already *seventy-nine* missionaries in the Sandwich Islands, and had circulated nearly one hundred million pages of printed matter in the

(1) Ch. VI, p. 117.
(2) *The Western World Revisited*, ch. IX, p. 257.

Hawaiian tongue. (1) In 1853, the salaries alone
which had been paid to the missionaries up to that
date amounted to more than fifty thousand pounds
sterling, an expenditure which seems excessive, but
which is perhaps partly explained by the fact that
« nine of the mission families, » of which there
were forty, « numbered fifty-nine children. » (2) The
total « cost of missionary enterprise, » we are informed, exceeded nine hundred thousand dollars. (3)
The cost of a single « deputation » from the London
Missionary Society to their agents in the South Sea
was 7,920 l.; though this pleasant expedition was
described by the missionaries themselves, irritated
by the supercilious vanity of these luxurious tourists,
as only « a tour in search of the picturesque. » (4)

We are now to trace the effect of this enormous
expenditure, defrayed mainly by the generous contributions of the American people, who have a lively
interest in Christian Missions, display unbounded
liberality in their support, and have certainly a right
to ask how far it has accomplished the end which
it was designed to promote. But we must first notice
a fact, anterior to the operations of the American
missionaries, and too significant, as a presage of
events which occurred at a later period, to be altogether omitted.

In 1819, the year previous to the arrival of the
Protestant missionaries, the Abbé de Quélen, a cousin

(1) *Religion in the U. S. of America*, by the Revᵈ Robert
Baird, book VIII, ch. III, p. 691.

(2) Cheever, *The Island World of the Pacific*, app. p. 397.

(3) *Sandwich Island Notes*, by A. Haolé, app. p. 483.

(4) Forbes, *Unrefuted Charges*, etc., p. 31,

of the Archbishop of Paris, visited the Sandwich
Islands, on the occasion of the voyage of the French
frigate *Uranie*, of which he was the chaplain. Among
the visitors to the frigate was the chief minister of
the king; and this man, after a conference with
the Abbé, was converted and baptized. The Cross,
therefore, had won its first conquest; and it is perhaps to this occurrence that we may attribute the
phenomenon which the American missionaries remarked with astonishment, — the disappearance of
idolatry, « as if by miracle, » even before they commenced their labours.

Mʳ Jarves, an American writer who published in
1843 a History of the Sandwich Islands, apparently
with the sole object of defaming the Catholic Church,
and defending his countrymen from the reproaches
which then began to assail them from all quarters,
affects to regard the success of missions in the South
Sea as a struggle for « supremacy » between France
and America, and a question of « commercial advantages. » And this seems to be a popular view with
many of his countrymen. Mʳ Hursthouse, however,
remarks, with considerable force, that it was evidently intended to make the South Sea islands « a
select preserve for a handful of missionaries; » (1)
and the statement is confirmed by the proceedings
which we are about to relate.

It is undeniable that apparent success promptly
followed the appearance of the Protestant missionaries. The natives of Hawaii, like those of New
Zealand and Tahiti, easily comprehended the solid

(1) *New Zealand*, etc., by Charles Hursthouse, p. 51.

advantages which they might derive from association
with their new and opulent guests. Even M' Jarves
admits that « interest more than intelligence conspired
to produce an outward conformity, » and that the
barbarians accepted the religion of their masters
« because their importance was increased, and their
chance of political preferment better. » (1) And this
view of the subject has prevailed up to the present
time. « My subjects naturally wish, » said the king of
the Sandwich Islands in 1854, « to learn the English
language, which is employed in all public transactions. » (2) No doubt the words were written for the
poor savage by his advisers, who, as we shall see,
had long before that date relieved him of the care of
all « transactions, » both public and private.

The missionaries were now installed, and then
begon, once more, that eager race after wealth and
power, — cruel, greedy, and unscrupulous,— which
their own friends have so often narrated, but which
even they have rarely attempted to palliate. M' Bingham was for many years their leader, and Dingham
is thus described. « Dingham meddles in all the affairs
of government, » says Kotzebue, « pays particular
attention to commercial concerns, and seems to have
quite forgotten his original situation, and the object
of his residence in these islands, finding the avocations of a ruler more to his taste than those of a
preacher. » And again ; « that Bingham's private
views may not be too easily penetrated, religion is
made the cloak of all his designs.... Perhaps he al-

(1) *History of the S. Islands*, ch. x, p. 299.
(2) *Annuaire Historique Universel*, p. 233. (1854).

ready esteems himself the absolute sovereign of these islands. » (1)

Lord Byron, who was struck by the same facts, observes; « M' Bingham loses no opportunity of mingling in every business. » (2) M' Bingham's example was effectually imitated by his companions, each in his own sphere. « It will hardly be credited, » says Captain Sir Edward Belcher, « that one of the chief Missionaries took an active part in destroying a considerable cane plantation; that the ground was given for school or religious purposes; and that the same individual is now cultivating the proscribed cane on the same ground! » This independent witness speaks, in the same page, of « the tyranny of fanatics, who have already caused a disgust for the Protestant creed, and will probably, in the end, be expelled. » « No slavery under the sun, » he adds, « deserves to be questioned so severely as that of the Sandwich Islands. » We shall see presently in what it consisted. Sir Edward also tells us a fact which we might have ventured to anticipate, and which we have encountered in other lands, — « several have already *seceded from the Mission*, and are enjoying their rich farms. » (3) These men are every where the same.

M' Melville, though a Protestant and an American, confirms the evidence of these distinguished navigators in the following energetic words. « There is something decidedly wrong in the practical operations

(1) *Voyage round the World*, vol. II, pp. 255, 261.
(2) *Voyage H. M. S. Blonde*, p. 117.
(3) *Narrative of a Voyage round the World*, by Captain Sir Edward Belcher, vol. I, pp. 264, 270.

of the Sandwich Island Missions. Those who, from pure religious motives, contribute to the support of this enterprise, should take care to ascertain that their donations, flowing through many devious channels, at last effect their legitimate object, the conversion of the Hawaiians. I urge this not because I *doubt* the moral probity of those who disburse these funds, but because I *know* that they are not rightly applied. To read pathetic accounts of missionary hardships, and glowing descriptions of conversions, and baptisms taking place beneath palm trees, is one thing ; and to go to the Sandwich Islands, and *see* the Missionaries dwelling in picturesque and prettily furnished coral-rock villas, whilst the miserable natives are committing all sorts of immoralities around them, is quite another. » (1)

Mr Wheeler, also an American, could not help remarking the « comfortable houses of the missionaries, built, as nearly as circumstances will admit, in home style ; » while Lord Byron attests, that the men who were so indulgent to themselves displayed only rigour towards others. « The Missionaries, » he says, « forbid the making of fire, even to cook, on Sundays ; they insist on the appearance of their proselytes five times at church every day. » And this extraordinary system attained at length such a character of gloomy severity, except within the immediate circle of the missionaries and the principal chiefs, that Sir Edward Belcher, who judged it as a frank and intelligent Englishman, proposes this question : — « Is it reasonable to expect, that the

(1) *The Marquesas Islands*, ch. xxvi, p. 220.

millions inhabiting the islands in these seas can,
from a state of the most unlimited enjoyment, be
brought by this to believe that the christian religion
is to ameliorate their condition, when the very habits
and countenances of their would-be pastors are almost *distorted by severity?* » (1) The italics are his
own.

Lastly, Sir George Simpson, also an English
Protestant, recounts his impressions in the following
words. « The missionaries were regarded as the in-
ventors of a servitude such as the islands had never
known before; and, even during our visit, some of
our party, who were black, found themselves objects
of suspicion and fear, till they disclaimed all con-
nexion with the ' mikancries. ' » (2)

One of the effects of the ceaseless tyranny under
which the Hawaiians were now groaning, and which,
as Captain Laplace notices, rendered the missionaries « odious to the greater part of the natives, »
was a depopulation so rapid, that a prejudiced writer
in the Quarterly Review calls it « as unaccountable
as it is ominous. » (3) We have seen, however, and
shall see yet more clearly, that it is a law which has
no exception in heathen lands tenanted by Protestants. In the Gambier Islands, occupied by Catholics,
the population has sensibly increased; (4) while in
the Philippines, so long subject to the same influence,
we have seen, by the testimony of M' Crawfurd, that
« an immense social improvement » has accompanied

(1) *Narrative*, vol. II, p. 27.
(2) Vol. II, ch. xii, p. 103.
(3) July, 1859.
(4) Laplace, tome V, p. 351.

the presence of the Catholic civil and religious authorities, and the progressive increase of population
has followed the usual law in European countries.
In the Sandwich Islands, however, where Protestantism reigned supreme, we find the same frightful
declension which has marked its influence in the
Antipodes, in North America, in New Zealand, and
in Tahiti, — where two thirds of the whole population melted away in thirty years. Already in 1841,
Mr Olmsted, an American writer, reported, that, « the
depopulation of the Sandwich Islands is steadily moving forwards, and, unless it is speedily arrested, the
total extinction of the nation is inevitable. » « The
annual decrease of the population, » was then, « upon
an average, over six thousand. » (1) In 1851, the
Rev. Gustavus Hines, an American Protestant minister, after observing that, « the astonishing rapidity
of the decrease of the Hawaiian population is perhaps
without a parallel in the history of nations, » adds,
that in the course of four successive years it diminished by 21,730. (2) And Mr Dana, also an American
writer, reports at a still later date, that they are now
disappearing « at the rate of one fortieth of the entire
population annually. » (3) Yet the robust vigour of
this « doomed people, « as Mr Dana calls them, was
wont to excite the admiration of all the early navigators; and forty years ago, Von Langsdorff, noticing their strength and symmetry, declared, that
« many of them might very well have been placed
by the side of the most celebrated chef-d'œuvres of

(1) *Incidents*, etc., ch. xx, p. 262.
(2) *Life on the Plains of the Pacific*, ch. xi, p. 210.
(3) *Two Years before the Mast*, ch. xxviii, p. 174.

antiquity, and would have lost nothing by the comparison. » (1)

And now that we have seen something of the character of the missionaries, of the nature of their operations, and the effect of their presence, let us introduce without further delay, and as usual in the order of dates, the witnesses who will tell us what they have actually accomplished, during their long sojourn, towards the propagation of Christianity, and the social improvement of the natives.

We will begin, as before, with Mr Ellis, in 1829. In this case he was not personally concerned, and therefore revealed the whole truth. « Idolatry had indeed been renounced, » he says, referring to the period of his own visit, but « the great mass of the people were living without any moral or religious restraint. » (2) Perhaps nine years was too short a period for the desired change.

In 1830, Kotzebue gives us an actual specimen of a « convert », the Queen of Hawaii. « I enquired the grounds of her conversion. She replied that she could not exactly describe them, but that the missionary Bingham, who understood reading and writing perfectly well, had assured her that the christian faith was the best. If, however, she added, it should be found unsuited to our people, *we will reject it*, and adopt another. » (3)

In 1831, Captain Beechey says, « the residents in Honolulu well know what little effect the exertion of the Missionaries have produced; » and he adds that

(1) *Voyages*, etc., ch. IV, p. 108, (1813).
(2) *Polynesian Researches*, ch. XVIII, p. 544.
(3) Vol. II, p. 208.

« the system of religious restraint was alike obnoxious
to the foreigners residing upon the island, and to the
natives. » (1)

In 1832, D' Meyen, a Prussian naturalist, travelling with a purely scientific object, and free from
all religious prepossessions, confirms the testimony
which we have already received from witnesses as
capable and impartial as himself. He also speaks with
disgust and indignation of « the doings of the Missionaries who oppressed these islands, » and proves, as
an English writer observes, that « almost everything
had certainly *deteriorated.* » (2) « Let us publish it
aloud, » says this candid German, « it is neither the
glory of the Supreme Being, nor the zeal of a noble
vocation, which has impelled these hypocritical missionaries to visit these distant shores, but a greedy
cupidity, and an insatiable thirst for honours. »
Several of them, he adds, had already amassed a
considerable fortune, at the expense of the natives,
« who by their detestable frauds are reduced to
penury. » (3)

In 1833, one of their own witnesses admits, that
« in all the islands, » (4) though thirteen years had
now elapsed, only 669 were deemed Christians even
by such masters; and in the same year they confessed,
in an official report to the American Board, —
« Great numbers forsook the schools; the congregations on the sabbath were reduced at least one half; »

(1) *Voyage*, etc., vol. I, ch. x, p. 319; vol. II, ch. III, p. 101.
(2) *Quarterly Review*, vol. LIII, p. 330.
(3) *Annales*, tome VIII, p. 11.
(4) Missionary Report, quoted in the *Chinese Repository*,
vol. II, p. 379.

and they explain the defection by saying, « Multitudes became christians in form, never expecting that any thing else could be required of them. » (1)

In 1835, M' Reynolds, a scientific American Protestant, whose candid evidence about the Catholic missionaries shall be quoted hereafter, says calmly, « The improvement and advancement of these islanders has been considerably exaggerated. » (2)

In 1838, D' Ruschenberger, an American writer of the same class, forgetting national and religious prejudices, writes as follows. « The friends of the Missionaries have drawn overwrought pictures of the prosperity and prospects of the islands... Though we are all ready to accord our praise to the pleasing fictions of a novelist, we expect rigid accuracy from the pen of the divine, and are not disposed to allow him to envelop facts in the glowing language of a poetic fancy. » And then he goes on thus : — « The Missionaries stationed at the Sandwich Islands as a class are inferior to all those whom it has been our fortune to meet at other stations during the cruise. Many of them are far behind the age in which they live, deficient in general knowledge,.... and deal damnation, in a peculiar slang, to all whose opinions and course of life differ from their own. This is no sketch of fancy; and we can only lament there is no power to shield the pulpit from the vulgar spoutings of unlettered ignorance. » He adds, however, — « I have no doubt the ‘ Board for Foreign Missions ’

(1) *History of American Missions*, by the Rev⁴ Joseph Tracy, p. 242.
(2) *Voyage of the Frigate Potomac*, ch. xxii, p. 417.

sends abroad the best they have at command. • (1)
Yet it was at this very time that these singular missionaries wrote as follows to the Society which paid
them, and which always rewarded such language.
• The strength of religious principle among the
people, and their preparation to act from their own
convictions of duty, are more manifest than ever! •

In 1840, Commodore George Read, an American
officer, and Mr Debell Bennett, an English traveller,
record their impression of the progress of religion
and civilisation in the Sandwich Islands, by the
efforts of more than seventy missionaries, and an
expenditure of a quarter of a million sterling. The
former observes, with evident reluctance, • I must
say that the mass of the natives, notwithstanding all
the efforts of the Missionaries, appear to be still
indolent, licentious in disposition, and quite ignorant
of the term virtue. • (2) Yet this very year the missionaries wrote to their employers in these words :
« The past year has been one of signal triumphs of
divine grace ; • (3) and their employers printed and
circulated the report.

It is worthy of observation, that nearly twenty
years later, an English Protestant, — of a class which
is not yet extinct, and whose extraordinary ignorance
of the religion of St. Anselm and Sir Thomas More
is wonderful even in an Englishman, — confesses
that he heard a sermon, preached by a • Reverend

(1) *Voyage Round the World*, by W. S. W. Ruschenberger,
M. D., ch. XLIII, p. 464.

(2) *Around the World*, by Commodore George C. Read, vol. II,
p. 309.

(3) Tracy's *History*, p. 181.

Mr Parts, « in which the preacher informed his audience, consisting of three or four hundred natives,
« that the measure of their iniquities being full,
offended Heaven was about to cut them utterly off
from the land, that their place might be filled by the
children of a worthier race. » (1) The poor natives
had by this time been robbed of every thing else, and
even the missionaries could find nothing more to steal
from them but their land, which, with the help of
« offended Heaven, » they were prepared to do.

Mr Bennett speaks as follows of what he saw in the
Sandwich Islands. « In worldly matters the Missionaries in this group are particularly well favoured,
few of the foreign residents possess better dwellings,
or more available comforts. » Of Maurua he says,
« the females were bold in their amours, and the
people generally were more prone to petty larceny
than was altogether creditable to their morals. » And
then he went to the Lobos Islands, and at St. Lucas
Day he writes thus. « The inhabitants live contented,
and consequently happy; and their conduct towards
each other, as well as to ourselves, was equally
courteous and hospitable. The women are notable
and modest. *They* profess the Roman Catholic religion. » « The Jesuit missionaries, » he adds, — protestant travellers always call a Catholic priest a
Jesuit — « would appear to have performed their
duty with assiduity and success; the native Indians,
with the exception of a very few tribes, having
adopted in a great measure the language, religion,

(1) *Travels in the Sandwich and Society Islands*, by S. S. Hill
Esq ; ch. xx, p. 329.

and *habits* of their civilised teachers. » (1) Have
we not reason to say that the contrast, always
attested by Protestant witnesses, is every where
the same?

In 1842, the Protestant missionaries in the Sandwich Islands begin at last to confess, in their own
peculiar dialect, that » the assiduous efforts of the
papists have not failed of success painful to every
benevolent mind; » and that « Romanism has un-
questionnably made some considerable advances, and
penetrated many districts where it was before unknown. » (2) A little later they will give us more
ample information of its progress.

In 1843, we have the unsuspicious evidence of
Sir Edward Belcher, who not only asserts that the
general influence of the Missionaries is ruinous to the
character and happiness of the natives, but furnishes
the following instructive details. « Is it not strange,
with all the influence the American Missionaries are
said to have over the king, that it is not properly
exerted to improve his moral character? To compass
any object having for its end injury to the interests
of their own merchants they are keenly awake,...
yet they permit the pattern, by which all law acquires
moral force and energy, to commit sins and inconsis-
tencies, not only without control, but without expressing their opinion in that manly form which they
pretend their mission so imperatively demands of
them. » And then he adds, as if to complete the picture, — « Perhaps the greatest excesses are commit-

(1) Vol. II, ch. 1, pp. 9, 10.
(2) *Missionary Herald*, vol. XXXVIII, p. 473.

ted *within the missionary circle*, which includes the
king and chiefs. » (1) M' Stewart, himself an American missionary, but who was perfectly candid because he had abandoned the work, confirms incidentally this statement of Sir Edward Belcher, when he
tells us, that Riho-Riho « attended all the services of
the day, » though during the week he had been « in-
toxicated four or five days. » He appears at last to
have died in that state. (2)

In 1845, M' Melville, though an American, says;
« Not until I visited Honolulu was I aware of the
fact that the small remnant of the natives had been
civilized into draught horses, and evangelised into
beasts of burden. But so it is! » And then he goes on
to describe « a Missionary's spouse, who day after
day, for months together, took her regular airings in
a little go-cart drawn by two of the islanders. » (3)

And this singular fact is confirmed by M. Duflot
de Mofras in 1844, who noticed that « the natives
now discharge the office of beasts of burden; » (4)
and by a correspondent of the *Sandwich Islands Gazette* in 1839, who relates that he saw « a heavy
horse waggon drawn by fifteen females, harnessed
like beasts of burden, and found that they were performing a penance imposed by the Missionaries. » (5)
But to return to M' Melville.

(1) *Narrative of a Voyage*, etc., vol. I, p. 261.
(2) *Journal of a Residence in the Sandwich Islands*, by
C. S. Stewart, p. 110. 2ᵈ edition.
(3) *The Marquesas Islands*, ch. xxvi, p. 218.
(4) *Exploration du Territoire de l'Orégon*, etc., tome II,
ch. III, p. 87.
(5) Quoted in *Asiatic Journal*, vol. XXXI, p. 48.

This vigorous though indelicate writer sums up his observations in these words. « How little do some of these poor islanders comprehend, when they look around them, that no inconsiderable part of their disasters originate in certain tea-party excitements, » — he alludes to the « missionary meetings » at home, — « the *object* of which is to ameliorate the spiritual condition of the Polynesians, but whose *end* has almost invariably been to accomplish their temporal destruction. »

But he cites facts also in confirmation of his opinion. When Lord George Paulet, in 1843, released the unfortunate natives from the tyranny of their missionary rulers, and gave them at length an opportunity of showing whether their profession of religion was voluntary, and how far the missionaries had really acted upon their hearts and minds,—then was revealed, as in Ceylon and in Tahiti, the true character of Protestant converts from heathenism. « Who that happened to be at Honolulu during those ten memorable days will ever forget them! The history of those ten days reveals in their true colours the character of the Sandwich Islanders, and furnishes an eloquent commentary on the results which have flowed from the labours of the Missionaries. Freed from all restraints of severe penal laws, the natives almost to a man plunged voluntarily into every species of wickedness and excess, and by their utter disregard of all decency plainly showed, that although they had been schooled into a seeming submission to the new order of things, they were in reality as depraved and vicious as ever. » (1)

(1) *Appendix*, p. 285.

In 1849, Mr Walpole, a gentleman whose prejudices against the Catholic religion even the facts
which he unwillingly records fail to admonish, writes
as follows. « The great interest I feel for the natives,
and my heart felt desire for their well being, lead me
to deplore much that the missionaries have done; and
happy indeed should I be to hear the grave aspersions
they labour under disproved. The bitter persecutions, *even to death*, of natives who for conscience
sake preferred to die, rather than betray their Roman
Catholic faith, and the undenied monetary dirtinesses
they are accused of, are grave charges indeed. » (1)
We shall hear presently what he says of the Catholics, and of *their* pastors.

In 1850, Mr Berthold Seeman, after noticing,
apparently with surprise, that « the majority of the
king's counsellers are seceders from the American
Mission, » — missionaries converted into officers of
the state, — adds; that their royal pupil still permitted himself « all kinds of unholy and immoral
practices; » (2) and in the following year, Mr Gerstaecker found that, owing to « a severe attack of
delirium tremens, he was not fit to be seen during
my whole stay in Oahu. »

In 1851, we come to a writer with whose evidence
we may terminate these extracts, — representing exclusively the opinions of eager Protestants — not
because he is the latest in date, but because his
confessions are so frank and abundant that it would
be superfluous to add to them. The Rev. Gustavus

(1) *Fours Years in the Pacific*, vol. I, ch. XI, p. 249.
(2) *Narrative of the Voyage of H. M. S. Herald*, by Berthold
Seeman, F. L. S.; vol. II, ch. IX, p. 153. (1853).

Hines, an American Protestant Missionary, whose extraordinary candour we can only attribute to the fact that the Sandwich Islands were not the permanent sphere of his own labour, has recounted with considerable detail the actual results of Protestant missions, after thirty years of uninterrupted effort. The imprudent and interested exaggerations of earlier days were now to be finally exposed and rebuked, and it was impossible that the sentence should be pronounced by a more competent or impartial judge. Two years later, Captain Erskine noticed the « exaggerated accounts, » the « phraseology repugnant to readers of ordinary taste, » the tyrannical spirit of the Protestant and the courtesy of the Catholic missionaries. Mr Dana also, though an American Protestant, registered the proverb, « that the greatest curse to each of the South Sea Islands was the first man who discovered it; » and again, that « the curse of a people calling themselves Christian seems to follow them every where. » And Mr Gerstaecker had remarked, in the same year, as a fact which met his observation every where, that « the Missionaries' estates are among the best on the island. » (1)

But neither of these writers could speak with the authority of Mr Hines. And it required some courage to tell the whole truth. For many years a certain section of American Society had been fascinated with romantic tales of the triumphs of Protestantism in the South Sea. One is almost ashamed to quote, even by way of specimen, the language which was addressed to every missionary meeting, and always

(1) *Voyage round the World*, vol. II, ch. II, p. 86.

greeted with enthusiastic applause. « The smiles of
Jesus, » wrote the Rev. M' Green, « on the efforts
made to convert the inhabitants of Hawaii have been
signal : » (1) and they immediately sent him five
thousand dollars as a reward for words in which the
profane and the ludicrous struggle together for the
mastery. Yet this was the common phraseology of
the missionaries, during a long course of years, in
the reports which they forwarded to the United
states: and it was the influence of such reports which
extracted from women and children — for we can
hardly suppose that grown men were amongst the
subscribers — upwards of one million dollars, to be
consumed by the missionaries and their families in
the Sandwich Islands. M' Hines will tell us, though
a Protestant, a Missionary, and an American, with
what effect this prodigal expenditure has been attended, and he will speak from his own experience
and observation.

« Notwithstanding all that has been done for their
benefit, the state of the native Hawaiians *is still truly
deplorable*, » after thirty years of uninterrupted missionary effort ! « To call them a christianised, civilised, happy, and prosperous people would be to
mislead the public mind in relation to their true
condition.... To an enquiry which I made of the
Rev. Lowel Smith, one of the missionaries in Honolulu, concerning the prosperity of the natives, I received this reply : ' The evident tendency of things
is *downward*. ' Downward it is rapidly, in point of

(1) Quoted by Strickland, *History of the American Bible Society*, ch. xxv, p. 211.

11.   11.

numbers, and if the ratio of decrease shall continue
the same for only a few years, it does not require the
eye of a prophet to see what will be the result. The
epitaph of the nation will be written, and Anglo-
Saxons will convert the islands into another West
Indies. » (1)

A little later, Mr Hines offers this summary of his
experience as to the ultimate results of missionary
influence.

« Religion, in every department of Hawaiian society, however genuine the system which is taught
there may be, » — it is due to him to say, that he
does not seem to have even suspected its genuine-
ness, — « is of a very superficial character. Of this
the missionary residing among them is more sensible
than any other man can be, and one of them, in
answer to the enquiry, ' How many of your people
give daily evidence of being christian? ' replied;
' *None*, if you look for the same evidence which you
expect will be exhibited by christians at home. ' »
And Mr Hines declares that this account of them is
true, « from the hut of the most degraded menial to
the royal palace. » Yet if the reader will consult the
annual « Reports » of the missionary societies, he
will find, that they never cease to represent the
triumphant progress of religion, education, and social
order, among these very people, of whom *privately*
the missionaries gave only such accounts as Mr Hines
received from them.

Let us hear Mr Hines once more. « In attending
the native churches one is struck with the listlessness

(1) *Life on the Plains of the Pacific*, ch. xi, p. 232.

and inattention which prevail in the congregation. No
matter how important the truths, or how impressive
the manner of the speaker, he seems scarcely to
gain the hearing of the ear. » (1)

Finally, as if he thought that such an account of
a missionary work continued for more than thirty
years, at enormous cost, without let or hindrance,
and by people claiming to be the only advocates of
« scriptural religion, » required the support of some
terrible and conclusive fact, Mʳ Hines informs us,
that the immorality of this nominally converted people
is so shameless and universal, that « it is not an easy
matter for an Hawaiian to tell who his father is. »

If perchance the reader has by this time forgotten,
in following the course of so different a narrative,
the account of Missions in the Philippines, conducted
by apostles and martyrs, with which this chapter
opened, he may now be conveniently reminded of it.
« In examining the new social state of the Sandwich
Islands, » says Admiral Jurien de la Gravière,
in 1855, « I was involuntarily reminded of the Indian
of the Philippines, joyous and free to this hour under
the yoke of the law which he confesses, finding in
the ceremonies of religion the recreation which he
most prizes, and in the doctrines of his simple faith
fewer subjects of discouragement than of hope. » (2)
Such, once more, is the contrast between Catholic
and Protestant Missions, between the work of God
and the work of man.

But that contrast admits of fuller illustration, and

(1) Ch. xIII, p. 253.
(2) *Revue des Deux Mondes*, tome III, p. 38, (1853).

it is the main object of these volumes to supply it
We have seen that the later history of Tahiti furnishes further evidence of it; but that evidence may
be supplemented by the still more striking incidents
which have occurred in the Hawaiian group, and
in the other islands of the South Sea. There was a
class of converts of whom Mr Hines makes no mention, though Mr Walpole has candidly told us that
they resisted, « even to death, » all inducements to
abandon the Catholic faith. Perhaps Mr Hines had
not mixed with them, or found it embarassing to
speak of them. Others will supply the defect in his
narrative, and disclose the facts which he seems to
have wished to suppress.

Seven years elapsed from the visit of the Abbé
de Quélen to the Sandwich Islands before another
Catholic missionary landed on their shores. In 1826,
a prefect apostolic, attended by two companions,
arrived at Hawaii. The ground was preoccupied, and
all human influences were against them, but they
immediately commenced their mission of mercy.
Protestant writers will tell us how they fared, and
what was the issue of their labours.

The intelligent historian of the *Voyage of the Potomac*, who saw and conversed with these first missionaries, generously says, and Dr Meyen uses almost
the same words; « They were men of learning, and
agreeable manners and conversation, and, in all their
acts and behaviour, appeared sincerely pious. Pleased
with their manners and instructions, the natives
came in numbers to be taught by them, so that the
school and place of worship began to be crowded...
They never attempted to draw the natives to them-

selves, except by amiable and kind deportment. Indeed, they were exemplary in all their actions. *But
their success was too great*, and they were ordered to
discontinue their worship... The natives were forced
from their houses of worship by native soldiers, ordered by authority... finally, the Missionaries were
conveyed to the coast of California, on board a little
rickety vessel, and there inhumanly set ashore, on a
barren spot, and distant from any settlement! » (1)
The deportation had been effected with such complete
success that one of them died on the passage, and it
was only the corpse of the Abbé Bachelot which was
carried to land.

In this first combat the Protestant missionaries
gained an easy triumph. But the day arrived, which
they should have foreseen, when they were summoned to justify an action which France was not unlikely
to chastise, and which all that was noble in England
and America condemned. Their defence contained
only two pleas, — the first, that the violence was
the act of the native authorities; the second, that the
Catholic missionaries were justly banished, because
« permission from the government to remain had
never been obtained, or even asked. » (2) With respect to the latter statement, we do not read in the
Acts of the Apostles that St. Paul was accustomed to
« ask permission » from the heathen to preach Christ
to them, or that he refrained when forbidden to do
so.

(1) Reynolds, ch. xxii, pp. 417-18.
(2) *Refutation of the Charges brought by the Roman Catholics
against the American Missionaries at the Sandwich Islands*, p. 14.
Boston, 1843.

It is true that it was once made a reproach to the Master Himself, « *contradicit Cæsari;* » but it was reserved for Protestant missionaries to rebuke His servants for presuming to preach the Gospel, without having first obtained the permission of that pitiful caricature of Cæsar, the king of the Sandwich Islands. Mr Mark Wilks — who eagerly defends them, and observes, with a well-timed pleasantry, that their Catholic rivals « were conveyed *to the diocese of California* » — gravely affirms, that the latter ought to have obeyed the Polynesian magistracy, and that it was « shameless effrontery to set its laws and police at defiance. » (1) The Jews, who imprisoned St. Peter and scourged St. Paul, were probably of the same opinion, and chastised the « shameless effrontery » of those Apostles with the same energy which Mr Wilks applauds in the Sandwich Islanders.

With respect to the plea that it was « the authorities » who banished them, we may leave the answer to Protestant writers.

Dr Ruschenberger, who had discussed the matter with Bingham, who was the real « government, » writes with the candour of an educated and liberal American. « A leading member of the Mission told me, » he says, « he had no doubt but that answers which he gave to questions on the subject by the chiefs had very considerable influence upon their determination... It is clear to my mind that the missionaries embraced every opportunity to present the Roman Catholics in the hideous aspect in which they themselves view them. I am convinced that the mis-

(1) *Tahiti,* etc., by Mark Wilks, p. 10. (1844).

sionaries were the cause of their expulsion. » (1) Sir
George Simpson also says, « some of the Protestant
Missionaries were, beyond all doubt, chiefly responsible; » and he adds, that it was not bigotry alone
which influenced them, but that « there is strong
reason for suspecting that their real motives were
in a great measure secular. » (2) Mr Gerstaecker,
though unfriendly to the Catholic missionaries, declares without hesitation of the same proceedings, « the
Protestant preachers, in their mad, intolerant zeal,
excited the easily moved natives more and more by
their sermons; » (3) and he evidently agrees with
Sir George Simpson as to their motive.

The conflict of which we have seen other examples
had now commenced in earnest, and was sustained
on the part of the Protestant missionaries by actions
which we should have refused to credit, if they were
not attested by their own friends. It seems impossible
that the scenes which we are about to describe should
have been enacted in the nineteenth century. From
the hour in which the « little rickety vessel » bore
away to California the exiles of whom only two were
destined to reach it alive, and who were inhumanly
exposed to such a fate, as Protestants tell us, for no
other crime than this, that « their success was too
great, » Hawaii and all the islands of the group were
filled with the loud clamour of their enemies. Europe
was many a league across the sea, and the avenger
seemed to tarry. And so from every hill and valley
went up the cry of rage and malice against the Catholic

(1) Ch. XLIII, p. 474.
(2) Vol. II, ch. XII, p. 115.
(3) Vol. II, ch. VII, p. 236.

missionaries, whose virtues were a perpetual rebuke,
like the calm face of Mordecai standing in the gate ;
as well as against the converts who had dared to
follow them for their wisdom, and to love them for
their truth. Protestant writers, generous and upright
men, declare with one accord, that nothing could
surpass the atrocity of calumny and invective of
which they were now the victims. Every pulpit re-
sounded with the maledictions heaped upon them ;
and even the native teachers, hired for wages to
repeat the lessons of their masters, hurried hither
and thither to re-echo words which they neither
believed nor understood. Mr Cheever, exulting in the
excesses which he records, recites the following extract from a sermon, probably of his own composition,
preached by « a native assistant missionary. » « Believe not that the Pope is God; he is nothing but a
man, whose dwelling place is in Rome. » (1) Such
were the instructions offered to the people of the
Sandwich Islands, in spite of their urgent need of
other precepts, day after day, and hour after hour,
by lips whose accents had long filled them with
terror and dismay. They might mock Christianity by
their lives, and outrage every enactment in its moral
code, so long as they consented to frequent the Protestant chapels, and forfeit their land and their goods
to Protestant missionaries; but they must at least
hate the Pope, and learn to revile his ministers,
even when inviting them to virtue. Let crime reign
through all the land, as Mr Hines says, « from the
hut of the most degraded menial to the royal palace, »

(1) *The Island World of the Pacific*, p. 157.

but let not the hated rivals who had shown that they could break its spell gain a footing amongst them.

But it is time to speak of events which, though cruel and barbarous, it is impossible to regard with unmingled regret, because they served to reveal the character of the Catholic converts, and prepared the way for the final triumphs of the religion which had made them what they were. It was by their sufferings, according to the immutable law of Christian Missions, and by the constancy with which they endured them, that thousands were led to embrace the faith which had inspired so much courage and fortitude. Long before the decisive act which led to the death of the Abbé Bachelot, the measures which the Dutch adopted in Ceylon, and the English in Tahiti, had been employed by the Americans, — not without indignant protests from their countrymen,— throughout the Sandwich Islands. M. Bachelot himself, not long before he commenced his last and fatal voyage, wrote thus to his friends in Europe. • Our Christians continue to be persecuted, but in the chains with which they are loaded their attachment to the faith seems to redouble. After years of seduction and violence, during which our enemies left no means untried, *there has not been a single example of apostasy amongst them.* • Even the examples which we have already seen of invincible constancy in the inhabitants of China, India, and Ceylon, hardly prepare us for such a display of fortitude in the Sandwich Islanders. But grace produces everywhere the same fruits. M. Bachelot continues as follows.

• The mode of punishment now adopted is to have the Catholics conducted in chains to the public

necessaries, and to oblige them to remove with their
hands the most disgusting ordures. The triumph
which the Methodists seem then to enjoy consists in
listening to the railleries of which the Catholics are
the objects. They, however, support all with joy,
because, they say, ' religion is our only crime. ' » (1)
And when this tale reached Europe, confirmed by
Protestant testimony which we will presently quote,
it awakened that righteous indignation of which
Captain Laplace was the worthy instrument, and
filled the sails of the frigate *Artémise*, which bore
freedom to the Hawaiian Catholics, in 1839, after
thirteen years of oppression and servitude. « History
will record, » said an eloquent French voice, « that
men who dared to call themselves ministers of a
civilizing religion, in the middle of the nineteenth
century, in the face of heaven and earth, condemned
Christian females to gather up daily with their hands
the ordures of a garrison ! »

And these were not the only tortures inflicted by
the Protestant missionaries upon the Hawaiian natives, who dared to believe in the midst of infidelity,
and to be virtuous when surrounded by corruption.
They were beaten, imprisoned, worn out with heavy
labour, and sometimes starved, but all in vain.
A Catholic woman being cruelly beaten with a stick,
because she refused to attend the Protestant worship, her husband made this observation, worthy to
be compared with the historic words of the early
confessors. « Before I became a Christian, I should
have thought it no harm to revenge my wife, by kill-

(1) *Annals*, vol. I, p. 353.

ing him who struck her; but I was silent, and recollected that the first Christians did not complain when their limbs were cut off, and that they offered their bodies to the flames for Jesus Christ. » And M. Bachelot, who relates this anecdote, adds; « Many of the natives were so touched by this example of truly christian patience and resignation, that they have asked to be instructed, notwithstanding the dangers to which they are exposed from the Protestant Ministers. » He tells us also, that « the English Consul, » a worthy representative of his great nation, « manifested his sympathy for the prisoners. » Some he took under his immediate protection, but his generous aid came too late, for « many of them died shortly after, victims of the hardships they had endured. » (1)

It is not to be supposed that such incidents could occur without exciting the lively indignation of the residents in these islands. We have seen in what terms they are noticed by English and American writers; and Sir Edward Belcher has told us, that « the tyranny of fanatics, » — « illiterate fanatics, » Mr Forbes calls them, « with cargoes of bibles and religious tracts, » (2) — inspired « disgust » in men of all classes. M. Casimir Henriçy, one of the officers of the *Artémise*, who « mingled with the natives day and night in their huts, » discovered that « the missionaries are cordially detested by the population. Their insatiable cupidity has made them objects of horror. Ferocious oppressors, shameless monopolisers, trafficking in the Word of God, they have pro-

(1) *Annals*, vol. I, p. 355.
(2) *California*, by Alexander Forbes Esq., ch. V, p. 237.

cured for themselves a concert of curses. » But they were wearing out the patience both of God and man, and the hour of their humiliation was at hand.

An American Protestant writer'informs us, in 1854, that when they ventured to confirm their failing dominion by the extreme measure of forcibly expelling the Catholic missionaries, so great was the sympathy in favour of the latter, that « their stay was encouraged by the *English* and French officials. » (1) And so universal had this feeling now become, even amongst the better class of Protestants, — perhaps because they found their commercial pursuits frustrated by the jealousy of the missionaries, who aimed at keeping the whole trade of the islands in their own hands, and after robbing the natives endeavoured to ruin their own countrymen, — that even the local journals began to espouse the cause of the Catholic victims. In the *Protestant Gazette* of the Sandwich Islands, of the 29th of June, 1839, the year in which M. Bachelot perished, the following anecdote is narrated. Two native women being « accused of the crime of Catholicism, » one of them was suspended from the branch of a tree, « her toes scarcely touching the ground, » the other to a projecting beam of a house, « her feet tied with a chain. » For eighteen hours they were left in this condition, when they were forcibly delivered by some Europeans, in an almost lifeless state. One of these charitable persons had previously gone to inform Bingham, the missionary dictator of Hawaii, of what was taking place. Mr Bingham, we are told, « came in his coach,

(1) *Sandwich Island Notes*, by A. Haolé, p. 55. (1854).

but contented himself with observing, that ' he would
not interfere with the execution of the laws of the
country. ' ' In saying this, he put his horses to the
trot, and drove off. ' » (1) Yet M' Dingham has written a book, filled with Scripture texts, from Genesis
to Revelations, and celebrating his own exploits, not
as a ruler or a merchant, but as a preacher of the
Gospel, and a minister of Christ.

And now let us record the final result of these
extraordinary proceedings. In July, 1839, Captain
Laplace arrived, and M' Dingham and his friends
were informed, in accents which they could not mistake, that the Catholic natives of Hawaii had found
a protector, strong enough to defend the oppressed
and to chastise the oppressor. The patient constancy
of thirteen years was now to receive its due reward.
« The natives who had been victims of persecution, »
says Captain Laplace, « and had confessed their faith
amidst the most cruel treatment, now manifested
the utmost joy. » But in the Sandwich Islands, as
in the other groups of the South Sea, they were as
moderate in the day of triumph as they had been
resigned in adversity. When the Captain of the frigate *Allier* resolved to make an example in the island
of Futuna, where Father Chanel, a French missionary, since Beatified, had been cruelly murdered; it
was Bishop Pompallier who solemnly protested
against the threatened vengeance, declaring that they
had no need of human justice, and that they would
perish to the last man rather than invoke its aid.
And when the ship had departed, her gallant crew

(1) Quoted in the *Annals*, vol. I, p. 530.

more filled with admiration of the missionaries than
hatred of their cowardly oppressors, Bishop Pompallier remained among this sanguinary tribe, till he
had converted the king of Futuna and the assassin
of the Blessed Father Chanel, and baptized one hundred and fourteen of his subjects with his own
hand. (1) At the present day, Futuna is said to be
not only wholly Christian, but to present the most
extraordinary example in the Pacific of complete and
effectual conversion, in its largest sense. (2)

But it was not the Catholic natives only who were
now released from their bonds, and able at length to
worship the God of Christians in peace and security;
the Protestants also, profiting by the interference of
Lord George Paulet and others, threw off the hated
yoke of the missionaries, and solaced their long privations by one immense and frantic debauch. *They*
also had a season of joy, but it was the joy of animals,
not of christian confessors, who had earned, by patient endurance in trial, the right to sing a canticle of
praise and thanksgiving. And now the conditions of
the conflict which had lasted so long were no longer
the same. The Missionaries of the Cross went about
their work in peace, and Protestants will tell us how
they prospered. They were still feeble in all human
resources, but upon these they were not accustomed
to rely. The Vicar Apostolic of Eastern Oceanica
wrote gaily from the Gambier Islands, in 1837, in
these words : « During the first years of the mission
we lay upon hurdles, and had no other seats than

(1) IV, 331.
(2) *New Glories of the Catholic Church*, ch. v, p. 254.

blocks of stone, or trunks of trees. I administered
baptism in one of our chapels to eighty persons, and
during the ceremony used for my episcopal throne
the back bone of a whale! « (1) « The priests are fortunate, » he added, « when they can find time to mend
their clothes and wash their linen. » And six years
later, in 1843, when the Bishop visited Fathers Chevron and Grange at Tongataboo, « the destitution in
which we found them drew tears from our eyes. » At
Wallis also, « we found Father Bataillon, » afterwards Bishop, « without hat and without shoes,
having only miserable clothes in rags. » (2) And then
they embraced, like St. Paul and his fellow missionaries, and went on their way rejoicing.

They had reason to rejoice, for all their desires
were accomplished; and in bringing this chapter to a
close, we will now briefly describe the results which
they have already obtained. Let us begin with Honolulu, because it is the principal city of that Hawaiian
group which Protestantism had made its own, but in
which Catholics had purchased, by patient suffering,
the right to a final and undisputed triumph.

In 1847, Sir George Simpson, a Protestant writer,
and a British official, who had closely watched their
operations in other lands, gives this report. « In
addition to being engaged in building a large cathedral, the reverend fathers kept two schools, which
were attended by about *nine hundred* young people of
both sexes, natives and half-breeds; and many of the
pupils had made great progress in various branches

(1) I, 230.
(2) VI, 28.

of education, while a few of them spoke French
with considerable fluency. The new faith *was daily
extending its influence among the natives,* through the
untiring zeal of its teachers; but though it was no
longer exposed to legal persecution, yet it was still
subjected to the rude anathemas, spoken and writ-
en, of the Protestant Missionaries. We had a good
deal of intercourse with the priests, visiting their
schools and occasionally attending their chapel, and
were, on the whole, strongly prepossessed in their
favour. • (1)

Perhaps it is due to this generous Protestant to
confirm his account by at least a specimen of the language which the baffled missionaries now habitually
used. At an earlier period, while they still hoped to
banish the Catholic missionaries by violence, they
had gravely reported to their employers; • It is matter of devout thankfulness that the islanders are so
well prepared for these events by the extensive prevalence of piety among them • — though they probably smiled at one another as they wrote it. A little
later, they begin to change their tone, and tell their
paymasters; • We are unable to measure the disastrous consequences which have resulted, and which
will continue to flow, from the introduction of • the
Catholic Missionaries, • and their efforts among this
people. We mourn that any of our flocks ' are so
soon turned aside into another gospel, ' but this has
been permitted by the great Head of the Church for
wise and holy purposes. • At last they lay aside all
restraint. • They have wandered after the Beast, •

(1) Vol. II, ch. XII, p. 113.

is now their account of the natives who were deserting them in thousands. « As the Man of Sin advances, » they say in one of their official reports,
« he developes more and more of his real character...
But his days are numbered; his bounds are fixed;
beyond these he cannot pass. » If they purchase the
temporary return of one or two of their fugitive disciples, they cry out; « They have escaped out of
Sodom » ! And then these men, fed with the spoils
of their unwilling hearers, and whose own religion
was perhaps the least attractive caricature of Christianity which the world has ever seen, say of the
Catholic Faith; « The spread of *this heresy* amongst
us has a tendency to humble our hearts. » (1) Sir
George Simpson does not appear to have done them
any injustice.

A little earlier, M' Forbes, also a Protestant writer, contrasting with much animation the two classes
of missionaries, whose proceedings he also had diligently and honestly compared in various regions,
commends the paternal wisdom of the Catholic pastor, « indulging the innocent foibles and propensities
of the natives; » and then notices « the sour, ascetic
methodist, who takes from his own followers, » but
not from himself, « all their pastimes and pleasures;
but it must be admitted, » he adds, « that the contrast in the numerical results of their conversions is
no less striking. » The Protestant, this traveller says,
« takes away the few comforts the poor savage enjoyed — and what does he give him in return? Why,
he promises him, that if he lay aside the song and

(1) *Missionary Herald*, vol. XXXVIII, pp. 480, 81.

the dance, foregoes all pleasure and mirth, puts on a sour instead of a laughing countenance, attends to the rapsody of the preacher — then he promises, that he may *perhaps* escape from being damned for ever, and avoid passing his eternity amid fire and brimstone prepared for him in the world to come. » (1) And this somewhat grotesque picture, as Dr Ruschenberger allows, « is no sketch of fancy, » but an exact image of what met the eye and ear of English and American travellers, wherever they directed their course among the islands of the Pacific.

In 1849, we have the testimony of Mr Walpole, who arrived after the epoch of persecution had come to an end. After describing the Protestant church, he says; « In the town now stands a Roman Catholic cathedral, » the building of which Sir George Simpson had marked the rapid progress; « and I much fear *the congregation of the one tends daily more and more to the other.* Of the Abbé, who is at the head of the Roman church here, no eulogy would be too high. Their schools are excellent, and they invite scrutiny... They have now about *twelve thousand converts;* one hundred schools; *three thousand pupils...* Most earnestly is it to be hoped, that by strict purification of *themselves,* and more strenuous exertions towards the natives, the teachers of the pure Gospel will endeavour to regain the ground they have lost. » (2)

And now we have heard enough of the Sandwich Islands. Here was the result of thirty years of Pro-

(1) *California,* p. 241.
(2) Ch. xi, p. 249. Cf. *The Natural History of the Varieties of Man,* by R. G. Latham, M. D., p. 201.

testant effort, and to this bitter humiliation, — the
scorn and compassion of their own friends, — the
« teachers of the pure Gospel, » as M' Walpole calls
them, had come at last. « In this single island, » says
a Catholic missionary, — and after hearing so many
Protestant witnesses, we may well claim to listen to
one at least of our own, — « more than five thousand persons have, within twelve months, forsaken
the ways of error to follow those of truth. » And then
he speaks, not with anger, but with a kind of gentle
compassion, of his mortified rivals, reaping at length
the fruits which they had improvidently sown; and
seems almost to pity men who, « after such vast
sums had been expended during many years, saw
what they used to call their Model-Mission more
than half overturned, in so short a time, by a few
poor missionaries, destitute of every thing, and
without any other support than the Cross of their
Divine Master. » And if the evidence of this victim
of their cruelty be deemed insufficient, here is their
own account, addressed to the Missionary Society in
America, of the same facts.

In 1843, they had confessed, « the number of
Hawaiians baptized by the Roman priests is 12,500,
besides some in a course of preparatory training; »(1)
and at another date they gave the following details.
« In the districts of Kona and Waimea on Hawaii
the papists number many converts and boast great
things. On Kauai the excitement in consequence of
the spread of Romanism is considerable. Two priests

(1) *United States American Board for Foreign Missions*, Reports, p. 186.

are there labouring with indefatigable zeal, and we
are sorry to say they have a good deal of success...
On the Niihau, where there is a population of about
one thousand, it is said a considerable number of
the people have joined them. On Oahu they number
many followers, and in the districts of Waialma,
Waianae, and Koolauloa it is thought that nearly one
third of the population have gone after them. » (1)

But it was not only in the Society and Sandwich
Islands, with whose religious history we are now
sufficiently acquainted, that the Catholic missionaries had defended their Master's cause. In the Philippines, as we have seen, they had carried His Cross
triumphantly through the ranks of Pagan and Mahometan legions; in all the other groups they had
used it as a sword to resist the cruelties of mercenary
zealots. And every where the result was the same.
From Tahiti, as we have seen, they were transported
to the savage shores of Wallis Island, where it was
hoped they might find an obscure and unknown
grave. Vain project! and cruel as it was vain. In
1841, Father Bataillon could report that « out of
2,300 inhabitants which the island of Wallis contains, 2,000 are already converted. » And in the following year his report is in these words. « The Bishop, Monseigneur Pompallier, is about to quit us,
after having baptized and confirmed all the inhabitants of the island. Glory and benediction be given to
the infinite mercy of God! Thanks be rendered to
Mary, our august Queen, to whom, immediately on
my arrival in the island, I consecrated it. This is-

(1) *Missionary Herald*, vol. XXXVIII, p. 473.

land, but lately abandoned to the most ridiculous
superstitions, to the grossest vices, now adores the
only true God, the Creator of heaven and earth,
and the one only Saviour, Jesus Christ, His Son.
The conversion of Ouvea is, in my opinion, one
of the greatest prodigies of our time. It was, according to the account of every body, the wickedest
island of Oceanica... How great is God in His works!
How do the weakest instruments become strong in
His hands! »

In the same year, Father Chevron, whose apostolic destitution forced tears from the eyes of his
Bishop, says; « A living faith, an ardent charity,
extreme delicacy of conscience, and an insatiable
avidity for the Word of God, such are the virtues
which we see flourishing here. The natives pass half
their nights in prayer, in mutual instruction, in the
singing of canticles, and in reciting the rosary. Their
ardour in the exercise of piety is solely the effect of
grace. »

Towards the close of the same year, Father Viard,
afterwards Bishop, mentions that sixty natives of
Wallis, who had been absent two years, and had
been baptized by Protestant missionaries in another
island, returned, under the guidance of a chief who
was the brother of the king. They were full of malice
and calumnies against the Catholic religion, of which
they knew only what the Protestant ministers had told
them; but Father Viard adds, « several of these
erring islanders have already been converted. » Of
the king himself, Father Chevron relates that he said
to Bishop Bataillou; « I thank thee for thy affection
towards me. I was ignorant. I repulsed thee. I wish-

ed to drive thee away. But thou didst love us. Thou
hast taken patience; thou hast suffered much. I thank
thee. In saying these words large tears filled his eyes.
How powerful is grace! *Potens est Deus de lapidibus
istis suscitare filios Abrahæ.* »

In the Gambier Islands equally auspicious results
followed the patient labours of the missionaries.
A few words will suffice to describe them. The Holy
Sacrifice of the Mass was offered for the first time in
this group on the 13th of August, 1834; and by the
9th of May, 1835, almost all the inhabitants had
been converted and baptized. In 1851, a Protestant
writer, a friend of M' Pritchard of Tahiti, thus
attests, in characteristic language, this surprising
fact. « Within the last seven years, three French
missionaries, of the papal persuasion, have established
themselves upon the island of Mangareva; and the
control they have contrived to acquire over the simple
inhabitants must be seen to be believed : it is so
absolute, that their very movements appear to be
guided by what the missionaries would think of
them. » (1)

It was not to be expected that this gentleman
should notice, what he probably did not know, that
in these islands is witnessed one of those marvellous triumphs of religion, which Protestants do
not pretend to emulate even at home, much less
among savages, and which only the immense power
of divine grace can explain. In 1841, six years after

(1) *Rovings in the Pacific*, vol. I, ch. xi, p. 284. « In modo
che nel 1838 non eravi più un pagano. » Wittman, *Storia Uni-
versale delle Cattoliche Missioni*, vol. I, cap. iv, p. 162. (Mi-
lano, 1843.)

their conversion, these islands had already produced
a large number of those peculiar «spouses of Christ, »
whose glorious privilege it is to be united to Him by
a kind of sacramental marriage. « They now amount
to *fifty three*, and are entirely separated from the
rest of the natives. For nearly five years they have
continued to live in the most edifying manner. Five
schools are kept by them in the great island....
amongst the boarders are all the young girls of the
royal family. » (1) Who will refuse to praise God for
such a fact? the crowning token and evidence of the
working of His Holy Spirit. A false religion can
indeed produce, at particular epochs, a few simulated
« religious, » of whom the best always end by becoming Catholics; while the rest are of that class of
whom the great Bishop of Hippo speaks as « *hæreticæ
sanctimoniales,* » and whom, with all the weight of
his great authority, he solemnly charges to bear in
mind, that « an obedient wife is better than a disobe-
dient virgin. » (2)

« I am sure, » says the Vicar Apostolic, — in a
letter to the Superioress of the Convent of the Sacred
Heart in Paris, — « that you would recognise in the
greater number of these young persons sufficient
obedience and piety to form excellent novices. I know
not whether you have amongst your own children
any of more grave or modest deportment. We do
not seem to attach any importance to their pious
assemblies, but we often admire the virtue and angelic
purity of these young hearts which have received in

(1) *Annals*, II, 255.
(2) *In Psal.* 45, tom. IV, p. 564.

Baptism a new creation. Of what is not the grace of
Jesus Christ capable! »

It is not surprising that missionaries who could
convert even the pagan savages of the Pacific into
humble and devout religious, capable of choosing
Mary's « good part, » and of dwelling alone, in
secrecy and silence, at the feet of Jesus, should find
no difficulty in teaching the same class those ecclesiastical principles which the best order of Protestant
ministers proclaim in vain to educated hearers in
England and America. A young native of Oahu, who
had made some progress in Latin composition, wrote
a letter to the superior of a religious community in
Paris, in which, after contrasting the success of his
Catholic teachers with the convulsive but sterile
efforts of the Protestants, he added this explanation.
« It is because *the net of St. Peter* is fit to catch
the fish. The net of the heretics takes nothing,
because Jesus Christ does not assist their fishing,
and has not entered their bark. » (1) Such is the
reflection of a converted savage on the contrast
which only divine grace could have taught him to
appreciate.

In the island of Akaman, Father Honoré Laval
relates that a chief, who had heard that a Protestant
missionary was coming from another island, informed
him how he proposed to deal with the expected
emissary. « I will ask him who sent him; if he does
not say, ' Gregory, ' » — the Pope who had sent the
French missionaries, — « I will say, begone, you
are no missionary of Jesus Christ. I shall ask him

(1) *Annals*, II, 258.

in the next place, to whom do those children and
that woman belong? he will answer, they are mine.
Begone, I will say, you are no missionary. Jesus
Christ had no wife, and His missionaries have none.
We are the children of Peter, and you are only a
man like us. » (1) It is probable that this worthy
chief was wholly ignorant of the fact, that he was
closely following the advice of no less a person than
St. Francis of Sales, who, long before the Gambier
Islands had been discovered, gave this exhortation
from his pulpit : — « O mes frères, tenez cette
preuve pour fondamentale, et demandez à ceux qui
vous veulent retirer du sein de l'Église : *Quis te
misit*? » (2)

We have almost completed our history, in which
these is no variation from the first to the last page.
In the Marquesas, Dʳ Russell confessed, in 1843,
that every Protestant effort had ended in utter failure; and Mʳ Melville repeats, in 1846, « the Protestant Missions appear to have *despaired* of reclaiming these islands from heathenism. » Of the
Church of England mission to the Falkland Isles
Mʳ Parker Snow says, in 1857, after a fruitless
expenditure of 10,000 l., — I could not shut my
eyes to the fact that the mission was a failure. » (3)
At Nukahiva, where Dʳ Coulter found three American
missionaries in 1844, « the insults of the natives
were scarcely endurable, and I was afterwards told

(1) *Annales*, tome IX, p. 156.
(2) *Sermon pour le Dimanche de la Septuagésime*, Œuvres,
tome II, p. 56.
(3) *Two Years Cruise off Tierra del Fuego*, vol. I, ch. XVIII,
p. 271.

that they were obliged to leave it. » (1) The terrible
Feejee islands, as Captain Laplace notices, they did
not even attempt, till others had prepared the way,
« leaving the field perfectly free to our poor missionaries; who, by force of patience and devotion, amidst
a thousand cruel fatigues and privations, supported
with a truly evangelical resignation, braving martyrdom every day, have partly effected amongst the
ferocious inhabitants of this sombre archipelago the
same admirable work which they had already accomplished in the Gambiers. »

At Upolu, in the Navigator Islands, M^r D'Ewes,
after noticing the absence of Protestants, describes
« the Catholic Cathedral, with a large establishment
and school attached to it, that appeared to be well
attended. » (2) In the Solomon Islands, where Bishop
Epalle was martyred, on the 16th of December, 1845,
we might trace the same facts; and so well was the
contrast between the two classes of missionaries
understood, even by American Protestants, that Captain Porter, who visited Madison's Island, where he
charitably endeavoured to « explain to the natives the
nature of the christian religion, » frankly says; « Had
a Catholic priest been with me at the moment, he
might have made converts of every individual in the
valley. » (3) Lastly, even a Secretary of the London
Missionary Society confesses of another island, far
distant from these which have been mentioned, —

(1) *Adventures in the Pacific*, by John Coulter, M. D., ch. xv,
p. 212. (1845)
(2) *China*, etc., ch. vi, p. 170.
(3) *Cruise to the Pacific Ocean in the U. S. Frigate Essex*,
vol. II, ch. xv, p. 114.

« With regard to Mauritius, the only party increasing rapidly is the Roman Catholic. » (1) The facts, then, are every where the same, and every where there is a Protestant witness to reveal them.

We have now examined with sufficient, perhaps with excessive, minuteness the history of Missions in Oceanica. Upon that history we need offer no comment. Protestant writers have sufficiently performed that task, and have even accepted, at least in part, some of the practical conclusions which it suggests. It is from *them* we have learned both the virtues of the Catholic missionaries, and the vices of their rivals,—the constancy displayed by the converts of the first, and the immorality and misery of the nominal disciples of the last. As early as 1843, M' Jarves, the anti-catholic historian of the Sandwich Islands, was already lamenting that « from present appearances it is to be presumed that Roman Catholicism will eventually settle into a flourishing sect. » M' Olmsted, a graver but equally prejudiced writer, had also told his American readers, that the Catholic missionaries had « gained a permanent footing upon many of the islands of the Pacific ; » and had added, with unconcealed regret, his own opinion, that « their religion is destined to have the ascendancy in most of these islands. »

We have seen how these anticipations were gradually accomplished, throughout all the islands of the South Sea, in spite of persecutions prolonged through many years, and of cruelties which would have been more consistent in Chinese mandarins

(1) *Tour in S. Africa*, by J. J. Freeman, ch. XVI, p. 387.

than in Protestant ministers. The whole narrative
is before us, — from that great « manifestation of
pious zeal » which was displayed in the voyage
of the ship Duff, whose passengers, we have been
told, exhibited religion « in her native purity, »
to the death of the abbé Bachelot, and the final
humiliation of his assassins. With the past, then,
thanks to the candid histories of Protestant travellers, we are sufficiently acquainted : and if we desire to look into the future, the actors in these varied
scenes are themselves willing to assist us in the attempt. It is a Protestant missionary who assures us,
in language worthy of himself and his cause, that
« the natives of the South Sea Islands appear to be a
people upon whom the Mother of Harlots» — that is,
the Catholic Church — « shall operate for the purposes of superstition and error. » (1) It is thus that
he confesses the unwelcome fact, which even he can
no longer deny, that the battle is over, and the victory won, — a victory so complete, that twenty
years ago, in 1840, there were already in Oceanica
7 Catholic Bishops, 1,200 priests, and so great a
multitude of converts that even this host of pastors
was insufficient for the work. And then this Protestant witness adds, in words with which we may more
fitly close this instructive history than by any observation of our own, that as he and his companions
failed to convert the natives while they were heathen,
their only remaining hope is to corrupt them now
that they are Christians. He admits indeed that this
will be considerably more difficult, and does not af-

(1) *Friendly and Feejee Islands*, p. 133.

fect to be sanguine of success; but he is willing at least to reveal the final issue of Protestant missions in Oceanica, and the real character of those who took part in them, in these notable terms. « Unless we bestir ourselves, the probability is, that wo shall have to convert many of the South Sea islanders from Popery, instead of from Heathenism, which is much more difficult and dangerous. »

———

CHAPTER VII.

MISSIONS IN AFRICA.

More than a thousand years after the Roman empire had passed away, the land of Africa — a name which once included only the provinces of Tunis and Tripoli — was still to the inhabitants of Europe only the narrow but fertile region which stretched from Egypt to Morocco. Of the vast continent which extended in an unbroken line nearly 5,000 miles towards the south, — far away beyond the Atlas mountains, beyond the great Desert, beyond the sources of the Nile, the Niger, and the Senegal, — Europe had no knowledge. And when at length, in the fifteenth century of our era, the mariners of Portugal weathered with slow and hesitating course the

Capes which had barred the way to all former navigators; planted colonies on the banks of the Rio
Grande and the Gambia; won for their king the new
title of « Lord of Guinea; » established their apostolic missionaries in the heart of Congo; and finally,
under the guidance of Bartholomew Diaz, gazed with
wonder and awe on the « Stormy Cape, » which from
that moment became to all Europe the « Cape of Good
Hope; » — even the boldest would hardly have ventured to predict that the flag of Portugal would soon
be carried past it in triumph by Vasco de Gama, on
his return from the Indies, in the last year of the
fifteenth century. It is of this land, of which every
bay and gulf and promontory have since become
familiar to us, that we are now to speak.

In attempting, however, to trace the outline of the
history of missions in this vast continent, we encounter for the first time a difficulty from which there
is no escape. In the narrative which we have now to
present there can be neither unity nor connection,
because there is none in the regions to which it refers.
The four extremities of Africa, corresponding with
the cardinal points, have been hitherto as completely
isolated from one another as though the united waters of the Atlantic and Pacific were spread between
them. Egypt is almost as effectually separated from
Guinea, Morocco from Abyssinia, Tunis from Kaffraria, Angola from Natal, as though the Andes had
been piled on the Himalays to part them asunder.
It is not one nation or people of which we have now
to speak, but many; distinct in their origin, their
history, and their customs. In one respect only they
seem to have a common destiny. When the prophet

of old proclaimed the curse of the Avenger upon
Egypt and Ethiopia, — when he said to the first,
« I will deliver Egypt into the hand of cruel masters; » (1) and to the second, « Woe to the land
which is beyond the rivers of Ethiopia, » (2) — the
malediction was not for a time, but for ages and
generations, mighty enough to over-leap the frontiers
of many lands, and to run like a consuming fire
through all the wide plains of Africa, from the Red
Sea to the Atlantic, and from the mouths of the Nile
to the Indian Ocean. And so enduring, as it seems,
has been this ancient curse, — though we are sure
it has changed its character since the coming of the
Redeemer, — that even at the present hour it appears
a kind of paradox to speak of religion in connection
with Africa, as palpable as if we were to search for
the snows of the Caucasus, or the cool streams which
they discharge, in the burning sands of the Sahara; so
that we are almost tempted to turn away, with doubt
and fear, from any enquiry into the religious annals
of a land whose history seems to be summed up in
this one fact — that it is still, after a thousand years,
the home of the Moor, the Negro, and the Kaffir.

Yet even here we shall trace once more the contrast which it is our purpose to illustrate in all lands;
even here we shall see, as we have seen elsewhere,
the unchanging beauty and power of the Church, the
feebleness and confusion of the Sects; even here we
shall learn what manner of men they are, and what
they can accomplish, who bear a divine commission;

(1) Isaias, XIX, 4.
(2) XVIII, 1.

and also, what comes of pretending to do an apostle's work without an apostle's vocation.

Let us begin with the northern provinces — Algiers and Morocco, the Numidia and Mauritania of the Romans; Tunis and Tripoli, the *Africa Propria*, whence Carthage sent forth her fleets against the mistress of the world; and Egypt, where even now the promise begins to be fulfilled which said of old, « In that day there shall be an altar of the Lord in the land of Egypt. » A few words, however, must suffice, for we have hereafter to pursue our way round all the long coasts of Africa; and it is not here that the Cross has won its accustomed triumphs, nor the Church her wonted victories, though here St. Augustine preached, and St. Louis died. « With St. Austin, » says a modern writer, « the Church of Africa expired. » (1) Already in the third century, schism and heresy, sure precursors of final apostasy, had spread like a plague along the Southern shores of the Mediterranean; till in the sixth, the avenging hordes came out of Arabia which in the fifteenth were to vanquish the last Constantine in the capital of the Western Empire, and barbarism swept away in a common destruction both religion and civilization.

It would be beside our purpose to offer even a sketch of the earlier history of these ill-fated provinces. Corrupted almost from the beginning by heresiarchs of every school, — at one time over-run by Donatists; at another convulsed by the Arian excesses; or cruelly scourged by the Vandal kings,

(1) *L'Afrique Chrétienne*, par M. Jean Yanoski, p. 45.

with whom the Donatists leagued themselves out of
hatred to the Church; (1) or yet more grievously chastised by the Arab inundation under the Caliph Omar
in 547, till 150 years later the Roman name was
finally effaced from Africa, and the Moors embraced
the religion of their Arab conquerors; — these unhappy lands are still paying the penalty of guilt not
yet absolved, and even at the present hour, with the
exception of a single region, are the special field of
that « great and momentous struggle between Islamism and Paganism » (2) of which Africa has been the
most remarkable theatre during nearly a thousand
years.

If, however, the provinces of North Africa have
not yet been reconverted from the Mahometan apostasy, it has not been for want either of apostles or
martyrs. In the single year 1261, more than two
hundred Franciscans were martyred by the Mussulmans; and not long after, as if this were an incom-
plete sacrifice, one hundred and ninety Dominicans
received from the same hands the baptism of blood. (3)
We may not stay to relate their history. They knew
what destiny awaited them; yet from Lyons and
Genoa, from Rome and Naples, they hurried to the
battle field, content to shed their blood that others
might one day gain the victory, of which that blood
was to be the price. Forty years earlier, in 1219,
St. Francis of Assisi left Ancona on the same errand;
but though even the ferocious Moslem bowed in re-

(1) *Histoire de la Domination des Vandales en Afrique*, par
Yanoski, p. 85.
(2) Barth, *Travels in Africa*, preface, p. 22.
(3) Henrion, tome 1, ch. vi, p. 61.

vereuce before him, and declared that « *God alone could have formed such a man,* » he gained admirers only and not disciples; and at length was forced to admit, in spite of the charity which filled his soul, that their hour was not yet come, and to speak to his fellow-labourers those memorable words — « Away from this place; let us fly, let us fly far from these too humane barbarians, whom we can neither compel to adore our Master, nor to persecute us who are His servants. » (1)

Yet Africa was not abandoned by Christian charity, ever as ingenious in repairing defeats as patient in enduring them. In 1630, the Franciscan John de Prado, still honoured as the patron of Tangier, sealed with his blood the new mission which he had founded, and of which a living writer observes; « There is nothing more sorrowful, from the beginning to the end, than the history of this mission, perpetually destroyed, yet perpetually springing up again from the ashes of the martyrs. » (2) In 1646, the institute of the Lazarist Fathers, who are now scattered through the whole East, from the banks of the Nile to those of the Yellow Sea, was founded by St. Vincent of Paul. Other religious societies had preceded it, and it was to the Fathers of the Order of Mercy that the captive Cervantes, while planning in his dungeon the liberation of 25,000 Christian prisoners, owed his own redemption from the Moors. (3) But of all the missionary communities which have chosen

(1) « Les Maures sont les hommes les plus doux de la Barbarie. » *Alger*, par M. P. Rozet, p. 0.

(2) *Le Maroc*, par M. Godard, p. 10.

(3) *Algeria, Past and Present*, by J. H. Blofeld Esq., p. 297.

Africa for the field of their labours, none have surpassed the children of St. Vincent; who, as Count St. Marie relates in 1845, not only « rendered important services to commerce, but many of them acquired great influence with the Deys, who often appealed to them for counsel in questions of difficulty. Their influence has protected the Christians from much misery. » (1) And another Algerian authority notices the still more striking fact, that when France, in a moment of delirium, cast out the family of one of her noblest sons, Tunis afforded them protection and succour. « The venerable establishment founded by St. Vincent of Paul, » says Baron Baude, « received protection from the Divan when, in an access of stupid impiety, the Convention destroyed it. A Catholic Church was consecrated at Tunis, and the ministers of the Dey contributed 16,000 piastres towards its construction. » (2)

Even in Morocco, it was not till the year 1822 that the Franciscans were finally restricted by the Sultan to Tangier, and that the Catholic Church ceased to be represented throughout the empire, except by a single religious of the province of San Diego in Andalusia. « The revolutionary follies from which Spain has failed to preserve herself have caused this result, » says a French missionary, filled with the generous ardour of his order and nation; « and if the province of San Diego has no longer strength to cultivate the heritage of its fathers, more energetic

(1) *Algeria in 1845*, by Count S¹ Marie. cb. v, p. 185, English edition.

(2) *L'Algérie*, par le Baron Baude, ex-commissaire du Roi en Afrique, tome II, p. 363.

workmen will receive from the Holy See its abandoned patrimony. » (1) But we must revert for a moment, before we consider the actual state of religion in North Africa, to an earlier epoch.

The story of the combats of the children of St. Dominic and St. Francis, by whose blood the sterile soil of Africa was so often moistened, and to whom its future conversion will be mainly due, need not be recounted here. Whatever divine charity could inspire, or superhuman valour attempt, was dared by men who were so little discouraged by what seemed perpetual failure, that it was the sure promise of tribulation which most powerfully attracted them to this thankless land. Some were captured even before they could touch its shores; others fell almost within sight of the vessel which they had scarcely quitted; while the rest carried hope and consolation to many a captive whose bonds they lightened by sharing them, or wasted away in dungeons which their presence converted into sanctuaries.

And the toils of these victims were not in vain, though the Moslem thought their defeat final, and the world deemed their work madness. The Church will yet reap the harvest of which they planted the seed. It is to what they did while on earth, and perhaps still more to what they have done since they quitted it, that we may attribute the blight which has now fallen upon Islamism, once so arrogant and mighty, and the ignominy and decrepitude in which the mortal enemy of the Cross is pining away before the eyes of Christendom, no longer united, in arms

(1) *Le Maroc*, p. 18.

or in faith, against the common foe. The dead have won the victory of which the living are to gather the spoils.

And already, as we shall see more fully when we enter the lands which lie to the east of the Nile, the blood of the martyrs is yielding its accustomed fruit. If St. Francis fled away from a people who offered to himself the homage which they refused to his Master, the children of St. Francis have at this day altars at Jerusalem, at Bethlehem, at Nazareth, « wherever the history of the Redemption has left a memorial. » This has been their reward. And the same recompense another Saint seems to have won for North Africa. When St. Louis lay on his bed of ashes, assisted in his last moments by the Bishop of Tunis, and exclaiming with his latest breath, — « For the love of God let us obtain the preaching of the Gospel in Tunis; » in that hour, as a Christian writer of our own age observes, « he obtained for France the privilege of one day regenerating Africa. » (1) Let us see how far France has fulfilled her mission, and with what prospects of future success.

Once more we shall be able to refer, as in former chapters, to Protestant writers, whom Providence seems everywhere to employ to this end; and our first witness is an eminent clergyman of the established church, widely known amongst his countrymen as an able and learned writer. This gentleman will inform us, with the candour which might be expected in so distinguished a person, that the Church still produces in the nineteenth century exactly the

(1) Baron Henrion.

same class of evangelists whom St. Augustine led in the fifth and St. Francis in the thirteenth.

Of the See of Algiers, and its two first occupants, Mr Blakesley speaks in the following terms. « The See has since its constitution been filled by prelates of great zeal and intelligence, and the influence of the clergy has done much towards improving the character of the European part of the population. » Their first efforts were directed, as charity required, to the amelioration of that vagabond class of soldiers and adventurers who swarmed in Algeria from the earliest period of the invasion, and whose coarse immoralities were a scandal even to the natives; so that the Kabyles, as Colonel Walmsley notices, were accustomed to say of the French — « they do not follow the doctrines which they profess. » (1)

They might well say it, considering the character which even French writers have given both of the military and civil colonists of Algeria. Not only the common soldiers, by their boastful impiety, have too often shocked both the Moor and the Arab; but even amongst the officers, as Count St. Marie relates, « there are few examples of honourable conduct. » If France has done more than any modern nation to promote the glory of God, she has also done more to outrage it. « Since your religion is so noble and beneficent, » said Abd-el-Kader to the Vicar General of Algiers, « why do not the French observe it? » (2) And the answer which some of them have made to this reproach is a cynical jest such as the following. « Depuis l'évêque et le procureur-général, » says

(1) *Sketches of Algeria*, by H. M. Walmsley, p. 138. (1858).
(2) *Annals.*

M. Pellissier, « jusqu'au sacristain et au garde champêtre, on pourrait à la rigueur se passer de tout en Algérie, mais on ne saurait se passer de l'armée. »(1)

It was with the embarassments resulting from the profaneness of his own countrymen that the first Bishop of Algiers had to contend, and amongst his greatest difficulties his successor still reckons « des discours d'une infernale perversité tenus aux indigènes. » (2) Even the civil administration, infected by the spurious liberalism of the age, and adopting the maxims of government which modern statesmen have consented to borrow from protestant sources, has often been openly hostile to the progress of religion. The Sisters of Charity were ordered to remove the crucifix from their hospitals, — a command which they refused to obey, — lest the sensitive conscience of the Arab should be wounded; and a formal censure was addressed by the minister of war to the Bishop of Algiers, in 1846, for not repressing efficaciously the « proselyting schemes » of the Sisters, (3) — which consisted in recommending their dying patients to have a care for their souls. As late as 1850, the celebrated Père de Ravignan presented a memorial to the minister, in which he solicited liberty to preach the Gospel to the Arabs, and the petition appears to have received no reply. (4)

(1) *La Colonisation Militaire en Algérie*, par E. Pellissier, p. 18.
(2) *Lettre Pastorale* de Monseigneur Pavy; *Orateurs Sacrés*, tome LXXXIV, p. 1082, Ed. Migne.
(3) *La Colonisation de l'Algérie*, par Louis de Baudicour, ch. VII, p. 265, (1856).
(4) *Vie du R. P. Xavier de Ravignan*, par le P. A. de Ponlevoy, tome II, p. 100.

It was in the midst of such discouragements that
the first Algerian prelate commenced his formidable
mission ; while two priests in Algiers, one at Oran,
and another at Bone, comprised in 1839, as Mr Blakesley remarks, « the whole of the ecclesiastical establishment in the French possessions of North
Africa. » Within seven years, however, the Bishop,
Mgr Dupuch, « had established, almost entirely at his
own cost and that of his friends, forty-seven churches
and chapels, and forty almouries, hospitals, prisons,
penitentiaries, and other institutions, which employed thirty-nine regular and three supernumerary
priests, besides a large number of Sisters of Charity. »

A French authority observes that, by the year
1846, he had 91 priests, 60 churches, and 140 Sisters of various orders. (1) Such were the works of
the first Bishop of Algiers, of whom the great leader
of the Arabs, even when flying from the French
arms, said to the Abbé Suchet ; « I know all that he
has done for Algeria, and have a great veneration for
him person. » (2) So universal is the admission both
of his private virtues and of the success of his labours, that M. St. Marc Girardin could say, with
general approval, « of all our establishments in Algiers, the strongest and most efficacious is the bish-
opric. » (3)

« M. Pavy, the successor of M. Dupuch, carried

(1) *Histoire de la Conquête d'Alger*, par M. Alfred Nettement,
p. 624.

(2) *Annals.*

(3) Quoted by the Revd Thomas Debary, *The Canary Isles*, etc ,
ch. xxiv, p. 301.

on the work which the other had begun with no less
tact than vigour, and so far as French power is con-
solidated in Northern Africa, it is mainly due to the
moral influence of the clergy. ' And then M' Blakesley, a witness as capable as he is truthful, describes, as far as a stranger could, by what process
that influence was acquired. ' They operate upon the
natives, not by formal attacks upon their creed, but
by those works of charity which are common to
Christianity and Islam, and which more than any
other religious act are appreciated by the votaries of
the latter. The hospitals especially, into which the
Moslem population is freely admitted, and the service
of which is, in many cases, performed by females of
one or other of the religious orders, exercise a powerful influence, and most deservedly so, over the
conquered race. I visited one of these — the civil
hospital at Oran — and was exceedingly struck with
the appearance of cleanliness, order, comfort, and
even cheerfulness, which reigned throughout. The
calm demeanour of the Sisters seemed to be felt like
a sun beam in the chamber of death. There was no
sourness of look, no parade of self-devotion, no expression of the least wish for any thing but more
ample space to enable them to receive all the patients
that offered. I talked of the unhealthiness of the summer season, when the wards would be full of fever
patients; but I could not elicit a word implying that
they themselves would then be exposed to greater
risk, or compelled to greater labour. The Apostle's
exhortation to let works of mercy be done with
cheerfulness came forcibly into my mind, when I
thought of the conventional unction in which the

philanthropists of London platforms are wont to indulge. » (1)

Other Catholic institutions receive from Mr Blakesley equally generous notice, and especially the orphan asylums originated by Père Brumault, of the Society of Jesus, and conducted with the most auspicious results, in spite of the vexatious meddling of the administration, which tried to extort from him a pledge that he would not convert the orphans to Christianity! The Maréchal Dugeaud, to whom he appealed, decided that as he was the real father of the poor outcasts, he had a right to do as he pleased « with his own children. » (2) In 1850, he had 270 orphans under his charge; in 1855, they had increased to 490.

Finally, Mr Blakesley observes that in the first fifteen years of the French occupation, in spite of the decay of noble traditions once dear to the heart of France, the civil administration, learning wisdom from experience, had provided thirty-seven new churches, « independently of others due to private efforts, » and that within the same brief period the ecclesiastical establishment had increased to four vicars-general and about one hundred priests, a number since largely increased.

Thus far France has proved that she is not unequal to the mission which Providence has imposed upon her. A century of revolutions may have changed her who once rejoiced to be « the most Christian » nation, — too many of her sons may have embraced the im-

(1) *Four Months in Algeria*, pp. 43-48.
(2) De Baudicour, ch. VII, p. 292.

pious maxims of a shallow and inept philosophy, —
even her soldiers, throwing away the banner of the
Cross under which their fathers fought, may have
proved that the same men can be physically brave
and morally cowards, can face with a smile the
assault of an enemy while they meanly cringe before
the sarcasm of a comrade; but France is still mighty
to atone for the crimes of her apostate children, still
rich enough in the treasures of grace and wisdom to
supply the demand which daily reaches her from
every land for evangelical labourers; and here is one
more proof of her inexhaustible strength, one more
company of that incomparable phalanx which she
offers, even in the nineteenth century, for the service
of the Church.

« On the spot where the battle of Staoueli was
fought and won by the French, » says a recent English writer, « a large convent now stands, » — fit
memorial of a victory which gave to North Africa the
first promise of Christianity and civilization. That
convent and its inmates are thus described in 1857
by another witness, an Anglican clergyman, candid
enough to avow the impressions which they produced
on a heart sufficiently delicate and refined to appreciate them. « The establishment at Staoueli, » says
the Rev. Mr Davies, « is remarkable enough in its
features to require no surreptitious aid to render it
an object of the deepest interest to every thinking
mind; and it is impossible for any one to visit it without pleasure and advantage to himself. » Mr Davies
was admitted into the chapel of the convent, and thus
describes what he saw. « Never was devotion more
fervent and fixed than theirs appeared to be; not an

eye was lifted nor a muscle moved to indicate that our
presence distracted their thoughts; body and soul
were engaged together profoundly in the great work
of adoration. The contemplation of this solemn scene
has left its impression on our memories, and we pray
for abstraction in prayer like that of the monks of
Staoueli. « And these monks, — whose « indolent »
and « useless » lives have long formed one of the
world's most popular jests, « have established, » as
Colonel Wulmsley tells us, « one of the finest model
farms in Algeria ; » and have even completed, as
Mr Blakesley adds, « the collection of a series of important meteorological observations. » Devotion, agriculture, and science are the occupations of the community at Staoueli ; and Mr Davies was probably not
mistaken when he inferred from « their mild and
smiling countenances, which indicated nothing but
rest and sweet contentment, » that « it was that
' peace which passeth all understanding ' which these
men so unmistakeably enjoyed. » (1)

Such are the men whom France sends to do the
work of God in Algeria. That they will ultimately
succeed in their holy mission, we may reasonably
believe ; and already the tokens of success are becoming manifest both to Christian and Mussulman. The
very legends of the Arabs, and those mysterious pre-
dictions which in all ages have issued even from
pagan lips, announce the future triumph of the
Christian law. Not only in Algeria, but even throughout the Sahara, such ominous voices are heard, de-

(1) *Algiers in* 1857, by the Revd E. W. L. Davies, M. A. Vicar
of Ardlingfleet, p. 63.

claring the coming fall of Islam. « This is so general
an idea, » says a recent African traveller, « that even
the ignorant Mahomedans of the East firmly believe
that the Amhara, or Christian population of Abyssinia, will at a future time seize Mecca, and destroy
the temple. » (1) One hundred and thirty years ago,
as General Marcy notices, the French invasion was
prophecied by the Hadji Aïssa, a Marabout of Laghou-
at; and the prophecy, which was repeated to the
General by a lineal descendant of Aïssa, contains,
amongst others, the following verses.

« A Christian army, protected by God, advances towards us. »
« The power of the Christians will have no limits. »
« The Mosques will be abandoned. »
« The religion of the faithful is dead at Algiers. » (2)

A succession of remarkable events has conspired
to confirm these anticipations. One of the earliest
converts was the wife of the Bey of Constantina, as
one of the latest has been a daughter of Abd-el-Kader,
now a Sister of Charity; and though hitherto insignificant in number, almost every class — Arabs,
Moors, and Jews — has proved itself open to Christian influence. But it is the gradual and almost universal destruction of ancient prejudices, and the tardy
recognition of the immense superiority of the Christian race, which more especially claims attention. By
the year 1843, three Mosques in the capital had

(1) *Travels in Southern Abyssinia*, etc., by Charles Johnston,
M. R. C. S., vol. I, ch. XVII, p. 267. (1844).

(2) See *Algeria and Tunis*, by Captain J. Clark Kennedy, vol. I,
ch. XI, p. 236; and *Algérie*, par M. E. Carette, pp. 121, 2.

already become Catholic churches; (1) and when the
central Mosque of Algiers was solemnly blessed for
Christian worship, it was the Mufti Ben Ekbati who
said to General Count D'Erlou, in words of which it
is impossible not to feel the significance, — « Our
Mosque will change its worship without changing its
master, for the God of the Christians is also our
God. » (2)

The change of feeling which such notable words
imply, is manifested in a thousand ways. Already
« the Arabs of Algeria, » says Count Saint Marie,
« respect the Catholic Priest as much as they do the
Marabout. » He notices also the extraordinary affection displayed by the Arab and Moorish students at
El Biar towards the Jesuits, and especially towards
Father Brumault, the founder of that institution,
from which the Bishop hopes hereafter to obtain a
native clergy. « It is but justice, » adds this writer,
« to the Jesuits, to say, that their conduct in this land
of misery and suffering is admirable... There is no
calamity which they do not endeavour to alleviate;
and the French soldiery, though little inclined to
bigotry, respect these men for their uniform courage
and devotedness to the cause of humanity. » (3)

Lastly, — for we may not linger in one province,
since so many others remain to be visited, — a German Protestant writer thus appreciates, in 1855, the
effect of the French conquest upon the inhabitants
and the religion of Algeria. « Closer acquaintance, »
says Dr Wagner, « has greatly conciliated the Mus-

(1) *Algeria*, by J. Reynell Morell, ch. v, p. 84.
(2) St-Marie, ch. v, p. 192.
(3) Ch. viii, p. 276.

sulmen to their antagonists in faith, and they do not
now consider the presence of Christians as desecrating
their places of worship. » And he sums up his candid
reflections with this comparison : — « A great improvement in the lot of the Algerine Arabs has been
the result of their conquest by France... In a moral
point of view, the French have some right to be satisfied with the results of their rule in Algeria, when
contrasting what *they* have done in twenty three years
with England's century in India ! » (1)

Let us quit Algeria, and going eastwards we come
to the province of Tunis. Here also the influence of
Christian France is yearly increasing. When the last
new church was built, the Bey refused to sell the site
for which application had been made to him, but
insisted upon presenting it as a free gift. (2) Here the
Abbé Bourgade, the author of the *Soirées de Carthage*, « has succeeded by his evangelical zeal in
erecting a hospital at Tunis, from charitable sources

---

(1) *The Tricolor on the Atlas*, from the German of Dr Wagner,
by Francis Pulaky, cb. x, p. 401. « Autrefois le maraboul seul
pratiquait la culture des lettres. L'homme d'épée, comme nos
barons du moyen âge, avait tout savoir en mépris... Les arabes
se sont aperçus que l'instruction était un titre à nos faveurs.
Nombre d'entre eux, enfin, se sont dit avec une résignation mé-
lancolique ces paroles que j'ai recueillies un jour : ' Autrefois
nous pouvions vivre avec l'ignorance, car le calme et le bonheur
étaient parmi nous; mais dans ces temps de perturbation que
nous sommes obligés de traverser, il faut que la science nous
vienne en aide.' Ainsi notre influence accomplit lentement, jusqu'au sein du désert, cette œuvre civilisatrice, etc. *Les Mœurs
du Désert*, par le Général E. Daumas, p. 384, (5ᵐᵉ édition).

(2) *Description de la Régence de Tunis*, par le Dr Louis Frank ;
2ᵈᵉ partie, ch. xviii, p. 205.

ǁ.   14.

alone, for the poor Christians. » He has also founded
« the European college, under the direction of zealous
and learned missionaries, where the Mussulman and
Jewish children are instructed together with the
Christian » — to the astonishment of all who witness
so unexpected a triumph over the most inveterate
passions and prejudices. Lastly, when the Bey,
Ahmed Pacha, visited France in 1846, he addressed
these parting words to the attendants who assisted
at his embarkation. « Others have aspired to the title
of ' pilgrim of Mecca, ' let mine be *hadjy frandjy*,
' the pilgrim of European civilization. ' » (1) Is the
prayer of St. Louis about to be accomplished?

One does not expect to find Protestant missions in
North Africa, and the only attempts which appear to
have been made are thus described. » A station was
occupied at Tunis by Mr Ewald and others, from 1829
to 1846, under the London Society. It has since been
abandoned. » (2) Mr Ewald himself relates, with
cautious indignation, that he had previously been
forced to quit Algiers by the peremptory orders of the
Duc de Rovigo against Protestant preaching. He
consoles himself, however, with the assurance, that
« many a son of Abraham had been made acquainted
with the Redeemer, » — an assertion which presently
dwindles into the statement, that « several hundred
copies of the Holy Scriptures had been circulated,» (3) which our knowledge of the effects of bible

(1) Dr Frank. p. 214.
(2) *The Land of the Morning*, by H. B. Whitaker Churton,
ch. IX, p. 155.
(3) *Journal of Missionary Labours*, etc., by Revd F. C. Ewald,
Introd., p. 7.

distribution does not permit us to accept as an equivalent fact.

The year after Mr Ewald departed from Tunis, where he only repeated his Algerian experience, a fresh attempt was made by some Scotch missionaries. Mr Margoliouth reported to Lord Palmerston, in 1847, that they had established two important schools, from which great results might be expected, and that they were about to « erect an edifice » for a church, which, he cheerfully anticipated, would effectually stop « the taunt in the mouths of the French Roman Catholics against British Protestants. » The result was not in accordance with his hopes. A few disciples were collected, of the same class which China and Hindostan have furnished to British missionaries, but of such extreme irregularity of conduct that they fell under the observation of the native authorities; and when their teachers appealed to Sir Thomas Reade, the Consul General, that officer, whose religious prepossessions did not blind him to the real character of these « sons of Abraham, » coldly declined to afford protection to « those wretches. » And then came the usual climax, unwillingly related by Mr Margoliouth himself in 1850, — « The mission, the chapel, and the schools were abandoned. » (1)

We have now reached Egypt, — still, as of old, a land of bondage and shame. « The Christians of Egypt, » says one whose mission it is to unite them in one household, « may be compared to the children of Israel, living under the dominion of Pharaoh; and

(1) *A Pilgrimage to the Land of my Fathers,* by the Revd Moses Margoliouth; vol. 1, pp. 281, 382.

this state of things will continue till European predominance, either by counsel or by the sword, like
Moses of old with his rod, succeed in freeing them
from the servitude of ages. » (1) Yet here also we
may trace the eternal contrast between the Church
and the Sects; here also the first has produced martyrs, the latter only merchants; the first has drawn
to herself the children of error, the last have been
sucked, one after another, into the abyss of apostasy;
the first has struggled to gather all into one fold, the
last to scatter even what was united; the first has
done the work of God, the last have been active only
in the service of the evil one. Here is the latest
example of the manner in which the sects do his
bidding.

The Christian Copts, now numbering only 250,000
— who have continually lapsed into Islamism, (2)
among whom the rite of circumcision is commonly
practised, whose priests, as M. de Chabrol remarks,
« are generally as ignorant as the lowest of the
people, » (3) and whom heresy has degraded almost
below the level of the Turk, — disposed themselves
on a recent occasion to seek by a return to unity the
gifts and blessings which they had forfeited. « Four
years had elapsed since the death of their last Patriarch, » — says the Franciscan Bishop Guasco, Apostolic Delegate in Egypt, writing from Cairo in the

(1) The Bishop of Fez, and apostolic Delegate in Egypt; *Annals*,
Feb. 1856, vol. XVII, p. 251.

(2) *Histoire de l'Égypte*, par M. J. J. Marcel, de l'Institut de
l'Égypte, ch. IV, p. 120.

(3) *Essai sur les Mœurs*, etc., ap. Pancoucke, tome XVIII,
ch. I, p. 19; ch. II, p. 61.

year 1836, — « and the Copts had not yet agreed in
the election of a successor. Finding it impossible to
come to an agreement among themselves, the Coptic
Bishops and the leading men of their nation unani-
mously resolved to have recourse to me for the choice
of their Patriarch. Of course I could not accept any
such mission, except with a view to reconcile Alexandria with Rome; and there is every reason to
believe that I should have succeeded, if the English
Methodists had not interfered. These men, although
they had nothing whatever to do with the matter,
and no one asked their interference, yet managed, by
means of intrigues with their consul, to induce the
viceroy of Egypt, by religion a Turk, to elect a Christian Patriarch, and to impose him upon the schismatical Copts as their administrator. The whole affair
was contrived by the power and intrigues of the
Protestants. » And thus, by the intervention of English Protestants, a quarter of a million of sectaries,
ignorant of the first elements of Christianity, were
replunged into the miseries from which they seemed
about to escape, in order that the Church might be
hindered from performing her divine mission by imparting to them religion and civilization.

But there is nothing in this fact to surprise us. It
is the mission of Protestantism to scatter and destroy.
In such triumphs its emissaries find their delight;
and we have seen, in various lands, that they openly
avow their preference of Buddhism, Islamism, or any
other form of evil, to the Catholic Church. Here are
fresh examples of the same fact. A Protestant clergyman, of the High Church school, though he represents
the schismatical Coptic Patriarch as spending his

whole day in smoking and sleeping, and hopelessly
sunk, like his flock, in ignorance and sloth, observes
with gravity that « he occupies the see of St. Mark; »
but this writer does not so much as once allude to
the Catholics of Egypt, whose prelates and congregations more candid Protestants will presently describe
to us, lest he should be obliged to confess their superiority. (1) « Mahommedanism, » says another Protestant minister, who bears the title of « Doctor of
Divinity, » and was not content with silent animosity,
« was some *improvement* upon the system which it
supplanted » — that is, « Christianity in the fifth and
sixth centuries ! » And then this professor of theology
says, — « It is really a relief to pass from one of
these idol-shrines into the stern simplicity of a Moslem
mosque. » He had just come out of the Church of the
Holy Sepulchre, and this was the reflection which
that place suggested to him. (2)

The language of this gentleman deserves a moment's attention, not perhaps for its own sake, but
because it reveals a condition of mind almost peculiar
to English Protestants. Mahometanism, he says, was
an « improvement » upon the Christianity of the fifth
and sixth centuries. Now it was during this very
period that the world was illumined by the presence
of such men as St. Chrysostom and St. Jerome,
St. Augustine and St. Cyril of Alexandria, St. Hilary
and St. Benedict, St. Simeon and St. Gregory of
Tours; and by such women as St. Geneviève and
St. Clotilde. It was during this period also, which

---

(1) See *Travels in the Holy Land*, by the Revd J. A. Spencer,
M. A. (1850).

(2) *The Desert of Sinai*, by H. Bonar, D D., ch. III, p. 63.

he selects for unfavorable comparison with Islamism,
that Christianity encountered and overcame the greatest trial which any system or polity, human or
divine, has ever survived. The Roman empire was
then in the agonies of dissolution, and the wave of
barbarism had inundated Europe from the Elbe to
the Mediterranean. Before this storm every thing
perished except the Church. « It was *the Christian
Church,* » says an eminent Protestant, « which saved
Christianity, which vigorously resisted both the
internal dissolution of the empire and barbarism;
which conquered the barbarians, and became the
bond, the medium, and the principle of civilization
between the Roman and barbarian worlds... Had the
Christian Church not existed, the whole world must
have been abandoned to purely material force. *The
Church alone* exercised a moral power. » And even
this is not all. « *From that epoch,* » says M. Guizot,
« the Church powerfully assisted in forming the
character and furthering the development of modern
civilization. » (1) And not only did she save at this
crisis in the world's history both Christianity and
civilization; not only did she preserve the Holy
Scriptures and the apostolic traditions; but she
rescued from destruction, in spite of the barbarians,
jurisprudence, letters, and philosophy. It was during
this very convulsion, which upheaved and shattered
the whole framework of society, that the monasteries became, as M. Guizot observes, « philosophical
schools of Christianity—it was *there* that intellectual
men meditated, discussed, taught. » And once more.

(1) *History of Civilization in Europe,* Lect. II.

Contrasting the intellectual life of the civil and ecclesiastical societies of this very epoch, the same distinguished person observes, that the latter alone « were
active and potent at once in the domain of intellect,
and in that of reality ; their activity is rational, and
their philosophy popular... philosophy and religion
were *saved* (by the Church of the fifth and sixth
centuries) from the ruin which menaced them. » So
that M. Guizot does not hesitate to declare, in spite
of prejudices as imperious and tyrannical as ever
oppressed a noble and generous heart, that « it may
be said without exaggeration that the human mind,
proscribed, beaten down by the storm, took refuge
in the asylum of churches and monasteries. » (1)

    « The *fifth and sixth centuries*, » says a learned
Prussian writer, — referring especially to the Armenians, the first people who as an entire nation
embraced Christianity, and at that time so remarkable
by the position which they occupied with relation to
the rest of Christendom, — « were *the brightest
period* of the Armenian literature, during which a
vigorous intellectual intercourse was carried on with
the West : the classical works of Europe were translated, with a profound comprehension, instances of
which I have before mentioned in the works of Plato
and Aristotle ; » while that version of the Bible was
then executed, « which, in the judgment of the
Mechitarists, and of many scholars, *is the finest of
all translations of the Bible*, and remains to the
present day a model of the pure Armenian language. » (2)

(1) *History of Civilization in France*, Lect. IV.
(2) Von Haxthausen, ch. x, pp. 337, 339.

And it is of such an epoch as this, so fruitful in
blessings to humanity, so inexpressibly glorious to
the Church, that a British Protestant does not blush
to say, that it was happily replaced by Islamism, the
great destroyer both of religion and civilization! Such
is the dull imperturbable audacity, not of lofty and
disciplined reason, jealously sifting its own conclusions, but of blind prejudice and contented ignorance.

Let us briefly notice, before we resume our progress in Africa, the actual state of religion in Egypt.
« Christianity has only remained among the mixt race
of Copts, » says a Protestant historian of Egypt. (1)
The Catholics he does not even mention; though
another English writer observes, apparently with
regret, the notorious fact, that « the Church of Rome
has induced some to forsake the tenets of their ancestors » — including the tenet of circumcision —
« and to join the community of Catholic Copts. » (2)
She has induced so many to take that step, that a
recent traveller in these lands tells us, that « of late
years the number of Coptic Catholics has greatly
multiplied, and it is now estimated at one third of
the whole Christian population of Egypt. » (3)

Dr Durbin, an American Protestant, also confesses
of the oriental christians generally, — « It is not to
be denied that their intercourse with the Roman
Catholic Church tends to elevate them in the scale of

(1) *History of Egypt*, by Samuel Sharpe, vol. II, ch. xix,
p. 345.
(2) *Modern Egypt*, by Sir Gardner Wilkinson, vol. I, p. 395.
(3) *Journal of a tour in Egypt*, etc., by J. Laird Patterson,
M. A., app. p. 403. (1852).

civilization, as the priests sent to serve them, being
generally educated men, diffuse European knowledge
as well as manners among them. » (1) D' Robinson,
a well known anti-catholic writer, gives this description of a catholic oriental prelate, who preached a
sermon in Arabic, at Cairo, which D' Robinson and
other Protestant ministers heard. « He was a man of
noble mien ; his manner dignified, full of gesture, and
impressive. His sermon, according to the judgment
of my companions, was well-ordered, logical, full of
good sense and practical force. » (2) And the increasing power of the Church in these unhappy lands
is freely admitted by all the better class of Protestant
witnesses. Thus Mr Jowett noticed, some years ago,
the opinion expressed by Mr Barker, at that time
British Consul at Aleppo. « *All* Syria and Egypt he
considers as comparatively occupied by the Roman
Catholics : even Aleppo, he says, is gradually drawing, and nearly drawn over to them. » (3) We shall
see more ample illustrations of these facts in the next
chapter.

On the other hand, here are the accounts which
Protestant writers give of the operations of their
co-religionists, backed by the wealth of England and
America, in the land of Egypt. A few examples will
suffice. « I am sorry to tell you, » is the report
addressed from Cairo to the « Malta Protestant College » in 1831, « that very little Protestant progress
has been made here, and that I find every thing poor

(1) *Observations in the East*, by John P. Durbin, D. D., Late
President of Dickinson College, vol. II, ch. 34, p. 287.
(2) *Biblical Researches in Palestine*, vol. II, p. 458.
(3) *Asiatic Journal*, vol. VI, p. 509.

and without life. But, on the contrary, wherever you turn your eyes you see Roman Catholic progress : buildings every where, churches three or four, and schools three ; missions in the villages, » etc. etc. (1) And exactly the same report is given, by another Protestant witness, of Alexandria. « Whilst the Roman Catholics establish schools, build convents and churches, and have a large number of their clergy here, » says Mr Ewald, the fugitive from Algiers and Tunis, « the Protestants have withdrawn all their missionaries, and Mr Winder is the only Protestant minister of the Gospel at this important place. » (2) Meanwhile, the progress of the *Catholic* mission appears to have been so well sustained, that in 1860 the Lazarists had « an admirable school, » attended by 200 boys « of every nation and religion ; » the Christian Brothers a second, which was equally successful ; and the Sisters of Charity a third, frequented by a still larger number of girls. » (3) At Cairo, by the same date, the school of the Sisters of the Good Shepherd counted about 300 pupils ; while the operations of the protestant agents are thus described.

« They have been, » says Dr Durbin, in 1845, « about fifteen years engaged in the mission at Cairo, designed for the benefit of the Copts ; but such is the jealousy of these native Christians that missionaries can have but little access to them. I twice attended divine service in the mission chapel, and found

(1) *Fifth Annual Report of the Malta Protestant College,* p. 10.
(2) *Journal,* p. 264.
(3) *Un Hiver en Égypte,* par M. Eugène Poitou, ch. XVI, p. 448. (1860).

perhaps twenty persons present, and most of these Franks. I think there were not half a dozen native christians. « Yet these missionaries had maintained schools, both male and female, for many years, and at great cost; but with the same results which have attended their educational efforts in every other land. « Most of them, » D' Durbin confesses, « *resume* the same religious views and feelings which prevail among their people. » (1) They are perfectly willing, in spite of their « jealousy, » to be taught and fed by protestant missionaries, but they go elsewhere for their religion.

And this fact became at length so apparent, even to those who were most reluctant to admit it, that an Anglican clergyman informs us, only six years after D' Durbin's visit, that « M' Lieder's school, the Church Missionary Institute, has, alas, been relinquished, owing to the expense of such an establishment, and the supposed inadequate appearance of fruit. » (2) Nor was the school the only instrument of conversion which sustained a check. Even the preaching appears to have languished, and to have lost, what it probably once possessed, the merit of originality; for a critical English traveller relates, a little later, that « M' Lieder gave us a good plain sermon, probably not his own composition, for I had heard it before. » (3)

D' Wilson had reported, indeed, and perhaps believed, that « a spirit of serious enquiry had begun

(1) Vol. 1, ch. VII, p. 67.
(2) *The Land of the Morning*, by H. D. Whitaker Churton, M. A., ch. I, p. 10. (1851).
(3) *Shadows of the East*, by C. Tobin, p. 83. (1855).

to appear among a few of the Copts; (1) but the enquiry seems to have been barren of results. Even D' Bonar, who prefers a mosque to the Church of the Holy Sepulchre, relates of the American missionaries at Cairo, that « the door, » at which they have been knocking for so many years, « does not seem by any means an open one. » (2) D' Yates also deplores that the protestant agents have so completely failed to persuade the natives to regard them as religious teachers, in any sense whatever, that « the less informed Mahommedan, » as he resentfully styles him, « supposes that the people called Christians » — he means Protestants — « have no religion at all. » (3)

The facts, then, which we have noticed in so many other regions of the earth, present themselves once more in Egypt. We need not multiply them. The characteristics of Catholic and Protestant missions are everywhere invariable.

« In Lower Egypt alone, » says the Apostolic Delegate whom we have already quoted, « seventeen martyrs are numbered as belonging to one order. Our Religious, immoveable at their posts, endured exile, imprisonment, every sort of trial and persecution, and death itself. Nothing but a special Providence could assuredly have preserved their establishments from destruction, menaced as they have been through ages of fanaticism; but at length the day has arrived

---

(1) *Lands of the Bible*, by John Wilson, D. D., F. R. S., vol. II, p. 528.

(2) Ch. III, p. 36.

(3) *Modern History of Egypt*, by W. Holt Yates, M. D., vol. I, ch. III, p. 85.

when Catholics are permitted publicly to open their
churches, and to found schools and hospitals. » And
then he shows what has been done of late under his
own eyes. « During the sixteen years that I have been
in the position of apostolic delegate, it has afforded
me great satisfaction to see Catholic churches erected
here for all the Oriental rites. New religious bodies
have also afforded us their zealous co-operation.
Thus, in 1844, this vicariate welcomed Priests of
St. Vincent of Paul, and Sisters of Charity, both of
whom are now in possession of very fine establishments at Alexandria. In 1846, the Sisters of the
Good Shepherd, from Angers, established themselves
at Cairo, where they now have a flourishing seminary, a house of refuge, and an orphanage. These
Religious also conduct a day school, which is well
attended by poor Arabs. In 1854, there was founded
in the same capital an excellent institution for the
education of youth, confided to the care of the Christian Brothers.... What can be the cause of so great a
change? Has not God, in His divine mercy, granted
it as a recompense for the past, in consideration of
the labours of the former Missionaries, of their patience in bonds, and, above all, of the blood which
they so generously shed for the faith? » (1)

Whatever may be thought of this reflection of the
apostolic delegate, it is at least certain, by Protestant
testimony, that his own colleagues are not inferior
in heroism and generosity to their martyred predecessors. « I allow, » says Dr Joseph Wolff, — in
explanation of his own residence at Cairo during the

---

(1) *Annals*, ubi supra.

outbreak of cholera, — « that the example of the
Pope's Missionaries at Cairo induced me more than
any thing else to prosecute my journey; for whilst
during the plague in Egypt the Lutheran Missionaries
shut themselves up, as I myself (I say it to my shame)
did at Beyrouth, when there during the plague with
my wife and child, the Missionaries of the Propaganda of Rome visited those infected with that disease, *so that six Roman Missionaries died out of
seven.* » (1)

The Christian heroism which excited the admiration of Dr Wolff was natural in men who were the
heirs of Claude Sicard, the representative, as has
been well said, « at once of the Church and of the
Academy of sciences » in Egypt; (2) who converted
in one week the Greek solitaries of the Thebaid, and
the next enriched Europe with those luminous essays
on the monuments, the geography, or the chemical
products of the land of the Nile, by which later researches have been aided; and who died at last at
Cairo, in 1726, a martyr of charity, ministering to
the victims of the plague, and falling himself by the
side of those whom he had no longer power to
bless.

Let us leave Cairo, embark on the Nile, and
journeying towards its source we shall come to
Khartoum. If we stay for a moment at this place,
which brings us almost to the frontiers of Abyssinia,
it is only for the sake of noticing an account of the
Mission of the White Nile, by one of those candid

(1) *Journal*, p. 334.
(2) Crétineau Joly, tome V, p. 17.

Protestants of whom we have encountered so many
in these pages. This Mission has lately been alluded
to by a French traveller, who is nominally a Catholic,
but who, like too many of his countrymen, seems
to think a reputation for wit the highest object of
man's ambition, especially when it is some religious
topic which inspires the sorry jest. M. Charles Didier
is of opinion that all « pacific missions » are necessarily failures, and that the only apostles who can
achieve success are those who travel, like Mahomet,
sword in hand. (1) An English writer thus describes,
almost at the same moment, the work in which the
Frenchman only saw an opportunity for an indifferent joke.

« One of the most interesting establishments in
Soudan, » says Mr James Hamilton, in 1857, « is the
Mission for the conversion of the pagans of Central
Africa, respectable both for its object and the cha-
acter of the men who compose it. » Mr Hamilton then
notices the untimely death of the well known Padré
Ryllo, from whose enlightened labours great results
had been anticipated, and continues thus. « Should
the Mission be crowned with success, the spiritual
conquest of the vast unknown regions of the centre
will be amongst the most glorious triumphs of modern
times. Artificers of various kinds, the pioneers of
civilisation and religion, are attached to the house,
so that the pupils may learn and carry back to their
countrymen many useful arts. The Superior takes
yearly journies of inspection up the White Nile,
where three stations have been established; and if,

(1) *Cinq cents lieues sur le Nil*, par Charles Didier, ch. III.

as I have every reason to believe, his patience and
discretion equal his zeal and that of his fellow-
labourers, they cannot fail in time to overcome the
immense difficulties which surround their undertaking. Both among Turks and Arabs, Abuna Suliman,
as D' Ignatius Knoblecher is called, enjoys the highest consideration; far and near I heard him spoken
of with respect, and even by the Copts, the least
likely persons to appreciate his qualities. This is
already a great success, alone worth the large sums
which the Mission has cost, for it is the breaking
down of prejudices of colour and religion, if not as
old as nature, older than history or tradition. » This
intelligent and conscientious writer next proceeds
to furnish details which appropriately illustrate the
primary subject of these volumes. « Many of the
missionaries have already fallen victims to the climate, and perhaps also to the excessive austerity of
their lives, but in dying they have done good. Those
who have been long enough in the country to be
known have left a memory venerated even by the
pagans, and the funeral chant of one who died last
year at his station up the river, Don Angelo Ninco,
a gentleman of Verona, is still sung in their assemblies, as composed by the blacks themselves. » (1)
Have we not reason to say, that Catholic missionaries are everywhere and always the same?

The honorable testimony of M' Hamilton is confirmed by an American Protestant traveller, who was
a guest of the apostolic prefect, whose « thorough

(1) *Sinai, the Hedjaz, and Soudan*, by James Hamilton,
ch. xiv, p. 332. (1857).

II.   13

cultivation • and varied knowledge he warmly eulo-
gises, and who frankly reports • the success attending the efforts of the Catholic priests in Khartoum
in educating children. • (1)

Mr Hamilton notices with regret the impiety of
the European traders, whom the desire of gain has
attracted to these regions, and then adds, — • Some
of the anecdotes which I heard when at Khartoum
of personal violence offered to the vicar general and
his colleagues, and submitted to, although they had
ample means of successful resistance, raised my admiration of their exemplary patience. •

It is curious that even in these remote and almost
unvisited spots, Protestant writers are found to trace
for us the contrast which we could hardly have
proved without their assistance. • A certain German
missionary • — said an English writer, only a few
months before Mr Hamilton wrote the above account
— • well known in this part of the world, exaspera-
ted by the seizure of a few dollars, advised the authorities of Aden to threaten the ' combustion ' • of
the place where he was mulcted. • A traveller, •
Mr Burton calmly adds, • even a layman, is bound to
put up with such trifles. • (2)

And now let us pursue our journey, and enter
Abyssinia. The history of missions in this kingdom
has been written, with their usual decision of style,
by certain Protestants, most of whom were never
within a thousand miles of the place, or had any
knowledge whatever of the events which they affect

(1) *Journey to Central Africa*, by Bayard Taylor, ch. XXIII,
p. 300.
(2) *First Footsteps in East Africa*, ch. I, p. 13. (1856).

to describe but what they had borrowed from the
reports of Catholic missionaries. Our acquaintance
with Abyssinia, Congo, and other interior regions of
Africa, was derived exclusively, as even the English
authors of the *Universal History* remark, « from the
missionaries who have penetrated into those torrid
and unwholesome climes, and amongst the most barbarous nations, with the utmost hazard, and through
the greatest hardships and discouragements, to propagate the Gospel among them. » These Protestant
annalists add, that heat, disease, and want of food —
to say nothing of continual martyrdoms — « made
such dreadful havoc amongst them, that scarce one
in ten outlived the first six months. » (1)

In spite of these notorious facts, some modern
Protestant writers — exulting in the certainty, as
they deemed, that Catholics had been finally driven
from Abyssinia, an anticipation which we shall see
hereafter has been signally disappointed — have published to the world their view of the circumstances
which led to this result. One official writer, willing
to borrow weapons in such a cause from any arsenal,
is not ashamed to quote what he truly calls « Gibbon's melancholy picture of the wicked arts practised
by the Jesuits. » (2) The Jesuits who went to Abyssinia, says the Rev. Professor Lee, in his preface to
Dr Gobat's Journal, were prodigies of infamy and
cupidity, — his actual words are somewhat coarser,
— and had no other motive but to pilfer the precious
metals and other treasures with which this opulent

(1) *Universal History*, vol. XI, p. 163.
(2) *Journal of a Deputation to the East*, vol. II, p. 849. (1854).

country abounded. It would be quite as rational to
say, that St. Paul went to Greece with the same
design.

Abyssinia, as M. Desvergers not long ago remarked, is a region so utterly destitute of wealth, though
fertile in agricultural resources, that « nothing but a
purely religious motive » could have induced the
educated and well-born missionaries of France,
Spain, and Portugal to enter it; (1) and a modern
missionary, Padré Montuosi, writing from Gondar
in 1840, tells us that he found one of the kings of
this country « clothed only with a pair of drawers,
and having for his throne a miserable rag of cloth
spread over a little straw. » (2) A recent English
traveller records also his astonishment at finding
« the capital of one of the most powerful kingdoms
of Ethiopia nothing but a large straggling village of
huts, mostly thatched with straw. » (3) Other writers will presently assist us still further in correcting
the fables of Dr Lee, in which a corrupt imagination
has supplied all the facts, and a malice verging on
frenzy has elaborated all the comments. Almost the
only book on which he founds his calumnies, is Ludolf's pretended History of Ethiopia, of which an
English Protestant has lately said; « it is such an
evident compilation of what ought to be the faith of
the Abyssinian Church, rather than what it ever
was, or is at the present day, that any account founded upon it would be one of the grossest impositions

(1) *Abyssinie*, par M.A. N. Desvergers, p. 10.
(2) *Annals*, vol. II, p. 348.
(3) Parkyns, *Life in Abissinia*, vol. 1, ch. XIII, p. 161.

that could be palmed upon the reading public. » (1)
Perhaps Dr Lee had partly derived his inspiration also
from Bruce, who calls Father Paëz an impostor, (2)
and Father Lobo « the greatest liar amongst the
Jesuits » — such are the amenities of Protestant
literature; although Dr Ncke, a learned and honest
Protestant, who visited Abyssinia at a recent date,
confesses, that « Paëz discovered and described the
source of the river Abai long before Bruce, » and
even hints that the latter probably « composed his
own account from the description furnished by the
very missionaries so much slandered and depreciated
by him. » (3)

But these are the weapons with which her enemies
assault the Church, and Professor Lee is willing to
reveal his own special qualifications as a christian
historian by informing us, with respect to the heresies of Nestorius and Dioscorus, that « the disputes
which have so long divided the Eastern Church
amount to nothing more than a battle about words. »
And that we may still more clearly appreciate his
zeal for the honour of God, he immediately adds;
« both Monophysites and Nestorians hold the Divinity of our Lord; their disputes respect *only* the
mode of His incarnation ! » (4) Why should Dr Lee
show more respect for the virtues of Catholic missionaries than he does for the Incarnation of our Redeemer?

(1) Johnston, *Travels in Southern Abyssinia,* vol. II, ch. v, p. 80
(2) *Travels,* vol. III, pp. 617, 623.
(3) *Mémoire Justificatif en réhabilitation des Pères Paëz et
Jérôme Lobo,* p. 69.
(4) *History of the Church of Abyssinia,* p. 5.

Let us turn from this gentleman to graver writers, who possess a more accurate knowledge both of Christianity and of its history in Abyssinia. From them we learn that Frumentius, the disciple of St. Athanasius, was its first Bishop; and M^r D'Abbadie reports that the Abyssinian Christians, fallen as they are, still celebrate a yearly festival in his honour. Ethiopia, subject from the first to the patriarchal see of Alexandria, embraced like it the heresy of Dioscorus, and from that hour its long history of suffering began. The empress Theodora, an eager partisan of the Eutychian errors, sent emissaries to propagate them in Ethiopia : and though it is now impossible to trace with minute accuracy the gradual progress of heresy in these regions, it seems probable that by the ninth century, at the latest, the work of destruction was complete. It was not, however, till the sixteenth that Abyssinia, still nominally Christian, was finally subjugated by the Mahometan forces which she had so obstinately resisted, and thus incurred the last and most grievous penalty which divine justice has inflicted upon all the heretical churches of the East. *They*, as De Bonald said of the Greeks, have become, like the Jews, an accursed people, « the only Christian nation subject to masters who are not so. »

And now the downfall of Abyssinia was accomplished. « Islamism, » as M. D'Abbadie remarks, « at the present day so much enfeebled in Europe, has revived in Africa. » Already it has « perverted to its doctrines the savage or half-christian tribes which surround Abyssinia, and having excluded it from the rest of the Christian world, this fatal sys-

tem keeps encroaching upon and gradually absorbing
this ill-fated country. » « The Turks and Arabs, »
says Werne, « are just as strenuous in *their* exertions to make proselytes as the expensive European
missionaries ; » (1) and heresy is too weak to resist
them. « It is said, » observes M' Warburton, « that
considerable numbers annually become apostate to
the Moslem creed, for the sake of marriage, or money, or both. » (2)

Such, in its outlines, is the history of the Church
founded by Frumentius, and once guided by the counsels of St. Athanasius; and such the results of its
separation from unity. And now let us see what Catholic charity has attempted towards the re-building of
this ruined temple.

In 1850, the Patriarch Nugnez, chosen by St.
Ignatius for this perilous mission by the request of
Julius III, sailed from Lisbon, together with the
small body of Portuguese troops by whose heroic
valour David, king of the Ethiopians, was assisted
against the Mahometans. In his suite was Father
Oviedo, by whom numerous converts were made, and
who subsequently became Patriarch in his turn ; but
after seeing many of his brethren martyred, was
finally driven into exile by the arts of his implacable
enemies, and exposed to perish by famine (3). Thus
far partial success, constantly checked by greater
reverses, had attended the Catholic missions. In
1589, as Gibbon scoffingly relates, « the patience

(1) *Expedition to discover the sources of the White Nile*,
vol. I, ch. II. p. 39.

(2) *Crescent and Cross*, vol. I, ch. xiv, p. 139.

(3) *Nouveaux Memoires du Levant*, tome IV, pp. 277 et seqq.

and dexterity of forty years (1) « seemed at length
to have triumphed; and Paëz received the solemn
abjuration of the king, who, as Mr Murray observes,
« not only professed himself a convert to the Romish
faith, but made it the established religion of his dominions, which it continued to be for a long series
of years. » (2) On the 11th of December, 1624, the
Abyssinian Church solemnly abjured the Alexan-
drian errors, and submitted to the Holy See.

In consequence of these events, which appeared to
establish religion on a solid basis, Mendez was sent
as Patriarch; but once again the people, capricious
and fickle as Greeks, revolted; and at the death of
Soclnios, in 1632, his successor Facilidas, harassed by
a civil war, once more ordered all Catholic missionaries to quit the kingdom. From that hour it was only
at the risk of death that they could force an entrance.
Invariably massacred, either by the Mahometans, or
by the still more ferocious Gallas tribes, they could
henceforth be victims only, not apostles. In 1698,
Louis XIV sent the physician Poncet, attended by
Father Brevedent of the Society of Jesus. « I may
truly say, » was the report which Poncet gave of the
latter, who died of dysentery after entering Ethiopia, « that I have never known a man more bold and
intrepid in all dangers, more firm and ardent in defending the interests of religion, more modest and
devout in his whole life and conversation. » (3)

Once more, in 1752, three Franciscan Fathers,
fearlessly braving death, penetrated even to Gondar,

(1) Ch. 47.
(2) *Discoveries in Africa*, vol. II, ch. i, p. 30.
(3) *Lettres Édifiantes*, tome III, p. 299.

in the time of Yasous II, and « instructed many of the
royal family in the Catholic faith ; » (1) but the king,
in spite of his attachment to them, was ultimately
forced, by the perpetual anarchy and disorder which
reigned among his ignorant and heretical subjects,
to dismiss them from the kingdom. And so this
unequal contest continued ; for the Church, like her
Divine Head, never abandons those whom she has
resolved to save, and never calls in vain upon the
servants whom she invites to such labours. She
knows that the sure prospect of suffering and death
will rather animate than discourage their zeal. Let
us briefly state, in conclusion, what they have since
done in Abyssinia, and what they are doing at the
present hour.

In 1840, Father Montuosi wrote in these words
from Gondar to his friend the Abbate Guarini, at
Rome. « Towards the middle of September, 1839, we
left Cosseir for Djeddah. We embarked on board an
Arabian vessel, engaged in carrying corn for the governor of Egypt. The voyage was far from agreeable,
but why speak of privations and dangers ? We accepted
them as the welcome augury of the sacrifice which
we were going to offer in the heart of Ethiopia... On
the 1st of November we reached Aduah, the first important city of Abyssinia ; Father Sapito came to
meet us... The Mahommedans have here more liberty
than the Christians. Father de' Jacobis and I were
obliged to recite the Office in a low voice, so as not
to be overheard ; we seldom celebrated Mass, and
whenever we did, it was always in secret, as if in

(1) Salt's *Travels in Abyssinia*, app. p. 34.

the catacombs. » Finally, leaving Father Jacobis at
Aduah, he at length reached Gondar, « the capital
whence have issued at different epochs so many sanguinary edicts against the Catholic Missionaries. »(1)
Let us leave him here for a moment, and return to
his companion, whom he had left, as he says, « not
without tears; » at Aduah, like Daniel in the den of
lions.

On the 23ʳᵈ of April, 1842, Father Jacobis wrote
as follows, from Massouah, to the Abbate Spacca-
pietra, at Naples. « On the 14ᵗʰ of February, the
day on which we quitted Cairo to pursue our journey
towards Abyssinia, we were witnesses of an edifying
sight. In that city, in the convent of the Franciscans,
were assembled Bishops and Missionary Priests;
some of whom, recently arrived from India and
Arabia, were proceeding to Rome to render an account to the common Father of the faithful of their
apostolic labours; while others were on their way
to Ethiopia or China, to fill the places which the
martyrs had left vacant. Prostrated at the foot of the
same altar, we renewed to our Lord the sacrifice of
our lives, and, after bidding each other a fraternal
and last farewell, we separated, appointing to meet
again in heaven. »

Their caravan was composed of ten Missionaries,
of whom six were destined for the interior provinces
of China. In four days and nights, travelling chiefly
on foot, « because of the humbleness of our means, »
they reached Suez. Here, a week later, « the whole
city, not excepting even the Mussulmans, rendered

(1) *Annals*, vol. II, p. 347.

homage to the Catholic religion, by hailing with admiration the arrival of a humble colony of Nuns, six
ladies belonging to the Society of Jesus and Mary,
who were on their way from Lyons, accompanied
by the Abbé Caffarel, to found a school for girls at
Agra, in the East Indies. • (1) It is pleasant to
know that these ladies accomplished their long pilgrimage in safety.

Father Jacobis, to whom we will now return, was
on this occasion on his second journey to Abyssinia,
having conducted to Rome, in 1841, a body of
Abyssinians whom he had induced to pay a visit to
the Sovereign Pontiff. Two laymen, Captains Gali-
nier and Ferret, officers of the Staff, have recorded
the results of his journey. « The Abbé Jacobis reached Abyssinia, » they say, « at a moment of universal
anarchy, in consequence of the defeat of Ubié, king
of Tigré, at the battle of Devra-Tabor. The road
which leads from Massouah to Aduah was full of the
greatest perils, yet M. Jacobis did not fear to return
to his post, and all the revolted chiefs whom he met
on the way treated him with the greatest respect.
A large number of the inhabitants of Aduah went out
to meet him, and greeted him as a father whom they
rejoiced to see again after so long an absence. » And
then these gentlemen continue their report as follows.

« The journey of M. Jacobis to Rome has already
produced its fruits. The Abyssinians who accompanied him are now Catholics from conviction, and
fear not to avow it before their countrymen. They
have the greatest veneration for the Holy Father....

(1) Vol. IV, p. 46,

The king, Ubié, has the highest esteem for M. Jacobis, and sent a messenger to him from the mountains of Semen, to congratulate him on his arrival, and to promise him that, if he should recover his kingdom, he would do his best to be of service to him. But although Ubié should not re-ascend his throne, M. Jacobis would not be without protection. The most powerful chief of Tigré, who knew by reputation the admirable Missionary, has also sent to compliment him, and has offered him a place in his country, Vojjerat, with permission to build a church and to celebrate the rites of his religion. Thus, whichever prince may triumph in this struggle, the Catholic Mission will be established in Abyssinia. This happy result we owe to the edifying conduct of our Missionaries, but above all to the inexhaustible goodness, the zeal and ability of the Abbé Jacobis. »

Let us add, that when Dr Beke visited Abyssinia a little later, he says, though a Protestant, « the Italian priests of the Roman Catholic mission, the Abbate de' Jacobis and his colleagues, received me more like a brother than a stranger; » (1) and Mr Mansfield Parkyns relates, with the candour of a liberal and educated Englishman, that « it was well known that the esteem and influence which his truly Christian conduct and well-regulated charity had earned for him among the people were sore subjects of jealousy and causes of dislike in the hearts of the (Abyssinian) priests. » (2)

(1) *Statement of Facts relative to the British Mission to Shoa*, p. 17. (1846).

(2) *Life in Abyssinia*, vol. II, ch. XXXI, p. 89.

And now let us leave Father Jacobis, in his turn, pass over an interval of eight years, and in 1850 we come to the recital of fresh events, communicated by Father Leon des Avranches in these terms. He writes from Massouah, on the Abyssinian coast, on the 12th of March in that year, after « three years of persecution. »

« The ancient Abyssinian empire, no longer in existence since the invasion of the Gallas, is at present divided into three kingdoms : Tigré Amhara, where Ubié rules; Shoa, mainly consisting of the Gallas tribes; and the kingdom of Gojam. » It was to Shoa that the English government sent a mission a few years ago, the failure of which shall be noticed presently; while of its inhabitants Dr Beke reports, in 1847, that they display « the lowest form in which the Christian religion probably exists on the face of the globe. » (1) Yet it is of such « christians » that Ludolf and other Protestant writers speak with sympathy and admiration, apparently for no other reason than that they reject the Catholic faith, and treat Catholic missionaries after the manner recited in the following narrative.

« Bishop Massaia , the Vicar Apostolic of the Gallas nation, » says Father Leon, « has just returned to this town, on the shores of the Red Sea. After spending ten months in visiting the various Christian tribes dispersed through the kingdoms of Shoa and Gojam, he found himself compelled to quit his Mission, on account of the persecution raised by the

_____

(1) *Christianity among the Gallas*, by C. J. Beke, Ph. D. (1847).

schismatical bishop of Abyssinia.... Although the Christians of Abyssinia profess the error of Dioscorus, which was condemned in the Council of Chalcedon, a great number of them live in total ignorance of the matter, and suppose that their Bishop, the Abouna sent to them by the schismatical patriarch of Cairo, is in communion with the Pope. According to the laws of the country, there can be only one Bishop in Abyssinia : the usurper of the title is subject to the penalty of death. This furnished the motive for the persecution raised against Bishop Massaia. The actual Abouna, before he became a bishop, was a poor youth, whose only property was an ass, which he let out to travellers. After studying two years at Cairo, he was deemed sufficiently instructed to perform episcopal functions; he was ordained, and despatched to Abyssinia, together with some Anglican ministers, who were subsequently expelled by the people. »

By this singular prelate Bishop Massaia was « excommunicated, » and condemned to death; « the sum of one hundred talaris being also promised to any one who would bring him the head of a Catholic missionary. » (1) But the project was thwarted by the precautions of Father Jacobis, and « this outburst only served to extend the knowledge of the Catholic creed. The name of the Right Reverend D' Massaia was thenceforth on every tongue; all parties spoke of the new Abouna sent by the Pontiff of Rome. » Preserved by the chief of a Catholic tribe from assassination, the Bishop finally escaped to

(1) *Annals*, vol. XII, p. 330.

Aden; the Christians declaring that if he gave himself up to the Abouna, — as he proposed to do, in order to save his flock from vexation, — they would all die with him.

During his temporary exile, a touching scene was enacted on the island of Dhalac, near Massouah, where he had found refuge, by the connivance of the Ottoman governor, together with Father Jacobis. For more than a year the latter had been in possession of Bulls from the Sovereign Pontiff, appointing him to the dignity of the episcopate, which his humility had resolutely declined to accept. Even the remonstrances of Bishop Massaia were fruitless; till at length he was obliged to « command him, by virtue of the holy obedience which he owed to the Church, to receive the episcopal consecration, » — and the humble missionary became Bishop of Nilopolis, and Vicar Apostolic of Abyssinia. Twenty-five *native* priests also received ordination from Dr Massaia, and « after a fraternal embrace, the two outlawed Bishops separated, » the one seeking a refuge in the mountains of Aliena, the other remaining a few days to converse alone with God on the rock of Dhalac.

And now a new incident revived the hopes of the suffering Catholics. Teclafa, an Abyssinian Abbot, the Superior of more than one thousand monks, appeared before Bishop Massaia, to make in his hands his abjuration of heresy. « After this astonishing profession of faith, he withdrew, and proceeded to proclaim at the court of the kings of Abyssinia, and in the very heat of persecution, that he had become a Catholic Priest. Such a courageous declaration, » adds Father Leon, « from the lips of a neophyte, made our enemies crest-fallen, and restored courage to our Christians. None ventured to lay a hand on Teclafa, from dread of a popular insurrection. On his return to his monastery, all his monks likewise declared themselves Catholics. But his zeal did not confine itself within these bounds. Like another St. Paul be now devoted himself to the conversion of his brethren, and already three Christian congregations have been associated, by his exertions, to the Church of Jesus Christ. »

The scattered missionaries had now all reached once more the frontiers of the Gallas tribes, and their Bishop could not restrain the desire to be again in the midst of his brethren. Leaving Massouah in disguise, Dr Massaia again entered Abyssinia, where a price was set upon his head. Having shaved his long beard, and put on a Turkish dress, he joined a caravan proceeding to Gondar, in the character of a poor trader. In thirteen days he reached the camp of Ubié, who sent him on his way, « accompanied by a soldier, with orders that the same honours which were shown to the king should be paid to the Bishop. » He reached Gondar, but only to be once more banished by the cruelties and exactions of his enemies; then ascending the Blue Nile to its source, for nothing could daunt his courage nor exhaust his patience, he sought the presence of Ras Ali, one of the most powerful of the Abyssinian princes, having at that time 100,000 men under arms. The Ras was baptized, but in heart a Mussulman, and little advantage resulted from his interview with one who resented in private the homage which he was forced to pay to Christianity before his followers. As he came out of the royal tent, he was accosted by M' Bell, an English traveller settled in Abyssinia, and a captain in the army of Ras. « He had a tent prepared for the Bishop and his companions, and though he was a Protestant, always showed himself their friend and protector. »

It would, however, be an error to suppose that the obstacles to the conversion of this country proceed mainly from the Abyssinian heretics, or their miserable Abouna. « Islamism, » says D' Massaia, « watches the whole coast of this vast continent, and an immense belt of fanatical populations, constantly excited by emissaries from Mecca, obstruct all transit for Christians towards the interior. Their means of action are unlimited, their proselytism ardent, their progress unfortunately rapid. Already two-thirds at least of the Gallas nation are Mussulmans. In Christian Abyssinia they form a third of the population. In the capitals of Gondar, Tigré, and Shoa, they are in the ascendant, in consequence of their wealth and influence... The Christians, who are only heretics by birth, would willingly embrace our religion, if they were not oppressed by the Abouna and the Mussulmans. »

In spite of these formidable difficulties, and of the grave fact affirmed by Bishop Massaia, that « Mahometanism tends to supremacy within a short period, » -- for none of the heretical communities of the East have life enough to resist its progress, — the Catholic missionaries still pursue their arduous toils, always in peril, yet never dismayed, and leaving the result to Him whose servants they are.

Already, six years ago, they had received the abjuration of more than *ten thousand* Abyssinians,
including their most eminent ecclesiastics; and
within the last two years their influence has powerfully increased, even their most inveterate enemies
being subdued by their unalterable patience and
charity. In May, 1860, one of the most intelligent
and influential of the Abyssinian princes « was
restored to Catholic unity, together with all his
people. » (1) A little earlier, Négoucié, another of
the native potentates, sent a solemn embassy to the
Pope, announcing the free exercise of the Catholic
religion throughout his dominions, and expressing
his own desire to be received into the Church. (2)

It is evident that but for the potent influence of
Islamism, and its ceaseless intrigues, they would
soon convert all Abyssinia. The Abbot of Guend-
guendic, one of the most important personages in
the country, lately exclaimed aloud in the presence
of Ubié, to some of the chief opponents of the
missionaries; « If you would combat the Catholics
with success, you must begin by leading as Christian
lives as they do. » Bishop Jacobis, who relates this
anecdote, adds, — « Thanks to our Divine Saviour,
the exemplary conduct of the Abyssinian Catholics
wonderfully justifies this reasoning. As for the
Abbot, he does not confine himself to barren
speeches; impatient to confirm them by his actions,
he solicits without intermission the favour of being
admitted into the number of the faithful. We should

(1) *Annals*, n° 120, p. 125.
(2) *L'Abolition de l'Esclavage*, par Augustin Cochin; tome II,
p. 522.

already have yielded to the eagerness of his desires, if the conversion of a personage placed so high in general esteem, on account of his perpetual fasting, did not require sundry precautions, suggested by the interests of religion itself. This is, however, a sure conquest, although adjourned, and our temporising only serves to mature it by fasting and prayer. » (1)

And now, since we have sufficiently manifested the character of Catholic influence in Abyssinia, and of the generous apostles by whose toil it is maintained, we may quit a subject which our limits do not permit us to exhaust. From Abyssinia, where the creed of St. Athanasius is evidently destined to triumph over the errors of Eutyches and Dioscorus, the faith is spreading even among the barbarous Gallas tribes. « I enjoy perfect liberty in the exercise of my ministry, » says Bishop Massaia, now Vicar Apostolic of the Gallas, at the close of 1853. « A few years of patient perseverance will enable me, I feel convinced, to enter into communication with Sennaar. » Seven years later, a Protestant missionary will tell us that the brave bishop had penetrated far beyond even that remote place. « I have with me here (Sondabo) two pupils, one an Abyssinian, the other a Galla; the latter exceedingly fervent, and whom, in the course of another year, I shall be able to ordain Priest. Nothing but death shall separate me from my neophytes; and if my corpse is not followed to the grave by a numerous procession of Christians, the land at all events is here cheap enough to afford sepulture to my unworthy remains.

(1) Vol. X, p. 307.

Let me only succeed, before that hour arrives, in planting the Cross, and in kindling the evangelical fire which already begins to burn in the hearts of a few individuals, and the whole Gallas nation will be saved. » (1)

Six years later, the apostolic labours of this courageous prelate had already produced so much fruit in this savage soil, — which only zeal like his would have dared to cultivate, far from all human succour, and deprived of all human means, — that he found it necessary to consecrate a coadjutor, and the *native* clergy consisted of five priests, a deacon, and seven religious.

It is of the labours of such a man as this, and of his venerable colleagues, — who, as Mʳ Hamilton observes with admiration, were not rarely « victims to the excessive austerity of their lives, » and who won the reluctant veneration of the Moslem, the Nubian, and the Galla, — that a protestant minister, Dʳ Wilson, could deliberately write as follows. « The apparent success of the agents of Rome at present in Abyssinia is to be attributed principally to bribery and corruption. Let them beware of all unrighteousness and hypocrisy, for the day of reckoning may come sooner than they expect. » (2) Has Dʳ Wilson forgotten that it will come for himself also?

Let us return for a moment from the country of the Gallas to Abyssinia, before we pass to other regions, in order to notice, according to our custom,

(1) Vol. XV, p. 178.
(2) *Lands of the Bible*, vol. II, p. 593.

the attempts of Protestant missionaries in the latter kingdom.

The Abyssinian christians, fallen as they are, still profess a sincere belief in the Seven Sacraments; and as M. Rochet d'Héricourt — whose salutary influence with the king of Shoa M' Johnston describes and laments — lately observed, display so much reverence for the Mother of God that they celebrate thirty-three annual festivals in her honour. (1) Such devotions, always rewarded by her Divine Son, will no doubt hasten their reconciliation with the Church, in spite of the defects which accompany them. Meanwhile, they have won for the Abyssinians the reproachful sympathy of Protestants, who reprove their agreement with Catholic doctrine as much as they laud their opposition to Catholic unity. In order to check the one and stimulate the other, M' Gobat, the gentleman who now represents, without believing, the Anglican religion at Jerusalem, — in spite of the ineffectual protests of men who are accustomed to « protest » without gaining, or expecting to gain, any thing by it — paid a visit to Abyssinia. He had been preceded by others, one of whom, apparently M' Isenberg, was happy enough, before he was expelled, to dissuade some of the natives from embracing Mahometanism. Let us hope that he may receive an abundant reward for this good action.

M' Gobat seems to have been less successful. His manner of life, he tells us, and especially his invincible repugnance to bodily mortifications in general

(1) *Second Voyage dans le Pays des Adels et le Royaume de Choa*, p. 227.

and to fasting in particular, did not attract the esteem
of the Abyssinian christians. « The greater part of
the monks, » he complains, « have become my enemies, and call me ' Mussulman, ' because I condemn
the adoration of the Virgin Mary, and have no confidence in her intercession. » (1) And so he found it
expedient to depart, the people obstinately refusing
to believe that a man could be any thing better than
a Turk who never fasted, had « no confidence »
in the all-powerful Mother of Jesus, and publicly
asserted that she « was a sinner. »

As such a statement may appear impossible, even
in the mouth of one who seems to be, at the same
moment, a German Lutheran, an agent of the Church
Missionary Society, and an Anglican bishop, it may
be well to add, that Mr Gobat records in his Journal,
for the advantage of English readers, the very arguments which he proposed without success to the
Abyssinians. The Immaculate Virgin was evidently
a sinner, he says, for two reasons; first because she
called our Blessed Lord her Saviour; and secondly,
because she allowed Him to wander from her on the
journey from Jerusalem! A French writer observes
that Mr Gobat might have proved, by the same reasoning, that our Lord was also a sinner, because He
submitted to be baptized, and because He voluntarily
left the company of our Lady and St. Joseph. (2)

But if the Abyssinians refused to believe that
Mr Gobat was a Christian, he was equally surprised
that they could resist the attractions of his lenient

(1) *Journal of a Three Years Residence in Abyssinia*, ch. IV,
p. 323.

(2) *Les Lieux Saints*, par Mgr Mislin, tome III, ch. xxviii.

religious code, and reject the cheerful form of
Christianity which he offered them. « If the Priests
choose to marry, » he remarks, severely reproving
their indifference to that source of enjoyment, « they
have nothing to fear, *except* a little contempt, together with the prohibition of their officiating as
priests. »(1) To this hour, Mr Gobat can neither understand why these Ethiopians took him for a Turk,
nor why they rejected his cordial invitation to « defile
themselves with women;» (2) because, as he observes,
all they had to apprehend was « a little contempt, »
and degradation from the priesthood. By such inadequate motives they were restrained from embracing
the religion of Mr Gobat.

If Mr Gobat had selected Kurdistan, instead of
Abyssinia or Jerusalem, as the scene of his labours,
there is reason to believe that in the former country
he would found the disciples whom he failed to attract by the rivers of Ethiopia or under the shadows
of Mount Sion. That Kurdistan would have received
him, if not with enthusiasm, at least with sympathy,
we may infer from the remark of a Kurd to an English traveller, to whom he confidentially observed,
that the English and Kurdish religions were evidently identical, — « for *we* eat hog's flesh, drink
wine, keep no fasts, and say no prayers. » (3)

Mr Gobat asserts, however, that he did make at
least one convert in Abyssinia, and we are able to cor-
roborate the statement by the testimony of a fellow

(1) Ch. v, p. 349.
(2) *Apoc.* XIV, 4.
(3) *Nineveh and Persepolis,* by W. S. Vaux, M. A., ch. II,
p. 23.

missionary. « Girgis, an Abyssinian, » says D' Joseph Wolff, « was converted by Gobat. » The fact, then, is authentic; but D' Wolff adds immediately, as if to check undue elation, that this solitary convert first sold two children into slavery who had been entrusted to his care, « and afterwards turned Muhammedan at Cairo. » (1)

It is characteristic of the levity which accepts and propagates such fictions, that in a biography of M' Gobat, published by what is called « the Evangelical Alliance, » this very Girgis is presented to the admiration of English Protestants as « a noble Abyssinian, » and a devout pupil of Kugler and Gobat, « whose instructions, combined with the diligent study of the sacred Scriptures, were blessed greatly to promote his advancement in divine things! » (2)

When M' Gobat retired from Abyssinia, to continue elsewhere his unfinished career, he was succeeded by D' Lewis Krapf, who appears to have resembled the Anglican bishop of Jerusalem, both in his views of Christianity and in the success with which he taught them. M' Gobat, indeed, was content to recommend matrimony to the Abyssinian clergy for its own sake; D' Krapf from higher motives. « My experiences convinced me, » says the latter gentleman, « that an unmarried missionary *could not* eventually prosper. » It might perhaps be suggested that this opinion betrays an imperfect acquaintance with the history of Christianity; nor does

(1) Wolff's *Journal*, p. 331.
(2) *Evangelical Christendom*, vol. I, p. 77.

Dʳ Krapf's own career encourage the belief that marriage is an infallible guarantee of missionary success. Everywhere he failed. « I am specially grieved, » he says, « by the indifference of the Wanika, » — who had largely shared in his « thirty chests full of Bibles. » « My dear fellow-labourer Rebmann had at one time collected a flock of children at Bonni, and begun to teach them; but they soon dispersed. » In the midst of these vexations, « it was very consolatory, » he observes, « to remember the words, Fear not, Abram, I am thy shield, and thy exceeding great reward. » The only reward, however, which he actually records is his appointment to a comfortable position in Germany, for which he abandoned the insensible Wanika.

Dʳ Krapf's view of the efficacy of marriage in promoting missionary work appears to have been modified by later observations. « The wish to settle down as comfortably as possible, » he remarks, « and to marry, entangles a missionary in many external engagements which may lead him away from his Master and his duty. This wish naturally prompts him to trouble himself about irrelevant and subordinate matters, such for instance as house-building, all sorts of colonizing schemes, etc., etc. » Dʳ Krapf appears, therefore, to have been at least partially converted to St. Paul's doctrine on the same subject.

Dʳ Krapf records one convert, like Mʳ Gobat, but Dʳ Krapf is an honest man, though an unsuccessful missionary, and tells us his real character. Wolda Gabriel, Dʳ Krapf's hired servant, was a native of Shoa, and having been sent to Jerusalem, « became acquainted with the Bible and the Protestant faith. »

He could even, says his master, « defend pure Christianity against Mohommedans and bigoted Christians
of the Greek, Romish, and Abyssinian churches. »
But this was the sum of his merits. He had reached
that point beyond which no disciple of Protestant
missionaries ever advances, and « in spite of all his
intellectual acquirements, his heart was still unrenewed and unregenerate. »

On the other hand, Dr Krapf, like Dr Smith in
China and Mr Tomlin in India, was able to detect
that the labours of Catholic missionaries, in spite of
their being unmarried, were more fruitful than his
own. We even learn something from him about Bishops Massaia and Jacobis, and the colleagues who
shared their toils. « The Abuna said that the Gallas
would not allow white people to visit Kaffa, especially if they were provided with fire arms. In spite
of this, some Romish missionaries seem to have succeeded in reaching Kaffa, where they are said to have
been very well received by the King of the country. »
« Some time ago, » he adds, « an Italian priest is
said to have penetrated to Gezan, which is apparently
twelve days south of Sennar, and thence to have
proceeded to Fadasi, the chief place of the tribe
Bene-Shongol. He seems to have purposed to reach
Enarea and Kaffa, where are some Romish missionaries, who went to Kaffa from Abyssinia. » The missionary executed his bold project, and at Fadasi
« gained the favour of the prince by curing his sick
son. »

But Dr Krapf has more to tell us. Unable, like his
co-religionists in other lands, to relate any victories of
his own, he is content to celebrate those of Catholics.

« The Romanists made converts in Halai, Dixan, Kaich, Kur, and in other places, on the frontiers of Tigre, as many priests in the interior played into their hands. » Towards himself, if we interpret his silence rightly, the same priests were less favorably disposed; yet their Abuna was willing to give him free scope, and he relates, with great simplicity, how bluntly that intelligent functionary intimated his personal conviction that he had nothing whatever to fear from Protestant missionaries. « The Protestant missionaries, » he told Dr Krapf, — who repeats the words without the slightest suspicion of their true meaning, — «do not injure the Abyssinian Church, for they circulate the Bible, and that only ; » a practice which the Abuna had good reason to know would lead to very harmless results, « such as the wrapping up of snuff, » as Mr Parkyns has told us, « and such like undignified purposes. » The « eight thousand Bibles » which Dr Krapf himself distributed had made no other conquest than the « unrenewed and unregenerate » Wolda Gabriel.

But « the Romanists, » the Abuna assured Dr Krapf, were insupportable, » and interfered with my government of the Church. » Moreover, *they* were making converts in all directions, especially among the higher ecclesiastics, and were in every way offensive. For this reason, when Kasai attacked Ubié in 1853, the Abuna promised his co-operation, if the former would banish the Catholic missionaries from Gondar; which that prince did, to the great but premature exultation of Dr Krapf. The Catholic religion is accustomed to outlive more formidable adversaries than Kasai, as Dr Krapf quickly dis-

covered. And so, he observes, « Ubié worked so
strenuously in the interest of Rome, » having learned
to venerate such representatives of the Holy See as
Massaia and Jacobis, « that the Abuna could not
prevail upon the prince even to cherish the Abyssinian church to which he belonged. It was therefore evident that the Protestant Mission must entirely
abandon Abyssinia, and seek elsewhere for a sphere
of labour; and such was the result. » Whereupon,
says D' Krapf, « I bid farewell to my household,
after prayer and scriptural meditation. » (1) And so
ended the Protestant Mission in Abyssinia.

M' Gobat and D' Krapf, and their immediate associates, were not, however, the only emissaries of
Protestantism who were ejected from Abyssinia. The
Moravians also, we learn from M' Mansfield Parkyns,
maintained a costly mission in that land, and this
was the result of their operations. « Having expended
a large sum in books and property distributed and
lost, they left not one single convert, nor even one
individual who would say more of them than that
they were good natured, open-handed people, but
that it was a pity they were such desperate heretics :
even those whose gratitude for what they might have
gained in lucre induced them to pay the good brethren such negative compliments, were few indeed
compared to those who openly spoke of them as infidels and worse than Turks. »

This verdict, however severe, was not altogether
arbitrary and unprovoked. Not only did the Moravi-

(1) *Travels in Eastern Africa*, ch. vii, p. 87; ch. viii, p. 110;
ch. xi, pp. 185, 437, 465.

ans resemble Mr Gobat in their contempt for the
Saints, and dislike of bodily mortification, — peculiarities which were far from recommending them to
the sympathy of the Abyssinians; they even adopted,
as Mr Parkyns relates, the decisive plan of « killing
meat in the Mission House during one of their most
solemn fasts, *to tempt the poor and hungry to sin
against their own consciences.* » But the famished
Abyssinian was only revolted by this characteristic
proceeding, which excited such universal loathing
and indignation, that « the missionaries were declared to be no Christians, » and when they finally
departed, « they left not a single friend behind. » (1)

Such, in a few words, has been the issue of all
the Protestant missions in Abyssinia. They have
failed to convert a solitary individual, and their conclusion has been greeted by the natives with a chorus
of maledictions. Without, however, employing the
vehement phraseology of the christians of Shoa and
Tigré, we may content ourselves with observing, —
that if Protestant missionaries, of all sects and ranks,
venture upon actions which shock the instincts, and
provoke the disgust and astonishment, of the least
spiritual races of the human family ; if even the best
of them lead everywhere, and with a kind of osten-
tation, a life which, however decent and orderly, is
as manifestly earthly and un-supernatural as that of
their own domestics; while their religion consists
only in periodical fits of emotion, and in an incessant
talk about mysteries which they never realise, and
doctrines which they never interpret, and graces

(1) *Life in Abyssinia*, vol. I, ch. XII, p. 148.

which they never display; they have no reason to be surprised at the judgment which has long ago been passed upon them, with a terrible unanimity of aversion, by the whole heathen world.

It was a rule of the great Apostle to be « all things to all men, » and even to adapt his exposition of divine truth, so far as the integrity of the faith permitted, to the ideas and perceptions of his hearers. He spoke even to the lascivious Greek and the effeminate Syrian of the vigil and the scourge; but if he had preached in Hindostan or Abyssinia, he would willingly have fasted all the year round. Protestant missionaries disdain these apostolic arts. Fathers of families, and absorbed by secular cares, they hate fasting, silence, and every other mortification, and never scruple to avow their antipathies, for which they have always a « scriptural » justification, to all who will listen to them. But in doing so, they effectually alienate, not only Christians, but even pagans and mussulmans.

« The people bother my life out about fasting, » says an English traveller in Africa. « Two young Touarick women came to me —

‘ Thou Christian ! dost thou fast? ’ (they having never seen a person before who did not fast.)

‘ No; the Christians dont fast. ’

The girls.—‘ *Dont the Christians know God?*’ » (1)

Major Cornwallis Harris, another English Protestant, was not less irritated by similar remarks on the part of Abyssinians, who used to ask one another,

(1) Richardson, *Travels in the Great Desert of Sahara,* vol. 1, ch. v, p. 149.

with respect to the members of the English mission
whom that officer conducted to Shoa, — « What can
they be? Are they Jews? or Mahometans, or what?»
And when some charitably suggested that they might
possibly be a kind of degenerate Christians, the
bystanders would reply; « Christians! Impossible.
They observe no fast. » (1)

Mr Gobat, Mr Richardson, and Major Harris might
have told them, if so disposed, that Christians of the
school of St. Paul *do* fast; not, like Mahometans, to
avenge at night the mortification of the body by day;
nor, like heretics, as if fasting, without measure and
without rule, were a substitute for more important
virtues; but with such a prudent and holy fast as
St. Paul enjoined, « to bring the body into subject-
ion, » and chastise its disorderly appetites — a fast
expressive of humility and contrition, inspired by
charity, imposed by law, and consecrated by obedience. They might have told them, too, if they had
remembered it, that the only two men who ever
appeared in glory with the Redeemer of the world,
were also the only two who ever received power to
imitate His supernatural fast of forty days and nights.

We have spoken of the English mission to Shoa.
Mr Johnston, alluding to its utter failure, says; « I
know, from personal experience, that the merchant
and the missionary must now seek other situations
for carrying out their interesting and philanthropic
projects for the regeneration of Africa. » The English mission, he seems to think, which was designed
to counteract that of Catholic France, ruined those

(1) *The Highlands of Æthiopia*, vol. II, ch. xxii, p. 184.

projects finally; and « the missionary, » he adds,
« now grieves for influence that is gone for ever. »(1)

The French mission, unlike the English, has been
supremely successful in all its aims. Aided by the
powerful influence of the Bishop and his apostolic
companions, the dignity of whose character has conciliated even their enemies, it has already import-
antly served the interests both of religion and of
France. The delegate of the Holy See is at length
enthroned in the capital of Abyssinia, and fresh conquests reward his patient and enlightened zeal. Only
the enemies of the Church, and of her work of regeneration, have reason to deplore this new triumph
of faith and civilization; but *they* do not conceal
their displeasure. A French Protestant lady, whose
deplorable language makes one forget her sex, met
in Mr Lieder's unsuccessful school at Cairo an Abyssinian youth, who seems to have made the usual
progress towards utter infidelity under his English
teachers, but who gave this candid account of his own
native district. « There was an English missionary in
my country, *but they sent him away;* there is now
an Italian missionary, who has built a chapel : they
love the French religion better than the English. »(2)
And an emissary of a London Society lamented a
little later that the contest was over, and that « the
endeavours of Protestants to send other agents into
the country have hitherto been frustrated by the intrigues of the Jesuits. » (3) The truth is, as we have
seen by Protestant testimony, that they were driven

(1) Vol. II, ch. v, p. 70, and 84.
(2) *Journal d'un Voyage au Levant,* tome II, p. 446.
(3) *Journal of a Deputation to the East,* vol. II, p. 849.

away by the indignation of the people, who needed
no stimulus from a few helpless foreigners to rid
themselves of teachers whose worldly lives and unchristian doctrines led the Abyssinians, in spite of
their own imperfections, to regard them « as infidels
and worse than Turks. »

And now let us turn our faces westwards, traverse
the vast regions which have already proved fatal to
so many of the apostles of human science, — Ledyard
and Park, Burkhardt and Bowditch, Lang and Clap-
perton, and, in our own day, Barth and Warrington, (1) — and without lingering in that great central
waste into which the Catholic missionary alone can
ever introduce religion and civilization, let us com-
mence on the opposite coast of Africa the investigations which we have already attempted to pursue
along its eastern frontier.

The Père Labat, in his account of Western Africa,
endeavours to prove that the Normans visited that
coast in the beginning of the fourteenth century. (2)
If it were so, they left no materials, and were not
likely to leave any, for the history which we now
propose to trace. Four nations have, since that date,
partly from religious and partly from commercial
motives, made settlements on different points of the
Atlantic coast. The Portuguese, who led the way in
the fifteenth century, now retain only in Lower Guinea — including the Kingdoms of Congo, Angola,
and Benguela — the authority which they once
exerted through a wider range; Senegambia, and

(1) *Statement of the Society for exploring Central Africa*, p. 7.
(2) *Nouvelle Relation de l'Afrique Occidentale*, tome I, ch. II.

the Mandingo race, acknowledge the influence of
France; the Cape Coast region forms part of the
ample colonial conquests of Great Britain; and
America seeks, by her merchants and her missionaries, to dispute at Cape Palmas and a few other
points, by the energetic action of the Maryland Colonisation Society, the religious and mercantile supremacy of Europe. Let us begin with Sierra Leone
and the contiguous districts, which, for more than
half a century, have been appropriated as their peculiar field by the agents of English commerce and
religion.

England has not usually been happy in the earlier
representatives of her church and polity in foreign
lands. It is true that the Anglican Church has, in
every instance, employed members of other communities to convey her doctrines to the heathen —
because her own ministers, salaried officials of a
civil corporation, invariably refused the task. As
in India and Ceylon, in Syria and the Levant, and
in many other places, so in West Africa, she
has been represented chiefly by Germans. Even the
Americans, each of whose multitudinous sects has
its own distinctive missionary organization, freely
remark upon the reluctance of the Church of England clergy to act as missionaries. « The Church
Missionary Society, » observes the Rev. Joseph
Tracy, in a work on this subject, « sent out Germans; for, after several years of effort, no English
missionary could be procured. » (1) This statement

(1) *Colonization and Missions*, by J. Tracy, Secretary of the
Mass. Col. Socy, p. 30.

may not be literally true; for the Rev. William
Moister, an African missionary, informs us, that the
« Society for the Propagation of the Gospel in Foreign Parts » sent a clergyman to Cape Coast Castle
as early as 1751. Possibly, however, this gentleman
was also a German; but whatever his nation may
have been, « very little impression, » we are told,
« seems to have been made upon the minds of the
natives. » And then Mr Moister adds a very instructive anecdote. The clergyman returned to England
after four years absence, bringing with him three
native boys for education. The fate of two of
them is not recorded; but the third, Quaque, received the highest privileges which England and her
national church could bestow upon him. He was sent
to Oxford, « ordained, » after completing his studies
at that venerable university, and finally despatched
to his own country as the government chaplain.
« This post, » says Mr Moister, « he continued to
occupy for *more than fifty years;* but it does not
appear that he was instrumental in turning any of his
fellow countrymen to the faith of Christianity. Nor is
this matter of surprise, when it is known that, on his
death-bed, he had, at least, as much confidence in
the influence of the *fetish* as in the power of Christianity. » (1)

Commencing our history with this characteristic
example of the combined influence of England's principal church and university, let us now examine the
successive events which that history records. Not

(1) *Memorials of Missionary Labour in W. Africa*, ch. i, p. 41.
Cf. *Ashantee and the Gold Coast*, by John Beecham, ch. x, p. 258.

that Quake was really the first representative of English protestantism in Africa; for as early as 1553, as Mʳ Hugh Murray relates, Windham conducted an expedition to these shores which came to naught, « through the flagrant misconduct of those entrusted with it. » The same fate attended a good many succeeding expeditions. When Granville Sharp, « the indefatigable benefactor of the Africans, » — at least in intention — sent Dʳ Smeathman in 1786 to found a settlement near Sierra Leone, « about sixty whites, but who were chiefly women of abandoned character, debilitated by disease, were embarked on board the transports furnished by Government. » Again, in 1792, when the island of Buloma was ceded to Great Britain, « the majority of those who went out with Mʳ Dalrymple were persons of the most infamous characters and vicious habits. » (1)

In 1795, two missionaries were sent, « but owing to indiscretion on the part of the one, » and the illness of the other, « the mission was speedily abandoned. » (2)

In 1796, the London, Scottish, and Glasgow missionary societies, after deliberating on past failures, resolved to make « a united attempt. » But unity and protestantism do not co-exist; so « this also, » we are told, « owing to sickness and dissension, was attended with no better success. » (3)

In 1799, the African Association sent out Frederic Horneman, the son of a German clergyman. When

---

(1) *Discoveries*, etc., vol. II, ch. IV, pp. 263, 281.
(2) *Western Africa*, by J. D. East, ch. XI, p. 277.
(3) *Ibid.*

he and his party reached Scivah, they were menaced
with instant death as Christians; and then was
enacted one of those curious scenes which are found
only in Protestant annals, but which are perhaps less
curious than the comments made upon them by
Protestant writers. « On this difficult occasion, »
says Murray, — a vehement satirist of the Catholic
religion, — « Horneman acted his part *with great
courage*. » Perhaps you anticipate that he gave his
life for the faith? But this was not Mr Horneman's
view of the value of life; so « he drew out a copy of
the Koran, and displayed his skill in reading and
interpreting that sacred standard of the Mussulman
faith. » Having produced « a deep impression, » says
the Protestant historian, by this unexpected action,
« our traveller, who had thus established his reputation as an orthodox Mussulman, left with the caravan. » Finally, in 1805, Sir William Young was
informed by the British Consul at Tripoli, that Horneman was living amongst the Mahometans, « highly
respected as a Marabout or Mussulman saint. » In
that dignity he seems to have died about 1809. (1)

In 1810, an Englishman, one Adams, was captured by Mahometans, and carried to Timbuctoo.
There he appears to have solaced his retirement by
certain irregularities, which might have been over-
looked, says Murray, but that they were deemed « a
truly unpardonable crime ' in a Christian who never
prayed. ' » (2)

Thus far the history is uniform, and Africa had

(1) Murray, vol. II, p. 445.
(2) *Id*., p. 501.

not yet incurred any sensible obligations to England.
And even a quarter of a century later, we still encounter the same phenomena, which the annalist of
Protestant missions, wherever their scene may be,
strives in vain to avoid. « It has happened to myself, »
says one who represented the British government in
these regions, in 1825, «to have seen one missionary
lying drunk in the streets; to have known a second
living with a negress, one of his parishioners ; and a
third tried for the murder of a little boy whom he
had flogged to death. » And then he adds; « That
system does not work well, in which the removal of
such individuals requires a representation from the
governor of a colony to the secretary of a private
society, who becomes the judge whether the govern-
or's objection shall be acquiesced in or not. » (1)

---

(1) *Travels in Western Africa*, by Major Alexander Gordon
Laing, p. 393. When we consider what is, in every case, the
ostensible profession of a missionary, and that he is voluntarily
pledged, before men and angels, to exhibit in the sight of the
heathen the loftiest type of Christian perfection, we may reasonably feel surprise at the apprehensions which the Directors of Protestant Societies appear to entertain of the probable frailty of
their agents. So diffident are they of the purity of their emissaries,
and so imminent do they consider even such calamities as Major
Laing records, that some at least of their number have devised a
special machinery to deal with these familiar cases. This singular
fact is incidentally revealed by Dr Morrison, of Canton, in forwarding to *his* Society certain disclosures « of an unpleasant
nature, » relating to some of his younger colleagues, which, he
suggests, « should be considered *in the secret department*. » (*Memoirs*, II, 34.) Dr Campbell relates, that in the solemn exhortation to the missionaries who introduced Christianity to Polynesia
« in her native purity, » the prescient clergyman who occupied
the pulpit gave this unusual but not superfluous warning : —

It is time to notice, without further delay, the
final result of operations which commenced so in-
auspiciously. We may state it in a few sentences.
We have seen that the first Protestant emissary
reached Sierra Leone in 1751, — the gentleman who
afterwards conducted Quaque as an undergraduate
to Oxford; more than a century has elapsed, therefore, since the inauguration of missionary efforts in
this colony. Afzelius, a Swedish botanist, relates
that « un bâtiment rempli de missionnaires métho-
distes, » started from London in October, in 1797;
and that a similar expedition the previous year had
been completely unsuccessful (1) What with « indiscretion » in some, and « dissension » in all, the earlier attempts were evidently a series of failures. At
length, the English Government being solidly established throughout the colony, and the natives not
only reconciled to their new masters, but full of admiration for the opulent missionaries who paid them
with unexpected liberality for their presence at school
and chapel, the constitution of the various missions
was permanently organised, and Sierra Leone rejoiced in the possession of *nineteen* different forms
of the Protestant religion. We cannot be expected
to trace the history of them all, still less of those
modifications of Christianity which the negroes have
invented for themselves, and which, being administered by black preachers, — such as « Domingo

« Sons of men, beware of the daughters of women! » The Catholic
Church, sure of the vocation of her apostles, is content to say to
them, as St. Paul said to St. Timothy, « *Neglect not the grace
that is in thee.* »

(1) *Précis sur Sierra Léona*, par C. B. Wadstrom, p. 87.

the Independent, » and « Hector the Baptist, »
— have attracted the special sympathies of enthusiastic congregations. Some of the sermons delivered in these chapels are not altogether such as
a refined ear would hear with satisfaction, and the
expositions of « the Bible » of which they are appropriate theatres would perhaps be more revolting to
a Christian than any sounds which were ever uttered
in these regions before Protestantism set its seal upon
them. Let us confine ourselves, however, to the operations of the Anglican missions, of which a volumi-
nous history has been compiled by the Rev. Samuel
Walker, and which may be taken as a type of the
rest.

There would be more profit in following Mr Walker
through the six hundred pages of his volume, if it
were really a history of benefits conferred upon this
unhappy population; but as his work consists mainly,
not to say exclusively, of panegyrics upon the extraordinary virtues of the missionaries and their wives,
and incessant records of their marriages and of the
fortunes of their children, the natives themselves are
only noticed parenthetically. Still we may glean
something even from his somewhat monotonous biographies, though they resemble one another so exactly
that a single individual might have been the hero of
them all.

In 1836, then, Mr Walker relates that « the journals of the Missionaries are this year abundantly
supplied with proofs of the obstinate adherence of the
natives, *although professing Christianity* » — he
means Protestantism — « to the superstitious usages
of their country. » And then he notices, that some

at least of these « obstinate » disciples were « communicants » of the Church of England! (1)

Elsewhere Mʳ Walker candidly intimates, that in spite of their wealth, and their long occupation of the field, they cannot compete with their Mussulman rivals. « The spread of Mahommedanism at Charlotte this year was most distressing to the Missionaries, who observe, in their report for the year, — ' the emissaries of the false prophet have manifest advantages over the teachers of the Christian religion in this colony, the latter having so few natives to support them. ' » (2)

Yet through the whole period, in spite of such confessions and many more like them, — in spite of the acknowledged paucity of their disciples, and the fact that the best of them, the « communicants, » obstinately adhered to pagan usages, — reports were forwarded to England exactly such as the missionaries used to transmit, with such courageous indifference to truth, probability, and common sense, from the islands of the Pacific. Thus one of the missionaries, the Rev. Mʳ Johnson, — who describes *his* congregation to his friends in England as « 500 black faces prostrate at the throne of grace » — declares, in language which one is ashamed to repeat, that « *all* the people seem to be hungering after the righteousness of Jesus. » And again, « it is really wonderful to see the dealings of the Lord with this people. » (3)

We should probably err, however, in supposing

(1) *The Church of England Mission in Sierra Leone*, p. 379.
(2) P. 305.
(3) *Africa's Mountain Valley*, ch. vii, p. 117. (1856).

these statements to be, in every case, deliberate untruths. They admit of another explanation. Mere physical excitement, which such teachers often mistake for religious emotion, though it comes and goes like a summer cloud, will partly account for them. And moreover, to receive a bible, to quote it as readily as a popular song, to come occasionally to chapel, and to assume the name of a Christian — these were the accepted tokens of « conversion, » and all who could do thus much, no matter from what motive, were sincerely described as « hungering after righteousness. » They satisfied the aspirations of their teachers by this remote imitation of Christianity, and the pastor and his flock were mutually content. (1)

(1) « If there be one thing more than another about the popular religion of the day, it is the cultivation of the *religious feelings*... For this reason it is that we see around us so many strange developments of a religion of mere feeling... In vain does reason point out that they can tell us but little of the deep heart within. They are the mere phenomena of our own consciousness; they are the mere lights and shadows which float over the surface of our being, and have but little to do with our real inward life. They come and go, and are dependent upon a thousand things, which are not our real selves... We do not perceive that we are mistaking the lights that play upon the surface of our souls for its deepest depths; so eager are we to hear news of God in our exile. We think that God is talking to us when we are, in fact, only talking to ourselves.

... Each of the errors which we have noticed is a desperate spring at the substance of God across the wide gulf which yawns between fallen humanity and its Creator... The conversion of the Methodist is the fanatical eagerness of the soul to know the day and hour of its reconciliation to God. Even the sickly self contemplation of the Evangelical arises from the same desire to feel the

Another, and a conclusive proof of effectual conversion consisted in their « observance of the Sabbath day. » « The Africans, » says a Protestant missionary, — who was evidently quite sure of his audience, and knew what they could bear, — « rose to the enjoyment of the Sabbath-day. » (1) To that enjoyment let us leave them, in the hope that they may one day aspire, not in vain, to a deeper and truer religion. Meanwhile, two facts represent the final results which we have no space to illustrate further. England has reason to be satisfied with her colony, because « the total gain to the industry and revenue of the mother country cannot be less than 600,000 l. per annum; » and England's religion is perhaps content with the modest success revealed in the following figures, supplied by M[r] Walker, who admits, in 1847, that although there were 3,311 children in the various schools of the Colony, the whole number of « attendants on public worship, » including those who did not even profess any definite religion, and the communicants who still adhered obstinately to their ancient superstitions, was only 6,376, after the labours of a century. (2)

That some good has been effected, at least by

present God. All long for repose in God, and so far they are right. They err with a fatal error in taking the phenomena for the substance, but it is better to *seek* the reality than to give up all search for God and to acquiesce in the world.

... The fall was the universal shipwreck, and men » — outside the Church — « are tossing about the wild waves on a broken raft, driven to madness by their thirst for the living waters. » F. Dalgairns, *The Holy Communion*, ch. III, pp. 69, 70.

(1) *Africa's Mountain Valley*, ch. X, p. 179.

(2) *Introd.*, p. 29, and p. 589

individuals, and especially in the diffusion of elementary education, we may easily believe, though we shall presently be warned by Protestant writers not to feel too confident even on this point; but that any thing like primitive Christianity has been established amongst this people, or could be by such teachers, who, at the best, were only examples of domestic propriety, we cannot venture to hope. Men whose chief employment, as Mr Walker shows, is « marrying and giving in marriage, » may display many natural virtues, and even persuade the heathen, in rare cases, to outward decency of life; but to make them Christians indeed is a work which God has reserved for those who begin by offering to Him the sacrifice of their own lives, and who, like Massaia and Jacobis, have the vocation of apostles, and the spirit of martyrs.

Let us add, however, — for it is pleasant to meet with even a solitary exception in the dreary history which we are tracing, — that, of late years, some of the Protestant missionaries in this colony have shown higher qualities than are commonly displayed by their class; and, though they have shared the incoherent opinions of their colleagues, have manifested a certain zeal and benevolence which deserves the sympathy of Catholics, and suggests the prayer which St. Augustine once offered for men of a similar character, « that God may teach them the truth which they think they know. »

Senhor Valdez, the latest writer on Western Africa, though professing to be a Catholic, appears to have spent most of his time with Protestant missionaries. They have « done all, » he observes, « that human ingenuity could suggest for the amelioration of the temporal, and for the promotion of the spiritual condition of the liberated Africans. » A little later, he is « astonished at their great knowledge of the Scriptures ; » and then he adds, like M' Cruickshank, M' Duncan, and other Protestant witnesses who shall be quoted, « I only wish their general conduct was more in unison with the divine precepts ; for I was informed that some of them were very partial to their heathen customs, especially polygamy, and were in other respects immoral. Man may give instruction, but he cannot give grace. » (1) It is pleasant, however, to be able to believe, from this gentleman's account, that some of the English missionaries, apparently of more than one sect, have displayed of late both zeal and perseverance in their attempts to improve the lot of the African, and if they cannot make him a Christian, have at least done all which they knew how to do with that object.

If now we leave Sierra Leone, and travel southwards, we shall come to the Gold Coast, and to the kingdoms of Ashantee and Dahomey. M' Drodie Cruickshank, of Cape Coast Castle, a friend of the missionaries, and a member of the Legislative Council, will describe to us the operations on the Gold Coast. Alluding to all that was attempted previous to the suppression of the slave trade, this gentleman says ; « It was one long, dark career of unfeeling selfishness, without a single aspiration for the im-

(1) *Six Years in Western Africa*, by Francisco Travassos Valdez, vol. I, ch. VI, pp. 274, 287.

provement of the natives. Our motives were perfectly understood by them, and placed us at once on
an equality of footing with them. » And then he enters
into details about the missionaries. « The pay given
by them, » he says, — and they corresponded with
him confidentially as one of their own school, —
« to the young men whom they employed as teachers
being fully equal to that given by the merchants, and
a greater number of them being required for this
service, the missionary employment became an object
of ambition with many, as much, we are assured, in
many instances, for the sake of the loaves and fishes,
as from a sincere and earnest desire to promote the
cause of Christianity. This inducement drew a
number of the best educated natives within the pale
of the Society ; » — while « masons, carpenters,
labourers, » and others employed by the missionaries
in building, « in like manner swelled the ranks of
the Christian community. » (1)

Thus far we have an authentic account of the mode
in which their congregations were collected; and
Commander Foote, of the United States navy, judi-
ciously observes, that the missionaries have this
additional advantage in their contest with the Mahometans, that the natives easily perceive that « Christianity now stands contrasted with Mohammedanism,
as being the deliverer, while the latter is still the
enslaver. » (2) In spite of these inappreciable aids,
M' Cruickshank gives precisely the same account of

(1) *Eighteen Years on the Gold Coast of Africa*, vol. II, ch. IV,
p. 68.

(2) *Africa and the American Flag*, ch. XXXIV, p. 388.

the Protestant converts which we have heard in so
many other countries. Of their use of the Bible, he
says, that « texts which seemed to bear some reference to the peculiar situation of individuals were
wrested to suit their views, and to minister to their
inclinations and wants. » And then he goes on thus,
though he was the associate of their teachers, and
the earnest advocate of their efforts.

« We are constrained to believe that many of the
converts were either labouring under a hypocritical
delusion, or that the frailty of human nature exhibited itself with a uniformity of weakness truly humil-
iating and deplorable. » « There are only a very few
exceptions, » he adds presently, « to a *general relapse*
into immorality, when motives of personal interest
no longer bound them. » And again, as if the picture
were not sufficiently gloomy, « it is lamentable to
have to state, that many of the *best educated* and
most intelligent men, who, some years ago, were
most distinguished for zeal for Christianity, and who
occupied the first rank among the *office-bearers* of
the Society, are now living without its pale, while
the offices are filled by an inferior class. » He allows
that some good is done by the numerous Protestant
schools, which the natives attend solely to qualify
themselves for advancement, but « it is rare for a lad
leaving the school to observe such a correct deportment as will admit him to the honour of membership. » Finally, after a painful description of the
« gloomy and morose austerity which seems to
pervade the ministrations of the missionaries, » he
concludes with these words; — « it has often been
a question, whether, with the pecuniary means pla-

ced at the disposal of the Gold Coast Mission, greater
results might not have been expected. » (1)

Throughout the whole region the same invariable
facts recur. Of the Episcopalian missionaries at Cape
Palmas, M' Tracy, a Protestant minister, reports
that, as late as 1842, « the chiefs entered into a
conspiracy to kill the missionaries and plunder their
premises. » (2) M' Kelly explains, in the same year,
that « the disorder originated in this way. The Protestant ministers *had forestalled almost all the trade
of the coast*, to the great injury of the American
merchants. Deplorable consequences flowed from this
rivalry... The king and his subjects took up arms,
and appeared resolved to set fire to the Protestant
establishments. » Meanwhile, we are told, the Catholic missionaries « continued to visit the sick and
to teach the catechism, without meeting with the
slightest insult; » — for even the angry natives
knew that *they* had no interest in the schemes of the
rival traders. (3)

Again; the American Board of Foreign Missions
confess, with respect to the operations conducted in
the same place under their special superintendance,
that even « the colonists, as a body, regard the missionaries and their enterprise with ill will; » (4) because they find them their most formidable rivals in
all commercial speculations. D' Morison tells also
the usual tale of a certain « M' H., » a Protestant

(1) Pages 73 and seqq.
(2) *Historical Examination of the State of Society in W. Africa*,
p. 25.
(3) Quoted in *Annals*, vol. IV, p. 246.
(4) East, p. 295.

missionary, who « fell into a state of mournful backsliding, and greatly dishonoured his sacred calling. »(1) Yet it is to maintain such persons and their
families in opulent idleness, that England and America consume annually nearly three millions sterling,
with no result whatever but to make Christianity a
proverb among the heathen. Most of them, too, as we
have seen in China and elsewhere, do not even take
the trouble to learn the dialects of the people to whom
they are supposed to preach. « I cannot but express
my surprise, » observes a Protestant minister, who
was deputed to visit the West African missions directed by his own community, « that *in eighteen years*
no attempt has been made to acquire and speak the
languages of the country. » (2)

Of Dahomey, Commander Forbes relates that « the
Mohammedan religion, spreading over the vast continent of Africa, is gaining millions of converts ; » (3)
while Mr Duncan, another friend of the Protestant
missionaries, gives this candid report as to the working of *their* schools. « All that these young men aspire
to, is to get something in the fashion of European
clothing, and to seek employment as clerks. » He
deplores the « little benefit » of « a partial education
by merely reading the Scriptures, » and adds that,
« in many instances this partial education is only the
means of enabling them to become *more perfect in
villainy.* » (4) Yet the missionaries, in order to swell

(1) *The Fathers of the London Missionary Society*, app. p. 596.
(2) *Life and Journals of the Revd D. West*, ch. VIII, p. 184.
(3) *Dahomey and the Dahomans*, vol. I, p. 170. (1851).
(4) *Travels in Western Africa*, vol. I, ch. III, p. 42; vol. II,
ch. XIII, p. 303.

their funds, could gravely describe these poor Africans as « prostrate before the throne of grace, » and « hungering after righteousness. »

And now let us attempt a brief review of Catholic missions in West Africa. From Senegambia to Congo and the southern limits of Guinea, through nearly forty degrees of latitude, on both sides of the equator, — and from the Atlantic towards Soudan and for three hundred miles into the interior,—the Catholic faith has been preached, with an efficacy, as Protestant writers will tell us, which sufficiently attests its divine power. It was in the fifteenth century that apostolic missionaries commenced their labours in the kingdoms of Congo, Loango, and the contiguous regions. To discover a new realm, and to despatch to it without an hour's delay the messengers of peace, was the unfailing practice of Spain, Portugal, and France, animated by still more zeal for the salvation of souls than for conquest and renown. About the year 1485, as Merolla relates, three Dominican Fathers entered Congo : the first was martyred, and the other two died of the climate. (1) Their successors, as well as the sons of St. Francis, « penetrated deep into Congo, » as D' Leyden remarks, « and even into the regions behind, explored by no other European. » (2) A little later, the Jesuits carried the Cross into the same country ; and that we may comprehend at once, by one prodigious fact, — revealed to us by Protestant testimony,— what was the nature of their work, let us hear an English witness, who writes

(1) *Voyage to Congo*, Pinkerton, vol. XVI, p. 215.
(2) *Discoveries and Travels in Africa*, by J. Leyden, M. D., vol. I, ch. I, p. 77.

from the Cape of Good Hope, in the year 1859. At that recent date, the Protestant editor of an African journal declares, that « the Jesuits, before their expulsion, effected so much, that the natives in the large districts are *still* taught to read and write, the work of education *being carried on by native teachers.* » (1)

This remarkable fact, characteristic of the strangely enduring influence of the Catholic apostolate, is more than confirmed by Dʳ Livingstone, who tells us, with the frank honesty which distinguishes that manly writer, that « the Jesuit teaching has been so permanent » — in spite of a century of abandonment and calamity — that even at this day « the Prince of Congo is professedly a Christian, and that there are no fewer than twelve churches in that kingdom, the fruits of the mission established in former times at San-Salvador, the capital; » (2) and further, that the poor deserted natives, to whom Portugal, fallen from the glory of other days, has no longer Jesuits to send, still try, in spite of their ignorance, « to keep up the ceremonies of the Church! » Woe to the men who robbed Africa of her apostles, and restored to the enemy so many victims who had been rescued from his dominion.

There is no need to trace in all its details the history of the missions of which Dʳ Livingstone and others have noticed the actual remains, and which declined because, — in consequence of the constant mortality of the missionaries, the forcible suppress-

(1) *The Cape and Natal News*, January 31, 1859, p. 80.
(2) *Missionary Travels in S. Africa*, ch. xxi, pp. 411, 426.

ion at a later period of religious societies in various
parts of Europe, and the total absence during a long
course of years of apostolic teachers, — there was
no one left to maintain them. It was the special misfortune of Western Africa to be connected with an
empire already corrupted, faithless to Catholic traditions, and rapidly hastening to ignominious decay,
owing to the gradual extinction of all religious principle amongst its rulers; and Proyart was probably
not mistaken when he said, that the immoralities of
the Portuguese accelerated the ruin of their missions
in Africa.

In India, the influence of Portugal, once a chosen
instrument in the designs of Providence, has for
many years been unfavorable to religion and morality. Since the hour when Pombal, too well imitated
by his successors, cast away the traditions which
had made her one of the noblest and mightiest of
European nations, and adopted the political philosophy of Protestantism, which refuses to the Creator
any share in the government of civil society, decay
and ruin have marked the history of Portugal; till
at length the « most faithful » kingdom has become
contemptible in the eyes of the world, and her colonies, with the exception of Brazil, are a proverb for
the feebleness and disorder which Brazil only escaped by timely separation. « It is deplorable, » says
Senhor Valdez, speaking of a colony of 3,000 Catholic Africans, in the island of Anno Bom, « to see
such destitution of religious services as exists among
them. » (1) And this is not a solitary case. But Por-

(1) Vol. II, ch. I, p. 63.

tugal, which has lost all religious fervour at home, except in the hearts of the poor, is unworthy to be any longer a nursery of apostolic missionaries, and the cloud which broods over the land of De Britto and Laynez casts its shadow even upon the « streamless deserts » of Africa.

From 1534 to 1626, eight bishops ruled in succession the Church in Congo ; but from 1648, « the kingdom remained without any clergy, » (1) and in 1814 the king vainly implored the Portuguese monarch to « send clergymen to Congo. » Yet we learn from Proyart, that when some missionaries visited the interior towards the close of the 18th century, they found a province (Sogno) in which, after their long abandonment, « the people still continued Christians, and publicly professed the faith, and their horror of idolatry, » and were accustomed to offer prayers to God to send them a missionary. (2) Such facts, proper to the history of Catholic missions, sufficiently indicate the influence once exerted in these countries by men, who, as Murray scornfully relates, « sometimes exercised an authority almost paramount to that of the sovereigns. »

The same unfriendly annalist repeatedly admits the courage and firmness with which they « insisted upon a strict conformity to the Christian rule. » Hoefer tells us of one of them who « converted the king of Mahongo and all his family, » and yet found leisure to publish a grammar and dictionary of the

(1) Valdez, vol. II, ch. ii, p. 85.
(2) Histoire de Loango, Kakongo, et autres Royaumes d'Afrique, par M. l'abbé Proyart, ch. xvii, p. 317. (1776).

Bondo language; (1) and an infidel French writer
confesses, that « there is something marvellous » in
the fact, that « a few ignorant missionaries, » as he
absurdly styles such men as Colombini and Caone-
cattim, « were able to snatch a whole people from
their ancient customs and their gods. » (2)

« It is astonishing, » says a Protestant writer already quoted, « to find what a hold the Portuguese
have got upon the tribes far into the interior, and it
is impossible not to conclude that the enlightenment
and happiness of Africa in future ages will depend
very much upon them. » (3) May Portugal once
more prove worthy of the sublime mission which
Providence entrusted to her in earlier days! Already
there are signs of her resurrection. It is Dr Livingstone who tells us, that « the good influence of the
Bishop of Angola, both in the city and the country,
is universally acknowledged, » and that he is especially active in « promoting the establishment of
schools. » The same excellent writer reports of the
abandoned district of Ambaca, which he traversed,
that « it is now quite astonishing to observe the
great numbers who can read and write in this district. This is the fruit of the labours of the Jesuit and
Capuchin missionaries, for they taught the people of
Ambaca ; and ever since the expulsion of the teachers
by the Marquis of Pombal, *the natives have continued
to teach each other.* These devoted men are still held
in high estimation throughout the country to this

(1) *Afrique Australe*, par M. F. Hoefer, p. 471. (1848).
(2) *Encyclopédie de Voyages*, par J. Grasset de S. Sauveur;
Mœurs des Habitans du Congo, p. 16.
(3) *The Cape and Natal News*.

day. All speak well of them — os padres Jesuitas. »
And then D' Livingstone utters a regret, — which
we also may share, though not for precisely the same
reasons, — that the Jesuits did not « give the people
the Bible, to be a light to their feet, when the good
men themselves were gone. » (1)

Yet this distinguished traveller will confess, that
to translate the sacred Scriptures into the African
dialects, — a work in which Protestant missionaries,
with all their leisure, have not hitherto been very
successful, — was hardly possible to men absorbed
by the toils of their apostolic calling, and speedily
worn out by exhaustion and the influence of such a
climate. And we may add, without disrespect to this
worthy man, that, from his own account — which
we shall have the advantage of quoting presently —
these very men effected so much more, without the
aid of such translations, than his own colleagues have
accomplished with them, that for upwards of a century their potent influence has survived them; nor
will he deny, with the facts of Protestant missions
before him, that while millions of Christians, during
the early ages, attained to the closest union with
God, though they never saw a Bible, — thousands in
our own day, who have almost learned it by heart,
are still as far from any saving knowledge of Him as
the pagans themselves.

We have now only to state, in conclusion, what
Catholic missionaries are doing in West Africa at
the present moment.

Twenty years have not elapsed since D' Barron,

_____
(1) Ch. xix, p. 382.

formerly Vicar General of Philadelphia, was appointed by the Holy See Bishop of Constantina and
Vicar Apostolic of Upper and Lower Guinea. Landing at Cape Palmas during the rainy season, with a
band of missionaries who were immediately dispersed to various points along the coast, but who
did not find so much as a roof to shelter them, almost
all were cut off by death in rapid succession. The
Abbé de Regnier fell first. « Tell my family and
friends, » were his last words, « that I rejoice at
having left all for our Divine Master. » Father Bouchet was the next to sink, followed in a few weeks
by Fathers Audebert, Laval, Roussel, and Maurice.
Finally, of seven who had arrived in health and
vigour, one only, the Abbé Bessieux, remained
alive.

Six months after, in June 1845, the solitary survivor wrote as follows from Gaboon. « I shall soon
see zealous colleagues succeeding the friends whom
I have lost, encouraging and sustaining my feeble
steps. For, God forbid that you should forsake this
poor Africa! » Already he had discerned that the
tribes on the sea-coast had formed their estimate of
Europeans from the miserable examples before their
eyes, and had judged the spurious christianity offered
to them; but, he added, there are tribes in the interior, « reared in privations, inured to toil, and famous for their courage. They know that there is
nothing in common between the Catholic Priests and
the foreign traders. To them we will go first : this is
a conquest which the ministers of error will not venture to dispute with us. »

Four months later, the same intrepid missionary

had twelve native children residing under his charge, and could say; « I do not fear to assert, that there is at Gaboon a multitude of souls ready to receive the heavenly seed. » But he was alone, and poor, without as he observed, the immense resources of the Protestant ministers. » (1) Let us leave him for a moment, to follow the steps of others.

In 1847, his colleague Father Briot de la Maillerie wrote from Ndakar, a station on the Gaboon. Already they had established a training seminary, in which were « twelve native Levites, whose good conduct and docility have singularly edified us, » and who had learned to sing in the Wolof tongue » the praises of Jesus and Mary. » In the same year these students were present at the ordination of the Abbé Gallais, and « their joy was at its height. They mutually excited each other to hasten the time for their ordination. Each fixed already the district which he would take! One would go to Cayot, another to Fouta,.... and thus the whole apostolic vicariate was appropriated ! » « Be persuaded, » said the Abbé Gallais, a little later, « that these negroes are not such as calumny has so often been pleased to depict them. » They were now in the hands of apostles who could not only talk to them of a far-off Saviour, but guide them to His feet.

In 1852, the Abbé Durand sends these tidings from the mouth of the Gambia. « Praise be to God, in spite of numerous obstacles, amongst which the snares of the Methodists are not the least, the Catholic religion has made rapid progress in this coun-

(1) *Annals*, vol. VIII, p. 76.

try. In the year that has just elapsed, we have had one hundred and thirty baptisms, and have admitted forty to their first communion. The dispositions of our neophytes are excellent. »

By the year 1854, out of a total of seventy-five Missionaries sent to Western Africa, *forty-two* had already perished; but there remained at that date two bishops, fifteen priests, eleven lay brothers, and nineteen sisters. « Our Christians, » says the co-adjutor Vicar Apostolic in that year, « are generally faithful to their religious duties, especially in localities not frequented by Europeans. We have forty pupils in the central house of studies at Ndakar, » — by the following year the number had increased to sixty; « henceforth many of the principal difficulties may be regarded as overcome; traditions have been formed, an administrative organisation has been established, and is beginning to work with regularity. » (1)

But the bishop was destined to encounter a trial which even Apostolic zeal could neither avert nor resist. Twice since the date of his letter every Catholic missionary, including all the Bishops, has been swept away by pestilence. Warned by these repeated calamities, the ecclesiastical authorities appear to have adopted the conclusion, that the evangelization of Western Africa must henceforth be mainly committed to a native clergy; and to secure a staff of competent native missionaries is now the aim of the Holy See. But the dead have not laboured in vain.

At Goree, by the year 1845, there were already twelve hundred Catholics; and a Protestant mission-

(1) Vol. XV, p. 330.

ary reports, in 1850, « the people of Goree were all
either Mahometans or Roman Catholics. »(1)

The native king, a Mahometan, assured the Abbé
de la Maillerie, that he had no objection to his commencing a school for his people, « since it was for
a good object; » and a little later Father Arragon
could give this encouraging account. « At Goree, as
in all Africa, the harvest to be gathered is immense...
The Marabouts are pleased to see us in this country;
they salute us when they meet us; they are fond of
saying that they esteem us, because we love the great
God. Again, the people are warmly attached to us,
and show themselves grateful for the smallest services... With regard to the Mahometans also, we
are not without grounds of hope... The blindness of
this people arises chiefly from their ignorance; for
from repulsing the truth, they in general wish for it;
and the progress of the Gospel will be commensurate
with the means of instruction. » He then relates this
anecdote. « One evening two Marabouts came into
our house while a little black was giving out prayers
to the other children. This sight filled them with
surprise. One of them observed to his companions,
‘ these people will be taking away the Koran from
us.’ Then addressing himself to me, he said;‘ If you
only stay two years at Ndakar, there will be no more
Mahomet — nothing but the Missionary.’ May his
prediction be accomplished, and God alone be adored,
served, and loved by a people to whom He has been
so long unknown. » (2)

(1) Moister, ch. II, p. 70.
(2) Annals, vol. VIII, p. 89.

Let us add, in conclusion, a single example — for
there is no need of many — of the manner in which
converts are made in this country, and in which they
subsequently display the evidence of their reconciliation to God. One of the missionaries, Father Poussot,
had been attacked in the night by a fanatic, and severely wounded. Shortly after, Vané, the chief of a
neighbouring village, presented himself before his
companion Father Bouchet, with these words. « Father, I have long been a Christian at heart, but I am
determined to be one in deed. Wash me with the
water of prayer (baptism)... You told me that your
God loved mankind, and sent His Son on earth to
save them; that this Son died for them on a Cross,
and that instead of taking revenge upon His execu-
tioners, He pardoned them, and even prayed for
them; and you planted a Cross in our village. I
thought all this very fine, but still I was not in heart
a Christian. » Then raising his voice, and continuing with great animation, he said; « But do you remember our coming home together one day through
the forest of Mpongues? You were told that the
Father, your companion, had been wounded the previous night by a slave, and that his face was cut
open. I was enraged at his cowardly and shameful
act, and if I had met the slave, I should have stabbed
him. But you, Father, said nothing; you raised your
eyes to heaven. I was watching what you would do.
You pardoned the slave; you begged that he might
not be punished. The wounded Father also came
some time after, not yet quite recovered. He was not
angry. He spoke and prayed with us in his usual
manner, and had a meeting with his intended mur-

derer. Then I said to myself and others; This Father
loves us; *he does what he says;* he pardons his enemies. His word, therefore, is true. From that moment I was in heart a Christian, and I am now
resolved to be so for ever. » (1)

The chief was instructed and baptized. « The
whole family, » Father Bouchet adds, « have followed the example of their chief, and form at the
present day a nucleus of fervent and courageous
Christians, already tried by persecution, and, if called upon, prepared for martyrdom. » The trial came
— destitution, cruelty, loss of friends and relatives,
and menaces of a worse fate. All, even the children,
endured it with unmoved fortitude. When the father
was loaded with chains by the infidels, and they were
about to carry him away, his second son exclaimed,
« Take me instead of my father; he is infirm, I shall
be of more use to you. » The offer was accepted, and
the youth consigned to prison, with no other consolation than a crucifix, which one of his sisters conveyed to him. The pagans proposed to restore the old
chief to his former position, if he would consent to
apostatise. « I am a servant of the great God, » he
replied, « and must obey His orders rather than yield
to your desires. I have said it, henceforth nothing
shall persuade me to depart from the will of God. »
« Admirable and holy old man, » exclaims Father
Bouchet, the witness of these scenes; « how often
have I wept for joy over his conversion! At Mass, in
a special manner, his devotion is beyond all praise,
when kneeling absorbed in meditation on the adora-

(1) Vol. XVII, p. 216.

ble mysteries. There it is that his faith is constantly
revived, and from this source he derives courage to
say with St. Paul : ' I can do all things in Him who
fortifies me. ' *

It is impossible to read the history of Christian
missions in this part of Africa, during the last twenty
years, without admitting, that if the Catholics possessed even a small portion of the immense temporal
resources which the two richest nations in the world
continually place at the disposal of the Protestant
emissaries, so as to enable them to found educational
institutions, and to promote the other works of charity so urgently needed in this land of poverty, the
conversion of the heathen would be immensely accelerated. But poverty is not the greatest obstacle
to the success of the Catholic mission. There is a
yet more formidable and fatal hindrance. When the
heathen or the muhometan has learned, in spite of
ignorance and prejudice, to venerate teachers who
lead an apostolic life, and who display even to his
dull apprehension the marks of a supernatural calling; when the power of the demon is already shaken,
and light begins to dawn upon the soul; the half-
awakened native is sure to be presently confounded
and embarassed by the apparition of others, also
styling themselves ministers of the Christian religion,
though attended by groups of females and children,
surrounded by comfort and opulence, and leading
before his eyes the common life of common men;
and when these teachers speak to him, in strange
and unnatural accents, about a Book of which they
comprehend nothing but the letter, and a Saviour of
whom they know nothing but the Name; the perplexed

enquirer begins to suspect that, after all, Christianity is only a delusion, its advocates only impostors. The grave and devout pastors whom he had begun to love and admire, he is now told, are but the insidious professors of a wicked and false religion; while the wordly and immortified men, who hasten to offer him their gold and their Bibles, are the only preachers of pure Christianity. What marvel if the angry heathen confound the religion and its professors in a common sentiment of contempt and aversion? or resolve, at the bidding of the baser instincts of his nature, to make the Christian religion a source of gain, and to sign a contract which leaves his conscience untouched, while it redoubles his repugnance to teachers who are themselves the first victims of the hypocrisy which they create and recompense? We have said, and it may be repeated without exaggeration, that Protestant missions are everywhere the worst and most fatal impediment to the conversion of the heathen; because they add to the difficulties which beset him, in common with those which were surmounted by the primitive converts, a multitude of others, unknown to the pagans of earlier days, which had no existence till Protestantism arose, and with which even the Apostles themselves would perhaps have contended in vain. Protestantism — let us once more declare it — is the last scourge of heathenism.

Before we approach the only region of Africa which now remains to be visited, it may be well to resume, in the words of a Protestant minister, formerly a missionary in these regions, the history which we have briefly traced. In 1856, nearly one hundred

and sixty years after England had carried Protestantism to Western Africa, the character and results
of missionary labour in these provinces were thus
appreciated by Mr Leighton Wilson. « The Church
of Rome deserves great praise for the zeal she displayed in following up all the Portuguese and Spanish
discoveries of the fifteenth and sixteenth centuries
with efforts to extend the Christian faith. The Portuguese government itself, at the commencement of
these enterprises, was influenced as much by a desire
to propagate the catholic faith, as by any expectations of commercial gain. In the course of time,
when unexpected sources of wealth were opened up
by these discoveries, she lost sight, in a great measure, of the former of these objects, and gave herself
up wholly to an absorbing pursuit of the latter. The
Church of Rome, however, was not diverted from
her purpose by any such motives. She addressed
herself to the one great object of converting these
newly discovered tribes to the Romish faith, and
she pursued her calling with an energy, zeal, and
perseverance worthy of a better cause. »

On the other hand, the emissaries of Protestantism, who have been described to us by their co-
religionists as often profoundly immoral, and almost
always engaged in the eager pursuit of wealth, are
thus noticed by the same writer. « Had Protestant
nations and the Protestant church pursued the same
work with half the zeal and steadiness, the moral
aspect of the world at the present time would have
been very different from what it is. » And then
he gives this account of the actual fruits of their
operations, backed by the support of England and

America, and aided by immense resources, during a
century and a half. « *As yet*, the missionaries have
done little more than possess themselves of the out-
posts; but, in accomplishing even this much, they
feel themselves greatly indebted *to what has been
done by the squadron*. » (1)

Once more we have received the confessions,
with which we are now familiar, and which we
shall hear again in every land which we have still
to visit. Once more we have been told by a Protestant missionary, who had himself abandoned
the unprofitable work, the accustomed tale, which,
in default of his testimony, we should have learned
from others. There was as much prudence as candour in M' Wilson's tardy admissions. In 1842,
the mission of *Baraka*, the principal station on
the Gaboon river, was inaugurated by that gentleman. In 1861, after twenty years of costly effort,
M. Paul Du Chaillu, the intimate associate of the
missionaries, records their own avowal, that they
despair of acquiring any influence over the adult
natives of Western Africa. They have some hope,
he says, of the children in their schools, — they have
always hopes which are doomed never to be accomplished, and have already educated *one* generation
in vain, — but « it is only upon the children that the
labours of the missionaries can have any important
effects. » They may well be « discouraged, » he suggests, « at the slight result of their hard labour. »
« The positive success of the mission, » he reluctantly

_____

(1) *Western Africa*, by J. Leighton Wilson, ch. III, p. 446;
ch. V, p. 481.

observes, « is not great; » and we may accept his
impartial estimate of it, when he relates that, after
the « inculcation of Bible precepts » during nearly a
quarter of a century, « the older natives adhere to
their vile superstitions, and are with difficulty influenced. If they come to church, it is too often ont
of curiosity, or to please the preacher, or from some
fancied advantage to themselves. » (1) In other words,
a human religion is incapable, in Africa as in every
other land, of effecting what only a divine ministry
can profitably attempt, or of imitating those triumphs
of a holier faith which the agents of Protestantism
are always occupied in recording, and always contrasting, in spite of themselves, with their own
blighted hopes and unfruitful toil.

The southern portion of the vast continent of whose
religious history we have now offered an imperfect
sketch still remains to be noticed. We have spoken
of the Moor and the Negro, some account must be
given in conclusion of the Kaffir and the Hottentot.

In 1652, Van Riebeck inaugurated the Dutch reign
in South Africa. Twenty-eight governors followed
in succession, till in the year 1793 Holland forfeited
her possessions to Great Britain. In 1795, General
Craig, the first representative of English power, assumed the government of the Cape Colony. It is of
the progress of religion among the heathen since the
commencement of the latter epoch that we now propose to speak.

The numerous writers on South Africa are in accord, as their own words will presently assure us,

(1) *Adventures in Equatorial Africa*, ch. i, pp. 5, 6.

on one point only, — that both the Hottentot and the
Kaffir have degenerated morally during the period
of English rule; but an eager conflict has arisen
amongst them as to the real cause of this deterio-
ration. While the missionaries assert in self defence,
that it is the colonists who have ruined both Kaffir
and Hottentot, the latter confidently retort, with
wonderful unanimity, — to whatever rank or class
they belong, civil or military, — that it is mainly, and
with rare exceptions, the teaching and influence of
the missionary which have corrupted all the native
tribes who have had the misfortune to come within
the reach of either. When we have considered the
evidence which they offer, we shall be able to judge,
without much danger of error, on which side is
truth.

The first facts which claim our attention, and
which constitute the distinctive features of Protestant missions in every land, are, enormous expenditure, and ceaseless multiplication of sects. Nearly
twenty years ago D' Grant remarked before the university of Oxford, that already the following religious
bodies had been transplanted to the Cape Colony :
— 1. Society for the Propagation of the Gospel;
2. Scottish Missionary Society; 3. United Brethren;
4. French Protestant Society; 5. German Missionary Society; 6. London Missionary Society; 7. Wesleyan Missionary Society ; 8. Baptist Missionary
Society; 9. American Board of Missions; 10. Rhe-
nish Missionary Society; 11. Paris Missionary Society. (1)

(1) *Bampton Lectures for* 1843.

We have seen in other lands the hopeless confusion
and disorder, as well as the perplexity occasioned to
the heathen, by such a *colluvies* of sects. In 1835,
M' Moodie, a judicious and temperate writer, com-
mented in the following words upon this disastrous
but inevitable result. « Unfortunately each sect has
some peculiar dogma, which they generally inculcate
to their followers, too often to the partial exclusion
of more important doctrines. » And then he proceeds
thus : — « Each sect is ambitious of increasing the
number of its followers; a spirit of rivalry amongst
them is the necessary consequence of this party zeal,
which, joined to that external gloom and austerity
which distinguishes them all, naturally creates a
further distaste for their instructions. » (1)

And time, the sovereign remedy of so many
human evils, only aggravates this. Thus, as late as
1855, the Rev. M' Holden tells us, even of the new
province of Natal, that he found *seven* different
religious denominations in one spot; « enough, one
would suppose, to meet the diversified creeds, tastes,
and desires of the inhabitants. » (2) Two years later,
we find D' Armstrong, a Protestant bishop in South
Africa, deploring in these words the same incurable
dissensions. « I could not but be saddened by the
thought of our religious divisions! No less than
three places of worship were visible, as I approached
the town — Cradock — besides the Church of England. This, in the midst of a population of some

_____

(1) *Ten Years in South Africa*, vol. II, ch. XIV, p. 280.
(2) *History of the Colony of Natal*, by the Revd W. C. Holden,
ch. IX, p. 240.

700 people, was indeed a melancholy spectacle. • (1) This gentleman had also to lament, as we shall see when we come to examine his testimony, the implacable divisions within as well as outside his own sect, and his own incapacity to heal them.

Such is the spectacle which, in Africa as in every other land, Protestantism displays to the heathen, with no other effect than to warn them against adopting a religion of which these are the invariable fruits.

Dr Morison relates of a number of missionaries sent out by the Scottish Missionary Society, that « they unhappily differed among themselves, upon some minor points of theology, and some of them failed to exhibit that spirit of charity and forbearance which ought to distinguish the Missionary of the cross. » (2) Mr Pringle also describes the voyage of some English Protestants, who were always « engaged keenly in polemical discussions under the guidance of two preachers. » They fought, he says, with so much bitterness, that they soon « ceased to regard each other with sentiments of Christian forbearance.» (3) Lastly, Dr Livingstone tells us, in 1857, that « in South Africa such a variety of Christian sects have followed the footsteps of the London Missionary Society's successful career, that converts of one denomination, if left to their own resources, » — which apparently means, when they cease to be paid, — « are eagerly adopted by another; and are

(1) *Memoir of Bishop Armstrong*, by the Revd T. T. Carter, p. 347. (1857).

(2) Vol. II, app. p. 593.

(3) *Narrative of a Residence in South Africa*, ch. 1, p. 7.

thus more likely to become spoiled than trained to the manly Christian virtues. » (1)

It would be superfluous to offer any illustrations of the other point, — the enormous expenditure of these jealous and conflicting sects, each outbidding the other. Even the Government adds its liberal contributions to those of the various missionary societies. Some years ago the Education Grant within the Cape Colony already exceeded 5,000 l. per annum; (2) and we are told, in the life of D' Armstrong, that Sir George Grey, the distinguished and justly popular Governor, « proposes to spend no less a sum than 30,000 l. a year on missions. » (3) D' Armstrong asked, for his own share, 4,000 l. a year. What the other sects spend, we may imagine, but need not stay to calculate. And now let us approach, without further preface, the grave question of *results*, after more than half a century of uninterrupted effort.

On this point there are, of course, two classes of witnesses; the missionaries, who loudly assert, — with the exception of truthful and respectable men, like Livingstone, Calderwood, Armstrong, and a few others — that they have rivalled the first Apostles; and the crowd of lay writers, who as vigorously proclaim, in spite of their sympathy with the missionary projects, that they have utterly failed, and even, as a rule, have proved most injurious to the character and welfare of the natives. We will hear both classes.

(1) Ch. vi, p. 115.
(2) *Acts of the Government of the Cape of Good Hope*, 1854-7.
(3) P. 309.

The 40th Report of the Glasgow Missionary Society announces to the British public — or at least to that portion of it who subscribe to such objects — that « religion was striking its roots deeper and deeper in the native soil. » Another report says, — « our missionaries are everywhere scattering the seeds of civilisation, social order, and happiness.»(1) It need hardly be said that the various Societies emulate, and indeed often surpass, this style of narrative.

Their agents also assist them with materials for such compositions. The reports of Mr Moffat — who seems to have proposed to himself the journal of Mr Morrison, of Canton, as his model — are worthy of particular attention. Speaking of the weekly assemblies of his Hottentot dependents, he says; « A delightful unction of the Spirit was realised, especially in our Sabbath convocations. » (2) If a poor savage, who had borrowed from civilisation nothing but its vices, dies in the neighbourhood of a « mission; » « his disembodied spirit, » we are told, « entered into the realms of eternal rest. » The singular favours of what these gentlemen call, apparently for the sake of euphony, «the Triune Jehovah», are constantly showered upon the privileged Hottentots. Bloodthirsty savages, who afterwards became the bitterest enemies both of England and of her missionaries — such as Tzatzoe and Africaner, Palo and Macomo — are described, at one time by

(1) *Researches in South Africa*, by the Revd John Philip, D.D.; preface, p. 9.
(2) *Missionary Labours in Southern Africa*, by Robert Moffat, ch. XI, p. 172.

the London Missionary Society, as zealous in « diffusing the name of Christ; » at another by D' Philip,
as « elevated to a surprising height in the scale of
improvement; » or, by an American Society, as
remarkable for « an experimental acquaintance with
the Bible! » And vast sums were collected from
women and children, both in England and America,
on the faith of these representations. But we shall
perhaps obtain a clearer view both of the character
of the missionaries and the results of their labours,
if we introduce the witnesses in chronological order :
the unvarying uniformity of their testimony, during
fifty successive years, will not escape the attention
of the intelligent reader.

The introduction of Protestant missions into this
part of Africa appears to be due to Van Der Kemp,
whom Colonel Napier calls « the foundation stone
of the South African missions, » and who has been
celebrated with much applause in missionary reports.
His history exactly resembles that of Buchanan, and
other luminaries of the same order. He became a
missionary, because every other profession was
closed against him. He was originally, we are
informed, a captain of dragoons in the Dutch service,
was dismissed from his regiment, and then became
notorious as a professed atheist. Ultimately he found
refuge in this remote dependency of Holland; and
Lichtenstein, one of his admirers, gave, in 1812,
this account of his disciples. « They could sing and
pray, and be heartily penitent for their sins, and
talk of ' the Lamb of atonement; ' but none were
really better for all this specious appearance. » It
was solely, he adds, the « convenient mode of getting

themselves fed, « which « attracted many of the
most worthless and idle among the people, and all
who applied were indiscriminately received into the
establishment. » (1)

Van Der Kemp himself was accustomed to report
of them officially as follows : « the zeal of our converted Hottentots is evidently an extraordinary gift
of God's spirit. »

From Lichtenstein we also learn that both Van
Der Kemp, who now assumed the title of « doctor of
divinity, » and his English colleague Mr Read, —
whom a lively biographer calls « devoted heralds of
mercy, » — married Hottentot girls; while of another
of their company, famous as a preacher, the same
friendly witness relates, that « his influence over
the minds of the female part of his flock was employed for the base purpose of seducing a young
woman..... » (2)

It would be necessary to apologise for introducing
such details, if it were possible for the annalist of
Protestant Missions to avoid topics which form so
large part of their history.

Lichtenstein lived amongst these missionaries, and
knew them intimately; and though he makes an
exception in favour of the Moravians, he declares
that « the English and Dutch missionaries, with few
exceptions, were idle vagabonds, or senseless fanatics. » Indeed the language of this traveller, who is
the earliest in date of our witnesses, is sometimes

(1) Lichtenstein's *Travels in Southern Africa*, vol. I, ch. XVII,
p. 236. (1812).
(2) Ch. x, p. 144.

II.   18

still more energetic; for he does not hesitate to call
them « a swarm of idle missionaries, who find it
more agreeable to be fed by the devout colonists,
than to pursue the proper object for which they
were sent out — the endeavouring to instruct and
civilize the neighbouring savages. » Of Kicherer,
who long shared with Van Der Kemp the homage of
English Protestants, and of whose work « so much
boasting has been made by himself and his friends
in England, » Lichtenstein says; « The Dosjemans,
when they found there was nothing left to eat,
hesitated not a moment to apostatise from Christianity. » (1) Such is the evidence of one who had
watched the work, and was himself an ardent
Protestant, and such the characteristic commencement of Protestant missions in South Africa.

Dr Sparrman, a learned Swedish Protestant, qua-
lifies Lichtenstein's eulogy of the Moravians, by
relating, that Smid, one of their number, « was
banished out of the country of the Hottentots, for
having illegally made himself a chief among the
Hottentots, in order to enrich himself by their labour,
and the presents they made him of cattle. » (2) Many
of the witnesses, however, seem disposed to contrast
the Moravians with the other missionaries, apparently on account of the greater simplicity of their
lives, and their habit of teaching mechanical trades.
Yet most, or all, of them probably felt that they had
gained promotion by settling in Africa; for, as

(1) Vol. II, ch. xLI, p. 183.
(2) *Voyage to the Cape of Good Hope*, by Andrew Sparrman,
M. D., ch. v, p. 213.

M' Thompson remarks, nearly all of them had « originally been common mechanics. » (1)

In 1822, M' Burchell, an unexceptionable witness, familiar by actual observation both with the missionaries and their work, writes as follows. « It is much to be lamented that the community at home are misled by accounts catching at the most trifling occurrence for their support, and showing none but the most favourable circumstances, and even those unfairly exaggerated. » The nominal converts, he reports, listen to the missionaries « as long as it suits their worldly convenience and advantages. » The motives of the missionaries themselves M' Burchell seems to have easily penetrated. « Two of them in particular, as I was informed at Klaarwater, had carried on the traffic in ivory with much success. » Finally, as an example of what even the best of their converts were really worth, he notices « the three converted Hottentots » who were taken to England by M' Kicherer, « and exhibited as specimens of missionary conversion, » (2) and whose history deserves a moment's attention.

Nothing could exceed the enthusiasm which they created among « the favourers of missionary labours. » Even country subscribers were allowed an opportunity of seeing these selected specimens of African Protestantism, and of thus appreciating the excellent use to which their own contributions had been applied. At length they were withdrawn from

(1) *Travels in Southern Africa*, by George Thompson Esq., vol. II, ch. viii, p. 91 ; 2nd edition.
(2) *Travels in the Interior of Southern Africa*, by William J. Burchell Esq., vol. II, ch. v, p. 155.

the public gaze, after reciting, with surprising accuracy, innumerable texts of Scripture, and otherwise manifesting to delighted audiences their intelligent zeal for the Protestant religion. The missionary, satisfied with such encouraging success, re-conveyed his disciples to Africa, where he took them at first into his house as domestic servants. But the drama was now played out, and the curtain dropped; and Mr Burchell informs us, that as they immediately resumed their real character, proved to be inveterate drunkards, « and in other respects immoral and undeserving, their protector found himself compelled to put them out of his house. » (1)

Unfortunately this climax became known in England; and the Missionary Society, — displaying a tardy repentance for the fraud which had been so beneficial to their funds — thought it expedient to affirm, for the instruction of their resentful subscribers, that « the Hottentots were not brought to England by the desire of the Society. » (2) We need only add that Mr Kicherer, whose indiscretion had been so profitable to « the Society, » and probably to himself, ultimately abandoned missionary work altogether.

In 1828, we come to Dr Philip, the most conspicuous amongst the whole body of missionaries, and a gentleman whose proceedings, as recorded by himself or his contemporaries, excite in us — to speak frankly — such overpowering sentiments of repugnance, that we must be careful to express them

(1) *Travels in the Interior of Southern Africa*, by William J. Burchell Esq., vol, II, ch. v, p. 155.
(2) *Missionary Transactions*, vol. II, Introd., p. 5.

only in the words of others. Let us hear first his account of his converts.

« John Tzatzoe, » he tells us, « is of great use to M' Brownlee in his labours; » and then he shows that he was, in fact, an assistant missionary. D' Philip, mindful perhaps of M' Kicherer's example, determined to renew the experiment. Tzatzoe, in his turn, as Colonel Napier remarks, « was paraded at Exeter Hall. » At the fifty-first general meeting of the London Missionary Society, long after he had returned to Africa, where the astute barbarian revealed himself in his true character, the following report was gravely communicated to an audience of whom the « directors » and their « secretary » probably felt quite sure.

« John Tzatzoe, and the other native assistant, have made extensive journies through the year, *for the purpose of diffusing the name of Christ* and the knowledge of His salvation. » Nor was this all. A painting was executed, of which engraved copies were widely circulated, in which D' Philip appeared in the foreground in an impressive attitude, and the « native missionaries, » with prayerful countenances, in the rear. The effect, as is invariably the case with such performances, was triumphant. It is true that it did not last long, though probably quite long enough to secure the objects aimed at. Tzatzoe, says Colonel Napier, « who excited such ill-directed sympathy in England, appeared foremost in arms against us during the late Kaffir war. » (1) And M'' Ward

(1) *Excursions in Southern Africa*, by L' Col. E. Elers Napier, vol. II, ch. xiv, p. 275.

adds, that when she saw the report of the Missionary
Society above quoted, « my first impulse was to
laugh, knowing that Tzatzoe, the propagator of
Christianity in 1845, has been foremost in the mischief of 1846; but it is melancholy to think *how we
have been imposed upon*. » A little later this lady adds,
« the British public was completely imposed upon
by this savage heathen, for such he is, was, and ever
will be. » (1) In the able reports of the London Missionary Society he was wholly absorbed, as we have
seen, in works of piety, and in « diffusing the knowledge of salvation. »

It is certainly worthy of observation, if we had
leisure to dwell upon such details, that the arts
practised by English Missionary Societies have been
frankly compared, even by friendly voices, to the
unhandsome « shifts » of traders and attornies. Their
operations, we are assured, exactly resemble, except
in their ostensible object, those of commercial associations of the meaner class. « No mercantile houses, »
says a well known Anglican clergyman, « take more
pains to solicit orders than do the ' societies ' »; of
which, he adds, « some are simply large trading
firms, dealing with the money of others. » Even their
« balance-sheets, » the same authority declares, being
designed rather to hide than to reveal the real distribution of their revenues, are not only « very often
intentionally delusive, » but exhibit « in several the
existence of *a system of deliberate fraud*. » (2) The

(1) *Five Years in Kaffir Land*, by Mrs Harriet Ward, vol. II,
ch. IV, p. 116; ch. X, p. 277, (1848).
(2) S. G. O., *The Times*, January 17, 1860.

facts already noticed, and which we will now resume, appear to indicate that the same spirit inspires
all their operations, in England, in Africa, and every
where else.

Another distinguished « convert, » who was for
some time a sure source of income to the Societies,
was Africaner, who, in the eloquent report of D' Philip, was « elevated to a surprising height in the scale
of improvement. » This account of him was forwarded even to America, where, however, it was
deemed too tame to be safely submitted to audiences
accustomed to the more violent forms of religious
excitement. In the United States, therefore, D' Philip's eulogy of his pupil was published in the improved and expanded statement, that « he was of
undissembled piety, and much experimental acquaintance with his Bible. » (1)

The real history of Africaner is less attractive. He
was originally one of the flock of a certain M' Ebner,
who candidly described his own disciples to M' Moffat as « a wicked, suspicious, and dangerous people,
baptized as well unbaptized. » (2) And apparently
M' Ebner was the only person not deluded by him,
nor anxious to delude others. Africaner, who manifested such undissembled piety, became, like Tzatzoe,
one of the most dangerous adversaries of the very
missionaries whose schemes he had unconsciously
served, and « a bitter opponent, » as M' Francis
Galton relates, of their work. (3)

(1) *Life of Africaner*, by the American Sunday School Union,
p. 23.
(2) Moffat, ch. VIII, p. 103.
(3) *Journal of Geographical Society*, vol. XXII, p. 142.

But if Dr Philip habitually represented wicked and
treacherous savages, such as Tzatzoe and Africaner,
as devout Christians and valuable assistant missionaries, and his employers willingly profited by the
fraud, there are not wanting grave and responsible
witnesses to inform us — they have already declared
it before the British Parliament—that it was he who
stimulated them, for his own purposes, to the very
excesses which cost so much blood and treasure, and
which even a British army had some difficulty in
chastising. It was his object to gain influence over
them at the expense of the British government, and
therefore, says Colonel Wade, he « drove the Kaffirs
to outrageous proceedings and depredations (1). »
Sir Benjamin d'Urban also, though well-affected to
the missionaries, reported officially to Lord Glenelg ;
that « among the causes of the Kaffir invasion was
the injudicious and most dangerous tampering with
their discontents, practised (doubtless without intention of mischievous consequences) by Dr Philip, of
the London Mission, and his subordinate partisans. »
And then he distinctly charges this person, that « he
never apprised the Governor » that the Kaffirs were
about to « shed blood, » though he was perfectly
cognisant of their intention. (2)

But enough of such a « missionary » as this, who
in obliged to confess that Lord Howden, another
African official, reported « that the disinclination to
increase, or even maintain, the missionary institutions
already established in the colony, « is almost uni-

(1) *Parliamentary Papers*, July 1835, vol. VII, p. 373.
(2) 1837, vol. XLIII, p. 380.

rersal; » and that in reluctantly consenting to the
continuance of the seditious « mission » at Klaarwater, he expressed the hope, that it might become
« something better than the refuge of many wicked
and disorderly persons, who are obliged to fly from
justice. » (1)

It would occupy to much space to trace the gradual modification in the tone of the *home* reports, in
consequence of the unwelcome statements of officials
and travellers, which now began to reach England,
and suggested to directors and secretaries the necessity of caution. A single example will show into
what language these unexpected revelations were
cautiously translated, in order to produce the least
possible shock upon their subscribers. Of one of the
very worst cases, where the native disciples had become notorious throughout the colony for idleness
and profligacy, Dr Smith observes; « the Directors »
— who could not afford to put out too gloomy a view
of the character of their pensioners — « lament the
prevalence of *a Laodicean spirit* among the greater
part of them. » (2) To have said that the so-called
christian natives were wallowing in vice under the
very eye of the missionaries, might have compromised
the annual revenue; so they were only affected by
« a Laodicean spirit. »

In 1827, Mr Thompson, a well known African traveller, accidentally reveals, evidently from inadver-
tence, the prudent inaccuracy of his missionary

(1) *Researches,* etc., vol. I, ch. xviii, p. 370; and vol. II,
app. p. 382.

(2) *History of the Missionary Societies,* vol. II, p. 182.

friends, and exposes the real character of those well
known « reports, » in which there was often nothing
authentic but the date and the signature. None have
surpassed, few have equalled, M' Moffat, of whose
« sabbath convocations » we have already heard.
M' Thompson became the guest of this gentleman,
and having ventured, with the blunt frankness of a
traveller, to express his surprise at the scanty attendance of the natives in chapel, — whom M' Moffat
had described *officially* as attending in crowds, —
received this hasty and unguarded confession : « *At
no time*, the Missionaries told me, *has the attendance
been considerable.* » M' Thompson adds, at a later
date, after personal examination, « Few or no converts have been made ! » (1)

In 1829, M' Cowper Rose — our witnesses are all
ardent Protestants — contents himself with protesting
against the popular delusion, that « the Missionary is
a man who has taken up the Cross, and renounced
all that the wordly minded seek.» And then he notices
their « convenient habitations, » and their « wives
and families, » and the fact which continually met
his observation, that they were « not deprived of
social enjoyments. » (2)

In 1835, we have the important evidence of
M' Moodie, a particularly moderate and careful
writer, who spent ten years in Africa, and visited the
numerous missionary stations with warm interest
and sympathy, which only painful experience was
able to extinguish.

(1) *Travels*, etc., vol. 1, ch. IX, p. 193.
(2) *Four Years in Southern Africa*, Letter VI, p. 138.

For more than thirty years the missionaries had now been at their work, without let or hindrance, and M' Moodie will assist us to appreciate accurately all that they had accomplished during that long period, in which one generation had already passed away. Of the Moravians, who are usually preferred by other writers, because they generally content themselves with following the trade or calling which they had pursued at home, he speaks thus. « I have generally found the Hottentots who have come from the Moravian stations *more* improvident and lazy than those who come from other missionary institutions » — which he attributes to their « obliging the Hottentots to deposit all their earnings in their custody. » (1)

Sometimes he speaks of individual missionaries, and here is an example. M' S., missionary at Laure Brack, being in reduced circumstances, « had taken up the trade of an instructor of the heathen. » He first made the Hottentots build him a house, « for which they were not paid; » then got them « to labour for months in leading out a spring of water from a ravine in the mountain, to irrigate a strip of rich land : this he kindly allowed them to clear from brushwood, and bring into cultivation on their own account for a year or two; and then, the moment the principal difficulties were overcome, he very coolly appropriated the ground to his own use, without giving them any remuneration for their labour. » He adds that « M' S. was allowed to remain for many

---

(1) *Ten Years in South Africa*, by Lieut. J. D. W. Moodie, vol. I, ch. IV, p. 82.

years to tyrannise over this hapless people. Nothing
could exceed the appearance of wretchedness in the
institution. » Finally, « his misdeeds, I am happy
to say, have at last occasioned his expulsion. » (1)

Again. « At *all* the missionary stations in Kaffre·
land, I could not help remarking the gloomy and
desponding expression which pervaded the countenances of the people ;... we cannot for a moment suppose that this could be the effect of true religion. »
Aud then he shows how the unnatural gloom of the
whole system, and the fanatical denunciation of the
most « innocent amusements » — which these teachers seem to regard as the essential tenet of christianity — fully accounts for « the general disinclination of the Kaffres for the Christian religion. » And
finally he observes, that « as most of the missionaries
must be fully aware of the total inadequacy of the
system hitherto pursued, they should confess the
truth, instead of flattering the hopes of their employers by sanguine if not exaggerated statements of
their progress. » (2)

There is much more in Mr Moodie's sensible work
which illustrates the real character of Protestant
missions to the heathen, but we must hasten to hear
others. « The improvement which has been effected, »
he says, in any measure, and in particular places,
« the missionaries must well know is chiefly to be
attributed to causes over which *they* have no control. »
Again; « I have often been surprised to find that natives who bore the very worst character among the

(1) Vol. I, ch. v, p. 94.
(2) Vol. II, ch. xiv, pp. 280-283.

farmers, and had conducted themselves very badly in my own service, were considered quite ' saints ' at the missionary stations, where they find it their interest to assume the greatest sanctity of demeanour.»
« I believe their system to be radically bad, and productive of the worst consequences as respects the interests and improvement of all classes of the community. » And finally he sums up in these grave words the results of missionary teaching. « It is notorious to all the colonists, that the Hottentots who have resided for any time at the missionary stations are generally *the most idle and worthless of their nation.* » (1)

In July of the same year, 1835, various witnesses were examined before Parliamentary Committees on the results of Protestant missions in South Africa. « Do you think that the Missionaries have improved the character of the Kaffirs, » was a question addressed to Captain Aitchison, who had lived long amongst them. « *Not in the least,* » was his reply; « with the exception of Kama, and one or two of his tribe, I have not seen the slightest improvement by the Missionaries among them; in fact, in the neighbourhood of Chumic, where the great missionary station is, *they are the worst behaved Kaffirs of the whole tribe.* » (2)

Major Dundas reported, on the same occasion, « I believe they have hardly christianised a single individual; » (3) and we shall find this admitted to be true, even by missionaries, twenty years later.

(1) Vol. II, p. 292.
(2) *Parliamentary Papers*, July 1835, vol. VII, p. 12.
(3) *Ibid.*, p. 142.

Sir Harry Smith, an ardent advocate of extreme Protestant opinions, observed, that « the .house of the Rev. M' Brownlee » — whom he calls « an exemplary man, who had resided years with these people» — was burnt to the ground, and shortly after that of *every other missionary*, except the Chumie and Burn's Hill, which were ransacked. » And the Rev. William Culmers, of Chumie, confessed that, after so many years, they had not acquired the slightest influence with the natives, when he said; « An angry look just now would be enough to send all the missionaries into eternity. » (1) At Burn's Hill they were rescued by the military, at the earnest solicitation of the missionaries themselves; some of whom afterwards protested, when the danger was past, that they had never been in the least danger amongst their attached flocks!

In one of the later Kaffir wars, that of 1850, a still more characteristic fact occurred, and one which shows, that as the Negro Anglican « converts » at Sierra Leone were at the same time « communicants » and « obstinate » followers of native superstitions; so in South Africa, the same class exhibit an equally remarkable duality of profession. At a place called the « Shilo Missionary Institution, » « The Church, or missionary chapel, was held most resolutely by the enemy, garrisoned chiefly by those very Hottentots who, not a month previously, had received the Holy Sacrament within its walls. » (2)

(1) Vol. XLIII, pp. 350, 371.
(2) *Narrative of the Kaffir War of* 1850-1, by R. Godlonton, ch. XVII, p, 215.

In 1837, Sir James Alexander, though favorable to missionary schemes, says of the missionaries, — « little care is taken at home in the selection of the instruments; » and of the missionary schools, — « schools of idleness they are, instead of schools of industry, as they ought to be, » in which « the Hottentots were kept in a state of pupillage, immorality, and concubinage. » (1)

In 1839, M' Bannister, a member of the Aborigines Protection Society, says; « Missionaries have for the most part proved themselves incapable of protecting the natives politically, or of improving them so rapidly that they might become their own protectors. » (2)

In 1842, we come to M' Moffat, and to his account of missionary labours in South Africa. If this gentleman announces in animated phrase his own continual triumphs, he at least permits no such pretentions on the part of his colleagues and friends. Of M' Edmonds he tells us, that he abandoned the work owing to « an insurmountable aversion on his part to the people. » (3) His companion, M' Ebner, as we have already heard, deplored the wickedness of *his* flock, « baptized as well as unbaptized. » Of a tribe of Namaquas, « which had long enjoyed the instructions of missionaries, » he

(1) *Voyage Among the Colonies of W. Africa*, by Sir James E. Alexander, K. L. S., vol. I, ch. XVI, p. 402; vol. II, cb. XX, p. 75.

(2) *Memoir respecting the Colonization of Natal*, by S. Bannister Esq., Member of the Aborigines Protection Society; preface, p. 10.

(3) *Missionary Labours*, etc., ch. II, p. 27.

says; « They had not *the least idea* of a God or a future state. They were literally like the beasts which perish. » (1) Again, of Mr Edwards and Mr Cox, two Protestant missionaries, who « settled in the Dechuana country, for the ostensible purpose of preaching the Gospel to the natives, » he gives this account : — they took to farming and trading, and « on this rock these men appear to have struck, and both were wrecked. » « Edwards, » Mr Moffat adds, « is now, or was some years since, a hoary-headed infidel. » (2) His own interpreter also, « brought home a concubine with him, and apostatising, became an enemy to the mission. » « Mr Evans relinquished the mission altogether. » Of the natives generally he confesses, that they were « sensible only of the temporal benefits enjoyed by those who have received the Gospel. » (3)

It appears, therefore, that Mr Moffat, though he does full justice to himself, is at least perfectly candid in his estimate of others. It is only necessary to add, that they, in their turn, speak with equal frankness of him. Thus, the Rev. Dr Brown, alluding to Moffat's florid narratives, says bluntly ; « of these awakenings, we confess, we entertain great doubts. » And again ; « flourishing accounts were at different periods given of the progress of religion, but some of those accounts were probably much exaggerated, while others were founded on mistaken judgments. » (4)

(1) Ch. ix, p. 121.
(2) Ch. xiv, pp. 215, 16.
(3) Ch. xxxiii, p. 608.
(4) *History of the Propagation of Christianity among the Heathen,* vol. II, p. 239.

M' Freeman also, a secretary of the London Missionary Society, confessed nine years *later*, after a visit
to Kolobeng, which had so long enjoyed M' Moffat's
presence; « The whole mission-work of the station
is quite in an incipient state. » And then, as he was
not speaking of operations in which he had any personal share, he proposes this candid question : —
How far is a Missionary justified « in remaining with
a heathen people, when, though they are glad of his
presence, from the shield it serves to throw around
them in their civil and political condition, they not
only do not embrace the gospel which he preaches,
but resist and oppose, and scarcely ever come to
him? » (1) M' Moffat should have remembered, when
he wrote home about « the unction of the Spirit
realised in our sabbath convocations, » that in these
days people travel far and fast, and almost always
publish an account of their travels when they are
ended.

In 1844, M' Backhouse, — who was apparently a
preacher, and whose work is a painful specimen of
complacent fanaticism, — was obliged to admit, with
respect to South Africa, « the little that has been
effected, as well as the tardiness of its progress. » (2)

In 1848, — for lapse of time brings no change,
and after half a century of barren effort not the
slightest sign of improvement is recorded, — M' Bunbury, a scientific Protestant traveller, thus remarks
on the pretended influence of the missionaries among
the Kaffirs. « Yet it is certain, that in the present

(1) *Tour in S. Africa*, by J. J. Freeman, ch. XII, p. 291.
(2) *Visit to the Mauritius and S. Africa*, by James Backhouse,
app., p. 51.

outbreak the Kaffirs have shown themselves far more
powerful and formidable, and at the same time have
displayed a *more* sanguinary and merciless spirit
than at any former time. The task of reclaiming and
civilising these people is evidently not to be accomplished by missionaries alone. » (1)

In the following year, 1849, we have the testimony of Colonel Napier to the same facts which so
many other equally capable and impartial witnesses
have already attested. « Notwithstanding those flaming accounts which have been published to the contrary, » this distinguished officer says, « it is notorious, it is a fact which cannot be contradicted, that
all attempts to convert the Kaffir race have hitherto
proved complete failures. » It is just the history of
China, India, Ceylon, and Australia over again.
« Kaffirs, Korannas, and Bushmen, spite of the
falsely asserted success of missionary labour, are
still in a state of most brutalized ignorance, as regards religion or worship of any description. »

Of the Hottentots, he says, — « their Christianity
consists in that love of idleness, and a lazy useless
state of existence, which they so fully enjoy at those
establishments formed by their soi-disant spiritual
instructors. » Their natural vices, he affirms, « are
shamefully countenanced and encouraged at most of
the missionary establishments within the limits of
the Colony; » which, he adds, « are hotbeds of
lazyness, and have moreover, in many cases, been
converted into nurseries for harbouring deserters and

(1) *Journal of a Residence at the Cape of Good Hope,* by
Charles J. F. Bunbury, F. L. S., ch. xi, p. 255.

vagabonds of every description. » It is here, Colonel
Napier reports — as Sir B. D'Urban and others had
already done — that « discontent and suspicion, and
in some instances open rebellion, » are fostered » by
men professing to disseminate among the heathen the
holy truths of the Gospel. » And then he complains,
with natural indignation, that « drunken ruffians, »
such as Macomo, Pato, and others, should be represented by the missionaries, with the most unworthy
objects, « as converts to Christianity. » Finally, after
describing the missionaries as « men sallying forth
to convert the heathen with a bible in one hand, and
a Hottentot ' vrouw ' in the other, » — he thus appreciates, in the same sentence, the teachers and
their disciples : — « The Hottentots are more drunken
and dissolute than ever, and some reverend personages have not — to their shame be it said — set them
the most rigorous examples of morality. » (1)

If we still multiply evidence which, during fifty
years, we have found to be absolutely uniform, and
which, proceeding exclusively from Protestants, ef-
fectively illustrates the real character of a religion
of which *these* are the unvarying fruits in every land ;
it is only in order that its weight and volume may
bear some proportion to the mass of prejudice and
ignorance which it may possibly assist to remove.
For this reason, let us continue the chain of witnesses
down to the present hour, and the next, in 1851, is
the Rev. Gustavus Hines, who thus describes the
influence of his brethren in South Africa.

(1) *Excursions in Southern Africa*, Introd., p. 10; vol. I,
ch. v, p. 58; ch. vii, p. 111; vol. II, ch. xxii, p. 442.

« Large numbers had professed to be converted,
but very few had *continued* for any length of time to
give evidence of a genuine change of heart. Indeed
it appears to be the case in Africa, as well as in
other heathen countries, that it is much easier to get
the people converted than it is to keep them so. » (1)
And in the same year an English writer, not less
favorably disposed than M' Hines towards the missionaries, makes the same revelations as all the other
witnesses both about them and their converts. Of the
first he deplores that they should « put down every
thing that is pleasant, connect the devil with the
most innocent enjoyments, and make hymn-singing
the only overt act of hilarity; » while of the last he
says, — « Any thing more dreary and uncomfortable
than a *converted* savage I have never seen in the form
of humanity. » And then he gives a specimen of one
who had been taught to sing about « the sufferings
of the Lamb, » but who « attached no meaning to
the words, and knew no more about the Lamb, or
His sufferings, than one of the lower animals. » (2)
In 1852, M' Cole, after five years of personal
observation, thus confirms all his predecessors. « Out
of every hundred Hottentot Christians (so called),
I will venture to declare, that *ninety-nine* are utterly
ignorant of any correct notion of a future state.
I speak from experience. I have frequently been by
the bed-side of the sick and dying Hottentot, who
has been *a constant attendant* at some missionary

(1) *Life on the Plains of the Pacific,* ch. XV, p. 308, Cf.,
Sketches of the Caffre Tribes, 1851.
(2) *To the Mauritius and back,* ch. V, p. 197.

chapel, and I have asked him whether he had any
fear of dying? He has smiled, and said,

' None. '

I have asked him whether he expects to go to
heaven? and he has answered,

' No. '

Where then?

' Nowhere. '

This I have heard, over and over again, from the
lips of some of the ' pet' Christians of missionaries. »

Is it possible to desire a more impressive demonstration of the incurable impotence of Protestantism?

Like all the other witnesses, Mr Cole explains the
fact that many Hottentots call themselves « christians » by the « great pecuniary advantage » which
they derive from the profession. At also, like Lichtenstein, and Burchell, and Moodie, and Napier, and
the rest, declares that « it is notorious that the people
living at the missionary stations are the idlest and
most useless set of people in the colony; » while at
some of them, he adds, « promiscuous intercourse
between the sexes was winked at, if not absolutely
sanctioned. » (1)

In 1853, Mr Galton explains, like Mr Cole, the
motive of the missionary in still continuing his unprofitable career. « The missionary is, » he says,
« to all intents and purposes, lord paramount of the
place. » (2)

In 1854, we have the evidence of Archdeacon

(1) *The Cape and the Kafirs*, etc., by Alfred W. Cole, ch. VIII,
p. 145.

(2) *Tropical South Africa*, by Francis Galton Esq., ch. II,
p. 29.

Merriman, whose frank and genial style can hardly
fail to attract the sympathy of his readers, as his
character seems to have won that of his friends.
« The reformed Church of England, » this gentleman
observes, judging it by its proceedings in Africa,
« has yet to learn *the elements* of real systematic
mission work. » With equal candour, he rebukes
« the exaggerated accounts of missionaries, » of whom
he does not appear to have formed a high estimate.
Excepting certain « foreign » missionaries, he says ;
« Not a few South African missionaries seem to quit
the employment as soon as an opening occurs either
to farm advantageously, or to enter the employ of
the Government. *I meet with examples of this
wherever I go.* »

The true missionaries of the Cross, from the time
of St. Paul to our own, have always died at their
work ; by martyrdom, by toil, by disease, or by old
age. *They* do not « retire upon their property, » like
the Anglican missionaries in New Zealand, nor upon
a pension, like those in India ; they never « cease
to call themselves missionaries, » like Mr Gutzlaff,
Mr Kicherer, and their fellows ; still less do they take
to farming, banking, or other modes of augmenting
their imperceptible resources. They give much to
the world, but they borrow nothing from it ; except
the grave in which, after having « confessed a good
confession before many witnesses, » (1) they lie down
in peace, expecting the day of account.

Mr Merriman seems to forget his own exception
in favour of « foreign » emissaries, when he after-

(1) Tim. VI, 12.

wards relates of the « French Mission Stations, »
that « the missionaries are extensively engaged in
farming on their private account. » Dr Hawks does
not increase our esteem for the same class, when he
notices the rumour, « that the Caffres have been
instructed in the art of war by a French missionary
settled among them, who passed his early life in the
army. » (1)

Another singular fact which Mr Merriman mentions agrees with Mr Godlonton's account of a parallel occurrence. Of certain rebels, who acted with
great ferocity against the English, he says ; « These
men had all partaken of the Holy Communion together the Sunday previous ! » Anglican communicants
in the colonies do not seem to be of a high class.

Lastly, Mr Merriman, who seems to have been
every where distressed and embarassed by what he
calls « our hateful religious disunion, » relates how
he tried to prevent its evil effects upon the heathen.
He was, on a certain occasion, about to preach from
a waggon, just as a Wesleyan missionary had taken
up a rival position under a neighbouring hedge. A
prompt resolution saved appearances. The next moment the savages would have seen Protestantism
under an unfavorable aspect, but a rapid colloquy
was followed by a reluctant truce, and Mr Merriman
offered to read Anglican prayers while the other
should give a Wesleyan sermon. The compromise was
accepted, and for the first time a pagan audience was
persuaded to believe in the unity of Protestantism.

(1) *American Expedition under Commodore Perry*, by Francis
L. Hawks, D. D.; ch. III, p. 103.

It is curious, however, that a little later we find this Anglican Archdeacon, who was far from being elated by so questionable a triumph, envying even the Dutch Calvinists in South Africa on this ground, that at least they all professed the *same* heresies. « Ten times the number of English, » he observes, « could not do, in consequence of their religious divisions, what the Dutch so easily achieve. » (1)

In 1855, a more remarkable witness appears, and one who will assist us to comprehend not only the failure of Protestantism to impress itself on the heathen mind, but also its real influence even upon some of the most respectable of its own professors. D' Colenso is, or was, an Anglican bishop in Natal; a man far beyond the reach of any imputation on the score of personal character, highly intelligent, full of honest zeal, and probably as superior to most of his companions in moral worth as he certainly is in intellect and attainments. Towards this gentleman personally it would be irrational to entertain any but kind and respectful feelings. Yet he is perhaps the most striking example in the whole history of Protestant missions of the withering influence of a religion which could make such a man, full of ability and good intentions, avow opinions such as that which we are about to notice.

D' Colenso, embarrassed by the obstinate adherence to polygamy which he observed among the Kaffirs, came to the resolution — after conference, it is said, with other Anglican authorities of the highest rank —

(1) *Journals of Archdeacon Merriman*, pp. 37, 52, 116, 178, 185.

to remove the difficulty by a process which, though adopted in a well known case by Luther and Melancthon, had not previously received the official sanction of Anglican bishops. As polygamy would not yield to Protestantism, D' Colenso agreed to consider polygamy a « scriptural » mode of existence. Here are his own words.

« I must confess that I feel very strongly that the usual practice of enforcing the separation of wives from their husbands, upon their conversion to Christianity, is quite unwarrantable, *and opposed to the plain teaching of our Lord.* » And then he proves, of course from the Bible, that polygamy is not inconsistent with the all-holy religion of the Gospel. Here is the proof. « What is the use, » he asks, « of our reading to them (the heathen) the Bible stories of Abraham, Israel, and David, with *their* many wives? »

One should have thought it easy enough to explain to them, as St. Paul did, that the New Law not only proposes a higher standard of holiness than the Old, but gives power, through the Sacraments of the Precious Blood, to attain it; and that while the prophet of Israel permitted divorce to the Jews, « by reason of the hardness of their hearts, » the Apostle of the Gentiles dissuaded Christians even from marriage. But the awful sanctity of the religion of Jesus is « foolishness » in the eyes of men who know it to be unattainable by themselves, and who do not blush to claim for the Christian a license greater than that which was a reproach even to the Jew. St. Francis or St. Ignatius is a portent as hateful to the Protestant, as St. Paul was to the Greek. When our Lord said

11. 12

of the counsel of virginity, « All men take not this
word, but they *to whom it is given;* » (1) we know
for whom He reserved, in all ages, the angelic
gift.

But D' Colenso was not without support in his
view of polygamy. « The whole body of American
missionaries in Burmah, » he observes, « after some
difference of opinion.... came to the unanimous decision to admit in future polygamists of old standing
to Communion — but not to offices in the Church » :
as if the last were a greater privilege than the first!
« I must say this appears to me the only right and
reasonable course. » (2)

Yet M' East assures us, and we hardly needed
the assurance, that « intimately connected with polygamy, and in part at least, resulting from it, is the
degradation of woman in Africa. » (3) It is certainly
a remarkable fact, that if any unusually strange doctrine is announced among Protestant missionaries, —
any new outrage upon the Incarnation, as when the
Anglican bishops in India solicited an alliance with
the Syrian Nestorians; or upon the Blessed Eucharist; or the Sacrament of Holy Baptism; or the
Creeds; or the Mother of God; or the Sacrament of
Marriage; it is sure to proceed, not from the unlettered Baptist or Wesleyan, but from some highly
respectable minister of the Anglican Church.

D' Colenso speaks favorably of the Kaffir character, and of their « faithfulness and honesty, » as

(1) S. Matt. XIX, 11.
(2) *Ten Weeks in Natal,* etc., by J. W. Colenso, D. D.,
Lord Bishop of the Diocese, pp. 140, 141.
(3) *Western Africa,* p. 50.

Levaillant (1) and other early writers on South Africa
were accustomed to do. But it seems to be the mission of Protestantism, by the testimony of its own
agents, to rob the heathen even of his natural virtues.
Dr Colenso declares, and we may safely trust so intelligent a witness, that the Kaffirs display « traces
of a religious knowledge, however originally derived,
which their ancestors possessed long before the arrival of the Missionaries. » Yet Protestantism, with
every human advantage on its side, could only succeed in exciting the antipathy of these vigorous barbarians; and Dr Colenso himself mentions a Chief,
who, after listening with courteous patience to a
sermon, enquired eagerly, the moment the preacher's
voice ceased, « How do you make gunpowder? » (2)

The only other statement which we need borrow
from this writer, is an expression of opinion, founded
no doubt upon personal observation, which is not
likely to be acceptable to Protestant missionaries.
« Wives *often ruin a Mission*, » he says, « by their
tempers and animosities, breaking up the harmonious
action of their husbands. » (3)

In 1856, that we may continue the chain of witnesses, Mr Andersson, a friend and associate of the
missionaries, gives such examples as the following
of the complete nullity of their efforts. Of Schep-
mansdorf, in the country of the Namaquas, he says;
« Although Mr Dam (the missionary) had used every
effort to civilize and christianize his small communi-

(1) *Voyage dans l'Intérieur de l'Afrique*, 1780-1785.
(2) P. 117.
(3) P. 52.

ty, all his endeavours had hitherto proved nearly abortive. « Of the Damaras, again, this is his account. « M' Hahn, who is liked and respected by the natives, never succeeded, as he himself told me, in converting a single individual. »

Speaking of the nominal converts, under all classes of missionaries, M' Andersson says; « So long as they are fed and clothed, they are willing enough to congregate round the missionary, and to listen to his exhortation. The moment, however, the food and clothing are discontinued, their feigned attachment to his person and to his doctrines is at an end, and they do not scruple to treat their benefactor with ingratitude, and to load him with abuse. » (1) Such a history, uniform in every land, and for every race, sounds like an echo of the prophetic malediction; « You shall be as an oak with the leaves falling off, and as a garden without water. And your strength shall be as the ashes of tow, and your work as a spark. » (2)

Five years later, to anticipate a case which exactly resembles that of the Namaquas and Damaras, we are told that the Makololos, in spite of their profitable intercourse with Protestant missionaries, had just robbed a party of them of every thing which they possessed, and driven them out of the country. M'' Price, the wife of one of the ministers, « was buried under an isolated tree in the immense plain of the Mabobe; » and, « after the party left, the Makololos disinterred the body, and cut off a portion

(1) *Lake Ngami*, etc., by Charles John Andersson; ch. II, p. 27; ch. IX, p. 103.
(2) Isaias, I, 30, 31.

of the face to exhibit in their town. » (1) Such was
the progress which the missionaries had made, during
the interval, in acquiring the reverence of their African disciples.

In 1857, the Rev. Joseph Shooter had arrived at
the conclusion, suggested by the unvarying experience
of half a century, that « we must not estimate the
results of missionary labour merely by the number
of converts. » Yet any other estimate would apparently be still less acceptable, for he adds that long
observation of their character only « tended to weaken
his confidence in the religious professions of this
people. » (2)

In the same year, Dr Armstrong, an anglican
bishop, confirms all the other witnesses, but with
special reference to the misadventures of his own
religious body. « If the Kaffirs, » he says, « abound
in the diocese of Grahamstown by thousands, the
Church of England has yet done nothing for them. »
The representatives of that institution were fully occupied, it appears, in dealing with the domestic
phenomena which the Establishment is now exhibiting to the Kaffirs, after offering them to the contemplation of the heathen in every other land. « Port
Elisabeth, where I first touch my diocese, » observes
Dr Armstrong, « is full of Church troubles. » He
adds, indeed, as might be expected, that « many
bright features present themselves, » and then reit-
erates the accustomed lament, « but there is something sad in beginning with internal strife. »

(1) *The Times*, May 2, 1861.
(2) *The Kafirs of Natal and the Zulu Country*, app.,
pp. 369, 371.

Dr Arsmtrong found, like the rest of his brethren, that the eud corresponded with the beginning, and the « bright features » became clouded. A little later he had to deplore « the secession » of part of his flock, who adopted this mode of protesting against a clergyman who preached in a surplice; and the event was the more painful, because, as his biographer remarks, « he made many efforts to retain the dissidents, but in vain. » At Uitenhage also, he found it expedient to suspend one of his clergy for a dispute about « the offertory. » Such anecdotes, no doubt, are trivial; but in speaking of the Church of England as a missionary body, the most industrious historian searches in vain for graver materials.

Dr Armstrong's principal clergy, like Heber's, seem to have been German Lutherans, with an infusion of English Wesleyans, both classes accepting the « orders » which he was able to offer them. Yet he suffered much annoyance, we are told, from « the opposition of the Wesleyans, » as Heber and his successors did from the hostility of the Lutherans. And meanwhile the heathen looked on, and formed their conception of the nature of Protestanlism.

« The reports, » Dr Armstrong says, — meaning, probably, the private as distinguished from the official reports, — « do not really speak of many converts. There are many *listeners*. A chapel will be full every Sunday, and yet but very few converted and baptized. As a fact there are very few Christian Kaffirs. » (1)

(1) *Memoir*, by the Revd J. J. Carter, pp. 264, 269, 281, 307. 347, 381.

The Wesleyans were even more candid than D' Armstrong; for Sir Benjamin D'Urban relates, that « they all acknowledged to him, that they could not flatter themselves they had ever made a lasting salutary impression upon one of the race of Kaffirs. »

In 1857, D' Livingstone published his interesting work on South Africa. From such a writer we expect the truth, and the expectation will not be disappointed. The first « element of weakness » which he noticed in his fellow missionaries, was their determination not to venture beyond the tranquil borders « of the Cape Colony itself. » « When we hear, » he remarks, « an agent of one sect urging his friends at home to aid him quickly to occupy some unimportant nook, because, if it is not speedily laid hold of, he will ' not have room for the sole of his foot; ' one cannot help longing that both he and his friends would direct their noble aspirations to the millions of *untaught heathen* in the regions beyond, and no longer continue to convert the extremity of the continent into, as it were, a dam of benevolence. »

D' Livingstone, with the freedom from prejudice which is the privilege of manly natures, proposes this question to his readers. « Can our wise men tell us, why the *former* mission stations (primitive monasteries) were self-supporting, rich, and flourishing, as pioneers of civilization and agriculture from which we even now reap benefits; and modern mission stations are mere *pauper establishments*, without that permanence or ability to be self-supporting which *they* possessed? » We may be allowed to regret that a writer of so much integrity and good sense did not attempt to answer his own question.

Of the actual and final results of the labours of sixty years in South Africa, Dr Livingstone gives this cautious but impressive estimate. « Protestant missionaries, of every denomination, all agree in one point; that no mere profession of Christianity is sufficient to entitle the converts to the Christian name. » (1) It is impossible, in presence of such facts, to think without horror of the multitude of sacrilegious baptisms which, in Africa as elsewhere, appear to be the sole fruit of Protestant missions.

In 1858, for there is no defect in the chain of evidence, the Rev. H. Calderwood gives this report. « If we view the Kaffirs as a nation, they may be said to have *refused the Gospel.* The Kaffirs, as a people, are just as uncivilized and degraded, their customs are as impure and cruel, and they are apparently as unmoved, as they were on the day when Vander Kemp first stood on the banks of the Tyume. » (2)

And so notorious is this result of all the English missions in South Africa, including the operations of nearly twenty different sects, that in 1850, President Pretorius, of the Transvaal Republic, could thus openly jest at them in a public speech. « It was his decided opinion, that the emissaries of the London Missionary Society have done, and continue to do, so much harm, and so little good among the natives, that it has become absolutely necessary for the Raad to decide, whether or no their continued labours, and

(1) *Missionary Travels*, ch. vi, pp. 116, 117, ch. ix, p. 190.
(2) *Caffres and Caffre Missions*, ch. vii, p. 98.

even their presence, to the north of Vaal River shall be longer tolerated. » It is true that the English writer who quotes this speech angrily retorts, that the Boers « are as a class far more dangerous to civilization than even the irreclaimable savages of Moffat and C°. » (1)

It would be idle to offer even a word of comment upon such a history, in which, though every sentence is penned by Protestant writers, we read only an unvarying record of covetousness, immorality, worldliness, confusion, and failure. St. Paul has written the same history, but in fewer words. When the Apostle enumerates « the works of the flesh, » he seems to sum up, in one brief sentence, the principal incidents in all Protestant missions :— « uncleanness, luxury, contentions, emulations, quarrels, dissensions, sects. » (2) Such, as we have seen in every land, are their only fruits; and it is to gather them once more in a new field, that vast sums of money, which might have alleviated the lot of thousands of our heathen population at home, have here been expended, during three quarters of a century. Two races of pagan men have in this case been submitted, during three whole generations, to all the influences which Protestantism could exert upon them ; the one « have refused the Gospel, » the other, wherever they have accepted the instructions of a Protestant missionary, have only become « the most idle and the most worthless of their nation. » If it were possible to admit that the agents in such a work are, as

(1) *The Cape and Natal News*, Jan. 31, 1859, p. 77.
(2) Galat, v, 19.

they assure their disciples, the interpreters of divine
truth, and of truth « reformed » by a kind of second
revelation, the supposition would perhaps involve
the most frightful satire upon the God of Christians which the subtlest impiety has ever conceived.

It is time to quit a subject which is full only of
regret and humiliation, and to endeavour to seek
more grateful scenes in other lands. But first we must
say a word, in conclusion, upon Catholic missions
in South Africa.

A Protestant writer has observed, with allusion
to the facts of which we have now completed the
survey, that in South Africa « the Roman Catholic
community, until these few last years, were a proscribed people. By an old law of India, Jesuits and
Roman priests were to be forcibly apprehended, and
immediately deported. » (1) Bishop Devereux, Vicar
Apostolic of South Eastern Africa, notices the same
fact, in 1850, in explaining the absence of Catholic
missionaries from these regions during the Dutch and
English occupation. « These provinces, » he observes, « have been hitherto, so to speak, a sealed book
for Europe. First the Dutch East India Company
forbade, throughout the whole Colony, the exercise
of our religion, enforcing the interdict by severe penalties. The English domination succeeded, which,
after manifesting an almost equally intolerant spirit,
concedes, even at the present day, only a reluctant
consent to our ministry. » (2) It was not till 1838
that the existing mission, in spite of the frowns of

(1) *The Cape of Good Hope*, by John C. Chase Esq., Secretary
to the Society for Exploring Central Africa, p. 138.

(2) *Annals*, vol. XII, p. 12.

hostile officials, was constituted by Bishop Griffith, the first Vicar Apostolic. For some years the insufficient number of the missionaries, and the necessity of attending to the wants of the Catholic population, forbade all attempts to organise systematic efforts for the conversion of the heathen. The « children of the household » had the first claim. In 1855, D' Colenso, who evidently does not share the vulgar prejudices of his order, and is too generous to employ their language, appears to have visited the Catholic Bishop in Maritzburg—« a very gentlemanly Frenchman, with a benignant expression of countenance, and an appearance of sincerity and earnestness about him which I was rejoiced to witness. He told me that there were not yet any missionaries of his Church among the natives; but he was about, without delay, to set some at work. » In 1856 the project was executed, and the Mission of St. Michael opened in Kaffraria. In 1858, the Rev. H. Calderwood, writing from the same part of the country, says; « the Roman Catholics are on the increase. There are two bishops and a number of priests, who are able and energetic men. It is quite clear that Protestants are not to have it all their own way in South Africa. » (1) Lastly, M' Cole very candidly intimates what the final issue of the new Catholic mission is likely to be, when he says, — « The Catholics are steadily progressing in numbers, and make, I verily believe, more genuine converts among the coloured classes than any other sect. » (2)

(1) *Caffres and Caffre Missions*, ch. 1, p. 12.
(2) *The Cape and the Kafirs*, ch. ix, p. 155.

We may now quit Africa, not without the consolatory belief that the work of true conversion has at
length begun, and that a later annalist will record the
same apostolic triumphs in this land which we have
already traced in so many others. Let the reader compare, for his own instruction, the historical facts
which we have now imperfectly reviewed; the warfare of the martyrs of North Africa, of Egypt, and
Abyssinia, — never more truly apostles than when,
like our Lord at Bethsaida or St. Paul at Antioch, they
seemed for a season to preach in vain, — and the later
toils of the generous men who in our own day have
succeeded both to their office and their gifts, with
the narrative of turpitude and confusion which we
have just closed; and let him apply once again the
divine rule, *By their fruits ye shall know them*. And
that he may comprehend the whole lesson which
this history contains, let him note in this case also
the accustomed fact, that the agents of the Sects have
not only failed, — in Africa, as in India, Ceylon, and
the Antipodes, — but that they have failed, in spite of
the advantage which in all these countries they enjoyed as the representatives of an irresistible power,
and the dispensers of almost unlimited wealth. Silver
and gold they had, but it could not purchase a single
soul, for even the pagan mocked the preachers who
came to him with such gifts, when he saw that they
could give him nothing better. The Catholic apostles,
penetrated with other truths and holier maxims, gave
the life which was all they could call their own, and
gave it with more than royal munificence, content
that a later generation should reap the fruits of a
sacrifice of which *they* tasted only the gall and vine-

gar. And they did not offer it in vain. Already from
the north of Africa the Cross has begun to cast its
healing shadow towards the mountains which bend
down to receive it, and the deserts which smile at its
approach; and from the Nile to the Ocean, from
Egypt to Morocco, the disciples of Islam are hiding
their faces before the mysterious Sign which tells
them that their hour has come. From the East also a
voice is heard, which reaches even to the West, and
is echoed from the mountains of Ethiopia and the
cities of Abyssinia, across the burning plains of the
Soudan, to the rivers of Senegambia and the parched
solitudes of Angola and Benguela; and if in the South,
long abandoned to unfruitful husbandmen, who sow
but never reap, and whose labour is as unprofitable
as their repose, the field seems to be pre-occupied;
yet here also the Church will accomplish the victory
of which we have lately followed the irresistible
march in all the Islands of the Pacific, and having
silenced the discordant cries of struggling and conflicting sects, will at length entone the hymn which
shall announce to heaven and earth that the curse is
removed from Africa, and that the blood of her martyrs has not been shed in vain.

CHAPTER VIII.

MISSIONS IN THE LEVANT, SYRIA, AND ARMENIA.

Many lands have now been passed in review, and each has proclaimed in turn the same unvarying tale. We have visited the Chinese and the Hindoo, the Cingalese and the Maori, the Philippine and the many tribes who people the island world of the Pacific. We have interrogated the Moor and the Copt, the Negro and the Abyssinian; and now at length the Kaffir and the Hottentot have added their voice, and have told us, that they too, in spite of the mists which cloud both heart and brain, are learning to discriminate between the apostles of Jesus and the emissaries of man. All have bowed in turn before the meek but fearless pastors who went amongst them bearing the Cross, and have confessed, in love or in hate, that *they* indeed came from God; while all have agreed to spurn, as only men like themselves, the crowd of rival teachers, having neither the gifts nor the calling of apostles, and to utter the testimony which the evil spirits have so often been forced to proclaim by the mouth of the heathen, — « Jesus I know, and Paul I know, but who are you? » (1)

And now we approach the regions where the mightiest races of the human family have in turn reigned or served, and the lands, immortal both in sacred and profane story, where Christianity yielded its first martyrs, and won its earliest triumphs. They have changed since then, yet not as other lands have changed ; for in this mysterious East, which still silently rebukes by its grave and solemn mien the fickle and clamorous races of the West, even error knows how to simulate the prerogatives of truth, and still wears the same outward form, after the lapse of centuries, in which it defied the sentence of God at Ephesus and Chalcedon. The lessons of a thousand years, and the abject misery of the last four hundred, have failed to admonish the disciples of Photius and Eutyches and Nestorius; until in these last days a new call to repentance and conversion has been heard amongst them, of which we are about to trace the noble results. We are going to speak of the Greek and the Syrian, — of the Moslem who rules over both, — and of the Russian who is planning in secret how he may set his heel on them all.

We have come from Africa, and must therefore

(1) *Acts*, xix, 32.

enter the Mediterranean through that famous strait
at whose mouth England keeps watch from her
strongest fortress. Let us begin our new voyage from
this spot; for even in Gibraltar, where but a few
thousand men are crowded together, we shall find
one more example, worthy of a moment's attention,
of the eternal contrast between the children of the
Church and the children of the world.

An Episcopalian clergyman, who had left his flock
in America, but addressed to them from every place
which he visited pastoral letters, of which the main
object seems to have been to keep alive during his
absence their aversion to the Catholic Church, found
materials for an animated discourse even in Gibraltar. He visited both the Catholic and Protestant
church in that place, and then despatched to his
remote congregation a description of what even he
was constrained to call « the striking contrast. » In
the Protestant church, he tells them, he never saw
« one of the attending soldiers on his knees; »
and then he exclaims, « to what advantage do the
Catholics appear in this striking contrast ! » « The
hundreds that stood *there*, » he adds, when he had
passed from the worship to the preaching, « were
all eye and ear; but *here* (in the Protestant church)
nothing could be seen but yawning, and drowsiness,
and inattention. » (1)

This unfavorable report of an American minister
is more than confirmed by an Anglican writer who

(1) *Glimpses of the Old World*, by the Rev⁴ John A. Clark,
D. D., Rector of Sᵗ Andrew's Church, Philadelphia, vol. I, ch. II,
pp. 56, 68.

observes ; • The state of religion when I was at Gibraltar was most disheartening... There is literally
no Church feeling in Gibraltar. • (1)

It is perhaps worthy of remark, that a Russo-
Greek traveller, the amiable Count Schouvaloff,
seems to have owed the grace of conversion to his
continual observation of the same • striking contrast • which produced only a transient impression
on Dr Clark. • What struck and edified me in the
Catholic churches, • he says, • was the profound
recollection of the faithful in the act of prayer. I
compared their modest and humble attitude with the
often unbecoming movements, the deep *ennui*, and
the distracted looks, of a great number of my co-
religionists during the divine office; and I was
obliged to confess, in spite of myself, that there was
more piety among the Catholics than among the
Greeks. • (2)

Let us stay also for a moment at another fortress,
also a symbol of Anglo-Saxon might, which we shall
pass on our way to the Isles of Greece. Malta has
been for more than a quarter of a century the head
quarters of Protestantism in the Levant. Nearly forty
years ago Mr Jowett recommended it to English missionary societies as a centre for their operations,
because, as he said, • it is very far from unhealthy,
British protection is here fully enjoyed, together with
a degree of comfort seldom to be attained in foreign
countries ; rendering it a peculiarly eligible residence

(1) *The Canary Isles*, etc., by the Revd Thomas Debary, M.A.,
ch. xviii, pp. 213, 225.

(2) Schouvaloff, *Ma Conversion et ma Vocation*, ch. iii, p. 209.

for a missionary family. » (1) These characteristic
considerations prevailed, and for thirty years an
eruption of tracts and bibles has flowed out of Malta,
and covered both shores of the Mediterranean. In the
single year 1831 they boast to have issued from this
eligible residence » 4,760,000 pages, all in modern
Greek. » (2) By the same year the Americans alone
had dispersed « about 350,000 volumes, containing
21,000,000 pages. » (3) Both English and Americans have been dispersing them at an increased rate
ever since. How many converts have been made by
this abundant literature, and of what sort, we shall
learn presently.

It is here also that the « Malta Protestant College »
has been established, with the object of providing
suitable instruction, as well as food and lodging, for
any orientals who could be induced to enter it. Of
the actual results obtained in this institution, which
appears to have been hitherto a kind of hospital for
astute adventurers of every class, we shall have a
sufficiently accurate notion when we have completed
our review of missions in the Levant. It was here that
Achilli found refuge ; and it may be doubted whether
any four walls in Christendom have contained within
them, at a given moment, so singular an assemblage
of adroit comedians as the Malta Protestant College.
Even Achilli is not, as we shall see, an exaggerated
specimen of its inmates. The gentleman who bears

(1) *Christian Researches in the Mediterranean*, p. 376 ; 3rd edition.

(2) *History of American Missions*, by the Revd Joseph Tracy,
p. 213.

(3) P. 235.

the title of « bishop of Gibraltar, » we are told,
« said he was not pleased with Achilli, as he expected, after the friendly intercourse they had had,
knowing the favorable opinion he had of the Church
of England, that he would have joined himself to our
Church, rather than have laid the foundation of another. » (1)

No doubt Achilli, who is said to have become
ultimately a Swedenborgian, had encouraged this
expectation, and found his profit in affecting esteem
for the Church of England. A person so fertile in
resources would find little difficulty in outwitting the
amiable gentleman of whom a well known traveller
gives this irreverent description. « Dr Tomlinson
acted like an episcopalian tight-rope dancer, always
balancing himself between Puseyism and Evangeli-
calism, and so distracted the few Protestants at
Malta. He is eminently a man of no decision of
character. » (2) Achilli and his companions appear
to have detected this infirmity. But the Malta College
wanted recruits, and was willing to accept them on
their own terms; and this fact becoming known
throughout the Levant, the revenues of the College
were constantly dilapidated by ingenious orientals,
who adopted the new drama of « Achilli and the
bishop of Gibraltar, » through every possible modification of comedy and burlesque, but always to their
own advantage. A few examples, recorded by Protestant writers, deserve attention.

(1) Dr Achilli, and the Malta Protestant College, p. 9. (1851).
(2) Richardson, Travels in the Great Desert of Sahara, vol. I,
ch VIII, p. 235.

The first is the case of Dr Naudi, reported at
length by Dr Clark. Professing to be a Protestant
convert, Naudi was long supported by the Church
Missionary Society, to whom he forwarded welcome
periodical reports, setting forth the rapid increase of
oriental protestants, and the inconveniently crowded
state of his own chapel in consequence. The « spread
of Protestantism in the Levant » became the theme
of many a glowing oration, till Dr Joseph Wolff,
always active and inquisitive, resolved to visit
« Naudi's place of worship, » in order to be an eye-
witness of his evangelical triumphs; — and then
was revealed an unexpected fact. « He ascertained, »
says Dr Clark, « that Dr Naudi *had never held
service here*, although he had *for years* made his
reports in relation to what he was doing, and received funds from England to enable him to carry on his
operations. » (1)

The next case is related by Dr Wolff himself.
« Antonio Fabri, the Cancelliere of the British
Cousul, told us he was convinced of the truth of the
Protestant religion. » But Antonio was a very inferior
performer to Dr Naudi, and betrayed his secret too
soon. « We found out, » says Dr Wolff, « that he said
this in order to induce us to give our consent to his
marrying our English maid-servant. » (2)

Stephanos Carapiet was another of the same class
of converts. « He arrived from Beyrout, and asked
me to give him money to go to Malta, to join the
American Missionaries there, by whom he said he

(1) *Glimpses*, etc., ch. VIII, p. 165.
(2) *Journal*, p. 161.

had been converted. He was a Greek priest. » Apparently Dr Wolff was generous enough to comply with
the request, for he adds, « after he had staid a few
days he got extremely drunk, so we sent him
away. » (1)

Dr Carne also tells us, amongst other examples, of
« two brothers, » who came from Mt Lebanon, —
the fame of the Protestant missionaries having evidently spread in all directions, — « clever and
designing fellows both of them, who *agreed to be
baptized* and become useful agents, on the promise
of some hundred pounds, to be paid them by a
zealous and wealthy supporter of the cause. » (2)
We shall hear of many similar cases when we get
into Syria, and these may suffice for the present.
It is curious that these playful orientals never even
attempt to practise their frauds upon Catholic missionaries, perhaps because they have detected that
the latter do not pay for conversions; and that it is
the English, who deem themselves the most discerning, and the Americans, who claim to be the keenest
people in the universe, who are their only victims.

Let us leave Malta and its college, the value of
which we shall learn to appreciate still more exactly
hereafter, but not without noticing words which it
seems to have chosen as its motto and device. « Here
we are, » says one of its officials, and the College
printed and circulated the announcement, « safe

(1) P. 148.
(2) *Letters from the East*, by John Carne Esq., vol. II, p. 115;
3rd edition.

from the withering influence of Puseyism, Romanism, and all the rest of Satan's isms. » (1)

And now we come to Greece, famous for great
actions which she has long ceased to imitate, more
fruitful in words than in works, abounding rather
in poets than in prophets, and as careless in the
nineteenth century as she was in the fifteenth of the
miseries which her errors have provoked, and the
blessings which her crimes have forfeited. If there
be a people in the world whose history may be
compared to that of the Jews, and who seem, by the
singularity of their fate, to have been struck by the
heavy hand of God before the face of all nations, the
Greeks are that people. From the hour in which the
Photian schism was accomplished, and Michael
Cerularius first uttered a curse, in 1053, against the
Vicar of Christ, they have never ceased to endure
such affliction and ignominy as no other Christian
people ever knew. (2) Again and again reconciled to
the Church, it was only to relapse into schism.
Vainly they were warned by prelates of their own
nation, perpetually affirming their allegiance to the
Holy See, or admonished by chastisements which
their pride refused to comprehend. But the Greeks
were fast filling up the measure of their crimes, and
judgment was at hand. Already, as Pachymeres,
Gregoras, and other Greek historians relate, « there
was scarcely a city in the empire which had not been

(1) *The Fifth Annual Report of the Malta Protestant College*,
p. 13. (1853).

(2) A few lines are inserted here from a paper, written some
years ago, on the « Russo-Greek and Oriental Churches » and
printed by the author in the Dublin Review, Dec. 1847.

twice or thrice in the presence of an enemy. «
Already they had this in common with that fated
race to whom their prodigious calamities have caused
them to be compared, that every fresh act of faith-
lessness was promptly followed by some signal
judgment. (1) The West had sent forth the avenging
hosts which scourged the one, and now the East was
arraying the more terrible armies which were to
crush the other. The fearful power which was
destined to trample them under foot was gathering
strength day by day. The Ottomans were knocking at
their gates, and, like raging lions, « demanding their
prey from God. »

At this moment, fear and dismay, false and hypocritical even in their deep abjection, urged them once
more to seek reconciliation with the Chair of Peter;
and at the Council of Florence, in 1439, *all* the
prelates of the Greek and Oriental churches again
confessed, with one voice, that « the Roman Pontiff
is the true Vicar of Christ and head of the whole
Church, » — and Joseph, the Patriarch of Constantinople, bequeathed from his death bed, as his last
legacy to his nation and people, that famous exhortation to obedience and unity of which he had himself given an immortal example, and in uttering
which he yielded up his soul to God. (2)

But Greek perfidy was still to provoke another and
a final judgment. Gregory, the successor of Joseph,
after struggling in vain against the new schism, re-

___

(1) Leo Allatius, *De Eccles. Occident. et Orient. Perpet.
Consens.*; Maimbourg, *Histoire du Schisme des Grecs.*

(2) Maimbourg, liv. 6, ann. 1439.

tired to Rome in 1451, predicting the coming fall of
Constantinople. Isidore, the metropolitan of Russia,
and delegate of the Patriarch of Antioch; and Bes-
sarion, once the ablest champion of the Greeks, followed his example. In vain the Sovereign Pontiff,
Nicholas the Fifth, warned the twelfth and last Constantine, in the spirit of prophecy, that « if before
three years they did not repent and return to holy
unity, they would be dealt with as the fig-tree in the
Gospel, which was cut down to the roots because of
its sterility. » (1) The prophecy was spoken in 1451,
the Moslem gathered round the devoted city, and in
1453, « struck by the hand of God, » in the words
of the Patriarch of Constantinople, the schismatical
metropolis fell. Two hundred thousand barbarians,
more merciless than the legions of Titus, ceased not
to strike till their weary arms could no longer hold
the sword. Here fell the last Byzantine emperor.
Here the most gorgeous temple of the Christian faith,
polluted by incurable schism, became a temple of the
Arabian impostor. « Weep, o weep, » said a Greek
Bishop, one of the captives of that sorrowful day,
« weep for your miseries, and condemn yourselves
rather than others; for like the Jews carried away
captive to Babylon, you have despised the prophet
Jeremy, foretelling the destruction and the captivity
of Jerusalem. » (2)

The judgment so long provoked was now consum-

(1) Gennadius, *Adv. Græcos : Theolog. Curs. Complet.* tom. V,
p. 480.
(2) Leonardi Echiensis, Episc. Mitylen, *Lib. de captivitate
Constantinopolis.*

mated. From that hour, misery, contempt, and oppression have been the bitter portion of the erring communities of the East. « Confounded with barbarians, »
says an eminent philosopher, « they bear the penalty
of their schism, and remain — signiſicant judgment!
— the only Christian people subject to masters who
are not so. » (1) The destruction of Constantinople by
Mahomed II, and the subsequent fate of the Greek
people, present, as Montesquieu observed, all the
marks of a divine judgment. (2) And to this hour,
with the exception of those who have been reconciled
to unity, and have recovered by a noble submission
the freedom and dignity which they had lost, the
Photian sects are still the most degraded of all Christian races. « Since they fell away from the centre of
unity, » says one who has long dwelt amongst them,
« they have been completely isolated from the movement of civilization and of science which is ever sti-
mulating the onward march of the other people of
Europe. All intellectual activity has died away among
them… In losing the.elevated sense of Christianity,
they have transformed it into a religion of purely
pharisaical ceremonies. The priests have no longer
the virtue of the celibate; and all the bishoprics, including the patriarchate of Constantinople, have become
the object and the prize of base intrigue, upon which
the temporal power eagerly speculates, while it
openly exposes to auction these sacred dignities. Si-
mony has spread itself like a leprosy over the whole

(1) M. De Donald, *Législation Primitive*, tome IV, § 5,
p. 175.
(2) *Grandeur et Décadence des Romains*, ch. xxii.

hierarchy, and they make merchaudise of holy
things. »(1)

« The sport which they make of the miserable dignities of the Greek Church, » said Edmund Burke,
« the little factions of the harem to which they make
them subservient, the continual sale to which they
expose and re-expose the same dignity,... is nearly
equal to all the other oppressions together, exercised
by Mussulmen over the unhappy members of the
Oriental church. » « The secular clergy, » he added,
« by being married... are universally fallen into such
contempt, that they are never permitted to aspire to
the dignities of their own church. » (2)

But enough upon the well known abasement of the
Greek and other schismatical communities of the
East. We shall visit them, one by one, in the course
of this chapter. « Notre plume se refuse, » says one
who had traced their earlier history, « à tracer des
tableaux qui ne sont que trop humilians pour notre
triste condition humaine. » (3)

The very Turks themselves, detecting the immense
distinction between the Latin and Byzantine Christians, denote by certain habitual and emphatic designa-
tions their respect for the one and their contempt
for the other ; and as two centuries ago they styled
Catholics *Beysadez*, or « the noble, » and the Greeks
Taif, or « the populace » —so they still call the former *Francs*, the term of respect and honour, and the

(1) M. Eugène Boré, *Correspondance et Mémoires d'un Voyageur
en Orient*, tome I, p. 152.

(2) *On the Penal Laws against Irish Catholics*, Works, vol. VI,
pp. 285, 290.

(3) *Grèce*, par M. Pouqueville, Membre de l'Institut, p. 447.

latter *Kafirs*, the Mussulman synonime for « a man without any religion. »

The Moslem, we are told by a modern traveller, « is astonished when he hears them classed amongst the great family of the Christians of the West. » « They have preserved, » he adds, « nothing of Christianity but the name. The clergy do not even comprehend the prayers of the liturgy. We have seen them selling prayers to Turkish women, who came secretly to drink the waters of some miraculous fountain. We have seen them selling brandy at the door of their church, and converting, so to speak, the sanctuary into a tavern, before the eyes of the Mussulmen, justly disgusted by the profanation. » Even woman, who owes all her dignity and influence to the Christian religion, has relapsed, throughout the schismatical communities of the East, into a kind of barbarism ; and while modern Protestants, who shall be quoted hereafter, notice the nobility and freedom of the *Catholic* women among the same races, sole exceptions to the general humiliation because they alone have kept, or recovered, the faith, « the schismatical Greeks and Armenians have caused their social system and their families to retrograde towards the Mussulman level. *Their* women fly from the sight of a Franc with a barbarism even more wild and senseless than that of the Turkish females. » (1)

The facts here indicated are all confirmed, with ample details, by English and American protestants of our own day, who have been eye-witnesses of them. « The utter desolation of the unhappy Greeks, »

(1) M. Doré. Cf. Ubicini, *Letters on Turkey*, vol. II, Letter 2.

says Dr Carne, « forces itself on one's notice every day. » (1) « The gross ignorance of the inferior clergy,» observes Mr Spencer, «not only in theology, but in the common rudiments of education, the dissolute habits of too many of the higher ecclesiastics, and the infamous practices carried on in the monasteries, have become household words throughout all Greece. » And this applies to Greece Proper, of which, he adds,« the inhabitants are *more* demoralised than they were under the rule of the Turk. »(2) « To the Greek, » says Mr Warrington Smyth, in 1854, « a large proportion of the crimes of the country is to be traced, » even within the Ottoman dominions. (3) « The Patriarchate, » an American writer reports, in 1861,« is a seat of barefaced corruptions. Nine tenths of the Greek clergy are ignorant, vulgar, drunken debauchees... They are, therefore, detested by a large majority of the members of that religion. » (4) «Divorce is nearly, if not quite, as easy,» says Sir Adolphus Slade, « in the Greek religion as in the Mussulman » — and as it is now in the Anglican or Prussian. » The licence is much abused, and the bishops, each of whom has the power, grant it on the slightest pretext. » And then he adds, by way of contrast, of the *Catholic* population, « divorce is not permitted among *them*. » (5) But we reserve the full exhibition of this contrast to a later period.

(1) *Letters from the East*, vol. I, p. 37.
(2) *Travels in European Turkey*, vol. II, ch. xv, pp. 280, 289.
(3) *A Year with the Turks*, ch. xiii, p. 205.
(4) Constantinople Correspondent of the *New York Herald*, April 16, 1861.
(5) *Records of Travel*, etc., ch. xxiii, p. 444. (1854).

Yet there are not wanting men in our own country, who have agreed, for party purposes, to exalt the Greek as a convenient ally of Protestants against the Catholic Church. It is true that the Greeks, and all the oriental communities, have again and again anathematized the Anglican religion, and vehemently declined, in spite of their own miseries, even the semblance of intercourse with any of its professors. Not long ago, as an English writer lamented in 1854, the schismatical Greek patriarch bluntly described its emissaries in the Levant, in an official document addressed to his co-religionists, as « satanical heresiarchs from the caverns of hell. » (1) But this does not deter Anglican writers, always soliciting a recognition which they everywhere implore in vain, from an affectation of sympathy with communities which display such repugnance towards their own ; and whose chiefs, after reciting on a solemn occasion — the deposition of Cyril Lucar — the tenets of Anglicanism as set forth in the « 39 Articles, » declared all who hold them to be « heretics who vomit forth blasphemies against God, » and then promulgated their decree, by the hands of Jeremy of Constantinople, as « A reply to the inhabitants of Great Britain, » to whom its anathemas principally referred. (2)

It is a notable feature in the oriental communities, that they spurn the modern errors which they have never accepted, as obstinately as they reject the ancient truth which they once held. When the advo-

(1) *Journal of a Deputation to the East*, vol. II, p. 816. (1854).
(2) Theiner, *Pièces Justificatives*, p. 363.

cates of Protestantism, vexed rather than convinced
by the terrible array of evidence in Nicole's celebrated work, *la Perpétuité de la Foi*, appealed in despair to the oriental sectaries in support of their profane denial of the Sacrament of the Altar, they did
not gain much by the appeal. Instructions were sent,
as Prince Galitzin notices, to all the ambassadors and
consuls throughout the Levant, and « professions of
faith were received from the patriarchs, archbishops, and bishops of all the various churches of the
East, affirming in the most positive terms the doctrine
of the Real Presence, and bitterly complaining of the
calumny » which they thus effectually refuted. (1)
Let us see how they have replied in our own day to
the same overtures which in earlier times they rejected with such vehement disdain.

We are going to trace briefly the efforts which
have recently been made by Protestants to introduce
their opinions in the Levant. It is from Protestants
exclusively that we shall, as usual, derive all our
information. But it may be well to observe, before
entering upon this subject, that when Anglican or
American teachers, of a particular school, contend
with one another to exalt the long extinct glories of
what they call « the Eastern Church, » — with the
sole object of defending, not the orientals, but their
own ecclesiastical theories, — they seem willingly to
delude both themselves and their disciples. There is,
in fact, no such institution as « the Greek Church, »
or « the Oriental Church. » There is no other con-

(1) *Un Missionnaire Russe*, par le Prince Augustin Galitzin,
p. 83.

nection between Athens and Constantinople, between
Alexandria and Jerusalem, or between Moscow and
any of them, than that semblance of fictitious con-
cord which unites the conflicting sects of Protestantism in a common hostility to the One Church. Indeed
they are not cemented even by this precarious tie.
« There is not at this day, » says Schouvaloff, speaking of Russia, « a single individual, priest or layman, who believes in the unity of his church. » And
much more is this true of the smaller Photian communities.

« I am sorry to learn, » said D͏r Wolff many years
ago, » that the Greek Church is no longer under the
Patriarch of Constantinople. » « The new kingdom
of Greece, » observes a more eminent person, *in
imitation, and by the counsels of Russia*, has withdrawn itself from obedience to the patriarch of Constantinople. » And this grave event, as the same writer
remarks, which would have convulsed with anxiety
and distress any portion of the Catholic Church,
« was accomplished in Greece without a shock, and
even without a rumour! So feeble is the tie which
attaches to the pretended chief of the oriental church
the churches most contiguous to him, even those of
which the bishops were his own suffragans ! » (1)

Nor is there any real unity or cohesion in the
severed communities which, after falling away from
the Chair of Peter, have at length renounced their
allegiance to the throne of the usurper. « Although
of the so-called ' Greek ' Church, » says a Protestant
writer, « the greater part of the Christians of Euro-

(1) *Persecution de l'Église Catholique en Russie*, p. 388.

pean Turkey have no affinity with, and no sympathy
for, the Greeks. • (1) And this solution of all
ecclesiastical affinity has become universal. Only
political ties now unite even the broken fragments
of what was once • the Greek Church. • • The
clergy of Georgia, » observes General Monteith
in 1856, long ago formed a connection with the
Archimandrite of Moscow, expressly • to separate
them from the patriarch of Constantinople, under
whom they had previously been. • (2) More recent
examples of the same kind have occurred in Bulgaria,
as well as in some of the islands of the Greek Archipelago.

The fallen prelate of Byzantium, who borrows
from his dependents the price of the see for which
he is obliged to outbid his competitors, must now
console himself with the empty sound of the titles in
which his predecessors delighted, and which, by an
appropriate judgment, are all that remains to their
successors. • The words Oriental Church, or Greek
Church, • as De Maistre observed, • have really no
kind of meaning whatever. It is not true that the
Russian Church belongs to the Greek. Where is the
bond of co-ordination? What jurisdiction has the patriarch of Constantinople over the Russian priesthood? • And then he proves, by notorious facts, that
he would no more dare to make his voice heard in
Russia, or even in Greece, than in France or Spain;
and that • all these bishops, thus independent of a
common authority, and strangers one to another,

---

(1) Warrington Smyth, ch. xii, p. 275.
(2) Kars and Erzeroum, ch. i, p. 17.

the miserable puppets of the temporal power which deals with them as with its soldiers, perfectly comprehend in their own hearts what they are — that is, nothing. » (1) We shall hear some of them presently bewailing their own shame. They have rejected, through jealousy and pride, the gentle rule of the Vicar of Christ, and are now the slaves of the Caliph or the Czar. As late as 1821, the Sultan, wishing to turn the schismatical Patriarch out of his residence, hanged him, without ceremony, with all his assistant priests, at the door of his church, on Easter Day. » (2) And his brother pontiff, the emperor of Russia, is a master equally absolute, and scarcely less unscrupulous. Such is the lot of men who have once made it their boast, « We have no King but Cæsar. » « I recognise, » said Peter the Great, when solicited to restore the Russian Patriarchate, « no other legitimate Patriarch but the Bishop of Rome. Since you will not obey him, you shall obey me alone. Behold your Patriarch! » (3) From that hour they have had no other.

It was to the vassals of such lords as these that the Protestant churches of England and America resolved to send ambassadors, by whom they hoped, after so many misadventures, to negotiate at last a treaty of alliance. For more than a quarter of a century they have dwelt amongst them, distributing on every side, according to their wont, bibles and gold, tracts and dollars. The Americans boast that by them

(1) *Lettre à une Dame Russe, sur le Schisme et sur l'Unité Catholique.*

(2) *Persécution*, etc., p. 171.

(3) *Theiner.* p. 46.

alone « the annual sum spent for several years » is
15,000 l. (1) The English, as usual, have been still
more profuse; and D' Wilson exults in the fact, that
« the whole sum expended by Protestants in missionary efforts is annually double of that expended by
Rome, » (2) though the former have neither churches
nor flocks, while the latter numbers its converts alone
by hundreds of thousands. Thirty years ago, the
active emissaries of the United States were circula-
ting, not only bibles and tracts which nobody looked
at, but « geographies and arithmetics, apparatus for
lectures, and compendious histories, » which received a much heartier welcome. (3) Indeed for many
years the education of the various sectaries of these
regions was mainly in their hands. We should not
perhaps exaggerate in supposing that the Protestant
missionaries in the Levant have consumed already
more than a million sterling. If we ask them what
has been the actual result of efforts prolonged through
so many years, they are willing to tell us.

Let us begin at Athens. The English, as usual,
have employed only agents who could persuade no
one to listen to them. An emissary of the British and
Foreign School Society, as D' Wolff relates, « was
sent for the purpose of establishing schools, but he
soon gave up that project, and delivered lectures
on political economy. » (4) The Americans have been

(1) *Journal of a Deputation*, etc., p. 826.
(2) *Lands of the Bible*, by John Wilson, D. D., F. R. S.,
vol II, p. 599.
(3) *Excursions to Cairo*, etc., by the Rev'd George Jones,
ch. xxi, p. 321. (1836).
(4) *Journal*, p. 97.

more successful. « Our country, » says an ardent
American, « has reason to be proud of its missionaries here. » (1) In the following year, another citizen of the United States, still writing from Athens,
exclaims; « The cause of education and Christianity
is making rapid progress. » (2) It was not quite true,
as we shall see, but it was hoped that it might be
verified later. « In Greece, » says a third trans-
atlantic writer, with equal complacency, « the only
schools of instruction are those established by American Missionaries, and supported by the liberality of
American citizens » (3) Nearly twenty years earlier,
an English writer had noticed, that 500 Greek children already attended the American schools in Athens;
and that in those which were taught by Mᵣˢ Hill, the
wife of a missionary, « the daughters of many of the
first Greek families of Constantinople, as well as of
the most distinguished of Greece Proper, » received
their education. (4) Dr King also rivalled Mr and
Mʳˢ Hill in influence and in the number of his pupils.

If, however, from these facts we infer that these
gentlemen and their companions were making progress *as missionaries*, the real aim to which all their
efforts tended, later events will dispel the illusion. Like
their brethren in all parts of the world, they were
tolerated for such benefits as could be derived from
them, but the moment they began to mistake their

(1) *Wanderings in Europe and the Orient*, by Samuel S. Cox,
ch. xiv, p. 197. (1852).
(2) *Yusef*, by J. Ross Browne, ch. xi, p. 100.
(3) *Incidents of Travel*, by J. L. Stephens Esq., ch. xxviii,
p. 212.
(4) *Greece Revisited*, by Edgar Garston; vol. 1, ch. v, p. 101.

position, and to venture upon the subject of religion,
grave incidents occurred to admonish them of their
error. In spite of the influence which they had acquired by their relations with the higher classes, —
in spite of the services which they had unquestionably rendered as secular teachers, and of the active
sympathy of the Queen of Greece, — no sooner did
they attempt to emerge from the humble function of
schoolmaster to assume that of missionary, than a
menacing murmur, which soon became a loud and
universal outcry, revealed to them their real position.
For twenty-four years Mʳ and Mⁿ Hill had conducted
their schools in peace, and might well consider their
permanence secured; but at the first hint they understood what was coming, « and thought it best to discontinue their school for boys. »(1) Dʳ King attempted to brave the storm, « in spite of episcopal and
patriarchal anathemas, » but the resistance was more
energic than effectual. The Greeks, though enfeebled
by schism, were at least resolved to fall no lower;
and so intense was their indignation at the attempt
to introduce Protestantism among them, that, as
Mʳ Irenæus Prime relates, « there were serious and
deeply concerted schemes for Dʳ King's assassination, » (2) — whose life was only saved by trans-
ferring the consular flag to his residence, « a flag, »
as a sympathising fellow-countryman observes, « containing quite a number of stripes, and more stars. »(3)

(1) *Notes of Travel in the East*, by Benjamin Dorr, D. D.,
ch. xv, p. 353. (1856).

(2) *Travels in Europe and the East*, vol. II, ch. xiv, p. 188,
(1855).

(3) Cox, ch. xiv.

Finally, an English traveller informs us, in 1854, that « last year at Athens, an American missionary, the Rev. D' King, was tried by the civil courts, and condemned to fifteen days imprisonment, *and to be banished the country*, for preaching the Gospel to the natives in his own house, and publishing a pamphlet opposed to some of the doctrines of the Greek Church. » (1) It seems that in his pamphlet he spoke against devotion to our Blessed Lady, a crime which even Greeks are not prepared to tolerate, nor able to witness with composure.

At the same time, a M' Buell, also a Missionary, who refused to allow a crucifix to be suspended in his school at the Piræus, was summoned before the tribunals, his school closed by order of the Government, and a fine of fifty drachmas imposed upon the profane schoolmaster. (2)

Such was the termination of the educational labours of a quarter of a century. The Greek conscience, though not fastidiously delicate, was outraged by the first accents of Protestantism, and while its agents were branded by the Patriarch as « heresiarchs from the caverns of hell, » the people answered its invitations by a shout, which came from the heart of the nation, of « anathema » and « banishment. »

It is not uninteresting to notice the effect of this popular outburst upon the Protestant missionaries and their supporters. Hitherto they had spoken, always with respect, often with a kind of reverence, of this « ancient » and « venerable » church, in the

(1) *Journal of a Deputation*, etc., p. 590.
(2) *Journal d'un Voyage au Levant*, pp. 281, 311.

hope that it might be induced to countenance their
own more recent institutions. The language of praise
was now to be heard no more. We have seen that in
India, as soon as the Nestorians, upon whom so
much courtesy had been lavished, declined the respectful overtures of the Anglican authorities, these
disdainful heretics were consigned to ignominy by
protestant prelates, whose precarious « orders » they
had refused to recognise, and even stigmatised as
« worse than Romanists. » The same thing happened
in Greece. « The Greek Church, » said D' Wilson,
recording the discomfiture of his co-religionists,
« agrees with the Church of Rome in most matters
of the greatest moment. It has the essential characteristic of Antichrist. » (1)

It was thus that these gentlemen revenged themselves upon the Greeks, once objects of almost timid
eulogy. « I would say, » adds D' Wilson, confessing
at length the futility of past missionary schemes,
« that at present it seems a very difficult matter to
impregnate the Greek Church with evangelical truth
and influence; and that its circumstances are much
less encouraging than those of the other Oriental
churches. » So they turned to these more promising
fields, with what success, we shall see in the course
of this chapter.

« In regard to the Greeks, » says D' Hawes, an
American protestant minister, « the success of efforts
made in their behalf has been less than was reasonably anticipated; » and then, as if he felt that this
was hardly an adequate account of the matter, he

(1) *Lands of the Bible*, vol. II, p. 466.

adds; « The missionaries have felt themselves obliged, for the present, *to withdraw*, in a great measure, from this field. » (1)

Messrs Eli Smith and Dwight, more emphatic in their resentment, confound the Catholics with the Greeks, and even seem to attribute their misadventures to the influence of the former. « A missionary, » they observe, « can hardly set his foot upon any spot in that field — the Mediterranean — without encountering some sentinel of the ' Mother of Harlots ', ready to challenge him and shout the alarm. » (2) Yet the Greeks do not appear to have needed any suggestions from that quarter, and would certainly have received them with surprise if they had been offered.

Lastly, a representative of English Protestantism swells the gloomy chorus, and discovers, a quarter of a century too late, that « the Greek Church is opposed to the general circulation of the Bible ; » and that « the priests have *always* strenuously opposed the distribution of the Bible in modern Greek. » (3) Yet the Bible Society used to assure its subscribers, as we have seen, that they had no more promising sphere of action, and that even the Greek soldiery fortified themselves with the Protestant version during the intervals of combat, « while encamped, and in expectation of the enemy. » It was, no doubt, to gratify this pious habit of the Greeks, that the English missionaries issued in a single year from

(1) *Travels in the East*, by J. Hawes, D. D., p. 168.
(2) *Missionary Researches in Armenia*, Letter XI, p. 210.
(3) *Journal of a Deputation*, p. 594.

their fortress at Malta « 4,760,000 pages, all in
modern Greek ; » and that the Americans had already dispersed, thirty years ago, « about 350,000 volumes, containing 21,000,000 pages. » And of this
enormous but perfectly useless distribution, since
increased fifty-fold, the Protestants of these two
enlightened nations have cheerfully, but not wisely,
defrayed the whole cost.

We must admit, however, before we pass from
Greece to Turkey, that Protestant teaching has not
been absolutely without effect in the former kingdom. Let us notice a single example of its influence.
An accomplished Greek lady, of rare intelligence and
attainments, the eloquent advocate of her race and
nation, had the misfortune to lose her parents, and
was brought up by a Protestant pastor. The result
of his instructions, if we may judge by her own
writings, has been to substitute for faith a cold and
arrogant scepticism, — to engender a fierce hatred of
the Catholic religion, which this lady calls « Christian Mahometanism, » — and to give her courage to
assert, that divorce, which has become a kind of
national institution in Greek and Protestant lands, is
not an evil, but an engine of morality! (1) There is
a good deal more of the same kind in the writings
of this distinguished lady, which it would be both
painful and unprofitable to notice, but which may at
least confirm our conviction, that Greece did well in
crying « anathema » to Protestant missionaries.

What the Catholic apostles have done for the

(1) *Les Femmes en Orient*, par Mme la C^{sse} Dora D'Istria,
pp. 71, 81. (1860).

Greeks, by their own confession, we shall see a little later, but will first follow their rivals to Turkey, that we may complete the history of their operations in the Levant.

In European Turkey, the English do not appear to have organized any systematic missionary efforts; and throughout the Levant the Anglican establishment has been represented, almost exclusively, as in India and elsewhere, by members of other communities. M' Perkins, an American missionary to whom we shall have to refer presently, remarks, that the employment of « so many men of a different religious communion reveals a painful deficiency in the missionary spirit of the Church of England, that men of devotion to the cause *cannot be found* in sufficient numbers within her pale to go in person and apply her missionary funds. (1) « At present, » adds a Protestant historian of American Missions, with quiet contempt, « she has more means than men. » (2)

Perhaps, however, the Church of England has no reason to regret this fact, considering the impression which her rare representatives usually produce upon the oriental mind. When M' Jowett, one of her clergy, was asked by a schismatical Greek bishop, what was the doctrine of his church about the « Double Procession » of the Holy Spirit, his answer must have astonished even such an enquirer. « It is a point, I replied, which, in the present day, has not

(1) *Residence in Persia among the Nestorian Christians*, by Rev⁴ Justin Perkins, ch. III, p. 52.
(2) Tracy, *History of American Missions*, p. 594.

been much controverted, being considered as somewhat indifferent! » (1)

Dut several years have elapsed since Mr Jowell's
visit, and the Greek prelates have had time to forget
both him and his church. So complete has been the
oblivion, that when Mr Curzon not long ago presented
a letter of introduction from the Queen's Archbishop
of Canterbury to the Sultan's Archbishop of Constantinople, the following curious conversation occurred.

« And who, quoth the Patriarch of Constantinople, the supreme head and primate of the Greek
Church in Asia, who is ' the Archbishop of Canterbury?'

What? said I, a little astonished at the question.
Who, said he, is this Archbishop?
Why, the Archbishop of Canterbury.
Archbishop of *what*, said the Patriarch.
Canterbury, said I.
Oh, said the Patriarch. Ah! yes! and who is
he? » (2)

The Americans have acquired more notoriety in
these regions. Their operations in Turkey commenced
in 1826, and by 1844 they had already thirty-one
missionaries in that country. (3) Not that they have
«attempted any conversion except of *the Christians*, »
as Mr Walpole remarks; the Turks, he adds, they
are « afraid » of provoking. (4) But they are active

(1) *Christian Researches*, etc., p. 17.
(2) *Monasteries of the Levant*, ch. XXII, p. 336.
(3) Daird, *Religion in the U. S. of America*, book VIII, ch. III,
p. 691.
(4) *The Ansayrii*, etc., ch. XVI, p. 366.

enough amongst the Armenian sectaries, both here
and in Armenia, as we shall see when we enter the
latter country. Meanwhile, it seems to be a tranquil
and jocund life which these thirty-one missionaries
lead in Turkey. « Personal trials are very few, »
says the candid wife of one of them ; « many are the
comforts and pleasant things about this life in the
East. » (1) And she was evidently not singular in her
keen appreciation of them. The Rev. Justin Perkins
tells us of a missionary wedding at Constantinople in
these terms. « Mr Schauffler was married to Miss Reynolds, February 25th. I could not help feeling that there
was a moral sublimity in the scene presented. » (2)
Perhaps there was; but another witness, Sir Adolphus Slade, who knows these regions even better
than Mr Perkins, and is evidently much less impressed by the moral sublimity of missionary nuptials,
gives the following candid account of the Protestant
missionaries in Turkey and the Levant.

« To what purpose do the missionaries on the
shores of the Turkish empire frequent them ? to
convert those *who are already Christians*. The utter
unprofitableness of these gentlemen cannot be sufficiently pointed out. One comes to Malta, and settles
there with his lady. Another comes to Tino, and
while learning Greek, to be enabled to labour on the
continent, falls in love, and marries an amiable Tin-
iote — his spiritual ardour takes another course.
Another fixes himself at Smyrna, finding that demi-
Frank city pleasanter than the interior of Turkey,

---

(1) *Memoir of Mrs Van Lennep*, ch. xi, p. 267. (1851).
(2) *Residence*, etc., ch. iii, p. 76.

whither he was destined. Another takes a disorder,
and dies of it on the shores of the Persian Gulf. Another quietly pursues his own studies at Alexandria,
regardless of others' souls, to qualify himself for a
situation in one of the London colleges. All are living
on the stipends granted by the Missionary Societies,
and occupied in forwarding their particular views.
Far be it from me to say that human weakness does
not merit indulgence; but they who embark in a
holy cause should quit it when they find that the
flesh overpowers the spirit. Religion is the last asylum where hypocrisy should find shelter. » (1)

Admiral Slade adds, — « It will scarcely be credited that Missionaries arrive in the Levant, to
preach, to convert, knowing absolutely no other
than their mother tongue! » Yet we shall presently
hear one of their number asserting, with perfect indifference to the more veracious testimony of a crowd
of Protestant writers, that he and his friends had
done more for education in Syria in twenty years
than « all the Catholic missionaries » in two centuries; though the former have had neither scholars
nor disciples, and were for the most part perfectly
incapable of teaching them if they had.

A few words will suffice on the final results of
Protestant missions in Turkey. The American Episcopalians sent Dr Southgate, one of their bishops, to
recommend their form of religion to the inhabitants.
He seems to have had some vague idea of ecclesiastical principles, and is even charged by his own countrymen, of other sects, with supporting the schisma-

(1) Ch. xxvii, p. 517.

tical oriental bishops in their resistance to the
proselyting schemes of the Protestant missionaries,
whom he openly taxed with introducing amongst the
Armenians « the revolutionary sentiments of European radicalism. » He had, too, sufficient courage and
honesty to confess, after ample experience, that the
Protestant converts are « infidels and radicals, who
deserve no sympathy from the Christian public. » (1)

Dr Southgate recommends also the employment of
missionaries « unrestrained by family ties, » —
though he does not suggest where they are to be
found, — and after deploring the activity of « our
brethren of other denominations, » predicts this as
the only fruit of their labours : « Horrid schism will
lift itself up from beneath, and rend and scatter the
quivering members of the Body of Christ. » (2) Yet
this gentleman, who had so much distaste for horrid
schism in others, actually intrigued to get a *firman*
issued against the Catholics, whom he could only
oppose by physical force, in favour of the Jacobite
heretics, whose « numerous points of affinity » with
his own sect he had detected with satisfaction. (3)

We are not surprised to hear that Dr Southgate
failed. For a long time, he confesses, his mission at
Constantinople received from a single congregation
in Philadelphia one thousand dollars annually. But
money could not save it. « The mission, » we are

(1) *Christianity in Turkey*, by Revd H. G. O. Dwight, ch. x,
p. 244. (1854).
(2) *Narrative of a tour in Turkey and Persia*, by Revd Horatio
Southgate, vol. I, ch. xxiii, p. 305.
(3) *Mr Southgate and the Missionaries at Constantinople*, p. 27,
(Boston, 1844).

told in 1852, « has been abandoned, at least for the
present, after a heavy expenditure. Bishop Southgate
has returned to the United States, and resigned the
appointment of Missionary Bishop to Turkey. » (1)
Two years later another Protestant authority says;
«the Bishop had to acknowledge the complete failure
of his mission, and was *recalled* by his Society. » (2)
It is exactly the tale which we have heard in so many
other lands. Not one of the customary incidents is
wanting, and they follow one another in their usual
and invariable order : first, « horrid schism; » then,
« heavy expenditure; » and finally, « complete failure. »

Of the operations of the other American sects at
Constantinople, there is no need to speak. We shall
presently survey them on a larger scale in Syria and
Armenia. M' Dwight, in a work which reveals the
real designs of his co-religionists in the East, declares
in 1850, that « at the capital the number of Armenians who declared themselves protestants rapidly increased. » (3) Their number is, in fact, perfectly
insignificant; and many Protestant writers will tell
us, before we conclude this chapter, as D' Southgate
has already told us, what an Armenian really becomes when he professes to embrace Protestant tenets. They will also assist us to comprehend what even
they consider the work of « corruption and demor-
alization » in which the American missionaries are
engaged, though happily, up to the present date,

(1) *Colonical Church Chronicle*, p. 396. (1852).
(2) *Journal of a Deputation to the East*, vol. II, p. 806.
(3) *Christianity revived in the East*, p. 32. (1850).

within a narrow sphere. It is true, however, that
they have succeeded, by lavish expenditure, — we
have been told that they consume thirty thousand
pounds per annum in Turkey, — in collecting together a few Jews and Armenians, who have more
admiration for their dollars than their doctrines, and
who abandon their old religion without adopting a
new one ; and that these form what they call the
« Protestant Church, » or, as Mr Dwight styles
them, « the people of God, » in Constantinople.
Such are the « wild grapes » of which they make
sour wine, to set their own teeth on edge. « The
Protestant Church of Turkey, » says Mr Cuthbert
Young, « is now recognised by the Government, »
owing to the energetic action peculiar to this branch
of the Anglo-Saxon family, « with an officer of the
Porte, *a Turk*, as its temporal head. This last circumstance cannot be regarded as auguring well for
the interests of vital Christianity. » (1) The Porte,
we shall see, was well advised in appointing an officer of its own to supervise such an assemblage, and
was probably quite as capable of promoting « vital
Christianity » as the Hebrew and Armenian disciples
to whom it lent a temporal head.

And now let us speak briefly, before we enter
Asia, of Catholic missions in the regions which we
are about to quit. Not that we can hope to give,
within the limits at our disposal, even a sketch of
labours as distinguished by supernatural patience and
charity as any which we have hitherto narrated. A
few examples must suffice, but they will abundantly

(1) *The Levant and the Nile*, ch. III, p. 76.

illustrate the familiar contrast which we have proposed to trace in all lands. We are going to speak,
though unworthy even to record their names, of a
band of apostles whom even a Protestant minister
calls, with honest enthusiasm, « *the best instructed
and most devoted missionaries that the world has
seen since primitive times.* » (1) We have heard what
sort of agents the Sects employ ; let us contemplate
for a moment another order of workmen, and see
what the munificent bounty of God can do for men
whom His own decree has called to the apostolic life.
Too long we have listened to the mean sounds of
earth, — it is time to open our ears to voices from
Heaven.

As early as 1610, the sons of St. Ignatius had
begun to convert both Jews and schismatics at Constantinople. So irresistible was the influence, here
as elsewhere, of men in whom religion displayed its
most fascinating form and *self* was all but annihila-
ted, that, as Von Hammer notices, the Grand Vizir
told de Solignac, the French ambassador, « that he
would rather see ten ordinary ecclesiastics at Pera
than one Jesuit. » (2) A century later, for these men
do not change, a schismatical Armenian patriarch
thus addressed a Catholic who had abandoned the
schism, and was about to be martyred : « Your blood
be upon the Jesuits who have converted you and so
many members of our Church. » (3)

In the single year 1712, for we must not attempt

(1) Williams, *The Holy City*, vol. II, ch. vi, p. 570.
(2) *Histoire de l'Empire Ottoman*, par J. Von Hammer,
tome VIII, liv. III, p. 166, ed. Hellert.
(3) *Ibid.*, tome XIII, liv. LXII, p. 186.

to trace the whole history, Père Jacques Cachod, to whom was given the noble title of « Father of the Slaves, » reconciled three hundred schismatics to the Church. (1) Five years earlier, nearly one third of the population of Constantinople died of the plague ; and it was at that date that Père Cachod, compelled by holy obedience to give an account of actions which he would have preferred to hide, wrote as follows to his superior, Père Tarillon.

« I have just quitted the Bagnio, where I have given the last sacraments to, and closed the eyes of eighty-six persons... The greatest danger which I have encountered, or to which I shall perhaps ever be exposed in my life, was at the bottom of the hold of a ship of war of 82 guns. The slaves, by the consent of their guards, had obtained my admission into this place in the evening, in order that I might spend the whole night in hearing their confessions, and say Mass for them very early in the morning. We were shut in with double locks, according to custom. Of fifty-two slaves whom I confessed and communicated, twelve were already plague-stricken, and three died before I quitted them. You may judge what sort of an atmosphere I breathed in this enclosed space, to which there was not the slightest opening. God, who by His goodness has preserved me in this danger, will save me also from many others. » Twelve years later he perished, struck down by the pestilence which he thought he might henceforth defy. And the only reflection which such a narrative, and such a fate, suggested to the other Fathers was this ; « If

(1) *Lettres Édifiantes*, tome I, p. 14.

we were more numerous, how much more good we could do ! » (1)

But if these generous apostles displayed a zeal which knew not fear, it was regulated always by prudence and forethought. « During the seasons of the plague, » says one of them, « as it is necessary to be close at hand in order to succour those who are seized by it, our custom is that only one Father should enter the Bagnio, and that he should remain there during the whole time that the pest rages. The one who obtains the permission of the Superior prepares himself for this duty by a retreat of some days, and bids farewell to his brethren, as one about to die. Sometimes his sacrifice is consummated, at others he survives the danger. The last Jesuit who died in this exercise of charity was Father Vandermans .... since his death, the only victim has been Father Peter Besnier, so well known for his genius and rare gifts. »

It is impossible to trace here the details of the apostolic history of which this is only a characteristic episode. The public cemetery of Constantinople, filled with the bodies of Jesuits who died between 1585 and 1756, is their only monument. Smyrna, Aleppo, Trebizonde, and many other oriental cities, gave a tomb to missionaries of the same class. At Smyrna, where ten thousand perished by plague in the same year, a Jesuit Bishop became a martyr of charity at eighty years of age. In Aleppo, Father Besson, — « who united to his immense labours perpetual mortification, allowed himself but scanty repose at night,

(1) *Lettres Édifiantes*, tome I, p. 23.

and rose long before the dawn in order to spend
many hours in prayer, » — « after having procured a
holy death to a large number of persons, found the
crown which he sought. » He was followed, both in
his life and death, by Father Deschamps ; and almost
at the same moment, Father de Clermont, of the
illustrious family of that name, was added to the
company of martyrs. It was at this time, and by
the labours of such men, that the schismatical Patriarchs of Armenia (Erivan), of Aleppo, Alexandria,
and Damascus, were all reconciled to the Church.

In 1709, Michael Paleologus becomes the disciple
of Father Draconnier. Father Bernard Couder is the
next in this band of Christian heroes. More than nine
hundred families in the city of Aleppo were formed
by him to a life of piety. Six times he solicited and
obtained the coveted permission to devote himself to
the plague-stricken ; and so perfect was his obedience,
that when ordered by his superior to quit a city in
which he had attracted a veneration which might
prove dangerous to his humility, « he began on the
instant to make his preparations for departure. »

In 1719, when the plague raged in Aleppo from
March to September, « I was often obliged, » says
the celebrated Father Nacchi, « to bend down between
two victims of the pestilence, to confess them by
turns, keeping my ear glued as it were to their lips,
in order to catch their dying sounds. » And when
death had done its work, these apostles, nurtured
themselves in delicacy and refinement, often the
most accomplished scholars of their age, and not
unfrequently members of illustrious houses, would
wash the bodies and clothes of the dead, « reeking

with a horrible infection, » and having borne them
with their own hands to the common cemetery,
hasten back to repeat the same office of charity for
others.

Such deeds, which Catholics have learned to consider natural in their clergy, of whatever rank, would
hardly deserve mention, but that we are tracing a
contrast. There is probably not one of the thousand
Priests in our own England who would not imitate
them to-morrow, and few of their number who have
not already exposed their lives, many a time, with
the same tranquil composure. It is not many years
since an English Bishop, and fifty Priests, died
within ten months, ministering to the victims of
typhus. « The good shepherd giveth his life for the
sheep. » But let us complete the narrative which we
have begun.

« Father Emanuel died in my arms, » says the
learned Nacchi, « after devoting himself incessantly
for four mouths to the victims of the plague. After
him I assisted Father Arnoudie, and Brother John
Martha, both destroyed by the same disease. » Father Clisson, after an apostolate of thirty years in
Syria, met the same death; and was followed by
Father Nau, of whom his companions used to say,
« he has received from heaven all the gifts necessary
for the apostolic life. » Then came the noble brothers
de la Thuillerie, Joseph and James, the elder dying
on the bosom of the younger. The next was Father
Réné Pillon, for they fell fast, whose only form of
recreation was to visit and console the sick, and
whose daily prayer it was « that he might die in the
service of the dying. » To him succeeded Father

Blein, whose humility so touched the hearts of the
Greeks that they flocked to see his dead body, and
though he died of the plague, carried away fragments
of his clothes as relics. Beyrout saw the last combat of Father John Amieu, « who predicted his own
death to one who lay ill by his side, but assured the
latter of his recovery. » (1) And these are only a few
names out of a multitude known to God, and written
in the book of life. Of them it may be truly said that
they resembled one another so exactly, that they
were like brothers of one family. And even the most
malignant spirit of heresy could not resist them.
« You seek only our conversion, » was a common
saying of the sectaries, « the others ask for our
money. » And they often contrasted their manner of
life with that of the Protestants who had already
begun to dwell amongst them. « The English and
Dutch in Aleppo, » one of the missionaries remarks,
« observe neither fast nor abstinence, to the scandal
of every body. The people of the country say that
they cannot be Christians, and even the Turks regard
them as void of religion. » And the results of a contrast which even pagans have noticed, in every region
of the world, were such as these. In Damascus,
where there were only three Catholic families when
the Jesuits arrived, there were in 1750 nearly
9,000 converts. In Smyrna and Aleppo, almost the
whole schismatical population has been converted;
the work being continued in our own day, as Protestant travellers will presently assure us, by men in
whom even *they* recognise the apostolic virtues of

---

(1) *Ibid.* p. 200, Cf. *Missions du Levant*, tome IV, p. 39.

their predecessors. Throughout all Syria, as we shall learn from the same witnesses, the heirs of the martyrs are now labouring with such fruit, that from the banks of the Orontes to those of the Tigris and the Euphrates, the wanderers are flocking to the true fold, and even Chaldea, as we shall be told by men who vainly strove to mar the work, has become a Catholic nation.

When the Society of Jesus was suppressed, the enemy triumphed for a moment in Turkey and the Levant, as in so many other lands. But the Fathers of the Order of St. Lazarus were chosen by Providence to supply their place, at least for a time, and we must now say a word of *their* labours in the East.

In 1840, there were already in Greece Proper 4 Bishops, 100 Priests, and 23,000 Catholics. At the same date, in the three principalities of Moldavia, Wallachia, and Servia, there were 3 Bishops, and 71,000 Catholics. In the kingdom of Turkey there were 11 Archbishops, 423 Priests, and 281,000 Catholics. (1) This total of 375,000 has probably trebled during the last twenty years, so that Ubicini reckons the whole number of Latin Christians in European Turkey alone, in 1856, at 640,000, of whom 505,000 were natives; (2) while the total number of Greeks under the sceptre of the Sultan had dwindled twenty years ago to 1,000,000. (3) It is even said that there is hope of the early recon-

---

(1) *Annals*, vol. 1, p. 406.
(2) See Ubicini's *Letters on Turkey*.
(3) *La Turquie d'Europe*, par A. Boué, tome II, ch. 1, p. 21.

ciliation of the entire Bulgarian nation, though the influence of Russia will no doubt be employed to prevent it.

At the close of the year 1840, the celebrated Lazarist Father Etienne gave this report to the heads of his Order. « The chief obstacle opposed by error to the progress of the Gospel is profound ignorance, the common basis both of heresy and Islamism. The first means, therefore, of favouring the triumph of the Gospel is the education of youth. The Koran has still its disciples, but only because it proscribes all education. At present, however, this prohibition is no longer regarded by the great, whose contempt for the law of Mahomet is only imperfectly concealed under a few exterior practices. » An English protestant traveller confirms this account, when he says, that the present religion of the Turks « is a kind of gross Epicurean scepticism. » (1)

Father Etienne, however, gives interesting proofs of the respect which they begin to manifest for the Catholic religion, and the remarkable acquaintance which some of them display with its doctrines; and he adds, that « once permitted to frequent our schools, the Gospel and science will find them equally docile to their instructions. From the moment the Turks are allowed to enjoy liberty of conscience and the blessings of education, the Church will be on the eve of counting them amongst the number of her children. » (2)

(1) *Two Years Residence in a Levantine Family*, by Bayle St John; ch. xxiii, p. 267.

(2) *Annals*, vol. II, p. 71.

Let it be permitted, at this point, to offer, under correction, a consideration suggested by the present aspect of Islamism. Perhaps there is nothing so marvellous in the annals of mankind as the history of the Mahometan religion, — its triumphant progress through the three continents of the old world, checked only by the union of the Catholic nations under the inspiration of the Holy See, — and its puissant dominion of a thousand years. What providential scheme was this mystery, strange and unique in the annals of our race, designed to serve? The present condition of Islamism seems to suggest the explanation.

When the East was enslaved by heresy and schism, *then* the legions of the false prophet came out of Arabia. For centuries they have been permitted to scourge the Oriental Christians, treading them under foot as vermin. In human history there are no such oppressors, no such victims. « Crushed and degraded below the level of humanity, » in the words of M'' Spencer, « generation after generation of the unhappy Christians have passed away like the leaves of the forest. » Nor is this the darkest feature in their history. It was from *apostate Greeks* and monophysites that the legions of Antichrist were perpetually recruited by tens of thousands. « Mahommedanism, » as Von Haxthausen forcibly observes, « represents the pure monotheistic direction which *the Eastern Church*, especially in its sects, had already indicated and followed, one-sided and dogmatical. » Even in our own day it continues to enlist the same class of fallen Christians, helpless because severed from unity, — Copts, Greeks, and Abyssin-

ians. At Trebizonde, in 1838, we are told, « the
Greeks professed Islamism abroad, but lived as
Christians in the interior of their houses. » « Apostasy is, in fact, so obvious a sin in these countries,»
says an English protestant minister, « that even
little children, as I was informed by the Bishop of
Smyrna, will sometimes, when in a violent passion,
threaten their mothers that they will turn Turk.» (1)
Damascus, once wholly Christian, became almost
entirely Mahometan; and the same fact occurred in
most of the cities of the East. « Issuing from Arabia,
*and absorbing in its passage the Christianity of the
East*, the Mussulman torrent traversed the Bosphorus, and carried forward the crescent to the European
provinces of the Greek Cæsars; for it was no longer
with the degenerate Christianity of the East as with
that which flowed, full of life and strength, from the
apostolic Roman fount. The latter had quickly *absorbed into itself* all the conquerors of the empire; the
former bowed down without resistance under the
code of the Caliphs, and the Christian populations
of Asia, deserting the faith of Christ, adopted, in
vast numbers, that of the false prophet, and recruited
the armies of his vicars. » (2)

Such is the contrast between the Christianity of
Rome and Byzantium; and such, for centuries, has
been the influence of the Mahometan over the corrupt
and schismatical communities of the East. But Islamism has done its work, and may now disappear. It
came to chastise, by an unparelleled judgment, an

(1) Jowett, p. 23.
(2) *Persécution et Souffrances*, etc., p. 240.

unexampled offence. And now, when the oriental
churches are visibly returning to unity, and the voice
of the Supreme Pastor is once more heard amongst
them, Islamism — as if conscious that it may no
longer play the part of the Avenger — is hastening
to decay. We seem to touch already that great epoch
of Catholic unity, — of which the recent definition
of the Immaculate Conception of the Mother of God
is the surest pledge and precursor, — that consolida-
tion of all believers into one household and family
which Her love will obtain for the Church before
the world is abandoned to its final judgment, and
even the Church shall plead for it no more.

Let us return for a moment to Father Etienne, and
to the account which he gives of religion in Turkey.
« At Constantinople, » he says, « the clergy of our
congregation are at the head of a college, in which
the children of the first families of the city are educated : they have also a school, which is frequented
by 150 scholars. » This refers to the state of things
twenty years ago. « Three other schools are directed
by the Sisters of Charity. The 230 pupils whom they
receive are not all Catholics; Russians, Arabs, Armenian and Greek schismatics come to the same
source to obtain knowledge and wisdom. » The
Sisters had also under their care a hospital, towards
the expences of which the Sultan contributed 100 l.
Even the Mussulmen, he adds, filled with admiration for the charity of the Sisters, « who neither
will nor can receive any recompense, » are accustomed to ask,— « Whether they came down thus from
Heaven? » » May we not presume, » says M. Etienne,
« that the Sisters of Charity are destined by Provi-

dence to effect the long wished-for union between
Turks and Christians? »

An English Protestant writer, in spite of customary prejudice, thus confirms the account of Father
Etienne. « Short as the time has been since these
zealous Christians have entered upon this new-field
of labour, it must be owned in all justice that the
progress they have made, and the beneficial effects
of their judicious efforts, are most surprising... The
admiration, as well as confidence, with which both
they and the Lazarists have inspired the Turks is
unbounded. » (1) And this is confirmed once more,
in 1859, by another English Protestant, who considers, « a visit to the Convent of the Sisters of
Charity interesting and instructive, as showing how
human beings possessed of education and personal
attractions can leave everything which makes life
dear for the sake of God. Here, as every where else,
these ladies do a great deal of good, particularly in
education of the Arab children. » Of their hospital
« for the special use of strangers, » of all creeds,
« who may chance to fall ill here » — Beyrout —
he adds that, the sufferers, « when tended by the
devoted Sisters, scarcely miss the absence of their
friends. » (2)

When we have shown that the missionaries have
not degenerated from their fathers, but still resemble
a Cachod, a Besnier, and a Vandermaus, we may
pass to other scenes. « M. Elluin, » says Father
Etienne, « catechises the poor in Greek, and with

(1) *Wayfaring Sketches among the Greeks and Turks*, ch. IX,
p. 184.

(2) *Two Years in Syria*, ch. XXVII, p. 235.

the most consoling success; his instructions are frequented every Sunday by 300 persons, children and
adults. M. Donnieux, another Missionary, whose
indefatigable zeal I could not but admire, spends his
life in hearing the confessions of the Catholics, scattered throughout the city and the environs. Every
morning he sets out, taking in his course both sides
of the Bosphorus, penetrating into the interior of
families, distributing consolation and advice, and
often returning without having tasted food, except
the morsel of bread he had taken with him. Often,
too, surprised by the night far from his home, he
passes it in some miserable hut, offers there the
Holy Sacrifice in the morning before he leaves, and
continuing his route of the previous day, returns at
length to his brethren full of joy. This laborious
ministry is never interrupted, either by the rigour of
the season or the ravages of the plague. »

Such are « the comforts and pleasant things »
which *these* men choose for their portion. And the
results of their patient charity are such as the following. M. Donnieux alone, in the course of a few
months, reconciled to the Church 122 heretics. The
most conspicuous among his converts was Mgr. Ar-
tin, schismatical Archbishop of Van, in Armenia.
An immense crowd of the former disciples of the
converted prelate assisted at the ceremony of his abjuration; and after listening to the fervent exhortation
which, from a heart newly kindled with divine
charity, he addressed to them, « more than twelve
hundred persons were found to imitate this memorable conversion. » (1)

(1) *Annals*, II, 76.

The impulse given to education by the toils of the same workmen, is the only additional fact which we need notice. « It is very certain, » says Ubicini in 1858, « that the number of the schools founded by the Lazarists, with the assistance of the Sisters of Charity and of the Christian Brothers, increases yearly in a remarkable degree. » And then he observes, that already in 1849, « the latter had six hundred children in their schools of Pera and Galata, » while the former had, at the same date, eight hundred and sixty pupils. (1) Other writers will inform us that they are diffusing the same benefits in the principal cities of Asiatic Turkey.

We have no space for further details. For twenty years the work has progressed, every where by the same agents, and always with the same results. Even Protestants attest its power. « The Catholic religion in the East, » says Admiral Slade, in 1834, appreciating these events from his own point of view, « has ever offered a secure asylum for wavering minds of the Greek and Armenian sects. » He declares, also, from actual observation, « that it has made men *live in peace* among each other, and under their government, whatever that government be. » (2)

Dr Wilson, — who has perhaps employed more intemperate language than any living writer, and has been more abundant in those vehement invectives which sound like imprecations, and remind one of the text, « Whoso hateth his brother is a murderer, » — is constrained by a Power which uses such men

(1) *Letters on Turkey*, vol. II, Letter 3.
(2) *Records of Travels*, ch. xxvii, p. 511.

to proclaim the very truths which they abhor, to make the following confession. The Greeks, he says, when they become Catholics, « are amongst the most liberal and intelligent native Christians in the East. » (1)

D' Robinson, an American writer of the same class, — who laments that the movement of conversion among the Greeks, after spreading though Syria, « has now extended itself into Egypt, » — admits with evident reluctance, that « the result is a certain elevation of their sect. » (2) D' Durbin also, another American protestant, declares without reserve of *all* the oriental communities, — « It is not to be denied that their intercourse with the Roman Catholic Church tends to elevate them in the scale of civilization. » (3) We shall hear many similar testimonies when we enter Syria.

We may now cross the Bosphorus, and continue in Asiatic Turkey the investigations which we have hitherto confined to her European provinces. Let us begin at Smyrna. If we would find Protestant missionaries in Pagan or Moslem lands, much experience has taught us to look for them *on the coast.* They abound in Smyrna. « The number of Missionaries who have been sent to *Turkey,* » says an English protestant, « and are established at *Smyrna,* is very considerable. » (4) « They find that demi-Frank city pleasanter, » we have been told, « than the interior of Turkey; » and, as a matter of taste,

(1) *Lands of the Bible*, vol. II, p. 581.
(2) *Biblical Researches*, vol. III, § 17, p. 456.
(3) *Observations in the East*, vol. II, ch. xxxiv, p. 287.
(4) *Wayfaring Sketches*, etc., ch. vi, p. 118.

they are probably right. M. de Tchihatcheff, a Russian traveller, found some of the American missionaries, in 1856, occupied in meteorological observations; a useful and honorable pursuit, for which he
seems to think they had abundant leisure. (1) What
else they have done, we may easily learn, either
from themselves or their friends.

The English, who have had representatives at
Smyrna for a long course of years, do not even claim
any success. A gentleman who is apt to exaggerate
their influence candidly admits, in 1854, that « although Smyrna has long had the advantage of resident Missionaries, and of the faithful ministry of a
devoted clergyman, in the Rev. W. B. Lewis, the
British Chaplain, there are few signs of religious
life among the native population. » (2) There are, in
fact, ample signs of life, but not such as this writer
could detect or appreciate, because they were all
external to his own communion. Within its narrow
limits his description is apparently accurate. « It is
in the spirit of enterprise, » says Mr Jowett, « most
especially, that the Church of Christ » — he means
the Church of England — « appears defective. » (3)
« There is little of a practical and active missionary
spirit to be found among the members of the Church
of England, » said the late Mr Warburton. « When
I was in Syria, there was not an English missionary
who had taken a University degree; nor, with one
exception, was there a Christian-born minister of

(1) *Asie Mineure*, par P. de Tchibatcheff; ch. 1, p. 5. (1856).
(2) *Journal of a Deputation to the East*, vol. II, p. 570.
(3) P. 392.

our church. » (1) Admiral Slade mentions a single
Anglican clergyman, whom he considers an exception by character to his companions, and adds;
« Where did his labours lie? — Among the Greeks,
and without effect! » (2)

The Americans, as usual, have been, not more successful, but more ambitious and aggressive. D' Durbin, their fellow citizen, informs us, in 1845, that
they had printed in Smyrna up to that date
32,247,760 pages. D' Wilson records, in his account, an increase of some twenty millions. What
the inhabitants of Asia Minor have done with all
this printed paper, — amounting to about 130,000
octavo volumes, — does not appear. Indeed the only
effect of the presence of the various Protestant sects,
in Smyrna, — who distribute pensions which are
much esteemed, and books which no body reads, —
has been to afford amusement to these languid Asia-
tics, though only for a brief space. The excitement
lasted a few months, and then both Turks and
Greeks decided, as Protestant travellers assure us,
that the missionaries had ceased to be entertaining.
« Even the Armenians themselves, » says D' Valentine Mott, with unfeigned astonishment, « though
professing Christianity, joined with the deluded
Turks in suppressing the Protestant schools! » (3)
And D' Durbin, also an American preacher, relates
that his co-religionists, of various denominations,
were too much occupied in their accustomed pastime

(1) Ch. VIII, pp. 117-18.
(2) P. 518.
(3) *Travels in Europe and the East*, by Valentine Mott, M.D.,
p 404.

of fighting with one another, to allow a combination
of their efforts against the oriental sects. « It is to
be regretted, » he observes, « that they have come
into collision with each other in the midst of these
ancient churches, and in the presence of the Turk.
The chief ground of collision is the validity and
authority of their respective ministries » (1) — a
question which, he seems to think, they might have
discussed more advantageously at home.

Another sympathising writer, who laments the
trivial superstition which makes « keeping the Sabbath » the chief article of the missionary creed, says,
« We draw down contempt on that which we seek
to further, when we make it seem as though our
religion consisted in the observance of the Sabbath. » (2) Yet the Protestant missionary always
begins and ends with this precept.

Both the English and Americans have been especially unsuccessful with the Greeks, the very class
to which they have mainly directed their attention.
Mʳ Arundell, a man of learning and intelligence, who
was for some years British Chaplain at Smyrna,
expresses much dissatisfaction with their « ingratitude, » as well as with the levities which they
practised in their conduct towards himself. He sent
a young Greek, after due instruction, and an expenditure from which he hoped better results, as schoolmaster to Kirkinge. Unfortunately he paid him in
advance. « He went to Kirkingè, looked at it, said it
was an *askemos topos,* ' a horrible place, ' and

(1) Vol. II, ch. xxxv, p. 298.
(2) *Wayfaring Sketches,* ch. VIII, p. 170.

settled himself in Syria, without deigning to write
me a word » — a discourtesy which M' Arundell
resented the more keenly, because he had « for some
time assisted in keeping him and his mother from
starving. » (1)

But these Greeks are incorrigible — until they are
brought within the influence of the Church. Anglicanism and Methodism are too weak to hold them,
and only succeed in inspiring their ingenious malice.
Nothing less mighty than the Church can baffle their
intrigues, or rouse them from their petulant indifference. « Are you acquainted with Ephesus, » said
the Count D'Estourmel to a Greek, whom he wished
to employ as a guide to the antiquities of the apostolic
city. « Yes, » replied the luxurious Demetrius;
« I have eaten larks there with M. de Stackelberg,
and drank Chian wine with M' Dodwell. » (2) These
were his recollections of Ephesus.

But there is a power in Smyrna which can stir
the hearts even of such men as these. « The success
which attended the Romish Missionaries, « says
M' Jowett, « evidence of which exists in their numerous converts throughout every part of this region,
should be an encouragement to Protestants. » (3)
He did not consider that if Protestants would emulate that success, they must first become Catholics.
Thirty years later, another English writer, though
he is unable to record any Protestant progress during
that long interval, observes, that « the Romanists
comprise probably *five sixths* of the Frank population

(1) *Discoveries in Asia Minor*, vol. II, ch. XI, p. 271.
(2) *Journal d'un Voyage en Orient*, tome I, p. 213.
(3) P. 368.

at Smyrna. » (1) In ten years — from 1830 to 1840 — they more than doubled their numbers, though *they* have not been able to purchase a single convert, or bestow a single pension, and are not only poor, but have sworn before the Altar to remain poor to the end of their lives.

« My greatest hope, » said the Archbishop of Smyrna some years ago, « is in our schools, in which the population of Smyrna, by the religious education imparted to them, are completely regenerated. » Already the Lazarist Fathers had 250 pupils in their male schools, and the Priests of the *Missions Étrangères* 120 students in their college. Twenty *native* priests, added to an equal number of European missionaries, attested the influence of the education which they had received. Noble institutions have since then been created, and Smyrna now rejoices in possessing those Sisters of St. Vincent who teach, by their presence and example, the charity which only the true Faith can inspire. « In seasons of sickness, » says Mr Wortabet, — whose profession of Protestantism does not prevent his admiring the Sisters of Charity, — « whilst others flee to the mountains for a better atmosphere, *they* have been seen going from house to house, heedless of contagion from cholera, fever, or holes steaming with heat and stench, enough to make any one sick. One by one falls down by the bed-side of the dying sufferer. They die, but their memory lives, and no wonder many rise up to call them blessed. » (2)

(1) Young, *The Levant and the Nile*, ch. III, p. 74.
(2) *Syria and the Syrians*, ch. xv, p. 104. (1856).

If any further proof of the influence of the Catholic
religion in Smyrna, and of the virtues displayed by
its teachers, be required, it is impressively conveyed
in the angry confession of a Protestant missionary,
the Rev. J. Calhoun, — a confession appropriately
recorded by the pen of D' Wilson, — that even
« among the Protestants there are few who are decidedly anti-Roman Catholic. » (1)

But there are other cities which claim from us a
brief visit. Beyrout is one of them. « There are ten
thousand Christians in Beyrout, » says the Rev.
D' Durbin, « the great majority of whom are Roman
Catholics. » Yet a few years ago they were insignificant in numbers, and moreover, « Beyrout is the
centre of the American Missions in Syria, » and
« the Missionaries have several presses here. »
M' Neale notices « the superb nunnery in course of
erection here for the Sisters of Charity, whose advent
has given great satisfaction to the Catholics of Beyrout; » as well as their « boarding school for young
ladies, day-school for poor girls and Arabs, and hospital for sailors. » (2) M' Cuthbert Young observes,
in 1848, that « the Jesuit establishment at Beyrout
is said to be one of the most efficient, and many
Maronite and Greek children are educated in their
school. » Lastly, the candid M' Warburton says;
« I was much struck by the zeal, talent, and tact
exhibited by the Monks. »

Aleppo is still more worthy of our attention. Even
D' Wilson tells us that the Jesuits here « applied

(1) *Lands of the Bible*, vol. II, p. 577.
(2) *Syria, Palestine*, etc., vol. I, ch. XIII, p. 211.

themselves to the study of the Eastern languages
with a devotion seldom surpassed. » And then he
adds, — « They brought a considerable number of
persons within the pale of the Romish Church, and
they paved the way for the ultimate establishment of
the papal-Greek, papal-Armenian, and papal-Syrian
sects. » But if this gentleman finds nothing to say
against the earlier missionaries, he seeks relief by
informing his readers, without the least hesitation,
that as to the present Jesuits in this region, « *their*
morality is of the loosest kind. » (1) Probably he
never saw one of them, and knows nothing whatever
about them; but it was a safe assertion, and was sure
to be welcomed by his readers.

We need not reply seriously to such an assailant;
but here is an example of these modern Jesuits,
whose loose morality D'' Wilson deplores. Father
Riccadonna wrote a few years ago to his superior
in these terms, in obedience to directions which required an exact account of his position. « I will tell
you, in confidence, that we are living in destitution,
without clothes, without shelter, without provisions.
What others cast aside would be precious to us. A
little thread, some buttons, and a packet of needles,
would be a most acceptable gift. For want of these
we go for months together with our clothes in rags.
Praise be to God! It is necessary to have tasted these
precious sufferings to know their value and their
sweetness. May it be my lot to suffer them always. » (2)

(1) P. 573.
(2) *Annales*, tome VII, p. 241.

Let us return to Aleppo. In 1818, the British Consul General reported that « Aleppo is gradually drawing, and nearly drawn over to the Roman Catholics. » (1) In 1834, a zealous Protestant relates, that of 20,000 Christians, 17,500 are already Catholics. (2)

Monseigneur Brunoni, Archbishop of Taron, and Apostolic Legate in Syria, gave this account of them, in October, 1855. « The Catholic community in Aleppo, governed by pious and zealous pastors, appear docile to their teaching, and animated with religious sentiments in a manner very consoling to witness. I speak of what I have seen, having been invited to celebrate the Holy Sacrifice in the churches of the different liturgies, on which occasions the evident devotion and fervour observable in all was very edifying. The day on which I officiated for the Armenians, the pious and learned Paul Balit delivered an excellent discourse in reference to the conversions of the previous year, and on the majesty and superiority of the Catholic religion. His words made the truth so evident that no inhabitant of the neighbourhood, who was a schismatic, and happened to be present, was convinced of his errors, and renounced them on the spot. » (3)

« In Aleppo, » says a Protestant minister, the Rev. G. Badger, in 1852, « where they once numbered several hundred families, not more than *ten* Jacobite families now exist, the rest having joined the Church of Rome. » This unwilling witness adds,

(1) *Asiatic Journal*, vol. VI, p. 503.
(2) *Journal of a Deputation*, vol. II, p. 822.
(3) *Annals*, vol. XVII, p. 137.

that « the same secession has left them only a name
at *Damascus*. The Jacobite community of *Bagdad*
has followed the example set them by their brethren
at Aleppo and Damascus. » And then he performs
the usual task for which Protestant travellers seem
to be employed by Providence in all parts of the
world. « If the truth is to be told, it must be confessed that however much to be deplored this secession may be, the Syrian proselytes to Rome are
decidedly superior, in many respects, to their Jacobite brethren. » (1) Yet this gentleman « deplores »
that they should cease to be heretics, sunk in corruption and ignorance, though they become « decidedly superior » as members of the Catholic Church.
He does more; he rails at the Catholic missionaries
for « forming a schism, » and then proposes to the
Anglican Establishment to re-convert these neophytes
from their « Romish » errors! It seems that if we
desire to find unequalled examples of this kind, we
must now look for them in the Anglican clergy of
the High-Church school. But we shall hear of
Mr Badger again.

The Turks appear to discriminate more exactly
than Mr Badger between heretics and Christians.
Bishop Donamie reports, that at the Catholic funerals
in Aleppo, « janissaries, who are themselves Mahometans, precede the Cross, and oblige all whom they
meet on the way, without excepting the Turks, to
behave with respect and reverence before this sign
of our salvation. » (2)

(1) *The Nestorians and their Rituals*, by the Revd G. P. Badger,
vol. I, pp. 93, 180.

(2) *Annales*, tome VIII, p. 553.

Of the Protestants in Aleppo,—for they have there also their usual printing press, which works night and day with the usual results, — an eager advocate tells us; « On more than one occasion have the ecclesiastical authorities ordered all Protestant books, all Bibles from Protestant presses, etc., to be burned, destroyed, or delivered into their hands. » (1) Of one school of missionaries in that city, M' Walpole says; « The Presbyterian mission here bides its time, and perhaps I may say *nothing* has yet been done by them. » He remarks also that the missionaries do not even « kneel » at prayers; which, he observes, « seems a cold form of adoration. » (2) Their Moslem neighbours are probably of the same opinion.

Returning towards the south, let us visit Damascus. Here also we meet the usual facts. « The Christians, » says M' Warburton, « for the most part belong to the Latin Church. » Times are changed since, in 1551, twenty-two Catholics were crucified in Damascus on the same day. (3) « I believe about 20,000 are Christians, » says M' Churton in 1851, « principally *Greek* Catholics. » (4) « The *Syrian* Catholics of Damascus, » D' Robinson observes, « are *recent* converts. » (5) It was in 1832 that the Syrian Bishop of Damascus was reconciled to the Church, together with his numerous household and relatives. (6) At the present day, D' Wilson informs us,

(1) *Journal of a Deputation*, p. 822.
(2) *The Ansayrii*, vol. I, ch. XIII, p. 205.
(3) Henrion, tome I, ch. XVIII, p. 195.
(4) *The Land of the Morning*, ch. XV, p. 271.
(5) *Biblical Researches in Palestine*, p. 462.
(6) *Annales*, tome VI, p. 291.

II.   II

the Catholics have « the most splendid church which
Damascus contains ; »(1) and then he adds, as if to
counterbalance these unwelcome proofs of their progress, « in its services it is difficult to recognise the
simplicity of Christian worship. »

The « simplicity » of his Presbyterian co-religionists, at Aleppo and elsewhere, who refuse to kneel in
the presence of that God before whom the Archan-
gels hide their faces, and even their Immaculate
Queen worships with awful fear, is more agreeable
to Dr Wilson. To insult the Most High, even while
they imagine they are adoring Him, is commendable
« simplicity, » — though Daniel « fainted away and
retained no strength, » even before the presence of
au Angel. (2) If Dr Wilson had seen that other Angel, « having a golden censer, » to whom « was given
much incense, » that he might offer it « before the
Altar » in Heaven ; (3) he would perhaps have suggested to St. John, who did see it, that it was a very
« unscriptural » ceremony, and extremely deficient
in simplicity. If he had entered that temple, in which
even the « nails of gold, » and the « wings of the
cherubim, » and « the curtain-rods » were all prescribed and fashioned by divine inspiration, and
where priests arrayed in jewelled robes offered a
mystical sacrifice by divine command, — he would
perhaps have ventured on the same criticism. It
would have been imprudent, for the Hebrews made
short work of blasphemers. Yet Calvin, the author of

(1) *Lands of the Bible*, p. 581.
(2) *Dan.* X, 8.
(3) *Apoc.* VIII, 3.

the Presbyterian religion, pushed the claims of « simplicity » still further, and marvelled that the Son of
God did not rebuke the « superstition » of the woman
in the Gospel, who was healed by touching « the
hem of His garment. » It was intolerable that God
should thus-sanction the principle of relic worship,
and the Genevan bade his disciples take note of the
error. (1) Surely the Prussian philosopher had
reason to exclaim, « the Calvinists treat the Saviour as
their *inferior*, the Lutherans as their equal, and
Catholics as their God. » (2)

Let us return to Damascus. Another English writer, of the same school as Dr Wilson, notices in
1854, that « there are in Damascus three Latin
Monasteries ; the buildings are good, and have li-
braries attached to them, containing good collections
of books in the Oriental and other languages ; there
are also large day-schools under the direction of the
priesthood : » (3) and then he scoffs at them as
« concealed Jesuits. » The Jesuits have not the habit
of concealing themselves, and the objects of his dislike were, in fact, Franciscans and Lazarists. That
their schools are more accurately appreciated by the
Damascenes than by this Protestant tourist, we learn
from Dr Frankl, who says ; « It is worthy of notice
that the Jews and Mohammedans sometimes send
their children to the schools taught by the French

(1) « Scimus quam proterve *Iudai superstitio*... Quod a veste
hæsit potius, forte *zelo inconsiderato* paululum a via deflexit. »
Comment. in Nov. Test. tom. I, p. 220, ed. Tholuck.

(2) *Dictionnaire des Apologistes Involontaires*, Introd., p. 31,
Migne.

(3) *Journal of a Deputation to the East*, vol. II, p. 488.

Missionaries of the order of St. Lazare. » Ubicini also relates, that « their two schools were frequented, in 1856, by four hundred and fifty children, » — which perhaps accounts for the irritation of their English visitors, — and that at Beyrout, Salonica, Aleppo, and *wherever* the Lazarist missions extend, « *hundreds of children of all creeds* receive elementary instruction freely and gratuitously. »

A well known German protestant, who visited the Franciscan schools at Damascus, expresses surprise and admiration at the patient charity of men who had abandoned all — they have since been massacred by Turks — to labour in this field, and exclaims ; « The natural and primitive simplicity with which they follow their calling delighted me much. » (1) Yet an Anglican missionary who, during a long residence in Syria, had only learned to defame the works which he knew not how to imitate; who spent his time in sneering at Franciscans and Lazarists, and even at those Sisters of Charity of whom the more discerning Moslem speaks with affection and reverence; affects to deplore the miserably defective education which attracted scholars of every class and creed, and of which other Protestants will presently describe to us the real character. (2) It is creditable to English and American travellers, that almost the only individuals of either nation who use such language are the missionaries themselves.

We should perhaps not err in attributing the exas-

(1) Countess Hahn-Hahn, *Letters*, etc., vol. II, Letter 21, p. 55.

(2) *Five Years in Damascus*, by the Revᵈ J. L. Porter, M. A.; vol. I, ch. III, p. 145.

peration which betrays itself in such expressions to
the mortification of personal failure. After many years
of lavish expenditure, they had so utterly wasted
their time and money, that M' Wortabet unwillingly
confesses, in 1856, that the *five* Protestant missionaries in Damascus had only secured *sixteen* precarious
pensioners, who were probably all their servants and
dependents; (1) and D' Frankl pleasantly adds, —
« the Missionary Society has as yet thrown out its
golden net at Damascus *in vain*. » (2)

On the other hand, English and American travellers attest in chorus the contrast to which they could
not close their eyes, and the continual triumphs of
the Catholic faith, throughout all Syria, in spite of
the poverty of its apostles. « At *Diarbekir*, some
years ago, » says M' Badger, « the whole Greek
community in the town became Romanists. » (3)
The Nestorians in the neighbourhood quickly followed their example.« At *Aintab*, an American missionary, » who had been distributing bibles, « was
driven out of the town by the Armenians, » says
M' Walpole; « not, I believe, without insults and
some violence. » (4) And so uniform are these facts,
as we shall see more fully hereafter,that a Protestant
witness observes; even in places « where a few years
ago there were no Roman Catholics, we now find a
fair share of the population belonging to that
faith. » (5) M' Jowett had reason to say, « All

(1) *Syria and the Syrians*, ch. vii, p. 203.
(2) *The Jews in the East*, vol. 1, ch. viii, pp. 292, 7, 9.
(3) Badger, vol. I, p. 3.
(4) Walpole, ch. xvi, p. 255.
(5) Wortabet, vol. II, ch. xiv, p. 86.

Syria is comparatively occupied by the Roman Catholics. »

Before we quit Syria to enter Palestine, it seems impossible to omit one or two reflections upon what we have already heard. It is proved, by Protestant testimony, that throughout these regions the Church is constantly attracting to herself great numbers from the various dissident communities. « Men of virtue and piety, » says a learned English writer, familiar with many of the forms of oriental society, « are often found to pass from the Eastern to the Roman Catholic communion, while no instance, perhaps, or scarcely an instance can be adduced even of an individual of acknowledged piety and learning passing over to the eastern church. » (1)

Some Protestant writers are still more emphatic, and we must not conclude this portion of our subject without noticing their remarkable language. « Not one of the ancient Churches, » says the Rev. George Williams, formerly a chaplain at Jerusalem, « but was visited by Missionaries of the Propaganda, or the enterprising members of the Society of Jesus... When we consider the zeal, ability, and persevering practice of the best instructed and most devoted missionaries that the world has seen since primitive times, it is no matter of surprise that their self-denying labours were crowned with abundant success. » (2)

« It is difficult, » says another English Protestant, familiar by long experience and observation with the

(1) Palmer, *Dissertations on the Orthodox Communion*, p. 13.
(2) *The Holy City*, vol. II, ch. vi, p. 570.

East and its various races, « to meet and converse
with the zealous and talented missionaries of the
Propaganda in the East, and not feel warmly for
their situation. They are exposed to no ordinary trial
of patience. Educated at Rome, accustomed to Italian
refinement and conversation, then sent to some
remote spot — remote from causes of association
rather than from distance — destined to pass their
lives with a people as far beneath them in mental
culture as separated by habits, they may be truly
said to be banished men in the sharpest sense of the
term. Still we might at times rather envy than pity
them. Commiseration is lost sight of in our admiration at the disinterestedness and perseverance which
they ever display in the performance of their duties —
a good conscience their reward, heaven their guide.
No shadow of preferment looms in the distance, no
hope of distinction cheers them on, not one of the
ordinary inducements to exertion prompts them.
Courteous with the gentleman, confiding with the
peasant, caressing with the distressed, they are, as
St. Paul expressed himself to be, ' All things to all
men. ' Multiply the generations since the Osmanleys
conquered the country, and it will appear that *millions of souls* have been saved by these advanced
sentinels of Christianity, ever at their post, to
reclaim the wavering and confirm the steadfast. » (1)

D' Durbin, an American Protestant minister, who
visited the same lands, contents himself with admitting the facts. « It is not possible, » he says, « to
estimate the success of the Romish Missions to the

(1) Slade, *Turkey, Greece, and Malta*, vol. II, ch. xx, p. 425.

Oriental Churches, but the general fact is clear, that they have divided them *all*; so that there is in Asia a Papal Greek Church, a Papal Armenian Church, a Papal Church among the Nestorians, a Papal Church among the Syrians, and also many of the Copts in Egypt. » (1)

Other Protestant writers, deeply impressed, in spite of incurable and fatal prejudices, with the grave lessons which they have brought away from the East, — and especially with the demoralizing influence of Protestant missions, — do not hesitate to avow their condemnation of efforts which lead only to evil.

« I frankly avow my opinion, » says the Rev. M' Spencer, who seems to be a Scotch-Episcopalian minister, « that missions from the various religious bodies who contribute to the support of the gentlemen labouring in Syria can *never be productive of permanent results*. I was astonished to learn how little had, after all, been done. » And again. « It deserves to be well weighed by Protestants at home, that no mission of theirs to the Oriental Christians has succeeded to any extent commensurate with the means, the men, the time devoted to their conversion : may it not properly be asked — are we ever likely to succeed any better? » (2)

D' Wolff says, — « I cannot help thinking that the Church Missionary Society, though they might send their Lutheran Missionaries to the heathen,

(1) Vol. II, p. 287.
(2) *Travels in the Holy Land*, by the Rev'd J. A. Spencer, M. A., Letter 22, pp. 483-4. (1850).

ought never to send them to the Eastern Churches.
It is a gross insult to them — « (1) and apparently a
very unprofitable one.

M⟨ Williams also observes, though probably without much hope of obtaining a hearing; « There is
surely an ample field in the East for the European
and American Missionaries, without encroaching on
other churches. » Jews, Druses, Mahometans, Arabs,
and others, are the avowed enemies of Christianity,
as he remarks, yet the luxurious emissaries of Protestantism hardly even attempt to make any impression on *them*, and invariably fail when they do.
«They are merely playing at Missions,» adds M⟨ Williams — and with this frank confession we may
conclude — « while they limit themselves to a task
involving no risk, and requiring no sacrifices. » (2)

It is impossible not to be struck by such unexpected language as has now been quoted, from Protestant writers of various and conflicting schools, in
illustration of the eternal contrast which even they
discern between Catholic and Protestant missionaries. But there is yet another emotion, more painful
than surprise, which such testimonies awaken. The
witnesses record their evidence, in spite of natural
prejudice, and careless of the resentment of their
less candid co-religionists; and this courage none
will refuse to applaud. But we may be permitted to
deplore that such men, so truthful and generous,
should have been equally successful in banishing
another kind of fear, more noble and legitimate —

(1) P. 232.
(2) *The Holy City*, vol. II, ch. vi, p. 597.
    II.   11.

the fear of Him who has said, « *Out of thine own
mouth will I judge thee.* »

And now let us go to Jerusalem. The project of
the King of Prussia, the chief of the Lutheran communities, was eagerly adopted by a Church always
striving to make alliance with other heretical bodies,
and always unsuccessfully. At last she has succeeded.
The Church of England — in spite of the unmeaning
protests of a class who seem to think, like Pilate,
that it suffices to wash their hands in order to secure
immunity for acts which they invariably make their
own by acquiescence — consented to exercise, alter-
nately with a Lutheran, the right of nominating a
Protestant Bishop at Jerusalem. The present holder
of the office is Dr Gobat, of whom we heard in
Abyssinia. An English biographer, of similar religious opinions, tells us, that « Gobat, far from re-
cognising the Church of England as the sole, or even
the most scriptural Church upon earth, long declined
receiving her ordination. » (1) This writer plainly
intimates that he would never have received it at all,
but it was the turn of the Establishment to nominate,
and he was obliged to submit. The accounts of the
Protestant mission at Jerusalem, and of its results,
are so absolutely uniform, with the exception of one
or two writers who shall be noticed, that we may
call our witnesses at random. The more serious class
of Anglicans are ashamed of the whole proceeding,
and would be glad to bury it in oblivion : we, however, have no motive for declining to discuss it.

Dr Gobat's biographer, who is almost indiscreet

_____
(1) *Evangelical Christendom*, vol. I, p. 79.

in his frankness, reveals the secret aim of his party,
when he says, — « The Jerusalem episcopate ought
to be a Protestant patriarchate. » Let us enquire
how far this project has been realised.

If we take the evidence in chronological order, it
will run as follows. In 1841, an English visitor to
Jerusalem says, « We went to church at the Consul's,
and our congregation amounted to only *ten*, including an American missionary, » and the traveller's
own party. « As to the advance of proselytism, » adds
the writer, « M' Nicholaison does not consider more
than five converts have been made during the last
period of his residence, nine years. » (1)

In 1842, an Anglican clergyman still reports the
congregation to consist of « the architect, the bishop's family, with a portion of his household, and
two missionaries. » But, on the other hand, this
gentleman found about *eight-hundred* Catholics at
Nazareth, « particularly well conducted and habited
for the country; indeed the children who attend the
school of the monastery were quite cleanly, and
spoke Italian with fluency. » (2) And one of the
most distinguished of the Anglican clergy remarks
of the same mission, where he heard Arab converts
sing the chants of the Latin Church, — « there is
no church in Palestine where the religious services
seem so worthy of the sacredness of the place. » (3)

In the same year, an American traveller, who

(1) M'* Dawson Damer, vol. I, p. 309; vol. II, p. 33.
(2) *Egypt and the Holy Land*, by W. Drew Stent, vol. II,
ch. II, p. 44; ch. VI, p. 148.
(3) *Sinai and Palestine*, by Arthur Penrhyn Stanley, M. A.,
p. 437.

omits even to allude to the« Protestant patriarchate, »
as if he had failed to discover it, writes as follows.
« Every traveller who has visited Jerusalem must
have been struck with the contrast between the intelligence, wit, and learning of the friars of the *Latin*
Convent, and the besotted and gross ignorance of the
Greek monks, whose superstitions fanaticism is but
little removed above that of the Mussulmen. » (1)
And this is confirmed, with characteristic felicity of
language, by the author of *Eothen*, when he says of
the « Padre Superiore, » and the « Padre Mission-
ario » of the Jerusalem monastery,— « By the natives
of the country, as well as by the rest of the brethren,
they are looked upon as superior beings; and rightly
too, for nature seems to have crowned them in her
own true way. The chief of the Jerusalem convent
was a noble creature; his worldly and spiritual
authority seemed to have surrounded him, as it
were, with a kind of ' Court, ' and the manly grace-
fulness of his bearing did honour to the throne which
he filled.... If he went out, the Catholics of the place
that hovered about the convent, would crowd around
him with devout affection, and almost scramble for
the blessing which his touch could give. » (2)

In 1843, Mʳ Millard arrives at the gloomy conviction, « that Jerusalem is of almost all other places
the least accessible by Protestant missionary labours. » (3)

In 1844, a witness of a different class appears.

----

(1) *Tour through Turkey, Greece*, etc., by E. Joy Morris,
vol. I, ch. VI, p. 116.

(2) Ch. X.

(3) *Journal of Travels in Egypt*, by D. Millard, ch. XVI, p. 262.

The reader may possibly remember the Rev. I. Tomlin, an Anglican minister, who visited China and so many other places, always in submission to « calls » which he had not courage to disobey. M'' Tomlin says, « the labours of the Protestant Bishop of Jerusalem have been remarkably blessed of the Lord. » He says it quite seriously, and evidently without forecasting what later witnesses might possibly record on the same subject. M'' Tomlin adds, — « the Roman Legions are gone forth, and are fast preoccupying the ground , » and then he exclaims, as if resenting a personal wrong, — « they covertly creep in by the way which Protestant Britain has opened! » (1) The observation betrays some defect of historical accuracy. There was once a Christian « kingdom of Jerusalem, » as M'' Tomlin might have remembered, which lasted nearly two hundred years; and as Catholic missionaries have now been there for a good many centuries, we may perhaps say, without too much severity, that the notion of their recent and covert arrival under British protection is altogether worthy of M'' Tomlin. Protestant Britain has not often been very generous to « the Roman Legions, » and has certainly not hitherto afforded them much assistance at Jerusalem.

In 1847, D'' Rae Wilson, who had perhaps not read M'' Tomlin, and was evidently unconscious of being « remarkably blessed » in his solitude, says; « At this time I was the *only* Protestant in Jerusalem. » (2)

(1) *Missionary Journals*, etc., Introd. pp. 13, 15.
(2) *Travels in the Holy Land*, etc., ch. XVIII, p. 385.

In the same year, Tischendorff gives this account of the operations of the « patriarchate » which D' Rae Wilson and M' Joy Morris failed to discern. « With respect to the baptism of converts in Jerusalem, it is, as far as I know, framed to an accommodation with the most modern Judaism. Six thousand piastres (about fifty pounds) are offered to the convert as a premium; other advantages are said likewise to be considerable. » (1)

In spite of these attractions, the results could hardly be deemed satisfactory; for in the same year Lord Castlereagh expressed this opinion, founded on personal examination. « The progress of conversion, and the interests of Christianity, do not at present seem to require or warrant so large a church establishment as is here maintained. I enquired in vain for any number of converts that could be properly authenticated. » And then he describes once more the scanty official audience with which we are already familiar; « the bishop has scarcely a congregation, besides his chaplains, his doctor, and their families. » (2)

D' Gobat, however, did sometimes make a convert, as we saw in Abyssinia, in the case of the « noble Abyssinian » Girgis, who abandoned the Anglican tenets for Mahometanism. Here is one more specimen of D' Gobat's success. A certain « Joseph, » was « acknowledged by the missionaries Gobat and Mueller as a sincere convert. » (3) Indeed Admiral

(1) *Travels in the East*, by Constantine Tischendorff, p. 159.
(2) *A Journey to Damascus*, etc., vol. II, ch. xix, p. 3.
(3) Wolff, p. 285.

Slade says, and it is perfectly true, that he « figured more than once in the reports of the Bible Society, and has been cited as an instance of the success attending the missionaries labour. » He was even « strongly recommended as one admirably qualified to preach the Gospel among the Arabs. » The qualifications of this favorite of the Bible Society were these. Dr Wolff, to whom he gave lessons in Arabic, says that he was « the most infamous hypocrite and impostor I ever met with » : and he had good reason to say it, for this « admirably qualified » missionary broke open Dr Wolff's trunk, stole all he possessed, and then ran away. (1) D^r. Gobat is evidently not happy in his converts, nor the Bible Society in its heroes.

In 1848, we have an official account by Dr Gobat himself. « Our little congregation, » he says, « goes its quiet way. I regret that we have not more spiritual life... I believe there is growth in grace with some, and there is less division. » (2)

In 1852, an English clergyman, who describes the singular use made of « the Bibles and tracts so profusely spread among the eastern nations, » gives this grave account of the converts who had been obtained up to that date. « Their belief is a blank, and their principles distinctly Antinomian. I maintain, from observation, that to one class or other of these all the proselytes made to Protestantism in the East belong. They are either worthless persons — or sceptics and infidels. The reports of the Missionary Societies

(1) Slade, p. 521.
(2) Margoliouth, vol. II, p. 295.

themselves exhibit the truth of these allegations...
The work of the Protestant Missions is simply *destructive;* they first make a *tabula rasa* of minds, on
which they never afterwards succeed in inscribing
the laws of a sincere faith or consistent practice. » (1)

Two years later, in 1854, the representative of
an English missionary society still confesses of these
ambiguous « converts, » that « they have not unfrequently some hidden motive of worldly advantage. » (2) We shall hear them presently discussing
the real motive amongst themselves.

Admiral Slade, in the same year, prepares us for
future revelations by this statement. « I will not say
that any of them are gained by actual bribery, but
they certainly are by promises of employment in
the missionary line — promises often not fulfilled,
in consequence of which the converts are reduced to
distress. » (3) The Rev. Moses Margoliouth, now an
Anglican clergyman, incidentally confirms this unfavorable statement. This gentleman, an associate of
Dr Gobat, while he deplores the exceeding frailty of
Hebrew Protestants, does not on that account permit
himself to be discouraged. He even derives consolation from an unexpected source. « I do not affirm, »
he says, « that baptized Jews do not afford instances
of consummate rascality. So do the clergy of our
beloved Church. » (4)

In 1855, Mr Bayard Taylor, an intelligent Amer-

(1) Patterson, *Journal of a Tour in Egypt*, p. 455.
(2) *Journal of a Deputation*, vol. II, p. 351.
(3) P. 519.
(4) *A Pilgrimage to the Land of my Fathers*, vol. II, p. 334.

ican, relates, that as they could not make converts at
Jerusalem, Protestant Jews « were *brought hither*
at the expense of English Missionary Societies, for
the purpose of forming a Protestant community. »
The process was costly, for he adds that « it is estimated that each member of the community has cost
the Mission about 4,500 l. : a sum which would
have christianized tenfold the number of English
heathen. The Mission, however, is kept up by its
patrons as a sort of religious luxury. » On the other
hand, this gentleman observes; « many others besides ourselves have had reason to be thankful for
the good offices of the Latin Monks in Palestine. I
have never met with a class more kind, cordial, and
genial. » (1)

« The Latins, » says a German Protestant, — for
all the independent witnesses use the same language,
— « receive all strangers with the greatest liberality,
I mean liberality of sentiment. » It is true this writer
adds that Protestants would imitate the hospitality
of the Catholic Monks, if they could, for they see
with displeasure their co-religionists dwelling as
guests within the Latin monasteries; but « a Protestant establishment is quite out of the question, »
for the following reason. « The several parties would
not easily agree to whom it should belong, whether
to the Calvinists, or to the Lutherans, to the Presbyterians, or to the Anglican church. » (2) A little
later, however, they escaped from their embarass-
ment : they could not unite in erecting a monastery

(1) *The Lands of the Saracen*, ch. v, p. 78; ch. vi, p. 100.
(2) Countess Hahn-Hahn, Letter 29.

or a church, but they combined their resources and
built an hotel.

In 1857, Mr Gibson repeats a tale which has now
become somewhat monotonous. « As yet, few Hebrews have been induced here to profess Christianity. Some even of these have *gone back* to Judaism. » (1)

The failure, after twenty years of prodigious expenditure, had now become so evident, and people
at home were beginning to talk of it so loudly, that
the missionaries seem to have resolved that they
must make a diversion amongst the Christian sects,
rather than continue to do nothing. But there was
this difficulty, that they were pledged not to attempt
to proselyte the oriental sectaries. Relief came to
Dr Gobat in this perplexity from an unexpected
quarter. The narrator of the incident is the Rev.
Dr Stewart, who tells us, that « Lord Palmerston
has *authoritatively* stated that the bishop has a right
to receive those from other communions who apply
to him for instructions. » This pontifical decision of
the eminent statesman removed, as might be expected, all difficulty — except that of procuring the ap-
plicants for instructions. In this Lord Palmerston
could not offer them any assistance. They were left,
therefore, to their usual methods; and Dr Stewart
sufficiently indicates what they were, when he expresses his regret that « there is no way of making
trial of a convert's sincerity before his admission
into the institution; » and then frankly allows, that

(1) *Recollections of other Lands*, by William Gibson, B. A.,
cb. xxxviii, p. 404.

« the principle of giving support to *every* convert I
deem faulty. » (1)

We have perhaps heard enough of the Jerusalem
Protestant Mission and its results, but we must not
quit the subject without a brief notice of three important witnesses — Dr Frankl, Dr Robinson, and
Mr Williams — a Jew and two Protestants, who
have all dwelt in Jerusalem, and who confirm each
other's testimony in an unexpected way.

The first of these writers, whose work has been
introduced to English readers by Mr Beaton, gives
this account. « The Protestants give earnest money,
and demoralize families. When a father sternly rebukes his children, it is not unusual for them to reply with the insolent threat, ' I will go to the Mission. ' » He mentions an example of a Jew who had
got into difficulties by stealing 2,500 piastres, and
who, when his co-religionists « refused to intercede
for him, out of revenge went to the Mission; » but
as the thief had still some religious prepossessions,
he implored Dr Frankl to lend him the sum abstract-
ed, « to save him, his wife, and six children from
being baptized ! » Dr Frankl adds, that this case
« may serve as an example of the morals and principles of those who are converted; » and that so
little importance is attached to the momentary profession of Protestantism by a Jew, that his family
content themselves with observing, « He will soon
come back, after he has helped himself. » Indeed we
are told by a friend and countryman of Dr Gobat,

(1) *A Journey to Syria and Palestine*, by Robert Walter Stewart, D. D., (Leghorn) ch. VIII, pp. 294, 303.

that the Hebrew proselyte, when he has exhausted Protestant benevolence at Jerusalem, « has become *more than ever a Jew* by the time he has reached Jaffa, Hebron, or Tiberias. » (1)

D' Frankl relates also the curious fact that « converts » from the Jews « receive baptism in different cities *before* they reach Jerusalem, » where they are finally re-baptized, with a fresh payment for the operation : an account which is confirmed by the amusing authoress of « Travels in Barbary, » who is much defamed by M' Margoliouth for presuming to say of one of *his* Jewish converts, — « This is at least the *twentieth* time he has been baptized. » And even this was so far from a solitary case, that a Polish Jew remarked to some of his friends, — « Baptism was the only good business we had, and who has spoiled it? The Jews themselves, *by underselling one another.* » (2)

D' Robinson, the author of a well known work on the topography of Jerusalem, confirms all the other witnesses. « The efforts of the English Mission » he seems to think unworthy of serious notice ; while of his own countrymen, the Americans, he gives the following account. « The house of — » one of the Missionaries — « was large, with marble floors, and had on one side an extensive and pleasant garden, with orange and other fruit trees and many flowers. It furnished indeed one of the most desirable and beautiful residences in the city.» We have been told by the wife of another American missionary, that« many

---

(1) Mislin, *Les Lieux Saints*, tome III, ch. xxviii, p. 65.
(2) *The Jews in the East*, vol. II, ch. II, pp. 53, 54.

are the comforts and pleasant things about this life in
the East, » and her countrymen evidently agree with
her. Surrounded by so many enjoyments, to which
they would probably have aspired in vain in Boston
or Philadelphia, we are not surprised to learn from
Dr Robinson, that « the plague and other circumstances » soon scattered these opulent missionaries,
and even « conspired to suspend wholly, for a time,
the labours of the American Mission in Jerusalem. »

There is another class of missionaries whom the
plague sometimes kills, but never puts to flight. The
Protestant agents, — who would undertake at any
moment to teach a St. Francis, a Bonnieux, or a Riccadonna, a more « scriptural » and enlightened piety,
— prefer to run away when danger knocks at their
doors; and so Dr Robinson relates, as if the precaution of his missionary friends was too natural to require any comment, that though on this occasion the
plague only acted « mildly, » « the Missionaries broke
off their sittings, and those from abroad hastened to
depart with their families. » (1)

It was almost at this moment that the author of a
celebrated English book published the following narrative. « It was about three months after the time of
my leaving Jerusalem, that the Plague set his spotted
foot on the Holy City. The Monks felt great alarm;
they did not shrink from their duty... A single monk
was chosen, either by lot, or by some other fair appeal to Destiny; being thus singled out, he was to
go forth into the plague-stricken city, and to perform with exactness his priestly duties... He was

(1) Pages 327, 368.

provided with a bell, and at a certain hour in the morning he was ordered to ring it, if he could; but if no sound was heard at the appointed time, then his brethren knew that he was either delirious or dead, and another martyr was sent forth to take his place. *In this way twenty-one of the monks were carried off.* » (1)

D' Robinson, who does not love Catholics, is fain to confess that they do not much resemble his own friends. Of their inflexible constancy, although surrounded by every evil example, he gives this instance. « The Christians of the Latin rite (native Arabs) are said to be descended from Catholic converts in the times of the Crusades. » Centuries have left *them* unchanged. The Catholic College in Kesrawân, in which they teach Arabic, Syriac, Latin, and Italian, « takes a higher stand, » he says, « than any other similar establishment in Syria. » What he relates of the Maronites, we shall learn hereafter. The Protestants, he superfluously observes, « do not exist in Syria as a native sect. »

Lastly, M' Williams, a highly respectable Anglican clergyman, and once a chaplain at Jerusalem,— who, like most of his order, remains wholly unimpressed even by the lamentable facts which he discloses, — gives us the following information. « It was an unfortunate circumstance for our Church that it was first introduced to the Christians of Jerusalem, in later times, by a Danish Lutheran minister. » The Church of M' Williams has usually been introduced by persons of the same class. This one, he says, was

(1) *Eothen*, ch. x.

admitted « to Orders in the English Church, on
grounds of convenience rather than of conviction. »
But the Church of England, if she cannot produce
missionaries of her own, is wealthy enough to pay
for the services of others. « A Church capable of ac-
commodating four or five hundred persons was
commenced, » M' Williams remarks, « while as yet
there were but eight or ten individuals for whom it
would be available, and even they were there simply
with a view to its construction. » They were, he
adds, « the clergyman, the architect and his clerk,
the foreman of the works, the carpenter, an apothe-
cary, and one other. » (1) For this professional
congregation a church was commenced which,
D' Durbin says, « will cost about 130,000 dollars. »

M' Williams next describes the operations of the
gentlemen who minister in this Church. « The Missionary operations of the Society's agents have not
been such as to exhibit to the Natives an example of
earnest zeal for the conversion of the Jews, nor the
treatment of the Converts such as to impress them
with a favorable idea of their discretion. » He laments
the « serious errors and defects in the faith, scandalous irregularities and excesses in the practice, of the
ill-instructed members of this small congregation. »
Finally, he observes, that « self-sacrifice and simple
trust were not taught *either by precept or example*
by the Missionaries at Jerusalem. (2) « Yet M' Williams has probably no doubt whatever that the system
will continue, at the same enormous cost, under the

(1) *The Holy City*, pp. 579, 587.
(2) P. 593.

direction of the same class of men, and with precisely the same results.

This amiable writer, who records facts but seems never to draw conclusions, describes also « the very unsatisfactory native Protestants » made by the Americans, — during the intervals of « the plague and other circumstances, » — and gives examples of the class generally. One, an unfortunate Greek apostate, « the most favorable specimen by far, » after being first an Independent, then an Anglican, « had fallen into a state of listless indifference and unconcern which it was most grievous to witness. » A second, a Greek monk, « offered himself to Bishop Gobat as a Protestant convert. » His sole motive was, « that the Patriarch had imposed upon him some discipline to which he did not choose to submit. » Another, « a monk from Mount Lebanon, told me he wished to become a Protestant. ' Why?' ' I want to marry. ' ' No other reason?' ' None.' » (1)

Such, by the testimony of her own clergy, is the history of the Church of England in Jerusalem. It resembles her history everywhere else, but in the Holy City such facts seem to acquire additional gravity. Nor is this all. Not only do Protestants fail, in Jerusalem as elsewhere, to propagate their own religious opinions; they appear even to lose, in no small number of cases, whatever sentiment of religion they originally possessed. None but a Catholic can safely visit holy places, much less the scenes where the Son of God passed the years of His human life. « It is useless to deny, » says Mr Stanley, « that

(1) Pages 578, 595.

there is a shock to the religious sentiment in finding
ourselves on the actual ground of events which we
have been accustomed to regard as transacted *in heaven rather than on earth.* » (1) In other words, only
the believer, whose religion is *faith* and not sentiment, and who is able to penetrate with unerring
glance all symbolical and sacramental veils, and quick
to recognise the Footsteps which the instinct of love
alone can detect, may venture to put himself in contact with Kebron, Gethsemane, and Calvary. They
are death to others. So like do they look to other
places, so little do they reveal to the natural eye their
stupendous secrets, that many who come to gaze
cease even to believe. « The commander of an English man of war told me, » says a writer of our own
country, « that he once accompanied a party of
twenty from his own ship to Jerusalem, and that, out
of that number, seven returned unbelievers, not
merely in the authenticity of localities, but in Christianity itself. » (2) Such is the value of « religious
sentiment. »

And even when the results of their visit are less
fatal than this, they are in a vast number of cases
sufficiently serious. It is hardly possible to find a
Protestant writer, of any country, who does not apply
to the Holy Places precisely the same tone of criticism in which he would discuss the ruins of Pom-
peii, or the fossils of Maine and New Jersey. Indeed
he displays, not unfrequently, a far deeper interest
in relics of the latter class than of the former, as

(1) Stanley, *Sinai and Palestine*, p. 426.
(2) Mrs Dawson Damer, ch. IV, p. 92.

well as a more intelligent submission to the testimonies of history and science. In Jerusalem he is « scan-
dalized » at every step. « The American, » says a
Missionary of that nation, « who has been pointed to
(*sic*) Plymouth Rock, Bunker Hill, or Mount Vernon,
and yielded to the hallowed impressions of certainty,
must beware how he carries the same reverential
feelings into the East. »(1) What, he seems to say,
are the true sites of the Scourging or the Anointing,
compared with Bunker Hill and Plymouth Rock?

But Mʳ Perkins is rivalled by English writers.
« The one spot, » says Mʳ Dawson Borrer, « which
arrested more especially my attention, » — in that
City which was to him only « a horrid atmosphere
of mockery, » — was, not Calvary, nor the Cœnacu-
lum, nor the Hall of Judgment ; but a certain « spot, »
on which it was *probable* that a bridge of Jewish
construction once existed! » (2)

Another English traveller, of great repute, the
learned Dʳ Clarke, tells his readers that St. Helena
was « the old lady to whose charitable donations
these repositories of superstition were principally indebted; » while of one tradition, referring to the
dwelling place of the Holy Family, a subject which
only excited his merriment, he briefly remarks, —
« A disbelief of the whole mummery seems best
suited to the feelings of Protestants. »(3) Perhaps he
was right.

(1) *Residence in Persia*, etc., by Revᵈ Justin Perkins, p. 275.
(2) *Journey from Naples to Jerusalem*, by Dawson Borrer Esq.,
ch. xxiv, p. 404.
(3) *Travels in Various Countries*, by E. D. Clarke, L. L. D.,
vol. IV, ch. iv, p. 174.

It is certain, at least, that most of his co-religionists agree with him. « As I toiled up the Mount of
Olives, » says a Protestant writer in 1853, « in the
very footsteps of Christ, I found it utterly impossible
to conceive that the Deity, in human form, had walked there before me. » And so, he adds, « I preferred
doubting the tradition. » (1)

Yet there is perhaps nothing in which all races of
men, save only Protestants, are so absolutely of one
mind, as in the traditions which relate to the holy
sites. « Even the Mussulmans themselves, » as a
learned archæologist observes, « have always been of
one mind with the Christians as to the authenticity
of our sanctuaries. » (2) « The voice of tradition at
Jerusalem, » says the author of *Eothen*, « is quite
unanimous, and Romans, Greeks, Armenians, and
Jews, all hating each other sincerely, *concur* in
assigning the same localities to the events told in the
Gospel. »

But there is no admonition in these facts for men
who would trace with a puerile enthusiasm the path
of some favorite hero or national idol, and even strew
it with costly monuments; but who, when it is a
question of One who is to them little more than an
historical phantom, or at best an object of « religious
sentiment, » prefer « doubting the tradition. »
« Many Protestants, » says a well known writer
already quoted, « look upon *all* the traditions by
which it is attempted to ascertain the holy places
of Palestine as utterly fabulous. » (3) The house of

(1) Bayard Taylor, ch. v, pp. 74, 84.
(2) *La Terre Sainte*, par M. l'abbé Bourassé, ch. IV, p. 65.
(3) *Eothen*, ch. IX.

Shakespeare, the birth-place of Newton, or the coat of Nelson, are relics which they defend against all comers, for in these they avow a personal interest; but the house of Joseph, the birth-place of Mary, or the robe of Jesus, — these are only the theme of a jest, or scouted as « utterly fabulous. » It is worthy of men and philosophers to guard in sumptuous shrines the mementoes of fellow men, who no longer afford nourishment even to worms; but it is only a feeble superstition which is careful about the despised relics which the God-Man, or His Immaculate Mother, have left on earth. Protestants prefer « doubting the tradition » which relates only to such memorials.

This method of obliterating importunate traditions which they desire only to discredit « meets with much approbation, » we are told, « in speculative Germany; » — where, however, they venerate Luther's inkstand, and other relics of the same value. « I have undertaken, » says a German writer, « to convey to the American missionaries at Jerusalem the pamphlet of a Protestant clergyman, who disputes the locality of the Holy Sepulchre, without ever having been at the place. » (1) If he had been there, he would perhaps have disputed the Crucifixion.

Indeed these gentlemen are prepared to dispute any thing. « Even the *Via Dolorosa* » Dr Robinson gaily remarks, « seems to have been first *got up* during or after the times of the crusades; » although, as Tischendorff observes, « the real road along which

(1) Countess Habo-Hahn, Letter 27.

Christ walked must have taken this direction. »
Dr Robinson appears in this case to have been guilty
at least of an anachronism. Half a century ago,
people used to accept language of this kind in place
of wit, and many reputations were cheaply gained
by such means. The world has grown more exacting,
and no longer regards a bad jest as a substitute for
modesty, wisdom, and learning. (1)

« Alas! for the pilgrim, » said the lamented
Mr Warburton, — to whose soul may God grant
rest — « who can scoff within the walls of Jerusalem! » But there are men who can do worse than
scoff, not only in Jerusalem, but within the precincts
of the Holy Sepulchre. In that spot, where Angels
tread with fear and awe, but where schismatics jest
and harangue, the writer was lately informed by a
relative, an Anglican clergyman, that « the only
visitors who were not prostrate on their faces were
Turks and English Protestants, but that the former
were much the more reverent of the two. » And this
very reverence at the tomb of Christ, before which
the holy women once watched with heavy hearts,

(1) How different is the temper of Christian faith! « The faithful have a special light, over and above tradition, » says one who
appears to have been taught by the Holy Ghost, « to keep them
right about the sites of the Holy Places. » The same writer observes,
« that devotion to the Holy Land is a hidden support to Catholic
Kingdoms, — that our Lady prayed that Catholics might always
have the sanctuary of Bethlehem in their hands, — that heathen
and misbelievers gain *temporal* blessings from living in the vici-
nity of the Holy Places, » — and finally, « that the sins of men
have forfeited the peculiar custody of the Holy Places which our
Lady established. » Maria Agreda, quoted by F. Faber, *Bethlehem*,
ch. VII, p. 382.

only moves the disdain of the disciples of Luther and
Calvin and Craumer. « I have never seen anything
so abject, » says one of them, « as the conduct of the
pilgrims before the altar in the Calvary chapel. You
can scarcely recognise them as men. » (1) To lie
prostrate, and to weep, at the tomb of the Saviour,
this gentleman deems abject degradation. And this
exactly agrees with the equally cynical remarks of
an Anglican missionary in Ceylon, who once witnessed certain ceremonies in a Catholic Church
which provoked a similar comment : — « The great
events of our Lord's conception, birth, and life; His
last agony, trial, death, etc. are all acted as upon a
theatre. The *poor enthusiasts* are pleased and affected
at these scenes. » (2) He seems to marvel that they
did not share his own indifference.

One effect of the temper displayed, with rare
exceptions, by Anglican and American missionaries
in the East, is to be traced in the intense scorn and
indignation which they have excited amongst the
oriental races. Thus the Maronites, we are told,
« now confound under the common name of *biblicals*
all who belong to the British nation, and the English
tourist can hardly traverse the Libanus without
peril. »

Mr Farley, however, while he patriotically declares
that, without compromising his personal opinions,
he enjoyed, in every part of Syria, the most courteous and cordial reception both from priests and
people, and that it is the fault of every English tra-

---

(1) *The Wanderer in Syria*, by G. W. Curtis, ch. xi, p. 211.
(2 Revd Mr Clough, quoted in *Asiatic Journal*, vol. 1, p. 582.

veller if he does not experience the same hospitality, allows that the Americans, whom it was not his business to defend, are universally detested. « This, I think, is to be attributed to the manner in which they speak of everything. Sterne says, ' I hate the man who can travel ' from Dan to Beersheba, and say, ' 'T is all barren; ' but such is the usual mode of expression with American travellers. The traditions of ages are overturned, and the local prejudices of the people are shocked by the bold and free manner in which they express their thoughts. Kefr Kenna is not the Cana of Galilee; the Grotto of the Annunciation is not the veritable grotto; Mount Tabor is not the Mount of Transfiguration; the Workshop of Joseph is a myth; and so on. They would even deny that the Fountain of the Virgin is the true fountain ; but, unfortunately, there is not another fountain in the place. What a pity there is not a fountain at the other end of the town, so as to afford some reason for doubt! » (1)

It is creditable to the more enlightened class of protestants, that the excesses of the missionaries are generally corrected by the spontaneous testimony, sometimes by the indignant rebukes, of lay travellers. The readers of M' Farley's work on Syria will remember the case of « the Rev. John Baillie, Minister of the Free Church of Scotland, » whose « vulgar and brutal bigotry » in the monastery of Mount Carmel was repudiated, with such eloquent disgust, by a multitude of English and Scotch tourists. But to return to Jerusalem.

(1) *Two Years in Syria*, ch. xxxiv.

It is true that the Holy City is the scene of almost
daily scandals, which dishonour Christianity in the
sight of the unbeliever; but this is only another of
the bitter fruits of schism. « Il s'y passait des choses
bien plus convenables à des salles de spectacles et à
des bacchantes qu'à des temples et à des cœurs con-
trits. » (1) Yet even these horrors are as nothing to
those which were enacted on the same spot eighteen
centuries ago, before the same two classes of spectators; of whom, then as now, the one « wagged their
tongues and shook their heads, » the other « smote
their breasts » and went home to weep and pray.

It is no doubt with regret that France, Austria,
and Spain, once the guardians of the Sepulchre of
Jesus, look on in silence, and suffer the Russian to
pollute by his monks that holy place. « The Greek
Easter, » says Mr Stanley, and here we may agree
with him, « is the greatest moral argument against
the identity of the spot which it professes to honour
— considering the place, the time, and the intention
of the professed miracle, it is probably the most
offensive imposture to be found in the world, » (2)
But the nations are no longer one, and with division
has come feebleness and dishonour. Hence the presence of the Muscovite, the Anglican, and the Calvinist in the Holy City— hence the scorn of the Moslem.
« It is much to be deplored, » says Mr Curzon, « that
the Emperor of Russia, by his want of principle,
has brought the Christian religion into disrepute. »
But he is only fulfilling his mission as the head and

(1) *Palestine*, etc., par S. Munk, p. 646.
(2) P. 464.

pontiff of a « national » church, nor does it concern him to purify this defiled temple. His spiritual subjects are only political agents, and both he and they know it. He knows too that the Protestants are his sure allies; that they, like him, would rather see the Turk ruling in Jerusalem than the Frank; and that even the « abomination of desolation » is less offensive in their sight than the Cross would be, if it were planted again on Mount Sion.

We have alluded to the influence of Russia in the East, and the selfishness of its aims. It will not be out of place to notice briefly, in this place, her pretentious as a missionary church.

We have seen that in China, in spite of her long residence and advantageous position, she has never even attempted, in a solitary case, to convert a Confucian to the religion of Christ. Her agents in Pekin, like her representatives in Jerusalem, are incapable of any nobler mission than that which Russia imposes upon all her subjects alike, — her own commercial or political aggrandisement. « It is quite impossible, » observes a spiritual writer of our own land, « for true love to co-exist with an un-missionary spirit. » (1) Yet Russia, as Schouvaloff observes, « has never produced, since her schism, either a single missionary, or one Sister of Charity who deserves the name. » (2) Not only does she neither possess, nor wish to possess, any missionary organization, — so supremely indifferent is she to all which does not concern Muscovite interests, — but even

(1) *The Creator and the Creature*, p. 242.
(2) *Na Conversion*, etc., p. 301.

within her own territories, if the increase and con-
solidation of national power can be better promoted
by the agency of pagan tribes, she willingly abandons
them to heathenism, and prohibits all attempts to
convert them. • It is to the Russian Church, • says
Theiner, • that we must attribute the disgrace which
attaches to Christian Europe, in seeing still iu the
19th century so many pagans within her bosom.
Whole provinces, united during many ages to the
Russian Empire, are still filled with Gentiles. •
And this strange fact is thus explained by another
writer.

• Not only do the Russian government, and its
slave the Synod, remain perfectly indifferent to the
sad destiny of so many souls perishing in ignorance;
the former even *opposes itself systematically* and by
policy to their conversion to Christianity. The emperor has formed and taken into his pay several
squadrons of cavalry, drawn from the populations
of the Caucasus. All these men are Mahometans;
they live in the midst of a Christian capital, where
they have mosques constructed and ornamented at
the expense of the treasury. Many children also from
the countries of the Caucasus are brought to St. Petersburg, and there receive a gratuitous education.
But it is most rigorously forbidden to admit them
to Christian instruction with their companions, or to
attendance at their church. • He even adds that
• you may often see them weep and lament » at this
forced separation from their Christian companions;
but the motive is imperious. • These children are
destined to return one day to their native country,
where their office will be to preach to their (heathen)

compatriots the advantages which they may derive
from absolute and irrevocable submission to Russia.»
It is supposed they will do this more effectually as
pagans than as christians,— *therefore*, it is forbidden
to convert them. « And the ' most Holy and most
Orthodox Synod ' has no remonstrance to offer against
measures so barbarous! *Dominus horum vindex
est.* » (1)

Dut whether Russia forbids the conversion of the
heathen, or attempts, for purely political objects, to
make proselytes either amongst them or amongst
Christian communities, she is always the same. « The
Russians, » says Gibbon, » refused a passage to the
missionaries of Rome, who aspired to convert the
Pagans beyond the Tanais. » And during the last
two centuries, down to the present hour, it is by
brutal force alone that she is able to bar the way to
Catholic apostles. Thousands of Armenians, as we
shall see presently, have been converted by living
missionaries of the Church, who have assumed the
functions which the Russian and Dyzantine clergy
were too indifferent to perform. But it is in Russia
that they have found their chief adversary. The
Russian government, solicitous about religious questions only so far as they affect national interests,
and eager to mar within its dominions the apostolic
works which it has neither the will nor the power
to rival, « forbids the priests to give instructions to
the Armenians who have passed into its territories,
and interdicts the approach of every foreign ecclesi-

(1) *Persécutions et Souffrances de l'Église Catholique en
Russie,* p. 519.

astic. » (1) And they still pursue this policy of Anti-christ. « The Catholic priests in Trans-Caucasia, » says D‘ Wagner, « are strictly forbidden to make any proselytes. One of the Capuchins informed me, that if they were allowed free scope, they could convert many hundreds of the Pagan and Mohammedan mountaineers. He added, that multitudes of Suan-etians and Abchasians, most of whom were genuine heathens, had announced their wish to receive bap-tism in the convent of Kutais, *but they were ordered away;* for every priest who endeavours to convert an idolater into a Roman Catholic is threatened with transportation to Siberia,— a specimen of oppression and compulsion that has never been devised by any Potentate before, as far as I know. » (2)

How the Czar, who thus stands between God and His creatures, has dealt with the Catholics both of Poland and Russia, Gregory XVI reminded Nicholas to his face, when the Pontiff summoned the Auto-crat, who not long after expired in a paroxysm of auger and mortification, to meet him before the judg-ment seat of Christ. Yet his successor, untaught by all that has gone before, is walking in his father's steps.

All writers who have actually examined the oper-ations of the Russian church or government, and the one is only the instrument of the other, appear to be unanimous in their judgement of both. Haxthausen, a friendly witness, notices « le peu de préparation du clergé Russe au rôle de missionnaire; » (3) and does

(1) Eugène Boré, tome I, p. 401.
(2) *Travels in Persia*, etc., vol. II, ch. III, p. 204.
(3) *Études sur la Russie*, tome I, ch. XIV, p. 441.

not hesitate to affirm that the sterility of what he
calls the « Eastern Church, » « is undoubtedly attributable to its separation from Rome. » Tourgeneff
describes the fallen condition of the clergy, and the
« haughty disdain » manifested towards them by the
upper classes in their own country; (1) by whom
they seem to be treated with as little ceremony as
Lord Macaulay says was displayed towards Anglican
chaplains in the seventeenth century. If a wealthy
proprietor, we are told by M. Golovine, himself a
Russian priest, ask an Archbishop to make a sa-
cristan a priest, « a priest he will be, even though
he know not how to write. » (2) And this aristocracy,
exercising an influence which such prelates dare not
dispute, are too often themselves perfectly indifferent
to the religion in whose ministers they recognise only
an inferior order of state police. « Noblesse légère, »
says M. Léon Deluzy in 1860, « superficielle, égoïste,
corruptrice, et corrompue. » (3) « They show a strong
tendency observes an English writer who has lived
among them, « to add infidelity to their immorality. » (4) But in Russia, as Madame d'Istria remarks,
« la religion est une partie de la consigne militaire, »
and under the rule of the Czar even unbelief submits
to discipline. « Every one knows, » says M. Golovine,
« that the number of unbelievers in Russia continually increases. » M. de Gerebtzoff also notices the
« general tendency — entrainement — to religious

(1) *La Russie et les Russes*, tome III, p. 103.
(2) *Mémoires d'un Prêtre Russe*, par M. Ivan Golovine, ch. x,
p. 202.
(3) *La Russie, son Peuple et son Armée*, p. 45.
(4) *Dissertations on the Orthodox Church*, p. 293.

incredulity, and the unbridled gratification of brutal
passions, » which began to manifest itself in Russia
during the last century ; » (1) and at the present day,
while corruption spreads like a gangrene through all
ranks, and only a thin varnish of decency covers the
universal license, the worst crimes of all are committed in the name of religion, and the titles of « Holy
Orthodox Russia » are gravely invoked by men who
have ceased even to believe in sanctity, and who
might boast more truly than the worst class of
French sophists, « Nous sommes les enfants de Voltaire. »

Even the so-called « Holy Synod, » — an institution
which has superseded all ecclesiastical authority in
Russia, and itself is governed, or was not long since,
by an aide-de-camp of the Emperor, who was a cavalry officer and a Protestant, — confesses in a Report not destined to be published in Europe, that
in 1837 the number of *ecclesiastics* condemned by
the public tribunals was 1 in 24; in 1838, 1 in 23;
and in 1839, 1 in 20. During four years, from 1836
to 1839, the Synod reports to its imperial master,
that 13,443 ecclesiastics, of all grades, or *one sixth*
of the whole number, were under judgment, and
that, as the « supreme procurator » adds, for infamous crimes. » (2)

What marvel if such a church and such clergy
should fail to convert the heathen, or even to make
the attempt? What marvel if in Russia, as in Eng-

____

(1) *Histoire de la Civilisation en Russie*, par Nicolas de Gerebtzoff, tome II, ch. XII, p. 519.

(2) Theiner, ch. VI, p. 138.

land, religious earnestness almost always leads to
separation from the state church? « It is by religious
divisions, « says de Custine, » that the Russian empire will perish; » (1) and at least one Emperor of
Russia appears to have confessed the truth of the
statement. « The Russians, » observes M. de Bonald,
« have a religion entirely composed of words, ceremonies, legends, and abstinences, which is to genuine Christianity nearly what the Judaism of the
Rabbis, followed by modern Jews, is to the Mosaic
worship. » (2) « It is, » says Schnitzler, speaking
of their ecclesiastical position, « stationary, withered
by the spirit of formalism, and deprived of every
principle of liberty. » (3) And if the *people* of Russia
still adhere, sometimes even with fervour, to the
profession of Christianity, we cannot doubt that
their constancy is due to the veneration which they
still pay to the Mother of God, and to that constant
habit of invoking her sweet name which has ever
been the surest guard of the doctrine of the Incarnation. If Russians should ever cease to be devout to
our Lady, they will become a nation of deists.

When we have noticed a few examples of the mode
in which « conversions » are made in Russia, we may
resume our enquiry in other fields. In 1838, the tribe
of the Bouriates, amounting to 150,000 souls, after
fruitless invitations to embrace the Sclavonic uniformity, decided that, in order to find repose, they
would indeed change their religion — but they se-

(1) *La Russie en* 1839, Lettre 22, p. 134.
(2) *Législation Primitive*, tome IV, p. 170.
(3) *Histoire Intime de la Russie*, Notes, p. 473.

lected that of the Grand Lama. Even when they are
persuaded to adopt the national profession, it is after
the manner described in the following cases.

Admiral Wrangell relates of the Tschuktschi, who
had all received baptism, « it must be admitted that
they are as complete heathens as ever, and have not
the slightest idea of the doctrines or the spirit of
Christianity. » (1) « The Ossets, of Georgia, » says
Lady Shiel, « have been subject to Russia since the
time Georgia was annexed to that empire, more than
fifty years ago. A portion of the tribe is said to have
adopted a sort of nominal Christianity. It appears
that, conversion being attended with certain advantages, the same proselytes had been repeatedly registered under different appellations. » (2) The same
thing is said to be true of many of the Tartars, who
are attracted by the present of a pelisse, and « converted » in considerable numbers at the approach of
winter, but, long before the spring arrives, « have
returned to their gods as before. » Haxthausen,
though well disposed towards Russia, says; « The
majority of the Ossets are nominally Christians, and
belong to the Greek Church;... they are, in fact,
semi-pagans, indeed some are wholly and avowedly
heathens. They offer sacrifices of bread and flesh
upon altars in sacred groves. » (3) Turnerelli notices
the same facts with respect to tribes on the banks of
the Volga. « A great part of the Tcheremisse, as
well as the Tchouvash, are still Pagans; » while of

(1) *Expedition to the Polar Sea*,'ch. VI, p. 121.
(2) *Life and Manners in Persia*, ch. IV, p. 51.
(3) *Transcaucasia*, p. 395.

the nominal converts he says, « in general, even these remain secretly attached to their ancient customs. » (1) And it has been thus from the beginning of the history of the Muscovite Church. Laurent Lange, who was sent on a mission from St. Petersburg to China in 1715, after relating the « conversion » of a tribe who were baptized by the order of Prince Gargarin, adds; « but they have not the slightest conception of the difference between Christianity and paganism. » (2)

Lastly, a distinguished English writer notices, in grave and weighty words, that even where every political influence is in her favour, and every motive conspires to stimulate her to religious zeal, or at least to the affectation of it, Russia still remains speechless and inactive, when it is only the glory of God and the salvation of souls which invite her sympathy. The Convent of Mount Sinai, M[r] Stanley observes, « is a colony of Christian pastors planted amongst heathens, and hardly a spark of civilisation, or of Christianity, so far as history records, has been imparted to a single tribe or family in that wide wilderness. It is a colony of Greeks, of Europeans, of ecclesiastics, in one of the most interesting and the most sacred regions of the earth, and hardly a fact, from the time of their first foundation to the present time, has been contributed by them to the geography, the geology, or the history of a country, which in all its aspects has been submitted to their investigation

(1) *Kazan*, etc., vol. II, ch. IV, p. 155.
(2) *Journal du Voyage à la Chine*, p. 93. Cf. *Nouveaux Mémoires de la Moscovie*, tome I, p. 193.

for thirteen centuries. » (1) It is not surprising that
such an observer as M' Stanley should have detected,
and frankly proclaimed, « the superiority of the Latin
to the Greek monastic orders. » (2)

Enough, then, of Russia and her « Holy Synod »
as a missionary power. The Russian Church, which
resembles the Anglican in its sterility and in its sub-
jection to the civil authority, differs from it in this;
that whereas the latter attempts, sometimes sincerely and religiously, to make *Christians*, the former
only seeks to make *Russians*. They equally fail, but
the one in result only, not in intention; the other in
both.

If now, after this long digression, we resume our
journey in Palestine, and leaving the Holy City behind set our faces towards the north, we shall come
to the forests and mountains of Lebanon. Here consolation awaits us and refreshment. Here we shall
find a nation profoundly Catholic both in its social
and religious life, contrasting in every feature with
the less privileged tribes of the East, constant in the
faith, stedfast in filial devotion to the Holy See, and
recompensed by a generous Providence with gifts
and qualities which have not only merited the bene-
dictions of the Church, but extorted the admiration
of her enemies.

When we consider the position of the Maronites,
surrounded on all sides by Mahometans, idolaters,
or heretics; exposed to every evil influence which
has gradually corrupted the other christian natives

(1) *Sinai and Palestine*, p. 56.
(2) *Ibid.*, p. 346.

of this land; weak, except by the nature of their
country; owing all their security to their own valour, all their prosperity to their patient and cheerful industry; we are tempted to ask in surprise, by
what mystery have they alone preserved through
ages the dignity of character, the purity and simplicity of life, which even the most prejudiced travellers agree in ascribing to this favoured race? The
answer, which we need not anticipate, will be sufficiently revealed in the evidence which we are about
to produce.

We have not hitherto had recourse to Catholic
testimony in proving the contrast which it is the
main object of these volumes to trace, both because
the controversial value of such testimony would be
insignificant, and because Providence, as we have
several times observed, has forced Protestants to
collect everywhere and to publish to the world, all
the facts which illustrate that contrast. We shall
adhere to our rule in this case also, though it would
be pleasant to quote some few at least of the magnificent eulogies which eminent writers have pronounced on the Maronite nation, the nobility of their character, and the unswerving constancy of their faith.
Let us claim, for the first time, this indulgence.

« In spite of their great numbers, » says M. Achille
Laurent, — they are estimated by the French consular agents at 512,500 in the Libanus, and 30,000
in the plain, (1) « and though surrounded on every
side by infidels, heretics, and schismatics, never, in
relation to the faith, has the least difference been

(1) De Baudicour, ch. VI, p. 246.

known amongst them; never has any schism disturbed their unity; never has one individual amongst
them corrupted the purity of the Catholic doctrine. » (1) « This Catholic colony, » says M. Jules
David, « seems to recall by its charity, by the simplicity of its manners, by its smiling industry and
community of labour, the primitive Christian society;
a society of united and active brothers, a society of
equality before God, a veritable *communion* of which
the Church is the sublime centre. » (2) Lastly, —
for we may not linger even over testimonies which
are like music to the ear, — an apostolic missionary,
one of that noble band of discalced Carmelites who
have dared to imitate their Lord in His utter poverty,
gives this account of them, in 1858. After describing
their various neighbours, — the barbarous Moslem,
the pastoral Turcomans, the reckless Ansayrii, the
false and hypocritical Druses, the haughty Metualis,
— disciples of the anti-caliph Ali, « of whom it
would be difficult to say whether they hate a Christian or a Turk the most » — and lastly, the schismatical Greeks, « the ignorance of whose priests is
only equalled by the moral degradation of the people, » he continues as follows. « We come now to
the Maronites. The heart has been dried up and the
soul saddened by the confused disorder of idolatry
and schism. It is now our turn to rejoice. The ardent
faith of primitive Christianity, its sweet piety, inno-
cence, and simplicity of manners, is found repro-
duced amongst the Maronites. They appear like a

(1) *Relation Historique des Affaires de Syrie*, tome 1, p. 403.
(2) *Syrie Moderne*, p. 21.

people fresh from the hand of the Creator, or from the regenerating bath of the Baptism of Jesus. Oh, blessed people! how great are you in your oppression! how rich in your poverty! » (1)

It is not thus, of course, that Protestants speak of them, for they have attempted to creep into this Paradise and have been somewhat rudely ejected; but their language, though tinged with resentment and mortification, abundantly confirms the reports of more impartial witnesses.

« The Maronites, » says Colonel Churchill — who does not share the petty passions of the Protestant missionaries, « are still the ' fideles ' who welcomed Godfrey de Bouillon and his associates. » (2) While all has changed around them, centuries have left them unchanged. They are « the stanchest Romanists in the world, » says the Rev. Mʳ Williams — which only means, that they resemble true Catholics everywhere. « So bigoted is this Romanist sect, » says Mʳ Drew Stent, « that very little can be effected » — that is, they spurned the heresies of Anglican and Calvinist teachers, and stoned the false prophets who tried to find an entrance amongst them. « The missionaries, » says Mʳ Wortabet, alluding to the Protestant emissaries, « had to retire before pelting stones, and an angry mob. » « They were driven out, » says Mʳ Walpole, « by the fanatic population, and I do not believe they ever procured the satisfaction they ought. The Maronites are very proud of the victory.»

(1) *Annals*, vol. XIX, p. 271.
(2) *Mount Lebanon*, by Colonel Churchill, vol. III, ch. VI, p. 66.

He confesses, however, in spite of wounded sympathies, that « the attempt was worse than folly. »
And so purely spontaneous was the popular movement which expelled the foreign teachers,—because
they came, with money in their hands, blaspheming
the Mother of God, the Sacrament of the Altar, and
the Communion of Saints, — so wholly independent
of any political or ecclesiastical influence, that a Protestant association confesses, in 1854, that « a strong
proclamation came out from the Maronite and Greek
Catholic Bishops at Beirût to all their people, requiring them to guard carefully and protect all the members of the American Mission. »(1)

Let us hear other witnesses. « They are most
bigoted adherents of the Papacy, » observes one writer, « allowing not merely the claims of his Holiness
as Head of their Church, to dictate their creed, but
submitting also to his paternal government in matters
of discipline. »(2)« The Maronites, » says Dr Robinson, — and all Protestant writers use the same language,—« are characterised by an almost unequalled
devotion to the see of Rome. » They have lately converted, he adds, two Emirs of the Druses, together
with their families, « so that now almost all the
highest nobility of the mountain are Maronites. » (3)

This may suffice. No one will deny, in the face of
such testimony, that the Maronites are devoted Catholics. But perhaps they are servile, ignorant, and
priest-ridden? The Rev. J. L. Porter, of whom we

(1) *American Board for Foreign Missions*, Reports, p. 110.
(1854).

(2) *North American Review*, vol. LXXXI, p. 78.

(3) *Biblical Researches*, etc., p. 460.

heard at Damascus, and who had to avenge both his
personal misadventures and those of his colleagues,
says with emphasis; « They are as ignorant a set of
priest-ridden bigots as ever polluted a country, and
no stranger » — he means no Protestant missionary
— « can pass through their streets without meeting
insult, and often abuse... they are as tyrannical, as
unjust, and almost as bloodthirsty, as the haughty
Moslems. » (1) We have said that it only English
and American missionaries, but chiefly the former,
who soothe their mortification by outbursts of this
kind; and as it is quite true that the Maronite nation
owes it character, habits, and institutions solely to
the influence of the Catholic religion, it may be well
to compare Mr Porter's account of them with that of
other Protestants, not less prejudiced, but having
more respect for truth, for themselves, and for their
readers.

« They are, » says Colonel Churchill, in 1853, « a
community of Christians who are virtually as free
and independent as any state in Christendom. »(2)

« They are, » exclaims Mr Bayard Taylor, in
1855, « the most thrifty, industrious, honest, and
happy people in Syria. » « The women, » he adds,
« are beautiful, with sprightly, intelligent faces,
quite different from the stupid Mahometan females; »
and their home « is a mountain paradise, inhabited by
a people so kind and simple-hearted, that assuredly
no vengeful angel will ever drive *them* out with his
flaming sword. » (3)

(1) *Five Years in Damascus*, vol. I, ch. XVI, p. 279.
(2) *Mount Lebanon*.
(3) *The Lands of the Saracen*, ch. XII, p. 174.

« They are, » writes the Countess Hahn-Hahn,
« that industrious band of Christians who have
adorned these mountains with cornfields and vineyards, with villages and convents. » (1)

Thus speak an English, an American, and a
German Protestant. Let us confirm their testimony
by other witnesses. M'' Farley has told us that their
kindness and hospitality, even to Protestant travellers, were so universal, until they were irritated by
the selfish intrigues and impertinent bigotry of missionaries whom they would have been content to despise if they had not been constrained to abhor them,
that any Englishman was sure of a cordial welcome
amongst them, and that he could never forget the
« extreme courtesy » of the Maronite clergy towards
himself.

M'' Monro, an intelligent Anglican clergyman, who
had the good sense not to insult his hosts, and had
no personal motive for libelling them, not only contrasts their frank hospitality with the suspicious ex-
clusiveness of other Syrian races, but adds; « The
kind manners and energetic carriage of these people
afforded a striking instance that where industry prevails, the flowers of happiness will blossom, and
abundance ever be the fruit. » (2)

M'' Walpole, in spite of strong religious antipathies,
declares that their valour is as conspicuous as their
industry. « The Maronites rose against their oppressors, the Metuali, and drove them fairly out of the

(1) Countess Hahn-Hahn, Letter 21.
(2) *Travels in Syria*, by the Rev'' Vere Monro, vol. II,
ch. XXIV, p. 107.

district... The Metuali have a high character for warriors and courage. This shows what the Catholic population might become if united. « The general prosperity, he says, was so remarkable, that « it exhibited a scene which made one feel proud that at last the Christian dared improve. » He observes also, that the family of Sheebal, descended from Mahomet, had just been converted, and adopted into the Maronite nation. (1)

M͏͏ʳ Keating Kelly cannot speak of them without enthusiasm. « The condition of this people is essentially happy. Its religion is free and respected; its churches and its convents crown the summits of its hills; its bells that sound in its ears as a welcome token of liberty and independence, peal their summons to pray night and day; it is governed by its own hereditary chieftains and by the clergy it loves; a strict but equitable system of police preserves order and security in the villages; property is respected and transmitted from father to son; commerce is active; the manners of the people *perfectly simple and pure.* Rarely is there seen a population whose appearance more bespeaks health, native nobility, and civilisation, than that of these men of Lebanon. » (2)

Lastly, even a Syrian Greek, who cordially hates both their religion and their nation, and who seems by converse with English Protestants to have become indifferent to his own religion without adopting theirs, makes the following confession. « They are

(1) *The Ansayrii, with Travels in the Further East*, vol. III, ch. I, p. 7; ch. XVIII, p. 434.

(2) *Syria and the Holy Land*, by Walter Keating Kelly, ch. VIII, p. 97.

a most industrious, contented, happy people... and
so manly and courageous that, until the year 1843,
they had never been conquered by the Mahometans;»
and then he adds the most magnificent eulogy which
it was possible to pronounce upon a Christian people, that, « owing to the influence of the Bishops,
*crime is in a great measure unknown amongst the
Maronites.* »(1)

In reading these impressive testimonies, from writers of various creeds and nations, to the virtues of
a Catholic people, we have almost forgotten Mr Porter. Let us quote him once more, for the sake of adding a new example of the language in which passion
finds vent while reason is mute, and of the class of
agents whom Protestantism sends forth into every
land, but only to augment everywhere the repugnance
which is entertained, by all races of men, towards
England and her representatives.

The Maronite clergy, Mr Porter says, « are ignorant, bigoted, and overbearing, » and their religion
« senseless mummery. » It is of the Syrian clergy,
professors of the same faith, that a more enlightened
English Protestant says ; « It is a sublime spectacle
to contemplate these men devoting themselves to deeds
of charity and mercy, and welcoming a long martyrdom for conviction's sake. »(2) « I can imagine St. Ba-
sil the Great, » says another educated Englishman,
« or the Gregories, just such persons in appearance. »(3) « If Titian were about to paint a Doge of

(1) *The Thistle and the Cedar of Lebanon*, by Riek Allah
Effendi, ch. XVI, pp. 209, 273.
(2) Farley, *Two Years in Syria*, ch. XXXIV, p. 291
(3) Patterson, p. 322.

Venice, » says an accomplished French traveller, speaking of the Maronite Patriarch of Cilicia, « he would ask for no other model. » (1) Even M' Porter, in an access of involuntary admiration, confesses « their staid dignity and noble bearing. »(2)

But M' Porter speedily resumes his usual tone. « The education of the people, » he observes, « they never think of; » and as if even this statement admitted of improvement, he adds, « the idea of imparting religious instruction is quite out of the question. » Presently, as if the accounts of other Protestant travellers suddenly occurred to him, and suggested the necessity of caution, he says; « It is true a few schools have been established, but these are got up by the people » — who, although « igno- rant, bigoted, bloodthirsty, and polluters of the soil, » he now represents as going beyond their pastors, to whom he declares they are slavishly subject, in pro- moting education.

Yet M' Ubicini has told us, that in every province of Asiatic Turkey, Catholic schools are multiplying in all directions, and are eagerly frequented by child- ren of all sects. D' Robinson declares of the Maronite college of Kesrawân, in which the Jesuits teach Arabic, Syriac, Latin, and Italian, « that it takes a higher stand than any other similar establishment in Syria. » M' Farley speaks in the same terms of the Lazarist college at Antoura, « where some hundreds of students, who come from Beyrout, Aleppo, Da- mascus, and other towns in Syria, as also from

(1) *La Syrie avant* 1860, par Georges de Salverte, ch. VIII, p. 100.

(2) Vol. II, ch. XVI, p. 296.

Persia, Egypt, and even from Nubia and Abyssinia,
are taught, » in addition to « the usual branches of
education, » « the Arabic, French, Italian, and Latin
languages. » M. de Salverte reports, in 1861, that
the ecclesiastical seminary at Ghazir, in which he
found ninety students, is so efficient, that its excellence dispenses them from seeking education in the
colleges of Rome. (1) Mʳ Wellsted relates, that even
in Aleppo, « most of the children can read and write
at an early age. (2) And lastly, Risk Allah, though
he affects, in order to please his English readers, to
deplore what he has learned to call the « Romish
tendencies » of the Maronites, honestly confesses that
« their schools are really excellent; » and whereas
the Protestant missionary affirms that the Maronite
clergy « never think of education, » this Syrian
Greek avows, in spite of national and religious antipathies, that « one great advantage which the Maronites possess, and which must eventually prove very
beneficial to them, is the fact, *that education is
spreading universally amongst them.* » (3)

But in all this there is no lesson for Mʳ Porter.
He had a defeat to avenge, and after five years of
unprofitable labour had convinced even himself, that
it was time to quit Syria. And so in his anger he for-
got prudence as well as truth. Education is so literally *universal* among the Maronites, though their
clergy « never think of it, » that whereas, in the
words of the late Mʳ Warburton, « there is not an

(1) Ch. viii, p. 96.
(2) *Travels*, etc , by J. R. Wellsted Esp., F. R. S., vol. II,
ch. v, p. 91.
(3) Ch. xvi, p. 270.

Egyptian woman who can read and write, except a daughter of Mehemet Ali, and the few who have been educated in the school of M' Lieder, the Maronite women of the Lebanon, though of the same Arab race, are generally instructed. » (1) « Education, » says M' Kelly, « though limited to reading, writing, arithmetic, and the catechism, » — we have seen that for the class above the peasants the course includes Arabic, Syriac, Latin, French, and Italian, — « is *universal* among them, and gives them a deserved superiority over the other tribes of Syria. » (2) Whether such an amount of education can be said to be « universal » in England, we need not stay to enquire.

But M' Porter had still something to add. It was possible to clothe his enmity in still more impressive language. The Maronites, like all the Oriental tribes, severely exacting in their estimate of a Christian apostle, had rejected him and his companions, with an energy proportioned to the ardour of their faith, as ministers of the Evil one. M' Porter repays the indignity with the following announcement, in which he appears to have uttered his last farewell to Syria and the Syrian mission. « The protestant missionaries have done more for the advancement of education within the short period of twenty years than the combined priesthood of all Lebanon and all Syria has done during centuries. » It is our turn to bid farewell to M' Porter, to whom we have perhaps given an undue share of attention, and we cannot do

(1) *The Crescent and the Cross*, vol. I, ch. xi, p. 100.
(2) *Ubi supra*.

so more filly than in the words of his co-religionists.

From Mr Williams, himself a protestant minister, we have learned, on the one hand, that the Protestant missionaries in Syria « are merely playing at Missions, » and that « self-sacrifice and simple trust » are not to be learned from their example; and on the other, that the Catholic Church has sent to this land « the best instructed and most devoted missionaries that the world has seen since primitive times. » Dr Southgate, a Protestant bishop, has assured us that the rare disciples of Mr Porter and his colleagues « are infidels and radicals unworthy of the sympathy of the Christian public; » and Sir Adolphus Slade has added, that many of the missionaries themselves, who have « done more for education, » though they have neither schools nor scholars, than all the Catholic clergy for centuries, « know absolutely no other than their mother tongue. »

Finally, the same Protestant writer, long resident in Syria, conversant during many years with all which has occurred in that land, and full of admiration of the apostolic men by whom, as he observes, « millions of souls have been saved » in these regions, lends us the following appropriate words with which to take leave of Mr Porter. « Protestant missionaryism is much extolled; it certainly costs a great deal; but the good it may effect *is as a drop of water, compared with the sea of benefits spread by the Roman Catholic Church*, silently and unostentatiously, all over Turkey. » (1)

It is time to quit the mountains and valleys of

(1) *Turkey, Greece, and Malta*, vol. II, ch. xx, p. 423.

Lebanon, where we have found, in the heart of a land long abandoned to every error and impiety, a picture which a Christian may well love to contemplate. On the one hand, deep religious conviction, unshaken through ages, and that instinctive horror of heresy which is one of the surest signs of election; on the other, as even enemies allow, valour, dignity, purity, gentleness, industry, prosperity, and peace. Such, by protestant testimony, is the influence of the Catholic religion upon generous natures, penetrated by its healing power, and such its results even amongst a people of Arab origin, though surrounded by races and tribes with whom faith is a dream, and virtue a jest.

It is characteristic of that singular form of religion which seems instinctively to prefer crime and ignorance in union with heresy to virtue and enlightenment in connection with the Church, that the only reflection suggested to another episcopalian clergyman, of the same class as Mʳ Porter, by the contrast which we have just delineated, found expression in these words. « How sad, » exclaims the Rev. George Fisk, « that Popery should taint even the remains of the glory of Lebanon ! » Greeks and Armenians, sunk in mental and moral decrepitude, Mʳ Fisk would embrace with love, because, as he seriously observes, they hold « the great leading truths of the Gospel; » and though « in many respects superstitious, and manifestly corrupt, » they have this merit, which amply supplies the want of every other, that « they have never merged in the apostasy of Rome. » (1)

(1) *A Pastor's Memorial*, ch. ix, pp. 398, 400, 410.

M⟨r⟩ Fisk has apparently not read, or perhaps forgotten, the testimonies of Protestant writers, who
declare — as we have already heard and shall hear
again presently — that the only Greeks and Armenians who deserve the name of intelligent or consistent Christians are precisely those who have derived new life from reconciliation with the Catholic
Church.

Allusion has been made to the Druses, the implacable and hereditary foes of the Maronites. If we add
a few words with respect to the former, it is only for
the sake of noticing the characteristic relations of the
Protestant missionaries with them. Banished by the
Maronites, with every mark of contempt and disgust,
they took refuge among their hostile neighbours, and
endeavoured to make alliance with them. The infamy
of their character, and their indifference to any form
of religion, was no impediment to the negotiations
which now ensued. To protestantise the Druses, and
to vex the Maronites, would be a double triumph;
but it was one which they were not destined to
enjoy. « The Druses, » said D⟨r⟩ Yates, with great
confidence, « will unite with the Protestant Christians, and the power of the Osmanlis will cease. » (1)
M⟨r⟩ Fremantle, an Anglican clergyman, was of opinion that they would become « independent Episcopalians; » and as if this were not enough to stimulate
the hopes of his co-religionists at home, he gravely
added, — in a report which was actually published
by the « Society for Promoting Christian knowledge, »
— that « they desire to be united to the English

(1) *Modern History of Egypt*, vol. II, ch. IV, p. 158.

Church. » (1) Whether M' Fremantle really believed this, we need not question. The Druses, as
M' Chasseaud observed in 1855, are unscrupulous
hypocrites, and will affect to be of the religion of any
society in which they happen to find themselves. (2)
They pretend, says M' Paton, to be Mahometans
when it suits them. (3) All European writers agree
in describing them as impious, false, and bloodthirsty. D' Clarke says, « some among them certainly offer their highest adoration to a *calf.* » (4)
Risk Allah declares, apparently from his own observation, that « while they profess to be Mahommedans,
they have no hesitation whatever in denouncing
Mahommed as a false prophet; » and he adds, that
the Druses, like the Kurds, have formed such an
estimate of the creed of « English Protestants » as to
assert, « that their religion is a species of free-ma-
soury, which very much resembles their own ; » and
one of their leaders assured him that « a tall English
emir » had told him so. (5)

How surely these atheists of Syria reckoned upon
the sympathy of « English Protestants, » and how
much reason they had for doing so, is sufficiently revealed in the comments made by the latter upon the
Turco-Druse insurrection of 1860. All their apolo-
gies are for the Druses, all their sarcasms for the
Maronites. « The Maronites are mere savages, » says

(1) *The Eastern Churches*, pp. 44, 40.
(2) *The Druses of the Lebanon*, by George Washington Chasseaud.
(3) *Modern Syrians*, p. 309.
(4) *Clarke's Travels*, vol. IV, p. 136.
(5) *Ubi supra*, p. 292.

one of the ablest organs of intellectual Protestantism;
and as if this were not venturesome enough, he
gravely adds, that until « the hour of their triumph
the conduct of the Druses had been unimpeach-
able! » (1) It is but a new version of the old cry,
non hunc sed Barabbam. The worshippers of a calf
are preferred before the disciples of the Cross; and
the latter, though travellers of all sects confess with
enthusiasm their nobility and virtue, are peremptor-
rily described, by that instinct of hate which can corrupt even genius into imbecility, as « mere savages. »

An equally eminent authority observes, that
« the great Druse Chief Mohamed En-Nasar, the
instigator of these butcheries, *counted on English
support*, and therefore it need not be added on an
English reward. » (2) His calculation has been
abundantly justified. « The Druses, » observes a
traveller who has lived amongst them, « seek refuge
in the arms of England, because they know that
every other nation of Europe has judged and condemned them; » (3) while another relates that he
heard an Englishman say to a Maronite sheik, that
England gave her support to the Druses solely in
order to counterbalance the influence of France
with the Christians. « You admit, then, » replied
the Maronite chief, « that as soon as France begins
to labour for God, England takes up arms for the
devil. » (4)

(1) *Saturday Review*, April 20, 1861.
(2) *The Times*, September 1, 1860.
(3) *La Vérité sur la Syrie*, par Baptistin Poujoulat, Lettre 43,
p. 489.
(4) Mislin, *Les Lieux Saints*, tome I, ch. vi. p. 156.

It appears, however, that in spite of the avowed sympathy and alliance between the Druses and the English, the former only amused themselves at M' Fremantle's expense when they encouraged his cheerful expectations; for M' Walpole tells us, — eleven years after that gentleman's sanguine prediction, — « With the Druses the Protestant Mission-aries have made, I believe, no progress. » They are not yet affiliated to the « English Church, » nor is there any immediate promise of that event. « Many professed themselves converts, » says M' Walpole, « but directly the minister refused them some re-quest, turned round and said; We will listen to you as long as you pay us. » (1) This was their view of the value of Protestantism.

These are not the only operations of Protestants in the Lebanon, though precisely the same result has attended all their efforts. We have heard of the two « designing brothers » who went to Malta, and « agreed to be baptized » on condition of receiving some hundred pounds. Others have imitated these neophytes of the Lebanon with still greater success. D' Carne relates the story of « the noted Eusebius, bishop of Mount Lebanon, » who far surpassed, as became his more elevated rank, the performances of his ingenuous flock. This Greek prelate « was chap-eroned through many of the colleges at Oxford by one of the Masters. » In such society his anti-Roman views made him a welcome guest; but the crafty oriental was only speculating on the inexhaustible credulity of his sympathising hosts, by which he and

(1) *The Ansayrii*, ch. XVI, p. 356.

his class have so often profited. Eusebius obtained, says D' Carne, « a capital printing press, and about 800 l. in money. When we were at Sidon, we found that this eastern diguitary was living in a style of excessive comfort, and to his heart's content, at a few hours distance. With this money, which was a fortune in the East, he has purchased a good house and garden; not one farthing has ever gone to renovate the condition of the Christians of the East, and the printing press, or some fragments of it, were known to have found their way to Alexandria. » (1) Oxford should have learned by this time to mistrust pseudo-converts, especially when they come from the East.

We may now take our departure from Syria, in order to pursue in Armenia the investigations which we have almost completed. It is in the latter province that the Protestant emissaries from America boast to have obtained the greatest numerical results, and are at this moment engaged in operations which deserve particular attention. But we must first say a few words on Catholic Missions to the Armenians.

Nearly twenty years ago D' Joseph Wolff announced to Europe, that « about *sixty thousand* Armenians have joined the Church of Rome. » (2) Since that date, the great movement of reconciliation among the Armenian nation has steadily progressed; and it may be said without exaggeration that, at the present time, hardly a week elapses without a fresh instance of conversions, often on a large scale, and all attesting the wonderful restoration of this people to unity.

(1) *Letters from the East*, vol. II, p. 115.
(2) *Narrative of a Mission to Bokhara*, ch. III, p. 114.

And this remarkable fact is perpetually recurring, in spite of that « strong national bond » which, as Haxthausen notices, assimilates the Armenians to the Jews, « whose nationality no human power can destroy, » and which knits them all into one tribe and family, from China to Morocco. So powerful is this ineradicable instinct of nationality, — a sentiment always more or less fatal to Christianity, — that Armenians, when converted to the Church, are obliged, like converts from certain European races, to repudiate that false and exaggerated patriotism which has rent Christendom into twenty jealous, selfish, and hostile bodies, « and proudly renounce the name of Armenians, to call themselves Catholics. » (1)

During the last two centuries this consoling movement has received a constant impulse from the labours of European missionaries. In 1711, Père Ricard reconciled 1 Bishop, 22 Priests, and 875 lay persons. (2) Three years later, in 1714, Père Monier received the abjuration of more than 700, and shortly afterwards, in company with Ricard, penetrated into Kurdistan. They were both chained and imprisoned by the Pacha of Kars, at the instigation of the Armenian schismatics, whose vengeance followed them to their new field of labour. By such men, and with similar results, the combat has ever since been maintained, the heretics always invoking Moslem aid, and seldom in vain. And these incidents have marked the conflict up to the present hour. « Recently, » says

(1) Haxthausen, ch. vii, p. 224.
(2) *Nouveaux Mémoires du Levant*, tome III, p. 290.

M. Eugène Boré, « the schismatical patriarch purchased from the vizir for 2,000 purses the right to
prevent a member of his church from becoming a
Catholic. » (1) So uniform is their practice of seeking Mahometan auxiliaries in all their difficulties,
that, as M.r Walpole notices, in 1851, the Bishop of
Van « bribed the Pacha » to assist him in ejecting
the American missionaries from the neighbourhood
of Etchmiadzin.

Even Protestant travellers are almost unanimous
in affirming two facts, — the worthlessness of the
schismatical and the superiority of the converted
Armenian. « The Armenians, » says the Rev.
M.r Dwight, « appear to hold even a lower place in
the scale than either the Greeks or the Latins » (2)
— after which he evidently felt that he had nothing
more to say. He confesses, however, that even they
are witnesses for the Church, since they hold all the
Catholic doctrines controverted by Protestants; a
fact confirmed by a Prussian writer, who lived in
intimacy with the heads of the sect, and was led to
make the following important reflections. « The Armenian Church bears a marked testimony to the antiquity of the Catholic Church. All the dogmas
attacked at and since the Reformation are held by
it, — the Saints, the Seven Sacraments, Transub-
stantiation, the Sacrifice of the Mass, and Purgatory.
The dogmas which the Armenians hold in common
with the Catholic Church must be of high antiquity,
for as early as the Council of Chalcedon, in 451, the

(1) *Arménie*, p. 138.
(2) *Christianity in Turkey*, p. 7.

Armenian Church possessed an organisation of its own, and jealously guarded itself from foreign influence. » (1) This learned writer also observes, and proves by well known examples, that « the Armenian Church not only acknowledges that its founder, St. Gregory the Illuminator, received the Armenian Patriarchate *from Rome*, but it has several times submitted to the Pope, as the centre of Unity and the Supreme Patriarch. » He had reason to speak with confidence of the sentiments of the highest class of Armenian prelates, since Narses, the patriarch of the separated Armenians, gave him the following explicit assurance with his own lips, when he met him at St. Petersburg in 1843. « On the whole we are in harmony with Rome : the Armenian Patriarch usually sends a notice to the Pope of his elevation to the Patriarchate... There is no essential difference in doctrine between the Armenian and Latin churches ; indeed perfect agreement has been repeatedly attained. Jealousies and disputes have been much more frequent with the Greek Church. » It was impossible to omit testimony so interesting, though it probably reveals more accurately the convictions and wishes of Narses himself than of the corrupt and ignorant colleagues whom he nominally governs, and of whom Haxthausen declares with regret, — « avarice, envy, hypocrisy, and even gross sensuality are common amongst them. »

Such are the penalties of separation from the Holy See, even where the apostolic doctrine is nominally retained. Captain Wilbraham observed at Etchmi-

(1) Haxthausen, ch. IX, p. 313.

adzin itself, the head-quarters of the schism, and in
the cathedral, the « want of attention, and even of
decorum » which was displayed by the congregation;
and added, « there was none of that apparently sincere, though perhaps blind devotion, which I have
so often remarked in Roman Catholic chapels. »
« The Catholicos, » he says, or Patriarch, « nominally presides over the Synod, but a *moderator* has
been appointed by the Russian government, without
whose approval nothing can be done, which makes
the Emperor virtually the head of the Armenian
Church throughout the world : » (1) a fact of which
Narses bitterly complained to Baron Von Haxthausen, in these expressive words. « How undignified
is the position of the Patriarch! Every letter must
pass through the hands of the Governor General of
Caucasia, and is opened in his office, where every
clerk may read it! » Narses, a man superior to most
of his race and order, might have reflected, that this
is the usual fate of those who consent to preside over
« national » churches.

Mr Walpole declares, from his own observation,
that « the falsehood of the Armenian monks was
dreadful, as they asserted that so and so was the belief of such and such a church. »

Dr Moritz Wagner, also a Protestant, confirms
these dismal statements. « Gross ignorance, stupid-
ity, covetousness, and immorality, are the predominant characteristics of these ecclesiastics... They
readily assume an external show of virtue and self-

(1) *Travels in the Trans-Caucasian Provinces of Russia*,
ch. ix, pp. 95-98.

denial, whilst, in secret, they indulge freely in vice. Envy and jealousy reign supreme among them. They do not appear to have a shadow of brotherly or neighborly love, or of kindliness and courtesy, in the Christian acceptation of those terms. » (1) And these are the men who perpetuate the schism.

D⁻ Friedrich Parrot notices also « the moral corruption in which their priesthood is sunk, » and gives this explanation of their profound and universal ignorance. « Every laic, provided only he be chosen by the congregation, and have passed fourteen days in the prescribed fastings, and ritual observances in a church, may get ordination from the bishop, without either preparation or subsequent education. » He agrees with Colonel Drouville, that « their priests and Bishops are all as ignorant at it is possible to be; » and notices the usual phenomenon in all heretical bodies, that they have split into three sects. « There is an *independent* Catholicos at Sis, in Cilicia, and another, who has maintained himself in this dignity for 700 years, in the island of Akhthamar, in the lake of Van. » (2)

Lastly, D⁻ Wilson observes, — though he would probably have said nothing about it if they would have welcomed his friends, — « the Armenians partake in the monothelite as well as the monophysite heresy » — a statement which is not true of the whole nation, especially in Western Asia.

Such, by Protestant testimony, are the unfortunate communities who are paying the penalty of he-

(1) *Travels in Persia*, etc., vol. III, p. 51. (1856).
(2) *Journey to Ararat*, ch. IV, p. 92; ch. V. pp. 105-110.

resy and schism, and whom the Church, with the
patience and zeal of a mother, has resolved to restore
to truth, charity, and obedience. How far she has
succeeded in this aim, we may now briefly state.

We have already heard from Dr Wolff that sixty
thousand had been reconciled when he visited them.
Captain Wilbraham admits that « a considerable
proportion have returned to the Catholic Church,
from which this nation seceded, when, in the year
491, they rejected the authority of the Council of
Chalcedon. » (1) Dr Parrot, though a Russian Imperial Councillor of State, allows that « no small
portion of the clergy, and laity also, have attached
themselves to the Roman Catholic Church. » (2)
« Romanism, » says the Rev. Justin Perkins, of
whom we shall hear more presently, « is taking root
and extending, » — which he considers « the conversion of the Armenians from bad to worse. »
« Very few of the Nestorians now remain, » he adds,
« on the western side of the Koordish mountains,
who have not yielded to the intrigues and usurpa-
tions of Papal domination. » (3) This gentleman is
apparently of opinion that the operations of the
Americans, which shall be described immediately,
involve neither intrigue nor usurpation.

But the conversions effected by Catholic missionaries have not been confined to Armenia Proper. « At
Constantinople, » says Mr Curzon, « a great number
of the higher and wealthier Armenians give their ad-

(1) Ch. xxxi, p. 352.
(2) P. 110.
(3) *Residence in Persia*, p. 4.

herence to the Roman Catholic creed. » Of the *Chaldean* Catholics, Dʳ Wilson observes; « they form, I am sorry to say, a great portion of the Nestorians west of the mountains of Kurdistan. » Bagdad and Mosùl have yielded to the same beneficent power. « Emissaries from Rome, » says Mʳ Perkins, « have been laboring with a zeal and perseverance worthy of a better cause, to effect the conversion of the entire Nestorian church... Mʳˢ Perkins received a letter from a pious English lady who resides in Bagdad, in which the writer says, ' the religious state of this city is very unsatisfactory — the Roman Catholics carry the day in every way... A large body of bishops and priests are going to Mosùl in a day or two, to form a convention to endeavour to bring over all the Chaldeans to the Papal faith. ' » Fortunately, we can trace the results of this expedition; for a little later Mʳ Walpole tells us, with an angry commentary hardly worthy of so intelligent a traveller, that of « the fourteen Christian churches at Mosùl belonging to the different sects, several are now in the hands of Roman Catholics... whether by right or otherwise, » — how could a few poor missionaries gain them except by persuasion ?— « the Catholics have gathered to themselves many congregations. »

The expedition from Bagdad was evidently successful; indeed Dʳ Southgate was able to report, with unfeigned regret, that « the whole body of the Nestorian Church is now a branch of the Church of Rome, and with a sad propriety may the Papal Nestorians assume the *national* name of Chaldeans. »(1)

(1) Vol. II, cb. xvi, p. 183.

« The Nestorians who once inhabited the Mosùl district, » says Dr Asahel Grant, « have *all* embraced
the Romish faith. » (1) « The whole Chaldean notion, » adds an English traveller, « may now be esteemed Catholics. » (2)

Finally, the Patriarch of the Chaldeans, writing
from Mosùl in 1853, could already report that 55,000
wanderers from that nation alone had been restored
to the true fold, and that « the opposition of the Methodists » — he means the Anglican and other missionaries — was the chief impediment to the conversion of the few who were still in schism, but
whose imperfect faith was in danger from contact
with Protestant neology, as their morals were from
the lavish distribution of Protestant gold. (3) The
mission of Protestantism seems to be everywhere the
same. Its agents cannot make Christians themselves,
but they can prevent others doing so. By the banks of
the Tigris, as by those of the Nile and the Jordan;
in the cities of China, as in the villages of Hindostan;
in the islands of the Pacific, as in those of the Mediterranean; their aim is to rend unity, to mar the
work which they can neither understand nor imitate,
to confirm the heathen in his unbelief and the heretic
in his corruption; and the only triumph to which
they aspire is to keep back a few, when all around
are waking to a new life of truth and virtue, from
sharing the blessings which, but for their presence,
would perhaps regenerate the world.

(1) *The Nestorians*, ch. III, p. 27.
(2) Patterson, app. p. 401.
(3) *Revue Orientale et Algérienne*, tome IV, p. 357.

Let us return for a moment, before we conclude this part of our subject, to Armenia Proper. The movement of Catholic regeneration of which Western Asia is now one of the most conspicuous theatres, has at last penetrated to the very heart and centre of the Armenian schism. Rumours had reached Europe towards the close of 1839 of extraordinary and almost unprecedented conversions in the regions which surround Etchmiadzin. An Armenian gentleman, who arrived in England in the month of September of that year, brought intelligence of the almost simultaneous conversion of ten thousand Armenians in the neighbourhood of Erzeroum. Application was made to the proper authorities for authentic information with respect to so remarkable an event, and through the intervention of a venerable prelate a letter has been obtained from the Catholic Armenian Primate, dated Constantinople, October 26, 1839, which contains the following statement.

« I willingly communicate to you the details of the conversions which take place almost every week from the schismatical Armenian church to the centre of unity in these latter times, and especially during the last two years, in which so great a religious movement has been manifested in various parts of Asia, that it might more fitly be called a religious revolution — *che potrei meglio intitolare una rivoluzione religiosa.* In Karput and Arabghir, cities in the neighbourhood of Erzerum, more than five hundred families with some of their priests have been converted to Catholicism. In Tadem, Sartorici, and Garmir, regions adjacent to Karput, about one hund-

red families. In Mulatia and Adjaman, also contiguous districts, one hundred and fifty families with
their priest. Last week I received letters from Palo,
also in the territory of Karput, and containing more
than two hundred villages, which inform me that
fifty families have expressed their desire to be admitted to Catholic unity. In Marasci, near Diarbeker,
more than six hundred families, with some of their
clergy, have become Catholics, and other families in
the neighbouring districts. At Rodosto, near Adri-
anople, and again at Bandyrma, in the diocese of
Dyrsa in Dithynia, seventy families, beside others
similarly disposed, have addressed petitions to me
to be received into Catholic unity. » The illustrious
prelate does not state the exact numerical total of the
converts, which was probably unknown to him ; but
as they amount already to about fifteen hundred *families*, besides others similarly disposed, we may easily
form an approximate estimate. But even this is not
all, for the Archbishop immediately adds ; « I omit
to speak of other districts in the like condition, and
especially of one vast province, with respect to which
I am also conducting negotiations, in favour of more
than *ten thousand families*. »

Such is the work of God, in these last times,
among the schismatical communities of the East.
Worn out by the exactions of simoniacal priests and
bishops, scandalised by the ignorance and immorality
of their fallen pastors, conversant in many cases
with the superior virtue and dignity of their countrymen who have been reconciled to the Church, and
above all touched by the compassionate grace of God
and the purity, wisdom, and goodness of the apostles

whom He has sent amongst them, — they begin, in
this eleventh hour of their history, to turn wistful
eyes towards the source of unity and peace, and to
marvel that they have so long despised the blessings
which they knew not to be within their reach.

It only remains to show, — once more by Protestant testimony, — that as soon as they enter the
Church, they begin to acquire the freedom, virtue,
and enlightenment to which they had so long been
strangers. This also, thanks to the copiousness and
exuberance of Protestant literature, we shall be able
to prove.

« The Roman Catholics, » said an Anglican clergyman some years ago, « having compassed sea and
land, have made and still retain proselytes to the
Papal Supremacy from *every* Christian community
and nation, Abyssinia excepted. » If Mr Jowett had
written a little later, he would have been obliged to
omit the exception. Other writers, who share
Mr Jowett's prejudices, will now tell us, in language
more emphatic than could be expected from such
witnesses, though far below the truth, what influence
these conversions have produced upon the life and
character of their fortunate subjects.

Let us begin with the *Greeks.* Of the converts from
this nation we have been told, by men who can
hardly speak with composure of the Catholic Church,
such truths as the following. « They are, » says
Dr Wilson, in words already quoted, « amongst the
most liberal and intelligent native Christians in the
East. » They exhibit, since their conversion, says
Dr Robinson more cautiously, « a certain elevation. »
« Their intercourse with the Roman Catholic

Church, « adds D⁏ Durbin, « tends to elevate them in the scale of civilization. » And these are all vehement protestants.

Of the Armenian Converts, equally hostile witnesses give exactly the same account, though we may be sure they speak with reluctance and constraint. « Like the Christians in other parts of Turkey, » says Mess⁏ Smith and Dwight, eager partisans of Protestant missions, « they who have embraced the faith of Rome are more respectable for wealth and intelligence than their countrymen. » They add that « most of the native Christians employed by Protestants in the Levant are of the Romish persuasion » — a fact which they consider discreditable to the officials, merchants, and others, who employ them solely on account of their superior trustworthiness, because it encourages « the Pope's antichristian power. » (1)

« The Catholic Armenians, » says Captain Wilbraham, « are generally superior in education and intelligence to their countrymen » — which this gentleman attributes, « in some measure, to the circulation of knowledge occasioned by the literary labours of the Catholic Armenian Convent in Venice. » (2) In other words, they are brought by their conversion into contact with Catholic intelligence and learning.

« The Roman Catholic branch of the Armenian Church, » says M⁏ Curzon, « has done much more for literature and civilization than the original body. » Of the converts he says their minds are more en-

(1) *Missionary Researches in Armenia*, letter 1, p. 20.
(2) Ch. xxxi, p. 352.

larged, they are less Oriental in their ideas, » etc;(1)
an emphatic testimony, by a capable witness, to the
civilising influence of the Catholic religion. M' Curzon also observes, that « the Armenian Monks at
Venice printed the Armenian Bible in 1805; and
entirely by their energy, the small spark which alone
glimmered in the darkness of Armenian ignorance in
the East has gradually increased its light. » « The
Mechitarists , » says Haxthausen, « have printed
Armenian translations from all the languages of
Europe, and in every department of literature. »

Of the *Syrians*, even D' Southgate notices the
pregnant fact, that « the adherents of the Church of
Rome have all been themselves converted *individually*, » and that « they are zealously and intelligently
attached to their new faith. » (2)

Of the *Chaldeans*, we have heard that they have
become a Catholic nation ; and of the *Maronites*, who
owe all the « deserved superiority » which even
Protestants recognise in them to the influence of
their religion, we need say nothing more than has
been already related by English and American writers.

Of the converted *Jacobites*, M' Badger confesses,
in spite of that uneasy dislike and jealousy of the
Catholic Church which is now perhaps more intense
in Anglicans than in any other class; « If the truth
must be told, they are *decidedly superior*, in many
respects, to their Jacobite brethren. » (3)

Lastly, the eventual triumph of the Faith in all the

(1) *Armenia and Erzeroum*, ch. xv, p. 230.
(2) *Narrative*, etc., vol. II, ch. xxiii, p. 284. .
(3) Vol. 1, p. 63.

long-separated communities of the East appears so
certain to a German philosopher who had watched,
with cold but intelligent impartiality, its irresistible
progress, that he does not hesitate to announce in
these emphatic terms the inevitable issue. « *There is
no doubt* that the theology of the West will in time
penetrate the Eastern Church, with *all* its divisions,
Greek, Armenian, Nestorian, and Coptic. » (1)

And now we have heard enough of Catholic Missions in the Levant, Syria, and Armenia, of their
uninterrupted success, and of the character both of
the missionaries and their disciples. The history
exactly agrees with what we have heard in every
other land. On one side we have found God and His
gifts, on the other only man and his frailties. The few
Protestant converts, attracted only by offers of payment, and spurning the hand from which they receive
it, are, as Dr Southgate admits, « infidels and radicals ; » or, as Mr Williams, Mr Patterson, and others
report, notorious for « scandalous irregularities and
excesses — either worthless persons, or sceptics and
infidels ; » while even a Protestant minister not only
confesses the universal failure of his co-religionists
in Syria, but candidly asks, « Are we ever likely to
succeed any better? » Such is one more example of
the momentous contrast which has not hitherto been
revealed to the world, because neither genius nor
learning could have anticipated, much less dispensed
with, the facts which living writers have collected for
our instruction.

And what explanation do Protestants offer, in *this*

(1) *Transcaucasia*, by Daron Von Haxthausen, ch. III, p. 87.

case, of the success of Catholic missions and the failure of their own? In China, they assure us that,
« in becoming Papists, » and subsequently martyrs,
« they *give up nothing.* » (1) In India, « Popery is
better adapted » to the illogical Hindoo. In Ceylon,
and in other lands, it is « *ceremonial* » which
accounts for the contrast. And what is it in Syria?
In this province, the explanation is still more unexpected, and the very hypothesis which unites in itself
the largest measure of extravagance and impossibility
is precisely that which has been selected for the occasion. Who would have anticipated that, in the land
of the Moslem, « where, » as Mr Walpole observes,
« the Christian exists only on sufferance, » it is by
« cruelty and violence, » that a few Lazarists, Franciscans, and Sisters of Charity, win their way?
« Romish tyranny, » says the Rev. Mr Fremantle, for
the special instruction of the Anglican Church, « has
been insulting and *persecuting*, and assisting the
Mahommedans to oppress the fallen churches. » And
this account, which would be received with a shout
of laughter by a Druse or a Mussulman audience, is
repeated by other English writers, with various
modifications, as the true history of Catholic victories
in Syria.

Yet as late as 1845, we find a competent authority
making this declaration, in the form of an appeal to
Europe. « I know for a positive fact, that at this
moment all classes, sects, and denominations, are
crying aloud for European protection. » (2) Fourteen

(1) *The Land of Sinim*, ch. iv, p. 132.
(2) *Memoir on Syria*, by Charles Fiott Barker, formerly
Secretary to Mr Consul General Barker, p. 50.

years later, Mr Wingfield still reports, that « the assassination of Christians, even of the richer class, is unhappily of no very rare occurrence. » (1) Mr Warrington Smyth relates, about the same time, that he himself saw a new church in Bulgaria wantonly destroyed, « crushing in an hour the hopes of years. » (2) « The various Christian sects who occupy the plains of Syria, » says Colonel Churchill, « live in perpetual dread of some outbreak of Mohammedan fanaticism. » (3) How reasonable that dread was, the dismal tragedy of 1860 has once more proved. Even the Maronites, whose numbers and valour, as well as their geographical position, appeared to give them an exceptional security, fell, betrayed and ensnared, in that cruel conspiracy of Druse, and Turk, and Metuali; and were at all times so exposed, in spite of the nominal protectorate of France, whose generous designs were thwarted by the policy of a jealous and non-catholic nation, that as one of their Bishops observed to M. David, « *Dieu seul est bon pour la Syrie.* » In Antioch itself, though it is, as Mr Paton remarks, « nominally the metropolis of the orthodox Greeks, » « the Moslems are so fanatical, that they do not allow the Christians to have a church in the town. » (4) And it is in such a state of Society as this, in which the Catholics exist, like the sectaries, « only on sufferance, » and in daily peril of destruction; that helpless missionaries and religious

---

(1) *A Tour in Dalmatia.* etc., by W. F. Wingfield, M. A., ch. VI, p. 158.

(2) *A Year with the Turks,* ch. IX, p. 239.

(3) *Mount Lebanon,* vol. III, ch. XXVII, p. 387.

(4) *Modern Syrians,* ch. XIX, p. 220.

women, who attract tens of thousands by the sweet
odour of their virtues, from all ranks and sects, are
said to do so by « insults and tyranny, » and by
« persecuting the fallen churches! » Such is the
Protestant explanation of their success, and it is, as
usual, an Anglican clergyman who suggests it.

Before we close this chapter, let us add a few
words, in further illustration of the contrast, on
Protestant missions in Armenia. Hitherto we have
encountered grave and earnest men, fit preachers of
the evangelical truths of which their own apostolic
lives were the most impressive illustration; having
the counsels of Holy Writ in their hearts rather than
on their tongues, and still more eloquent by example
than in speech. Hence their peaceful triumphs, hence
their acceptance among all the Oriental races. We
have now, in conclusion, to notice briefly a class of
men towards whom we need not affect an esteem
which even their co-religionists have refused; men
to whom Holy Scripture appears to be every thing
except a teacher; men whose mouths are full of imprecations against the pure and the just, while they
do not even attempt to imitate their least merits;
whose whole life is one unbroken course of littleness
and self-indulgence, united with irrational contempt
for the manly virtues which they hate without understanding; whose mission seems to consist in marring
the Unity for which Jesus prayed, and in beguiling
others to reject the blessings which they have forfeited themselves; and whose own friends confess,
with one voice, that the few hearers whom they
entice are only ten times more immoral and unbe-
lieving than they were before.

The principal historian of Protestant missions in
Armenia is the Rev. Justin Perkins. Let us hear his
account of himself and his work.

Mr Perkins quotes the following passage from the
« Instructions » to the American missionaries by the
Society which employed them. « You are not sent
among these churches to proselyte. Let the Armenian remain an Armenian, if he will; the Greek a
Greek; and the Nestorian a Nestorian. » « The object
of the American missions to Syria, and other parts
of the Levant, » said Dr Robinson, « is not to draw
off members of the Oriental churches to Protestantism. » Such was perhaps the original programme,
and for a time caution restrained the American
agents. They offered only secular education, the use
of books, medical treatment, and other harmless
boons. When they thought their position assured,
they assumed their real character, and boasted, as
we have seen, of the very operations which their
nominal instructions forbade them to attempt.

They even claimed to have the field all to themselves, and warmly resented the intrusion of other
Protestant sects, and especially of Anglicans. The
Report of the American Board for 1841 protests energetically against the English for entering into communication with the Nestorians, because such a proceeding may « tend to awaken the thought among the
Nestorian ecclesiastics, that there are *rival* Protestant sects and interests, upon which they may practice
for the private gratification of avaricious desires. »
As a financial precaution, in order to keep down the
price of converts by having only one bidder, there
was much wisdom in this view; but the Anglicans an-

swered, by the mouth of M' Dadger, an episcopalian
minister, that the prudent suggestion was « as pre-
sumptuous as it is ludicrous. » M' Dadger even observed
that his American rivals « seemed to lay claim to
inspiration, and decided what was truth and what
was error with the assurance of apostles. » Meanwhile, the Nestorians looked on, and began to entertain « avaricious desires. »

We have seen that M' Dadger was no less indignant with the Catholic missionaries for their
endeavour to draw the Nestorians out of the pit
of heresy, ignorance, and corruption which even
Protestant writers of the most advanced school have
described to us. This Anglican clergyman, attracted
by their sounding titles, and rejoicing in their separation from unity, evidently thought them a far more
privileged class than either Catholics or Protestants.
It is true they deny the Incarnation, but they are
outside the Church, and were therefore welcome
allies for M' Dadger. « The Nestorian Church, » he
says, « abounds in noble gifts and rightful titles ! »(1)

There was a time when even the most advanced
Protestants, while Catholic traditions still lingered
faintly amongst them, professed to reverence the
Council of Ephesus, and to anathematize the Nestorian heresy. Now, it seems, they anathematize
nothing; and in this new Pyrrhonism they see only
a sign of their own progress and improvement.
Geneva itself once taught its students to say, —
« I *abhor* all the heresies which were condemned
by the first Council of Nice, *the first of Ephesus, and*

(1) *The Nestorians*, etc., vol. II, ch. XLVI, p. 351.

that of Chalcedon. » (1) We *detest* all sects and heresies, » said the French Protestant communities, at what they called « the Synod of Paris, » in 1559, condemned by the same Councils. (2) At the present day, even Anglican clergymen, especially those of the High-Church school, celebrate the « noble gifts and rightful titles » of Nestorianism! The Rev. Webb Le Bas calls the title θεοτόκος a « blasphemy, » (3) — though even La Croze was ashamed to say less than that « the title has nothing contrary to sound theology ; » (4) and the celebrated Calvinist Baldæus flatly asserted, that the Nestorians « teach points *contrary to salvation.* » (5) But an Anglican clergyman, when he once begins to speak against the Catholic faith, is pretty sure to surpass both Calvinists and Lutherans. The Rev. Dr Kerr, also an Anglican, called the monophysites of Malabar « a precious remnant of a *pure* and valuable people. »(6) Dr Southgate, a Protestant bishop, speaks of « the Nestorian heresy *if such it must be reputed* » (7) — implying that the Fathers of Ephesus were the real heretics. The Rev. Henry Townley considers the principal tenet of Nestorianism « a point of *orthodoxy*

(1) Ruchat, *Histoire de la Réformation de la Suisse,* tome VII, p. 291.

(2) Quick's *History of the Reformed Churches in France,* vol. I, p. 7. (1692).

(3) *Life of Bishop Middleton,* vol. I, ch. xi, p. 310.

(4) *Histoire du Christianisme des Indes,* tome I, livre I, p. 16.

(5) Ap. Churchill, vol. III, p. 576.

(6) *Report on the State of the Christians of Cochin and Travancore,* p. 8.

(7) *Narrative,* vol. II, ch. xix, p. 224.

on which we are agreed. » (1) Mr Layard says of
the Chaldean Nestorians, « there are no sects in the
East, and few in the West, who can boast of such
purity in their faith, » (2) and Mr Walpole adds
of the same class, that they are « pure and untaint-
ed, professing nearly as we profess. » (3) Lastly,
Mr Ainsworth, after enumerating the distinctive tenets anathematized by the Council of Ephesus, confidently asks, « In all this where is there any heresy? » (4) Evidently Mr Badger is not alone in his
admiration of the Nestorians — an admiration which,
however, he would perhaps have concealed, if he
had read the historian Evagrius, who relates that the
founder of their religion, the heresiarch Nestorius,
was not only anathematized by an OEcumenical
Council, but that he died, like Herod, by the judgment
of God, his tongue being gnawed by worms. (5)

Let us leave Mr Badger to accompany Mr Perkins
and his American colleagues. Here is a description,
by Dr Asahel Grant, of the country which they selected for their residence. « A plain of exuberant
fertility is enclosed between the mountains and the
lake, comprising an area of about 500 square miles,
and bearing upon its bosom no less than 300 hamlets
and villages. It is clothed with luxuriant verdure,
fruitful fields, gardens, and vineyards, and irrigated
by considerable streams of pure water from the adjacent mountains. The landscape is one of the most

(1) *Answer to the Abbé Dubois*, p. 230.
(2) *Nineveh and its Remains*, vol. I, p. 268.
(3) *The Ansayrii*, vol. II, ch. I, p. 10,
(4) *Travels in Asia Minor*, vol. II, ch. XLI, p. 272.
(5) *Hist. Ecclesiast.*, lib. I, cap. VII.

lovely in the East. » Some writers have suggested
that it was the site of the terrestrial paradise.

Here the Americans established their dwelling,
and here commenced the operations which Mr Perkins has described. A few extracts from his narrative, supplemented by other witnesses, will explain
their nature, and the character of the missionaries.

They hear that the Nestorian Patriarch at Jula-
merk is about to embrace the Catholic faith. In a
few hours a messenger is bearing across the plain
an urgent remonstrance, in which they address to
him, amongst other enquiries, this question ; « Is
there Paul, or Peter, or the Pope at Rome, crucified
for us? » (1) It does not appear how far he was
affected by this interrogation.

Mr Perkins professes much disdain for his Nestorian friends. « They are very degraded, » he says,
and their religion is « a revolting form of Christianity. » On the other hand, they feasted with him,
and jested with him, and by his advice took wives
and begat children ; and, above all, they accepted his
bibles and tracts, which, as he observes, « gives us
a glorious field of common ground. »

Here are some examples of his dealings with the
Nestorian bishops who became his pensioners. Of
one of them, he says, — « under the influence of *the
Mission*, he has got so much the better of his canon-
ical scruples on the virtue of episcopal celibacy,
that he has married a young wife, and is rearing a
family. » Mr Perkins was much encouraged by this
easy triumph, and his companions resolved to rival his

(1) *Residence in Persia*, p. 163.

success. « The American Missionaries, Mess™ Goodell and Bird, » says D' Wolff, « have succeeded in
converting two Armenian Bishops from the established Armenian symbols and ancient liturgy to the
vague and uncertain creed of the congregationalists
of America; from their attachment to their Patriarch
of Etchmiadzin to the half neological writings of
Professor Moses Stuart, of Andover. » (1) He adds
that they did this « merely for the sake of a wife, »
that both of them married immediately, and that in
order to quiet the troubled conscience of their wives,
they frequently expounded to them « 1 Tim III. 2 »
— with the interpretation which their American
friends had suggested.

And when they have pulled down these unfortunate men to their own level, they call it « bringing
them under Zion's king; » and having collected together a few such as these, by exciting lust, or avarice, or both,—having sapped all faith and religion in
them, and taught them to sing their shame in texts
of Scripture, — they call them « God's infant
church! » (2) « Wo to you, » said our Lord to such
as these, « because you shut the kingdom of heaven
against men, for you yourselves do not enter in, and
those that are going in *you suffer not to enter*... For
this you shall receive the greater judgment. Wo to
you, because you go round about the sea and the
land to make one proselyte, and when he is made,
you make him the child of hell twofold more than
yourselves. » (3)

(1) *Journal*, pp. 148, 9.
(2) *Christianity in Turkey*, ch. v, p. 130.
(3) Matt, XXIII, 15.

M' Perkins took Mar Yohannan, an ex-Nestorian
bishop, to the United States, — just as Tzatzoe and
Africaner were conveyed to England,—and when he
arrived there, the Episcopalian Protestants claimed
him as an ally. « You belong to us, » they said, in a
formal address, and they protested against the inde-
cency of his herding with methodists, presbyterians,
anabaptists, and other children of the « reformation, » from which they derived their own origin.
Under the tuition of his American guides, this poor
man, once a Bishop, made the following official
reply. « I do not wish to hear you say, you belong to
us ; I have not come here to make difference among
Christians. » And then he expounded his new ecclesiastical views. « I love Episcopalians, and Congregationalists, and Presbyterians, and Dutchmen, and
Methodists, and Baptists... there is no difference in
them with me. »(1)

Such was the general result of the influence of
M' Perkins. What the complexion of his theology
was, we may infer from the following facts. Of Nestorius, and his denial of the θεοτόκος, he says, « Protestant Christians would certainly never have thought
the worse of him : » and then, forgetting the description which he had himself given elsewhere, of « the
revolting form of Christianity » professed by Nestorians, he exclaims, — « their belief is orthodox and
scriptural ! » With respect to the sacrament of Baptism, he derides the oriental Christians because they
« appeared to suppose that this rite possessed some
mysterious charm that involved the agency of the

(1) *Residence in Persia*, p. 367.

Holy spirit. »(1) Such are the teachers whom America sends to promote the fortunes of Protestantism in the East.

M' Perkins would perhaps have remaiued in Armenia till the present hour, but the care of his wife and family, as usual, put an end to his labours. Armenia was a pleasant residence, but did not offer any career to his offspring. « The children of Missionaries, » he says, « should be to the Churches objects of deep interest, as well as of tender sympathy; » and for this reason, because the promise of our Lord to all who who should *leave* « father or mother, or wife or children, for His sake,» applies in a special manner « to the *children* of His missionary servants! » (2) It appears, therefore, that the divine promise of special benediction to all who *abandon* these worldly ties means, in the opinion of M' Perkins, that « they shall have a double blessing who *retain* them. » Finally, « M'' Perkins' health » suggested a return to America ; and as he seems to have suspected that his retirement from Armenia might possibly suggest malevolent interpretations, he complains apologetically, and by way of precaution, that « there is a *sensitiveness* in the Christian community on the subject of the return of Missionaries. » It is probable, in spite of the protest of M' Perkins, that this sensitiveness will continue.

Perhaps we have now sufficient knowledge of the character of American missionaries, but here is one more, and it shall be the last illustration. In a series

(1) P. 247.
(2) P. 344.

of volumes, bearing a grave title, and recommended
to public attention by one of the scientific societies
of America, the reader will encounter the following
passage. « K. is on her prancing pony, M⁰ T. is on
the lank, thin-chested , but deep-chested mountain
horse, Mʳ T... has mounted kicking Sâda, and I'm
aloft on tibn-devouring Mahjùb. » This is not, as
might have been supposed, a sportive account of a
pic-nic party, addressed by some Syrian Aspasia to
a sympathising friend, but the official narrative of« a
missionary tour, » extracted from « Notes of a Tour
in Mount Lebanon, by a Missionary of the American Board in Syria, » and solemnly read before the
American Oriental Society ! (1)

Here we might have terminated our notice of Protestant missions in Armenia, but that Providence has
provided a witness to their real character and results
whose remarkable evidence it would be wasteful to
neglect. In every country we have found Protestant
writers to tell us, from personal observation, what
the emissaries of England and America are really
doing among the heathen, and what are their relations with other sects. Armenia is no exception to
this rule. If there is a country in the world in which
the agents of Protestantism have been more boastful
and self-complacent than in any other, it is the province in which we are now going to resume their
operations. Catholic travellers could have told us
how fruitless, except in corruption and unbelief,
those operations have been — but we have resolved
not to hear Catholics on this point. It is from Pro-

(1) *Journal of the American Oriental Society*, vol. II, p. 237.

testants alone that we can receive such facts, since
only by their unsuspicious evidence could they be
adequately proved.

Dr Moritz Wagner, who seems to profess some
form or modification of Anglicanism, who was the
intimate friend and constant guest of Mr Perkins and
his colleagues, who warmly professes « esteem and
love » for his hosts, and considers « their devotion
entitled to all praise» — is exactly the witness whom
we should desire to interrogate. Fortunately that
intelligent naturalist has anticipated our wish, and
here is his account of the Protestant missionaries and of their work in the fertile plains of Armenia.

Let us hear first what he relates of the manner of
life of his opulent hosts. « The institution at Urmia, »
he says, « costs the North American Missionary Societies *about fifty thousand dollars annually;* » and
he will tell us immediately how that substantial revenue is spent. A writer of his own nation, also a
guest at Urmia, had already informed the world that
the mansion of the missionaries « is furnished with
so many conveniences and comforts, that it seemed to
me as if I were not under the roof of simple followers of Christ and teachers of the Gospel, but in that
of some wealthy private gentleman. Here were four
ladies, a whole troop of children, etc. » (1) — but
we will not pursue the narrative of a witness who, it
is fair to add, was so impressed by the uniform aspect of Protestant missions in all parts of the world
as to become ultimately a Catholic. Dr Wagner, who

(1) *Voyage round the World*, by Ida Pfeiffer, p. 221.

has not as yet, so far as we know, imitated this example, modestly laments that he has not sufficient power « to depict the charms and features of this missionary residence, » of which he declares with emotion that « the whole idyllic scenery » will never be effaced from his recollection. But this was only a portion of the missionary delights. They had also « a summer residence at Seir, scarcely four miles from Urmia, inclosed by a wall flanked with four towers, and covering the upper terrace of a hill, from which the eye commands a wonderful prospect of the vast, blooming plain of Urmia, with its three hundred and sixty villages. » And these palatial mansions, with a suitable income of more than ten thousand pounds per annum, were the selected abodes of *five* missionaries, and of what Dr Wagner calls, no doubt justly, « their amiable housewives. » We are not surprised to learn from their privileged guest, that « the missionaries not only live comfortably, but even luxuriously, as was testified by their stables, which were almost filled with horses of all Oriental breeds. » Dr Wagner adds, however, without the least intention of jesting, that his friends had generously quitted America, where both their dwellings and their stables were probably on a smaller scale, « for the propagation of Christianity. »

It was in these well furnished halls that Mr Justin Perkins held his court. « All the gentlemen, » says Dr Wagner, « were capitally mounted, » but Mr Perkins was distinguished even among his peers. « I have never seen throughout the East a finer horse than the snow white mare of Mr Perkins. Each movement of the beautiful animal, which had cost a considerable sum, was full of grace. It looked to the greatest advantage when kneeling down to drink. »

But M' Perkins and his friends had one trial, in the midst of these fabulous enjoyments; they were obliged to share their wealth with the needy Armenians, who positively refused their proferred alliance on any other terms. The « Patriarch » led the band. « He had good reasons, » our German informant observes, « for showing civility to M' Perkins, and allowing him to preach without interference the Gospel according to Presbyterian views, for he received a considerable subsidy from the Mission, exceeding, by twice the amount, the income he received from his congregations. The same motive applied to the priests of lower degree, whose cringing politeness to the missionaries was sufficiently explained by their poverty, their love of lucre, and their monthly salaries. »

And these were not the only classes who dilapidated the fifty thousand dollars which annually flowed into the missionary treasury from enthusiastic subscribers at home, who were perhaps not fully acquainted with the mode in which their contributions were consumed. « The missionaries showered their gold, » says their favoured guest, « with a liberal hand, and not only taught the youth gratis, *but gave them a weekly gratuity*... Each bishop receives from the Americans a monthly allowance of three hundred Turkish piastres, and ordinary ecclesiastics from a hundred and fifty to two hundred piastres. On the condition of this allowance being continued, the Nestorian clergy permit the missionaries to preach in their villages, to keep schools, etc. Without this payment, or bribery, of the priests for a good end, the missionaries could not maintain their footing in this country. Even the peasant is only carrying on a pecuniary speculation, in sending his child to school. Each scholar receives, weekly, a sal/efgeran; and though this gift is small, *the schools would become directly empty,* if it were to cease. »

Finally, if we ask D' Wagner to tell us frankly how many converts were really gained by this enormous expenditure — amounting, in thirty years, to one million and a half dollars, or more than three hundred thousand pounds sterling — he is willing to gratify our curiosity, and honestly confesses, that it has converted nobody! Even Nestorians, though willing to accept any amount of American money, do not cease to despise American doctrine. Amongst the domestic servants in the palace of M' Perkins were two, the one a Jew, the other an Armenian, who professed to be disciples. D' Wagner, a very amiable man, was charitably disposed to think well of the Armenian, who constantly expressed an earnest desire to visit Europe and America; but » the other missionary servant, a converted Jew, who had been my guide to Seir, hinted slyly that it was not so much the devout impulse of a pilgrim which prompted his friend John to visit Europe and Christendom, as selfishness and ambitious aspirations. He implied that the shrewd Nestorian fancied that, if he knew the English tongue better, he could play the part of Mess" Perkins and Starking among his countrymen.» These intelligent « converts » evidently appreciated each other, and the acute D' Wagner seems at last to have appreciated them all. « As a missionary ser-

vant, " he says, " John was a very unimportant personage in the land. But as Missionary, and supported
by the mission fund, even the higher clergy would
have paid court to him, which was enough to excite
the ambition of the Nestorian youth. " And then follow these grave words, in which the true character
of these costly missions, — always appealing to the
meanest sentiments of the human heart, and openly
conducted on the worst principles of human cunning,
— is exposed by this friendly and capable witness.
" If we except a few Jews, won over from motives of
gain, *these expensive establishments have made no
converts.* " This is all that has been accomplished,
he says, by " America's evangelical apostles, who are
so splendidly remunerated, and the wealthy members
of the societies, who have never yet raised their
voices against negro-slavery, and the hunting down
of the poor red-skins by rifle shots and blood hounds,
but who pay many hundred thousand dollars to support their *useless missions* in the East. " "The American Mission, " he declares, and with this final
testimony we may close our Armenian narrative,
" cannot boast of splendid results in relation to the
improvement of morality, stimulus by virtuous
examples, or the advancement of culture. *Even
M' Perkins admitted this.* " Yet in his official reports
that gentleman only spoke of his continual triumphs,
and even relates in his book such tales as the following. " The Rev. William Goodell dropped a copy of
the Tract entitled the Dairyman's Daughter in Nico-
media; " and this, he affirms, knowing what the
home subscribers could bear, created, without the
aid of any missionary, " a considerable number of

enlightened, spiritual Christians! » And the man
who could thus mock the well-meaning contributors
to his own luxury, privately confessed to D' Wagner,
who fortunately made a note of the words, that « he
thought almost all hope must be given up, in the case
of the present generation. » (1) Thus, by the aid of
a little patience and industry, we have arrived at
last, by exclusively Protestant testimony, at a full
knowledge of the character and results of all the
Protestant missions in Armenia, Syria, and Turkey.

We need not pause to offer any reflections upon
the history which we have now completed. Once
more we have traced a contrast, and one which
solicits no comment. Once more we have advanced a
step in that controversy which, as we have said, God
has already taken out of the hands of men, to decide
it Himself. He knows how to distribute His own gifts,
and we have seen upon whom He confers, to whom
He refuses them. But if we abstain from superfluous
comment upon the history of missions in Western
Asia, it is impossible to omit the truly remarkable
reflections which that history has suggested to a
learned German, familiar with the religious phenomena of these regions, and accustomed to estimate
them with the scientific precision of a mind which
professes to be wholly unbiassed either by preference
or hostility. It is surely a notable fact that a German
philosopher should attest, by his own experience and
observation, the universal law, that separation from
the Catholic Church is fatal to the life of religion;
and even confess, in express terms, the fitness of that

(1) *Travels*, etc., vol. III, ch. VIII, pp. 234-258.

glorious title, *Our Lady of Victories,* which the
Church in grateful love has given to the Mother of
God. « Rejoice, O Holy Virgin Mary, » says the
Spouse of Christ in one of her solemn offices, « because
Thou alone hast overcome all heresies throughout the
world. » It is in the following striking language that
Von Haxthausen, who had witnessed their influence
in Asia, seems to recognise Her royal prerogatives.

« In all the nations of Catholic Christendom, of
the Western as well as the Eastern Church, it is a
popular belief that the worship of the Virgin, the
invocation of the Mother of God, confers a peculiar
blessing, especially earthly happiness to the individual, and in families brings harmony and love. The
service of the Virgin has become the strongest basis
of nationality in its higher forms, as well as of political life, among the nations of Europe... The worship of the Virgin has unquestionably given rise to
a high degree of refinement, especially in the position
to which it has raised the female sex. It is worthy
of remark, that among the Sclavonic nations of the
Eastern Church, the Russians, among whom the
most fervent adoration of the Virgin prevails, are
those people who have become the most powerful,
by their capacity for civilization, warlike disposition,
and political success : whilst, on the contrary, we
see the Greeks, among whom the service of the Virgin
is spiritless and neglected, have fallen into a state of
semi-barbarism, oppression, and political feebleness,
notwithstanding their remarkable natural abilities.
Amongst the latter people, domestic and family life
is in general upon a low grade, because woman has
not her true position and respect, but is treated with

more or less Oriental oppression... perhaps the political weakness of the Byzantine empire may be mainly attributable to these considerations. How was it that the Romano-Germanic nations were so far superior to the Greeks in the Middle Ages, not only physically but morally, notwithstanding that the latter were so highly gifted by nature, the inheritors of classical refinement, and, individually, intellectual, brave, and warlike? If it be said that the Germano-Scandinavian nations, among whom the worship of the Virgin is no longer found, as the Swedes and English, nevertheless enjoy high political culture and prosperity, this is no valid argument. It must be remembered, that these peoples *have had* this worship, have been educated in and by it, and that they did not relinquish it until their political training was *completed*, and the whole structure of their national and family life was formed and settled. Among the Armenians unattached to Rome, the worship of the Virgin is neglected; and this has had an injurious effect on the position of the female sex and on family life... On the contrary, among those who are attached to the Church of Rome, the worship of the Virgin appears to have raised the position of the female sex to a greater freedom and independence, and humanized the domestic usages. » And then he adds these concluding observations, of which the gravity will be appreciated by every intelligent reader. « Until this humanizing influence, this recognition of the dignity of woman, shall become diffused generally among the Armenian nation, they cannot hope to attain a full measure of civilization. If ever Christianity spreads widely in the East, accompanied by a worship of the Virgin, *and without this it will never spread there*, the female sex will be emancipated from their present degraded position. The very trifling success which has attended the Protestant missions in that part of the world, notwithstanding the amplest means, may be in a great measure explained by the above remarks. » (1)

We might pursue our researches, at the risk of wearying the reader, in Georgia, and even in Persia, and every where we should find the same facts, every where trace the same contrast. In Georgia, — where, as early as the thirteenth century, Catholics were detected by being ordered « to trample on the crucifix, » and multitudes gained the crown of martyrdom, (2) — there are now German, American, and Scotch missionaries. Here is one example of each class. An English traveller, who visited the German colony near Tiflis, under the Lutheran missionary Dittrich, says; « I was sorry to learn from M' Dittrich that the German colonies had not flourished... He told me that great disunion prevailed amongst the colonists, principally from differences of religious opinion. » (3) Yet they thought themselves qualified to convert the Armenians to one or other of their own shifting creeds, or to all of them at once.

To the Americans at Shooshà, in Georgia, the Russian emperor sent the following admonition. « Learning by the real state of things that you, since the time of your settlement at Shooshà, *have not yet*

(1) Haxthausen, *Transcaucasia*, ch. x, pp. 344, 5.
(2) *Histoire de la Georgie*, par M. Brosset, tome I, p. 504.
(3) Wilbraham, *Travels in the Trans-Caucasian Provinces*, ch. XVII, p. 182.

converted any body, and, deviating from the proper
limits » — the conversion of the heathen — « have
directed your views to the Armenian youth, which,
on the part of the Armenian clergy, has produced
complaints, the consequences of which may be very
disagreeable; his Majesty's ministers have concluded
to prohibit you all missionary labours, and for the
future to leave it to your own choice to employ yourselves with agriculture, manufactures, or mechanical
trades. It has pleased his Majesty the Emperor to
confirm this decree. » (1)

It is true that the emperor tried to silence the
Catholics also, not because they had failed, like the
Americans, to convert the heathen, but because they
would have converted the whole country if he had
not prevented them. Yet Dr Wagner found eight
hundred Catholics « at or near Kutais, » who all
spoke the Imeritian dialect ; while the pupils of the
convent, to the number of thirty of forty, « could
read and write Georgian, and read Italian with tolerable facility. » He notices too « the respect and esteem which (the Superior of the Franciscans) had
obtained in the town and country, » and observes,
— « I frequently witnessed the child-like veneration
in which he was held by the Armenian boys. » (2)
Baron Von Haxthausen also mentions an Italian missionary, who « died thirty years ago, and the Geor-
gians number him among their Saints. » Such men
were opposed by the Czar, as the Americans were,
but for very different reasons.

(1) Quoted by Perkins, p. 221.
(2) *Travels*, vol. II, ch. III, p. 202.

It is a curious illustration of the different policy
of England, and of the deplorable influence which
she everywhere exerts in support of seditious fanaticism or meddlesome unbelief, that when Mr Perkins, whose operations we can now appreciate, solicited the sympathy of the Right Hon. Henry Ellis,
British ambassador in Persia in 1838, he received
the following characteristic reply. « The proposed
introduction of the pure doctrines of the Reformed
church among the Nestorian Christians in this country cannot fail to be a matter of deep and serious interest to His Majesty's government. » (1) Russia,
with more discretion, promptly dismissed the friends
of Mr Ellis as likely to prove, « very disagreeable, »
and suggested to them the more congenial pursuit of
manufactures or mechanical trades.

Lastly, — for we need not stay to multiply testimonies of which we have learned by this time to
appreciate the universality, — Sir Robert Porter
gives this account of the emissaries from Scotland.
« A Scotch colony of missionaries have established
themselves in the neighbourhood of Konstantino-
gorsk; but it may be regarded as an agricultural society, rather than a theological college. » (2)

In Persia, — where Jesuits once received honours
even in the tent of Nadir Schah, as their brethren did
in that of Akbar; (3) and where in our own day, Na-
poleon, comprehending with his infallible sagacity
all that such men could effect, stipulated, by the
treaty of 1808, for protection in favour of all Jesuits

(1) *Residence in Persia*, etc., p. 219.
(2) *Travels in Georgia*, vol. I, p. 47.
(3) *Crétineau Joly*, tome VI, ch. 1, p. 51.

II.   16

whom France might send to that land, — Catholic
missionaries, having the apostolic graces of chastity
and holy poverty, have won the respect even of the
disciples of the false prophet, while a crowd of
American missionaries dispense on every side the
enormous funds entrusted to them. « The money
they lavish, » says the Prefect of the Armenian missions in Persia, « presents a strong temptation to
certain Armenians, who follow them for a while, in
order to profit by their profusion, but invariably
adhere to the tenets of their own religion. » (1) The
Armenian clergy, we are told by the wife of a British ambassador, « receive salaries » from them, like
their fellows in the neighbourhood of Urmia. Of the
French Lazarists, the same lady says, « These gentlemen abounded in zeal and activity, but they were
poor, and wholly unable to contend against the treasures of Boston. » (2) Such is every where the influence, when they have any, of Protestant missionaries. To generate corruption and immorality,
without producing even the semblance of religious
conviction; to destroy faith, but never to inspire it;
and to hinder those who, in spite of their poverty,
know how to kindle the light of truth and charity in
all hearts — such is their deplorable work. And
their partizans at home are never weary of sending
them money to be employed in such aims.

They do not even attempt, as might be anticipated,
to convert the Persians, who suppose, like all Orientals, that they are atheists. Indeed Mr Perkins in-

(1) *Annals*, vol. I, p. 95.
(2) *Life and Manners in Persia*, by Lady Shiel, p. 356.

cautiously relates an anecdote which shows, that the
Persians are quite as likely to convert the Protestants
as to be converted by them. « A pious English family
in Persia, » he says, « were surprised and shocked
on one day finding their little girl, then four years
old, kneeling with her face towards Mecca, and lisp-
ing the devotions of the false prophet. » (1)

But it is time to close this chapter, already extended to undue limits, and we may conclude it with an
anecdote not less curious than that which we have
just heard. Not long ago, a French traveller, journeying from Ispahan to Bagdad, came upon a small
Catholic colony towards the close of a sultry day.
They were assembled together in the house of one of
them, and having recited vespers, were engaged,
when the traveller joined them, not in asking gifts
for themselves, but in praying for the conversion of
England! They seem to have understood, even in
their far home beyond the Tigris, that, in spite of
the zeal of some and the good intentions of many,
England is still, by her relentless warfare against
Unity, the great impediment to the conversion of the
heathen; and that the surest way to obtain for *them*
admission into the family of God, was to solicit for
her the recovery of the gifts which she has lost, and
of the faith which she has denied. And these Persian
Christians were right. If England had remained
Catholic, it is probable that at this hour there would
not have been a pagan altar in the world.

(1) P. 343.

TABLE OF CONTENTS.

VOL. II.

www.ingramcontent.com/pod-product-compliance
Lightning Source LLC
Chambersburg PA
CBHW021935110726
47901CB00003B/846